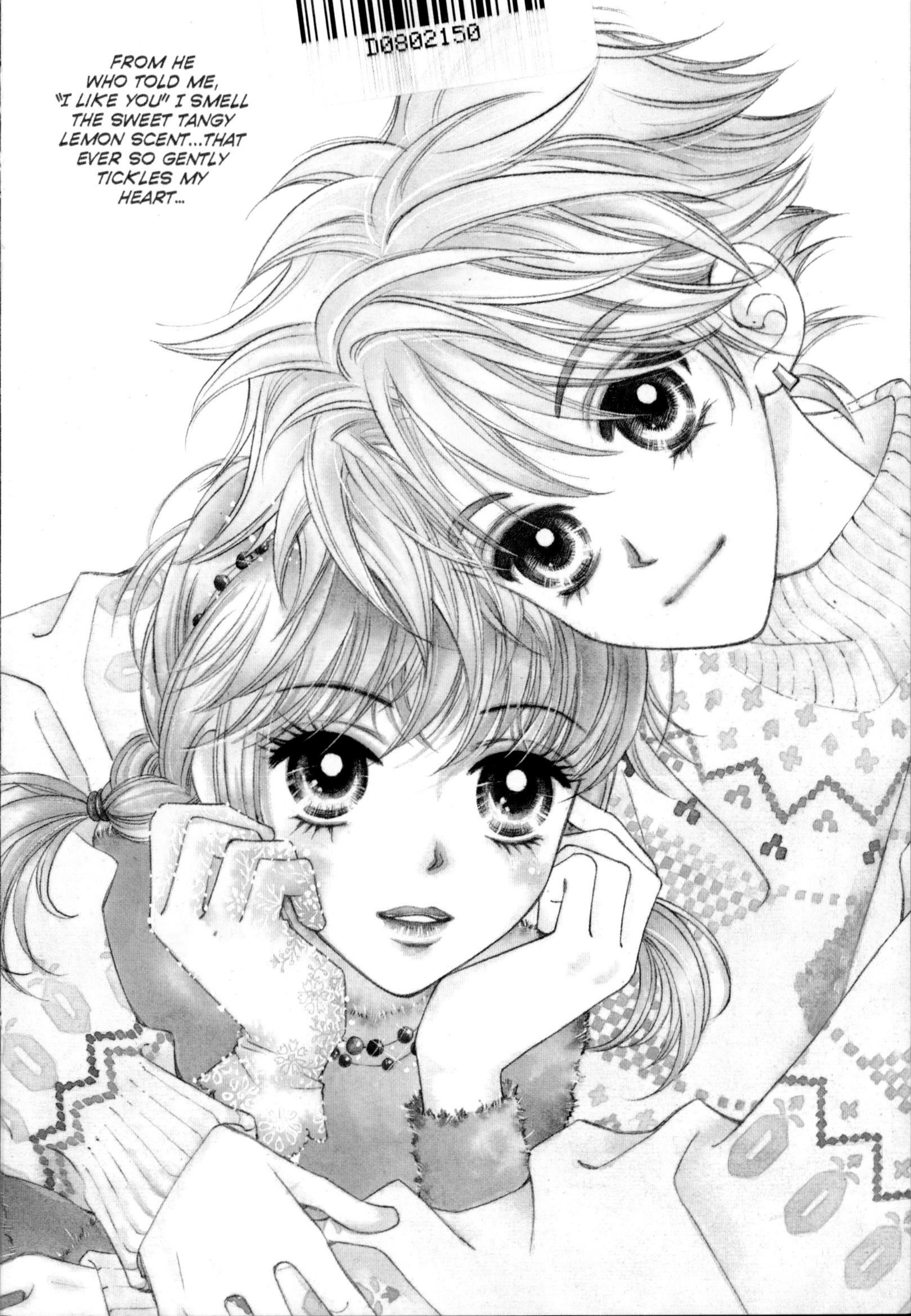
FROM HE WHO TOLD ME, "I LIKE YOU" I SMELL THE SWEET TANGY LEMON SCENT...THAT EVER SO GENTLY TICKLES MY HEART...

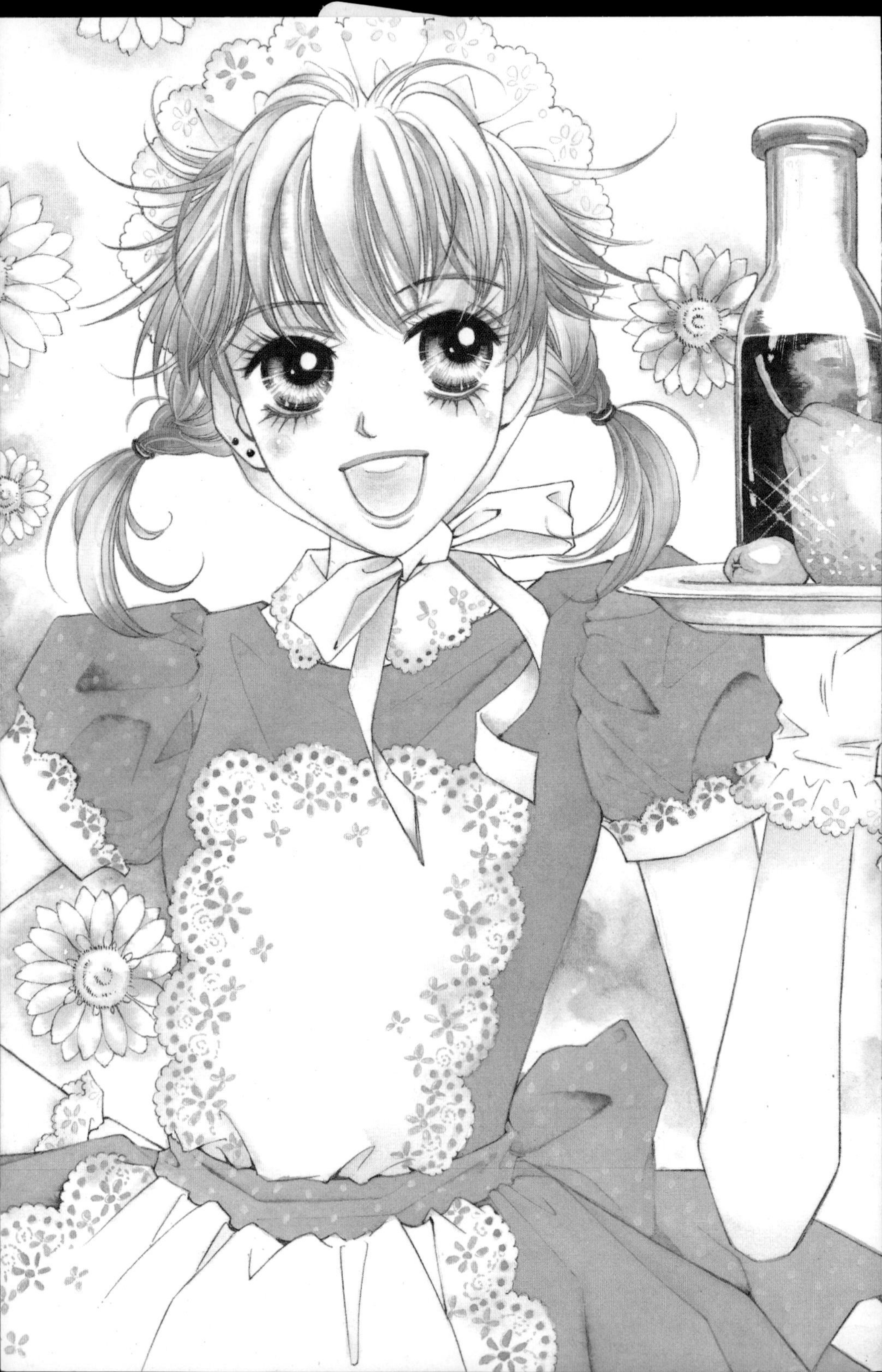

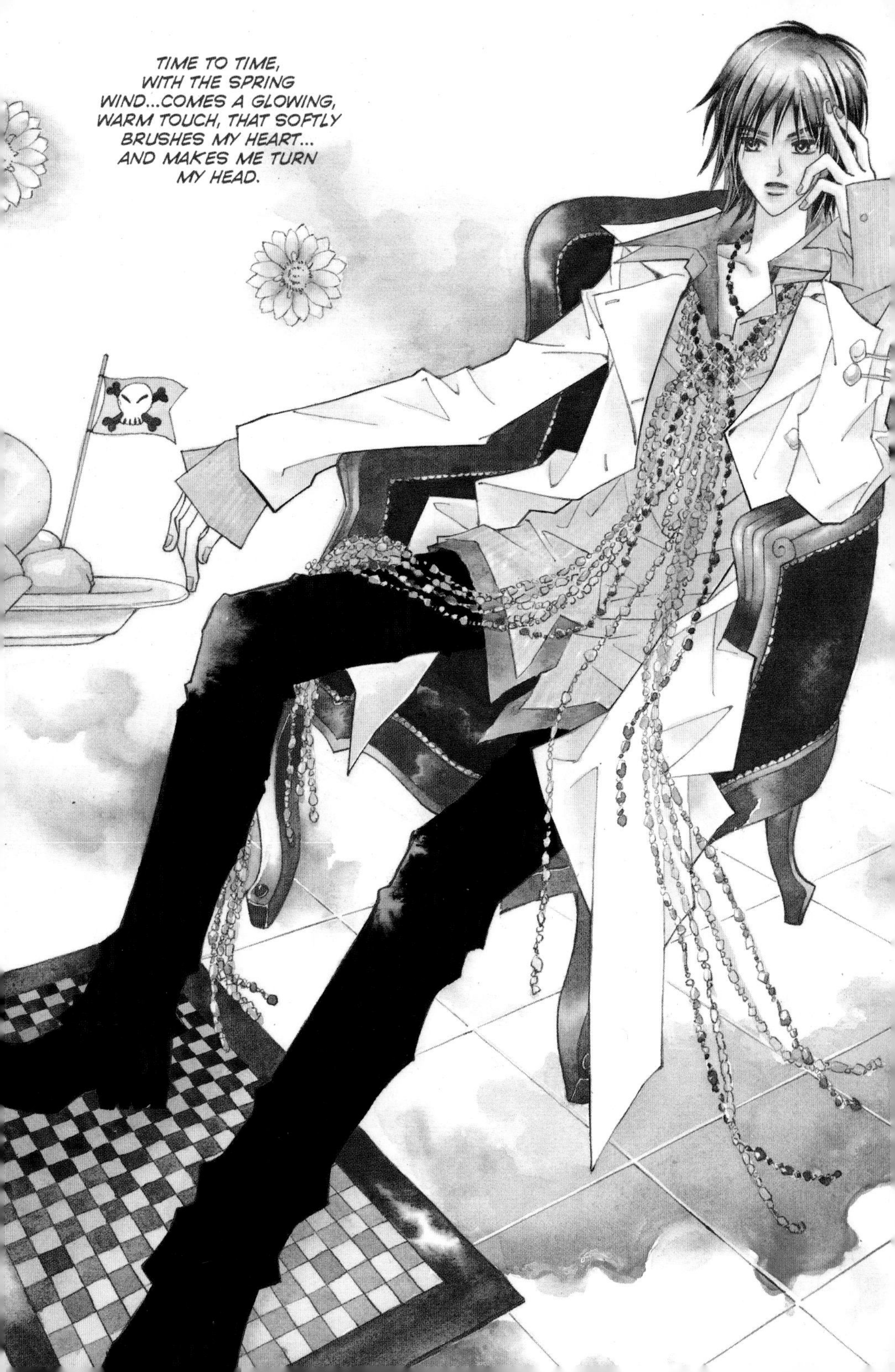
TIME TO TIME, WITH THE SPRING WIND...COMES A GLOWING, WARM TOUCH, THAT SOFTLY BRUSHES MY HEART... AND MAKES ME TURN MY HEAD.

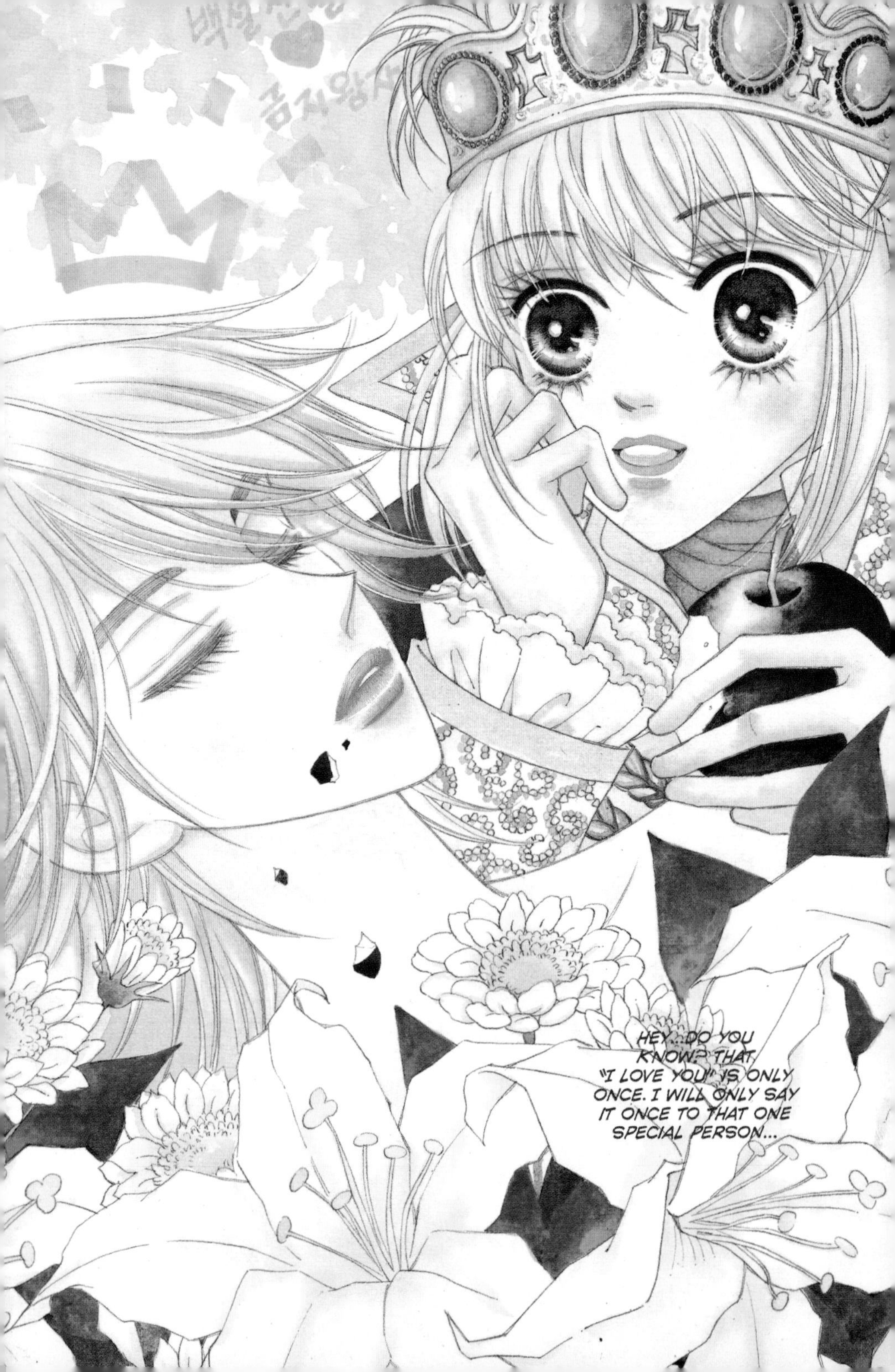
HEY... DO YOU KNOW? THAT "I LOVE YOU" IS ONLY ONCE. I WILL ONLY SAY IT ONCE TO THAT ONE SPECIAL PERSON...

giginal · Danbi Original · Danbi Original · Danbi Original · Danbi Original · Danbi Original · D

CHOCOLAT

vol.2

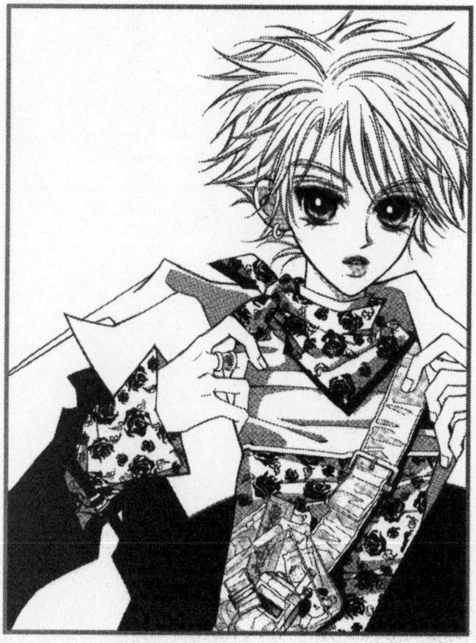

Shin JiSang ·Geo

ice Kunion

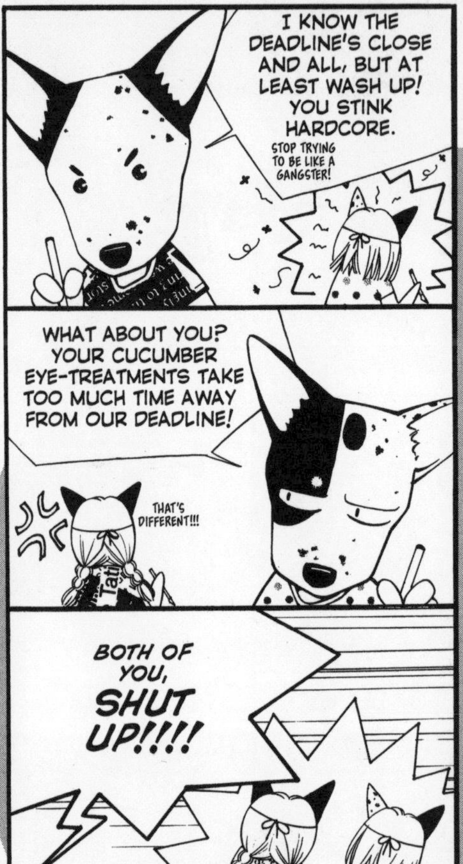
I KNOW THE DEADLINE'S CLOSE AND ALL, BUT AT LEAST WASH UP! YOU STINK HARDCORE.
STOP TRYING TO BE LIKE A GANGSTER!
WHAT ABOUT YOU? YOUR CUCUMBER EYE-TREATMENTS TAKE TOO MUCH TIME AWAY FROM OUR DEADLINE!
THAT'S DIFFERENT!!!
BOTH OF YOU, SHUT UP!!!!
FOR JUST ONCE IN YOUR LIFE, YOU GUYS NEED TO SAY "LET'S WORK HARD TOGETHER!" AND GET IT DONE! UNDER-STAND?!!!
YOUNGEST ASSISTANT.
SO SCARY...
YOU ARE RIGHT... YOU'RE SOOOO RIGHT... T.T

WORDS FROM THE CREATORS

IT SEEMS LIKE ONLY YESTERDAY THAT THE FIRST ISSUE WAS OUT, BUT IT'S ALREADY THE 2ND ISSUE... TIME FLIES BY SO FAST WHEN WE ARE WORKING SO HARD (LOL). I HOPE IT DID NOT TAKE TOO LONG FOR YOU WHO HAVE BEEN WAITING FOR THE NEXT ISSUE.

AT THIS POINT, IT MIGHT SEEM LIKE KUM-JI IS BEING LOVED BY TOO MANY BISHOUNENS, BUT WE WILL MAKE SURE SHE DOESN'T LOSE HER IDENTITY AND KNOWS WHERE SHE STANDS.

I HOPE YOU ALL ENJOY THE TASTE OF <CHOCOLAT> #2, AND HOPEFULLY WAIT FOR #3 AS WELL.

JI-SANG SHIN & GEO

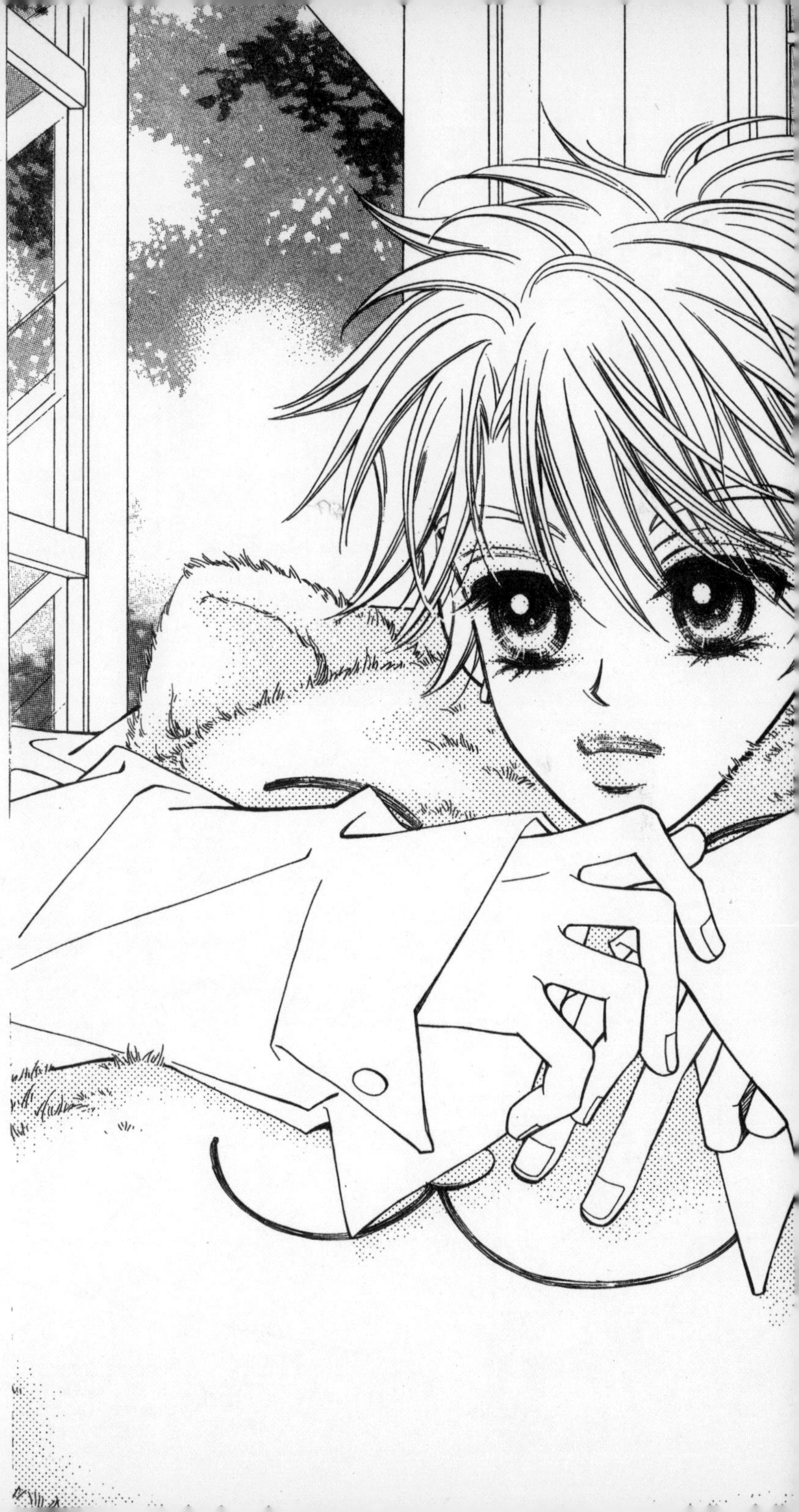

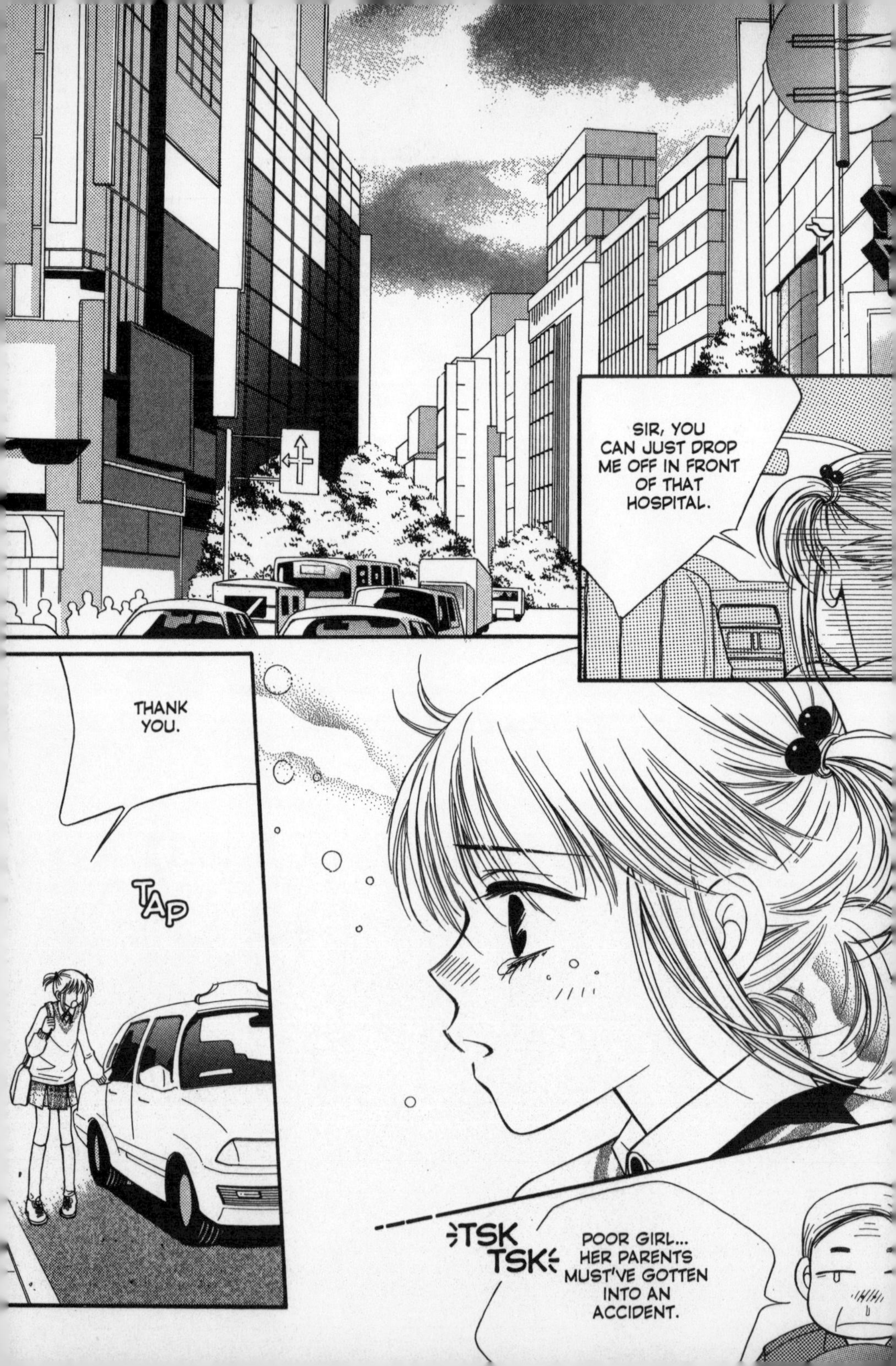
SIR, YOU CAN JUST DROP ME OFF IN FRONT OF THAT HOSPITAL.
THANK YOU.
TAP
TSK TSK
POOR GIRL... HER PARENTS MUST'VE GOTTEN INTO AN ACCIDENT.

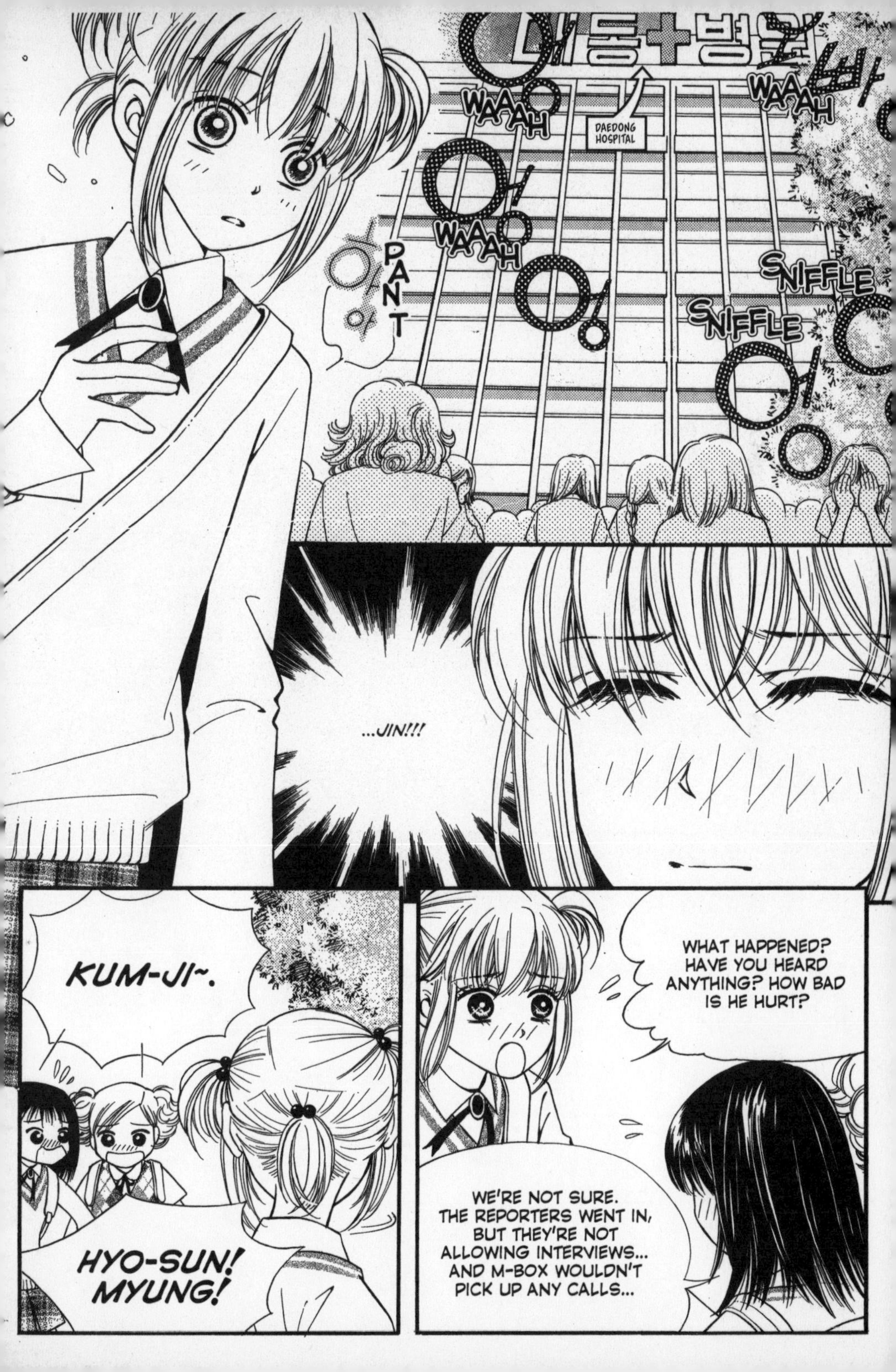
PANT
WAAAH
DAEDONG HOSPITAL
WAAAH
WAAAH
SNIFFLE
SNIFFLE
...JIN!!!
KUM-JI~.
HYO-SUN! MYUNG!
WHAT HAPPENED? HAVE YOU HEARD ANYTHING? HOW BAD IS HE HURT?
WE'RE NOT SURE. THE REPORTERS WENT IN, BUT THEY'RE NOT ALLOWING INTERVIEWS... AND M-BOX WOULDN'T PICK UP ANY CALLS...

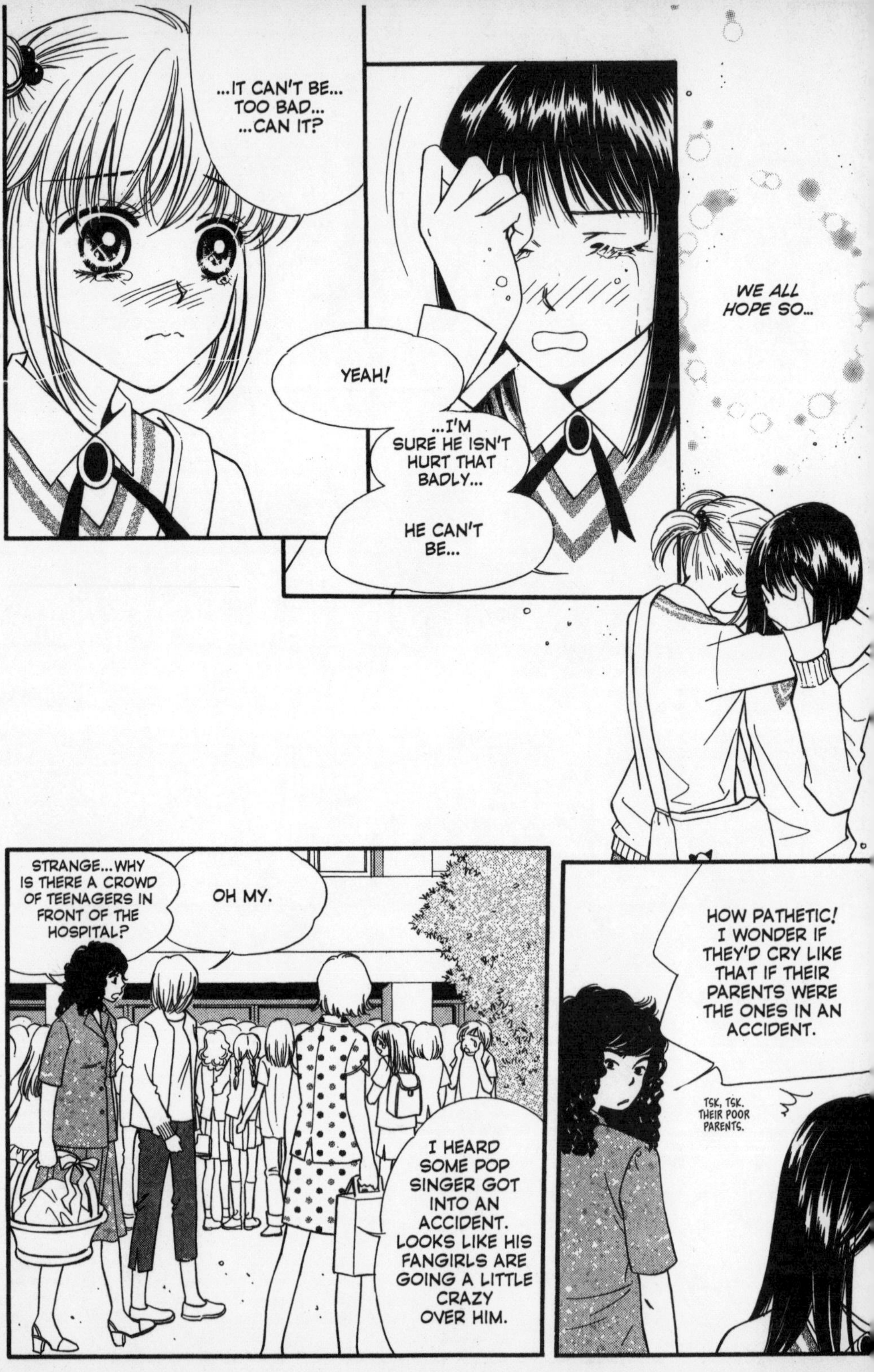
...IT CAN'T BE...
TOO BAD...
...CAN IT?
YEAH!
...I'M SURE HE ISN'T HURT THAT BADLY...
HE CAN'T BE...
WE ALL HOPE SO...
STRANGE...WHY IS THERE A CROWD OF TEENAGERS IN FRONT OF THE HOSPITAL?
OH MY.
I HEARD SOME POP SINGER GOT INTO AN ACCIDENT. LOOKS LIKE HIS FANGIRLS ARE GOING A LITTLE CRAZY OVER HIM.
HOW PATHETIC! I WONDER IF THEY'D CRY LIKE THAT IF THEIR PARENTS WERE THE ONES IN AN ACCIDENT.
TSK, TSK. THEIR POOR PARENTS.

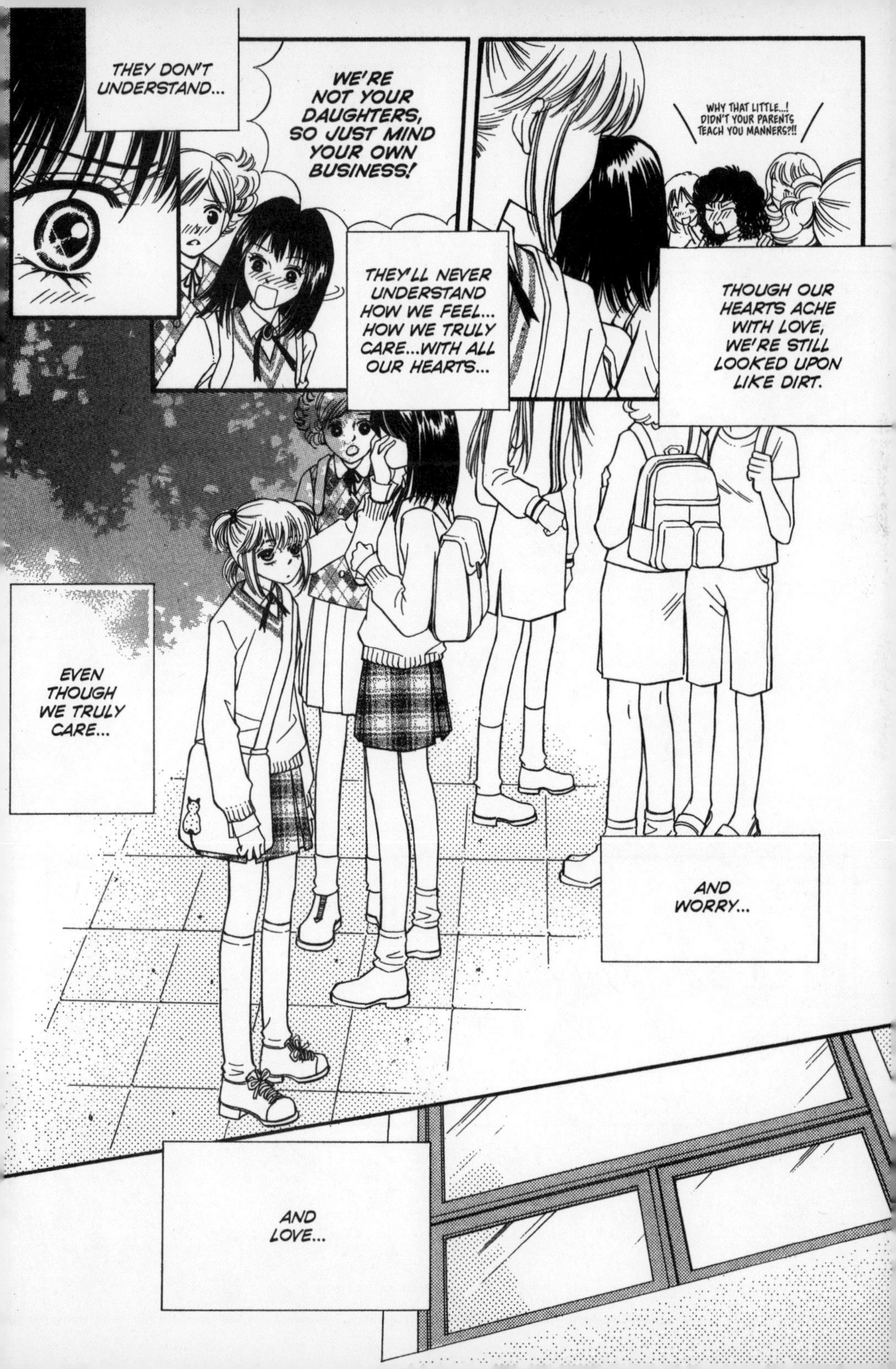
THEY DON'T UNDERSTAND...
WE'RE NOT YOUR DAUGHTERS, SO JUST MIND YOUR OWN BUSINESS!
WHY THAT LITTLE...! DIDN'T YOUR PARENTS TEACH YOU MANNERS?!!
THEY'LL NEVER UNDERSTAND HOW WE FEEL... HOW WE TRULY CARE...WITH ALL OUR HEARTS...
THOUGH OUR HEARTS ACHE WITH LOVE, WE'RE STILL LOOKED UPON LIKE DIRT.
EVEN THOUGH WE TRULY CARE...
AND WORRY...
AND LOVE...

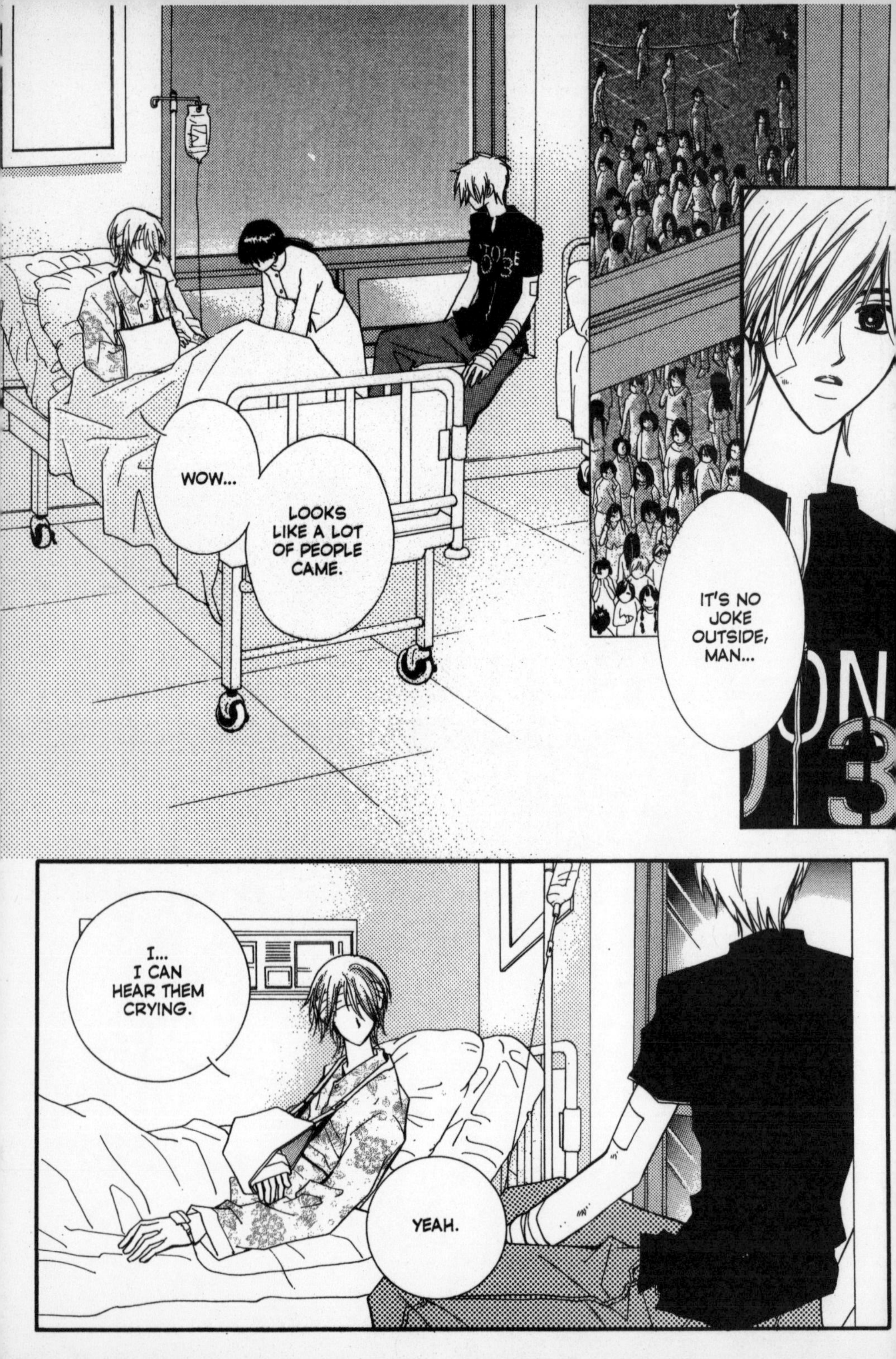
WOW...
LOOKS LIKE A LOT OF PEOPLE CAME.
IT'S NO JOKE OUTSIDE, MAN...
I... I CAN HEAR THEM CRYING.
YEAH.

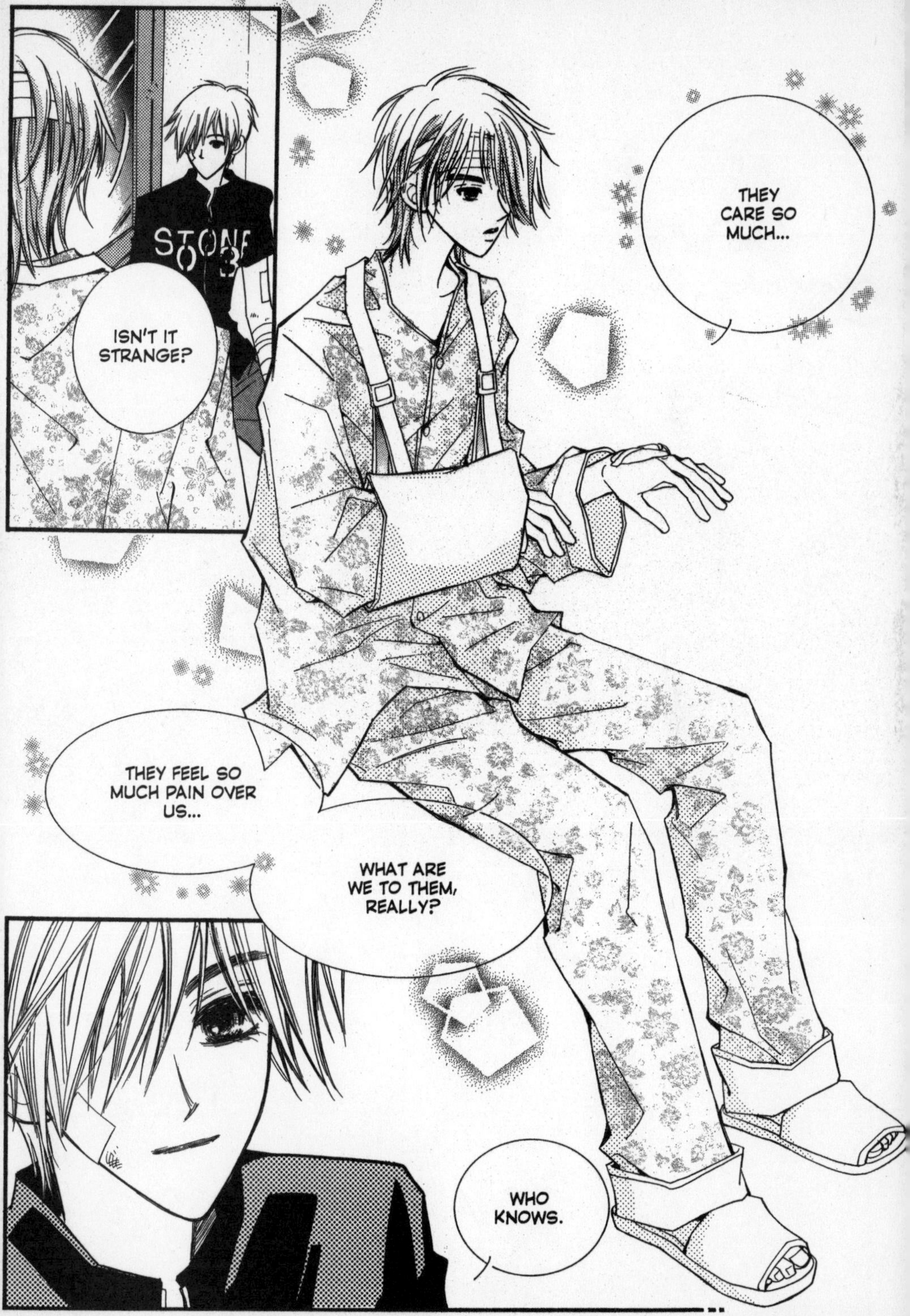
STONE 03
ISN'T IT STRANGE?
THEY CARE SO MUCH...
THEY FEEL SO MUCH PAIN OVER US...
WHAT ARE WE TO THEM, REALLY?
WHO KNOWS.

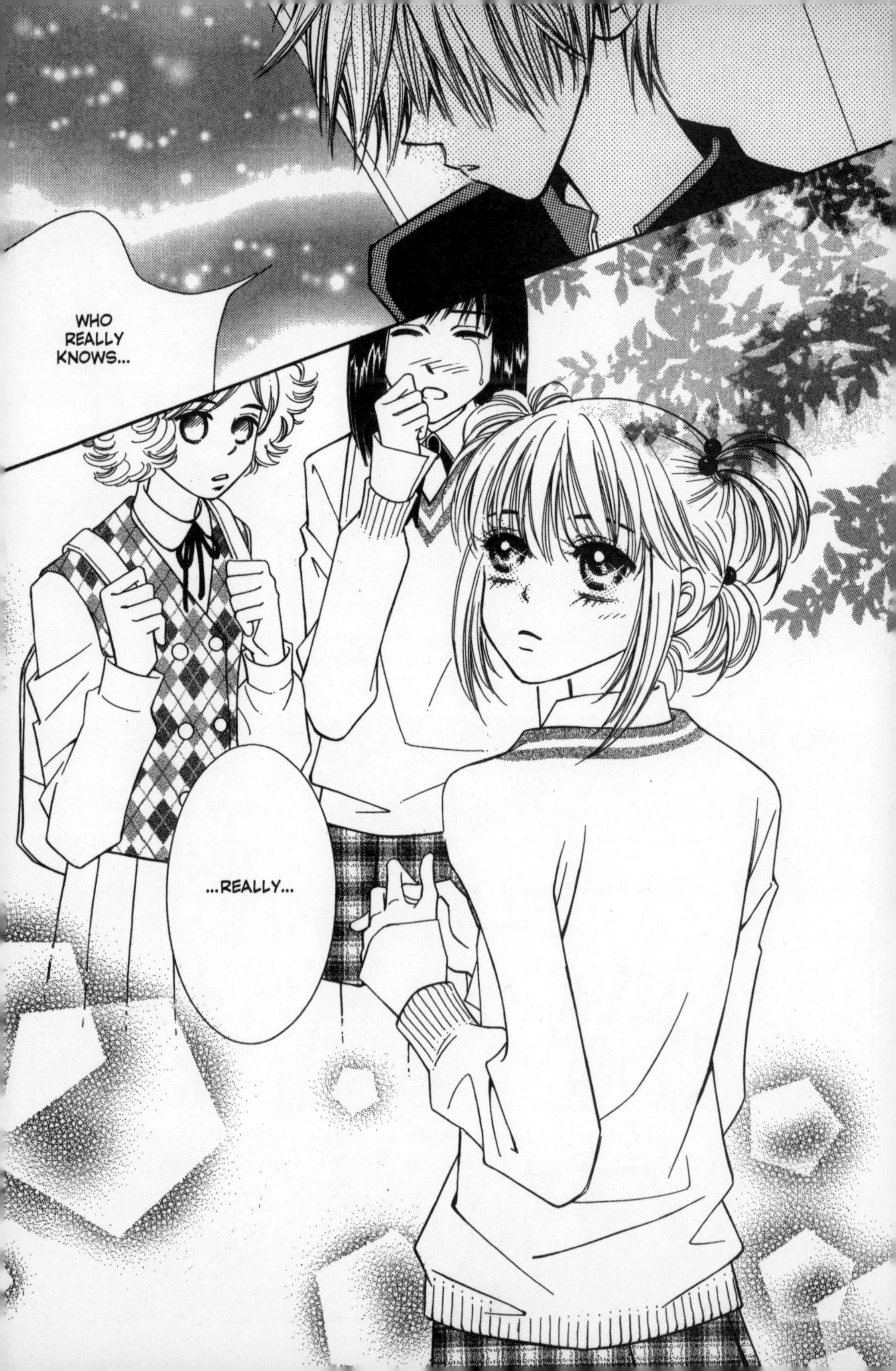
WHO REALLY KNOWS...
...REALLY...

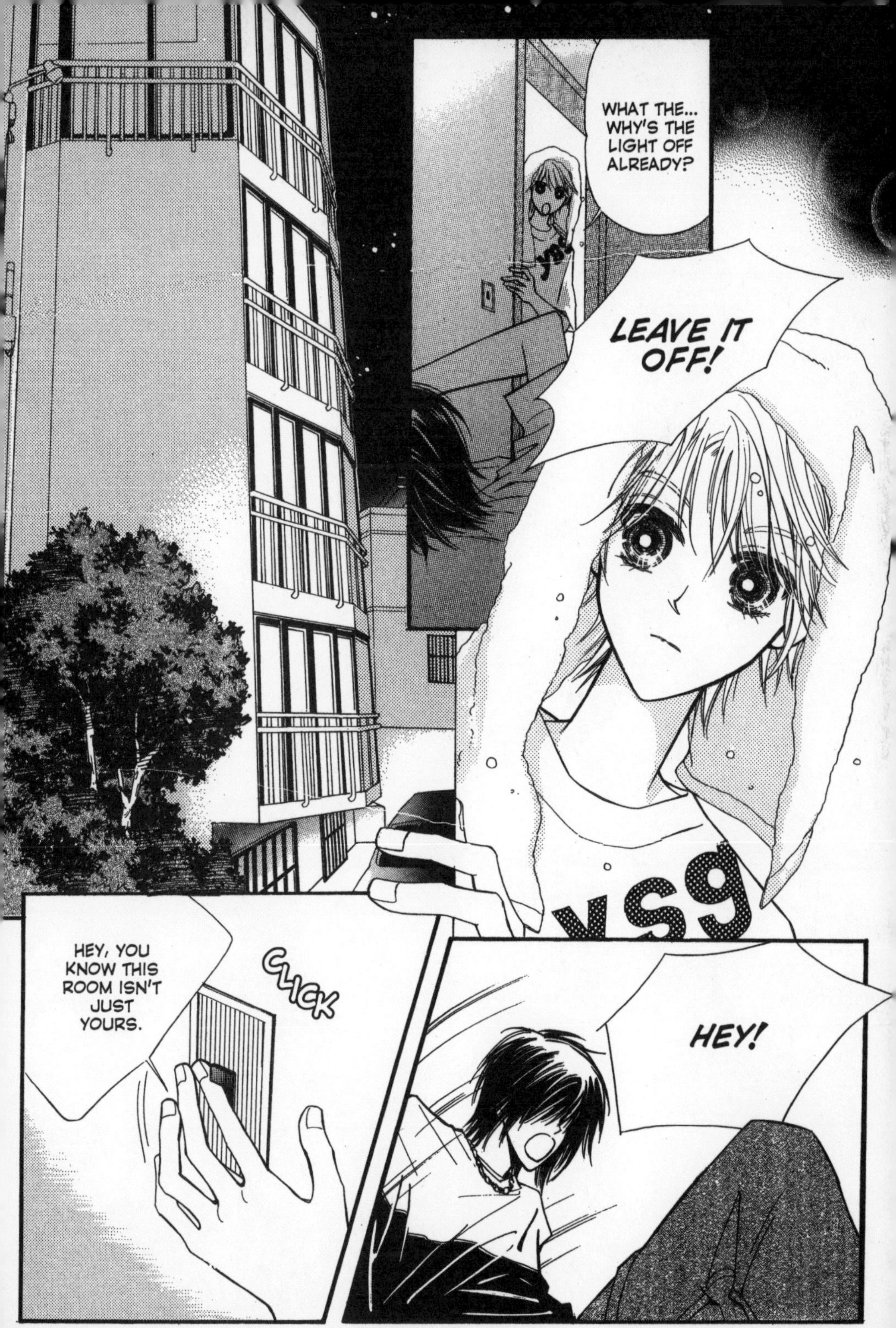
WHAT THE... WHY'S THE LIGHT OFF ALREADY?
LEAVE IT OFF!
HEY, YOU KNOW THIS ROOM ISN'T JUST YOURS.
CLICK
HEY!

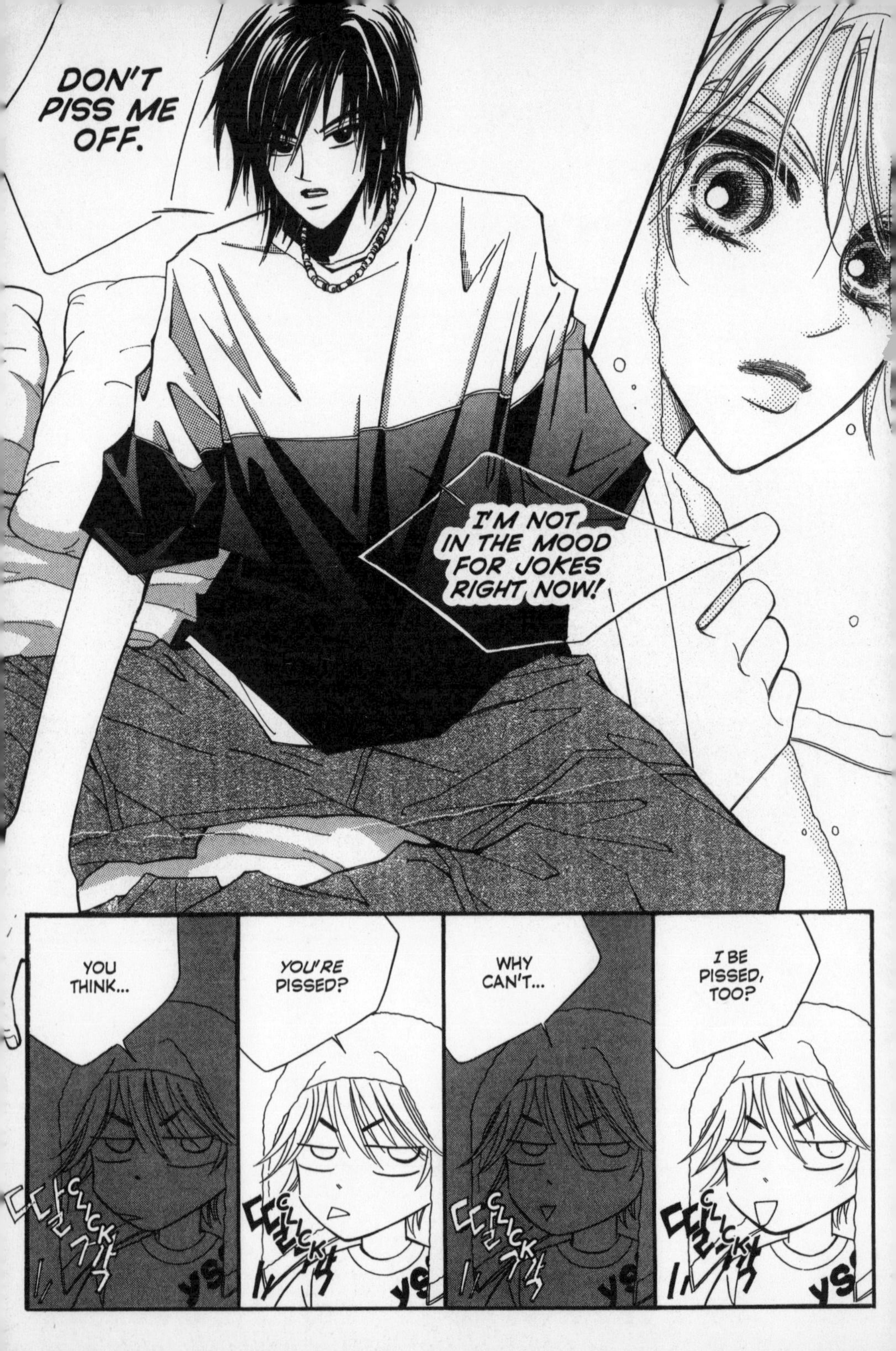
DON'T PISS ME OFF.
I'M NOT IN THE MOOD FOR JOKES RIGHT NOW!
YOU THINK...
CLICK
YOU'RE PISSED?
CLICK
WHY CAN'T...
CLICK
I BE PISSED, TOO?
CLICK

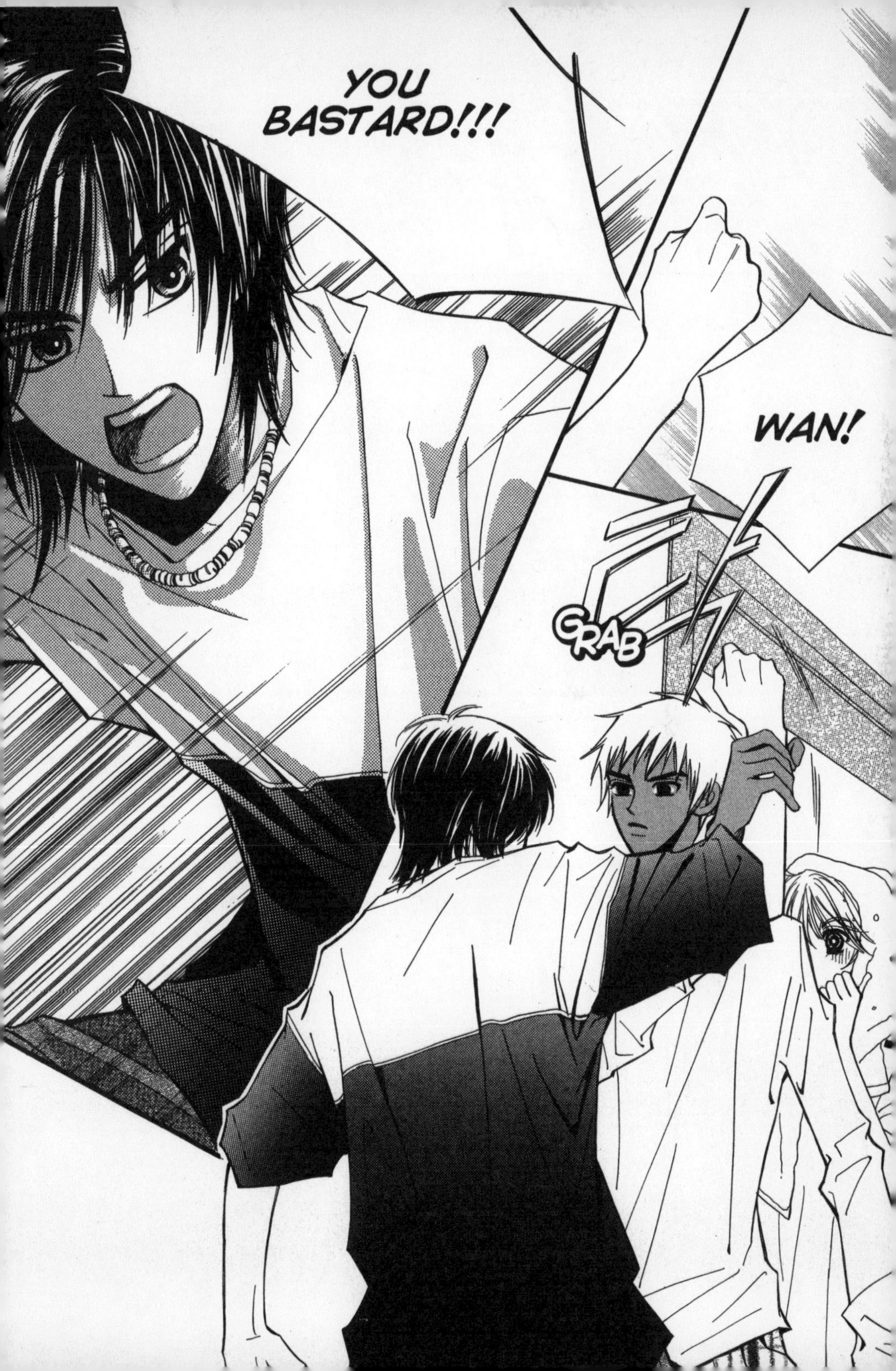
YOU BASTARD!!!
WAN!
GRAB

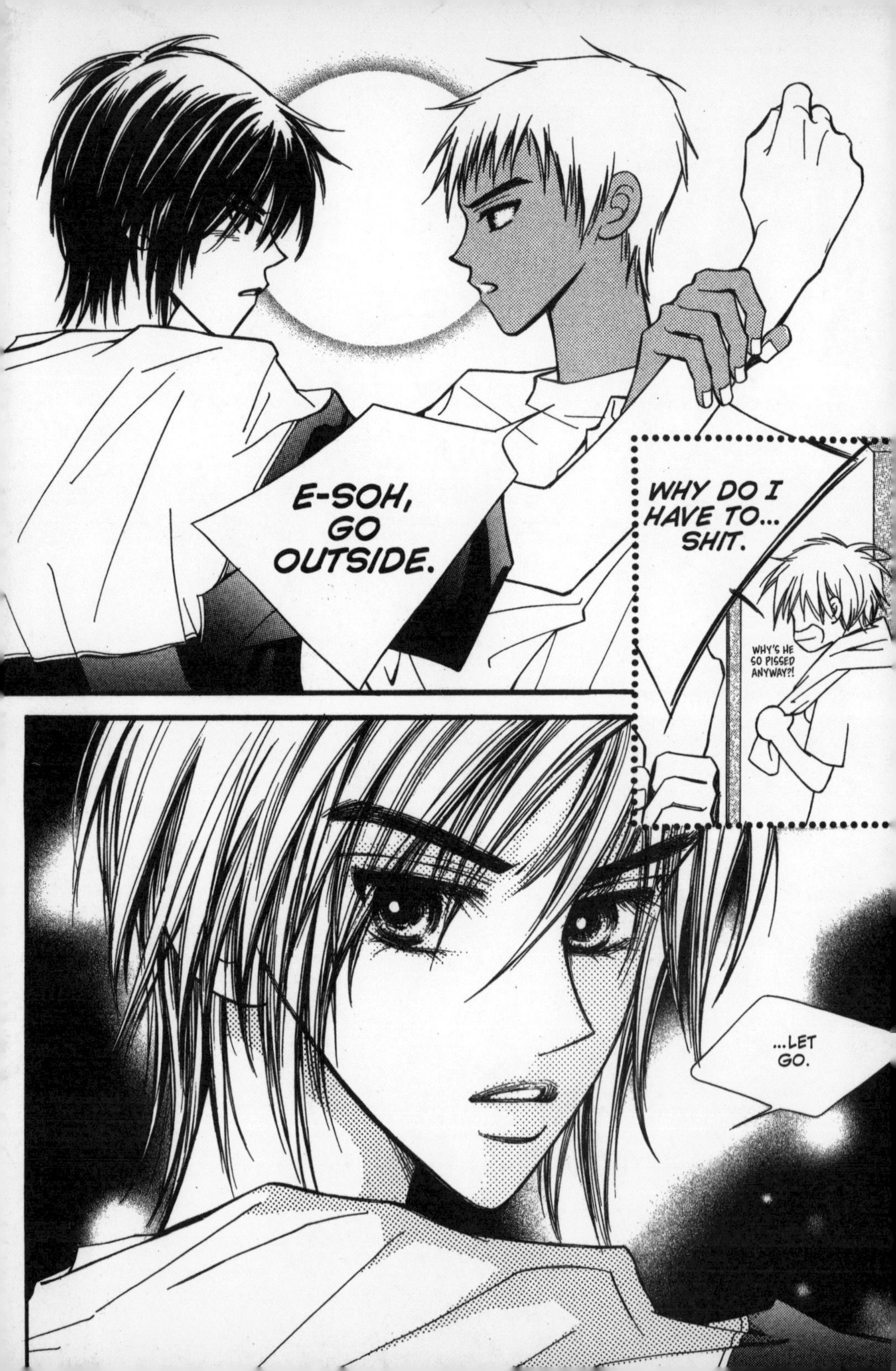
E-SOH, GO OUTSIDE.
WHY DO I HAVE TO... SHIT.
WHY'S HE SO PISSED ANYWAY?!
...LET GO.

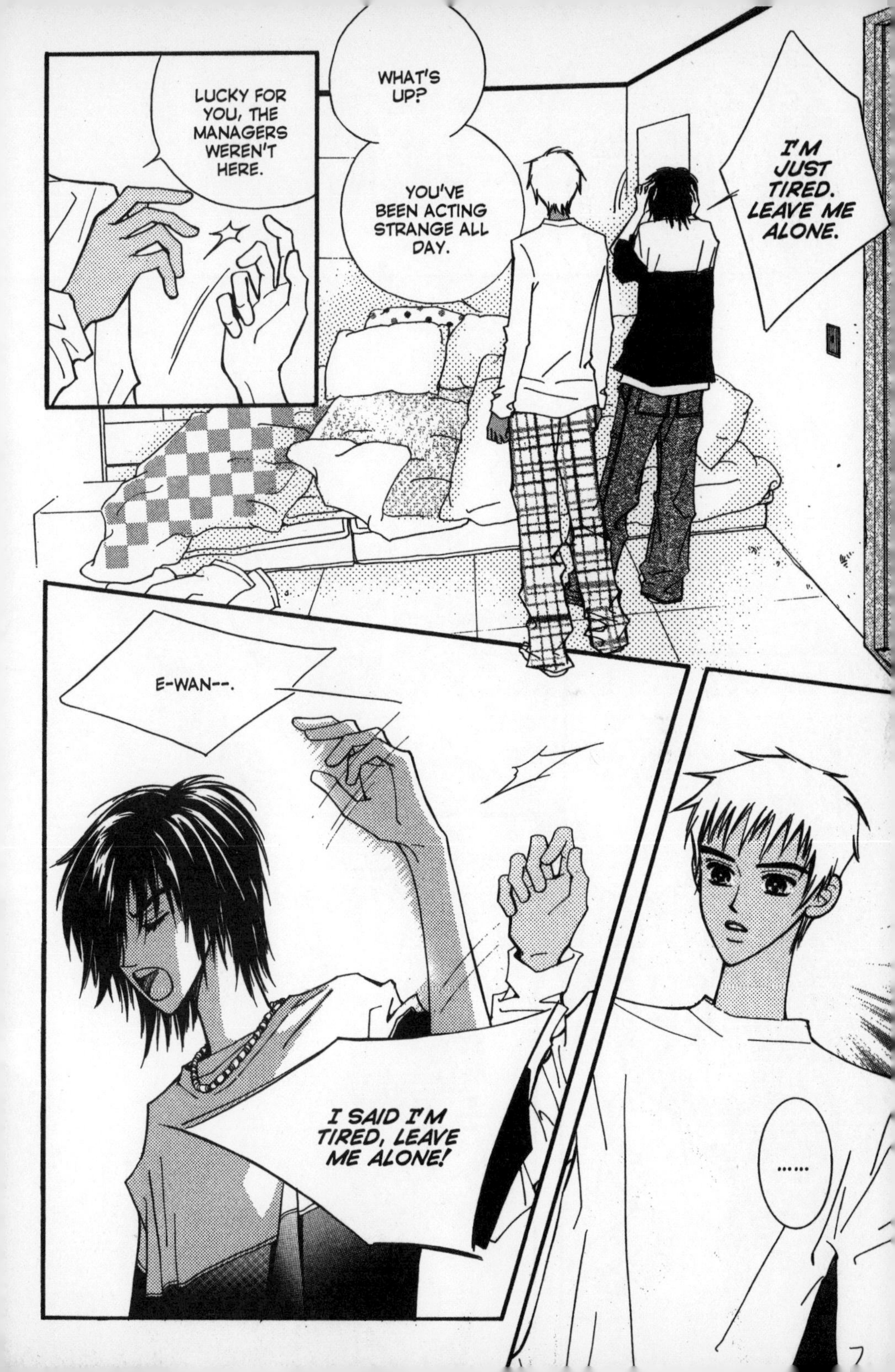
LUCKY FOR YOU, THE MANAGERS WEREN'T HERE.
WHAT'S UP?
YOU'VE BEEN ACTING STRANGE ALL DAY.
I'M JUST TIRED. LEAVE ME ALONE.
E-WAN--.
I SAID I'M TIRED, LEAVE ME ALONE!
......

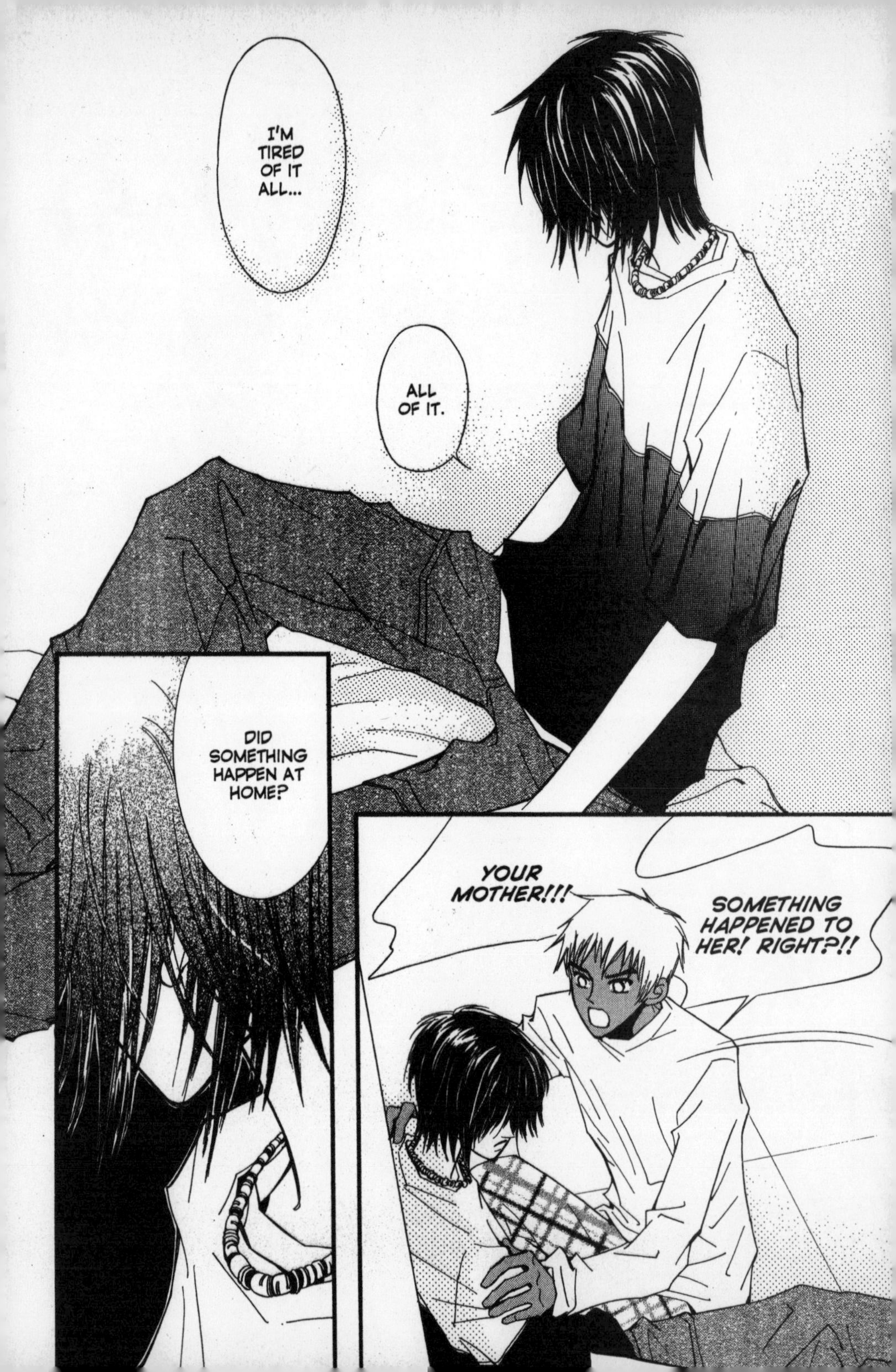
I'M TIRED OF IT ALL...
ALL OF IT.
DID SOMETHING HAPPEN AT HOME?
YOUR MOTHER!!!
SOMETHING HAPPENED TO HER! RIGHT?!!

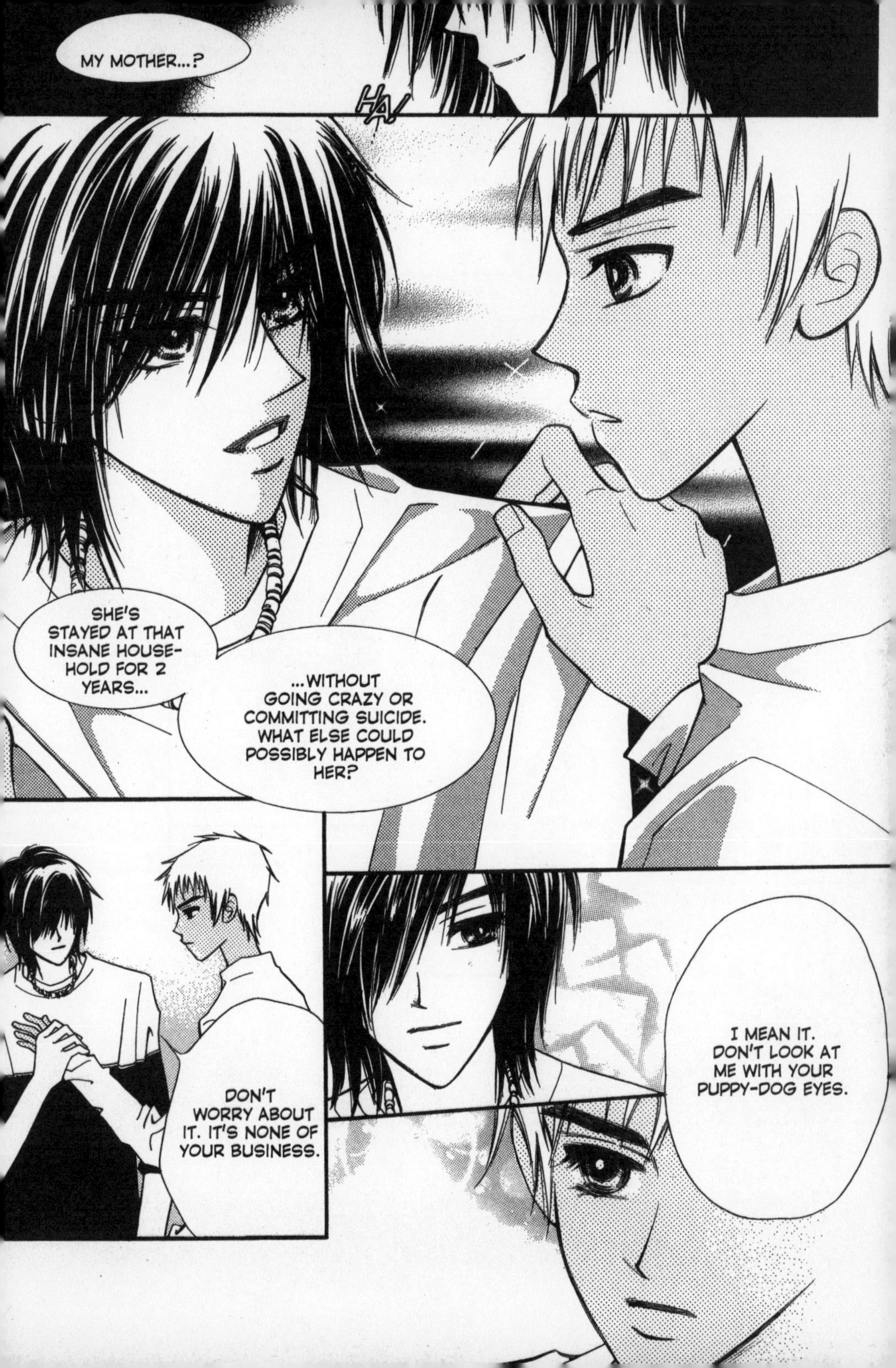
MY MOTHER...?
HA!
SHE'S STAYED AT THAT INSANE HOUSE-HOLD FOR 2 YEARS...
...WITHOUT GOING CRAZY OR COMMITTING SUICIDE. WHAT ELSE COULD POSSIBLY HAPPEN TO HER?
DON'T WORRY ABOUT IT. IT'S NONE OF YOUR BUSINESS.
I MEAN IT. DON'T LOOK AT ME WITH YOUR PUPPY-DOG EYES.

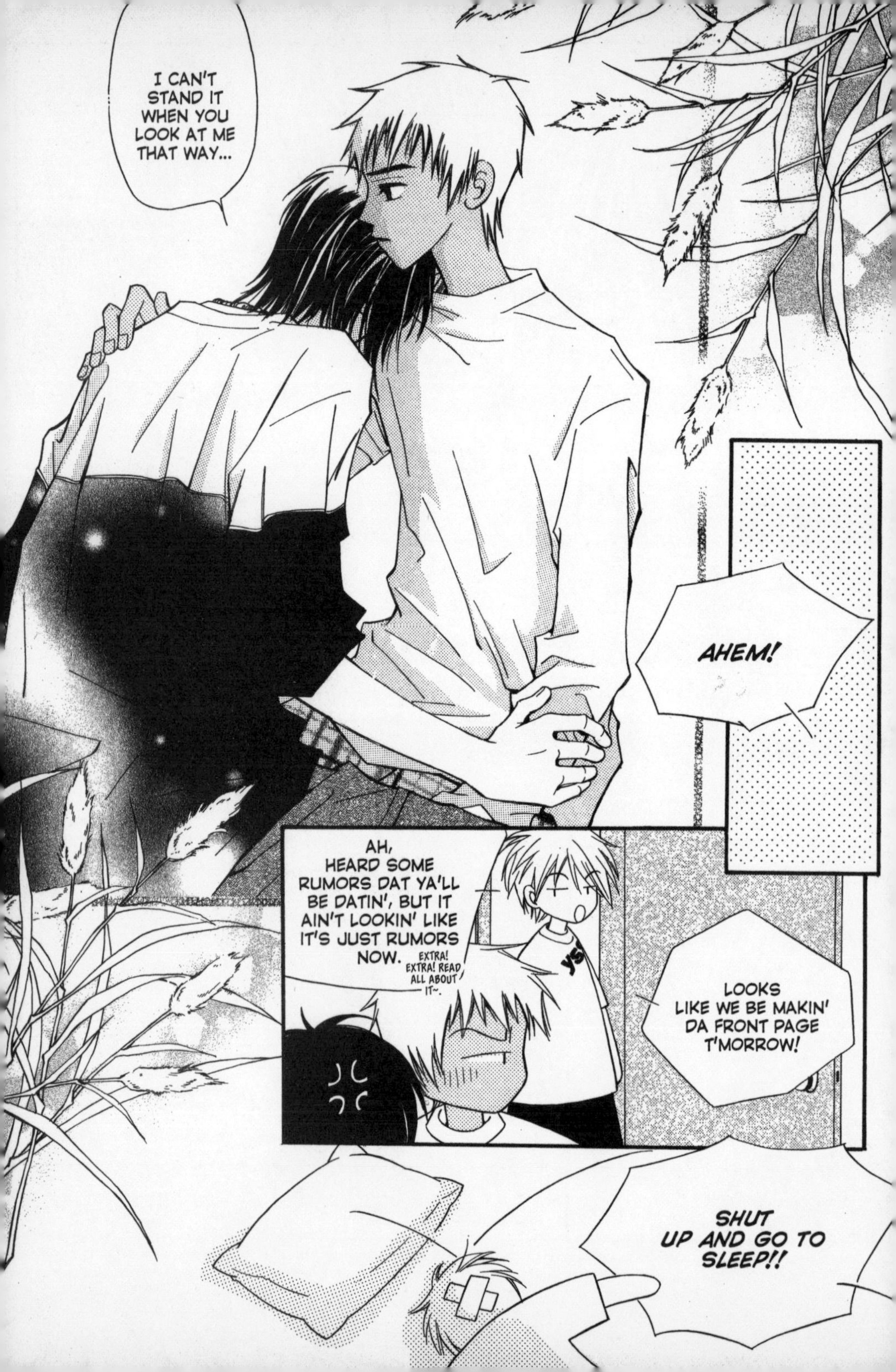
I CAN'T STAND IT WHEN YOU LOOK AT ME THAT WAY...
AHEM!
AH, HEARD SOME RUMORS DAT YA'LL BE DATIN', BUT IT AIN'T LOOKIN' LIKE IT'S JUST RUMORS NOW.
EXTRA! EXTRA! READ ALL ABOUT IT~.
LOOKS LIKE WE BE MAKIN' DA FRONT PAGE T'MORROW!
SHUT UP AND GO TO SLEEP!!

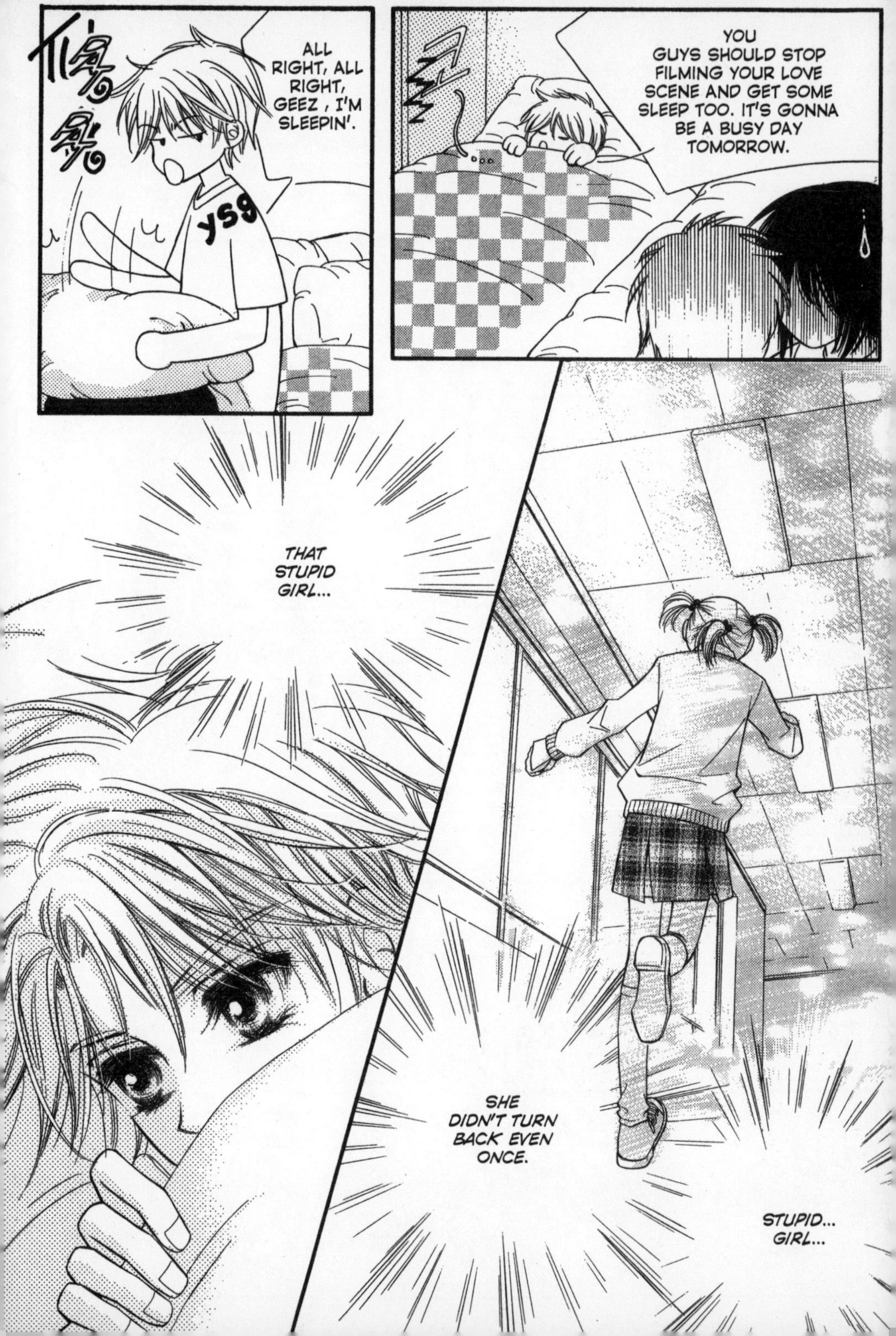
ALL RIGHT, ALL RIGHT, GEEZ, I'M SLEEPIN'.
YOU GUYS SHOULD STOP FILMING YOUR LOVE SCENE AND GET SOME SLEEP TOO. IT'S GONNA BE A BUSY DAY TOMORROW.
THAT STUPID GIRL...
SHE DIDN'T TURN BACK EVEN ONCE.
STUPID... GIRL...

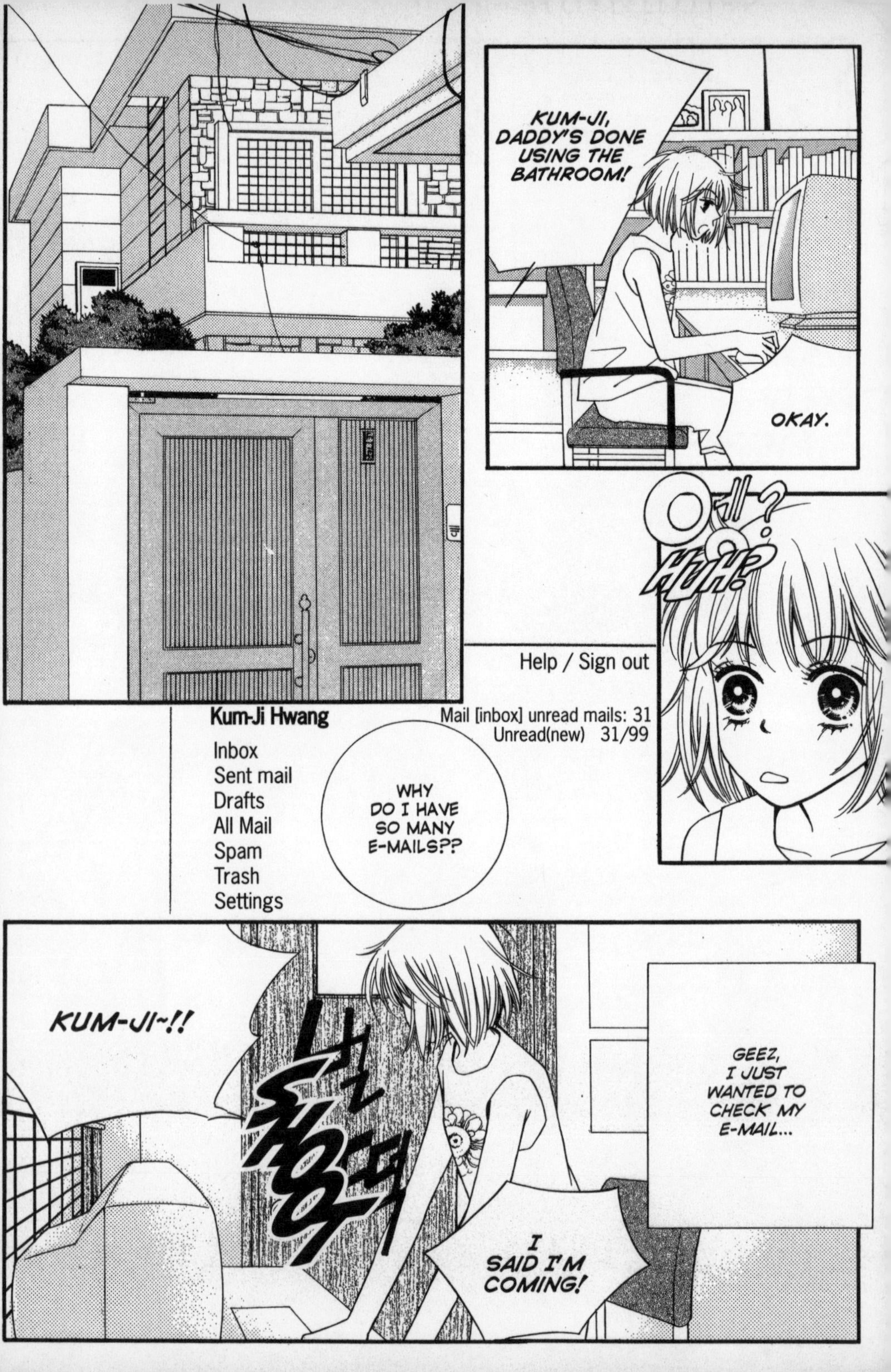
KUM-JI, DADDY'S DONE USING THE BATHROOM!
OKAY.
HUH?
Help / Sign out
Kum-Ji Hwang
Mail [inbox] unread mails: 31
Unread(new) 31/99
Inbox
Sent mail
Drafts
All Mail
Spam
Trash
Settings
WHY DO I HAVE SO MANY E-MAILS??
KUM-JI~!!
SHOOT
I SAID I'M COMING!
GEEZ, I JUST WANTED TO CHECK MY E-MAIL...

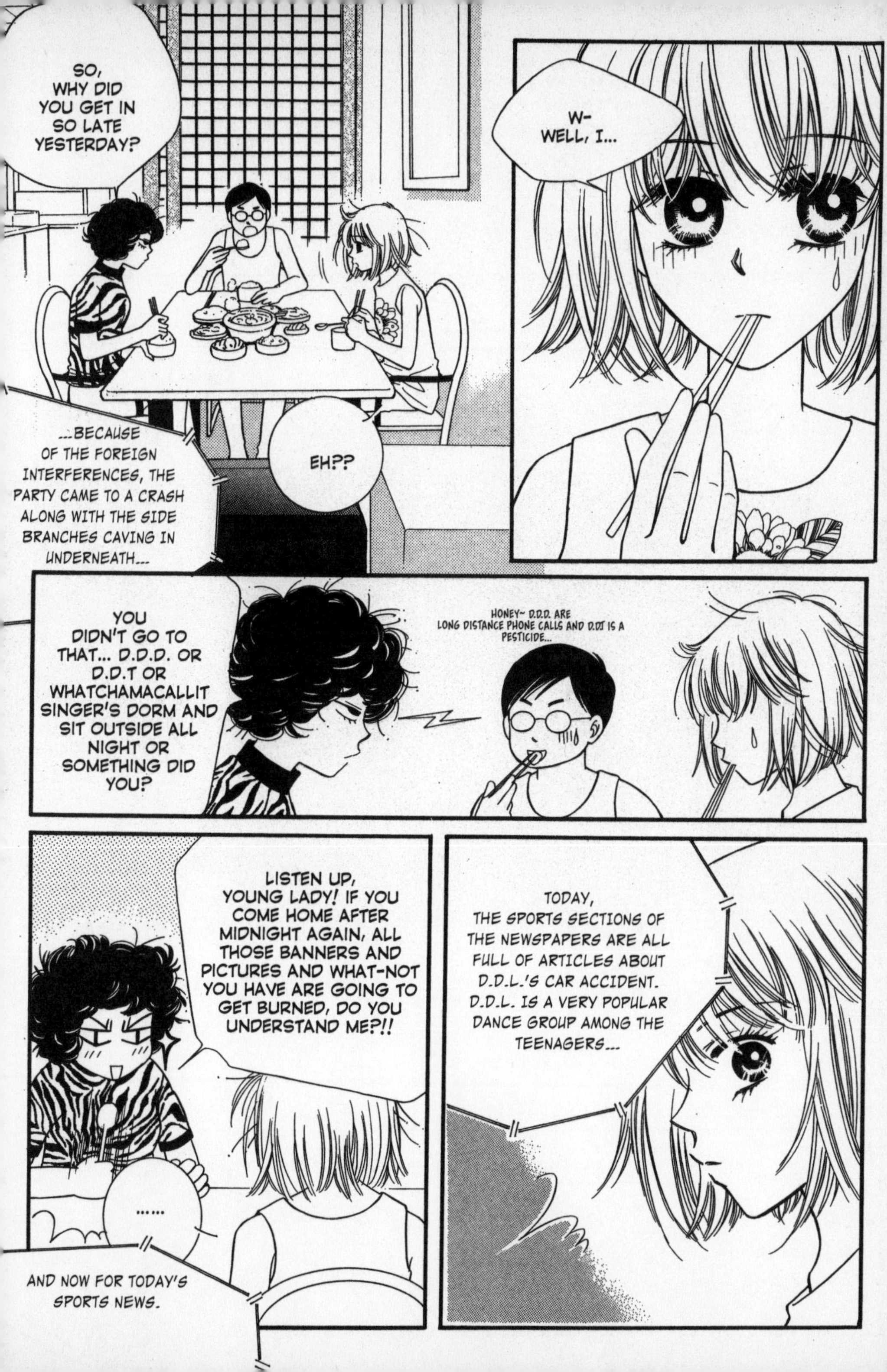
SO, WHY DID YOU GET IN SO LATE YESTERDAY?
...BECAUSE OF THE FOREIGN INTERFERENCES, THE PARTY CAME TO A CRASH ALONG WITH THE SIDE BRANCHES CAVING IN UNDERNEATH...
EH??
W-WELL, I...
YOU DIDN'T GO TO THAT... D.D.D. OR D.D.T OR WHATCHAMACALLIT SINGER'S DORM AND SIT OUTSIDE ALL NIGHT OR SOMETHING DID YOU?
HONEY~ D.D.D. ARE LONG DISTANCE PHONE CALLS AND D.DT IS A PESTICIDE...
LISTEN UP, YOUNG LADY! IF YOU COME HOME AFTER MIDNIGHT AGAIN, ALL THOSE BANNERS AND PICTURES AND WHAT-NOT YOU HAVE ARE GOING TO GET BURNED, DO YOU UNDERSTAND ME?!!
......
AND NOW FOR TODAY'S SPORTS NEWS.
TODAY, THE SPORTS SECTIONS OF THE NEWSPAPERS ARE ALL FULL OF ARTICLES ABOUT D.D.L.'S CAR ACCIDENT. D.D.L. IS A VERY POPULAR DANCE GROUP AMONG THE TEENAGERS...

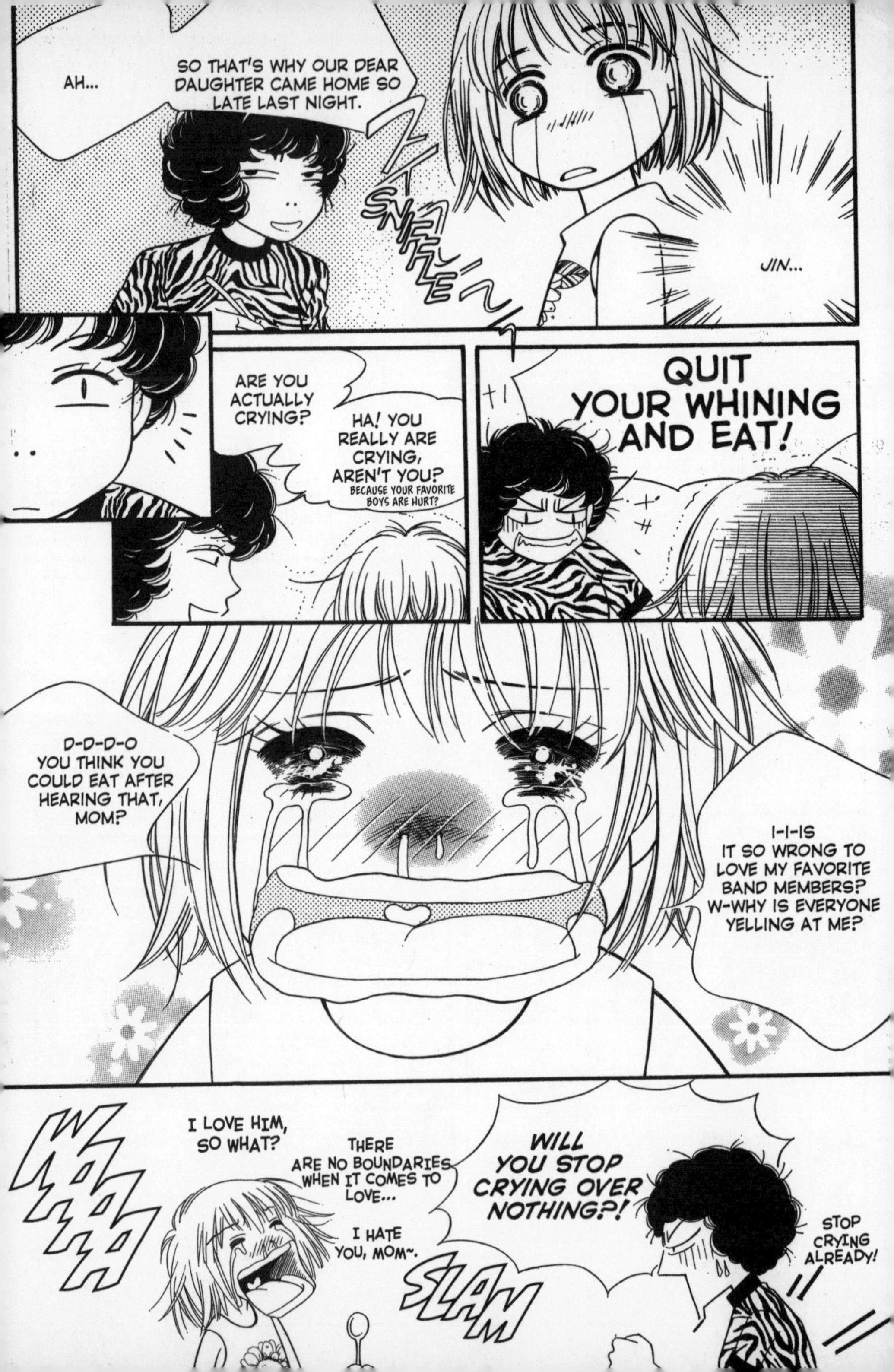
AH...
SO THAT'S WHY OUR DEAR DAUGHTER CAME HOME SO LATE LAST NIGHT.
SNIFFLE
JIN...
...
ARE YOU ACTUALLY CRYING?
HA! YOU REALLY ARE CRYING, AREN'T YOU?
BECAUSE YOUR FAVORITE BOYS ARE HURT?
QUIT YOUR WHINING AND EAT!
D-D-D-O YOU THINK YOU COULD EAT AFTER HEARING THAT, MOM?
I-I-IS IT SO WRONG TO LOVE MY FAVORITE BAND MEMBERS? W-WHY IS EVERYONE YELLING AT ME?
WAAAAH
I LOVE HIM, SO WHAT?
THERE ARE NO BOUNDARIES WHEN IT COMES TO LOVE...
I HATE YOU, MOM~.
SLAM
WILL YOU STOP CRYING OVER NOTHING?!
STOP CRYING ALREADY!

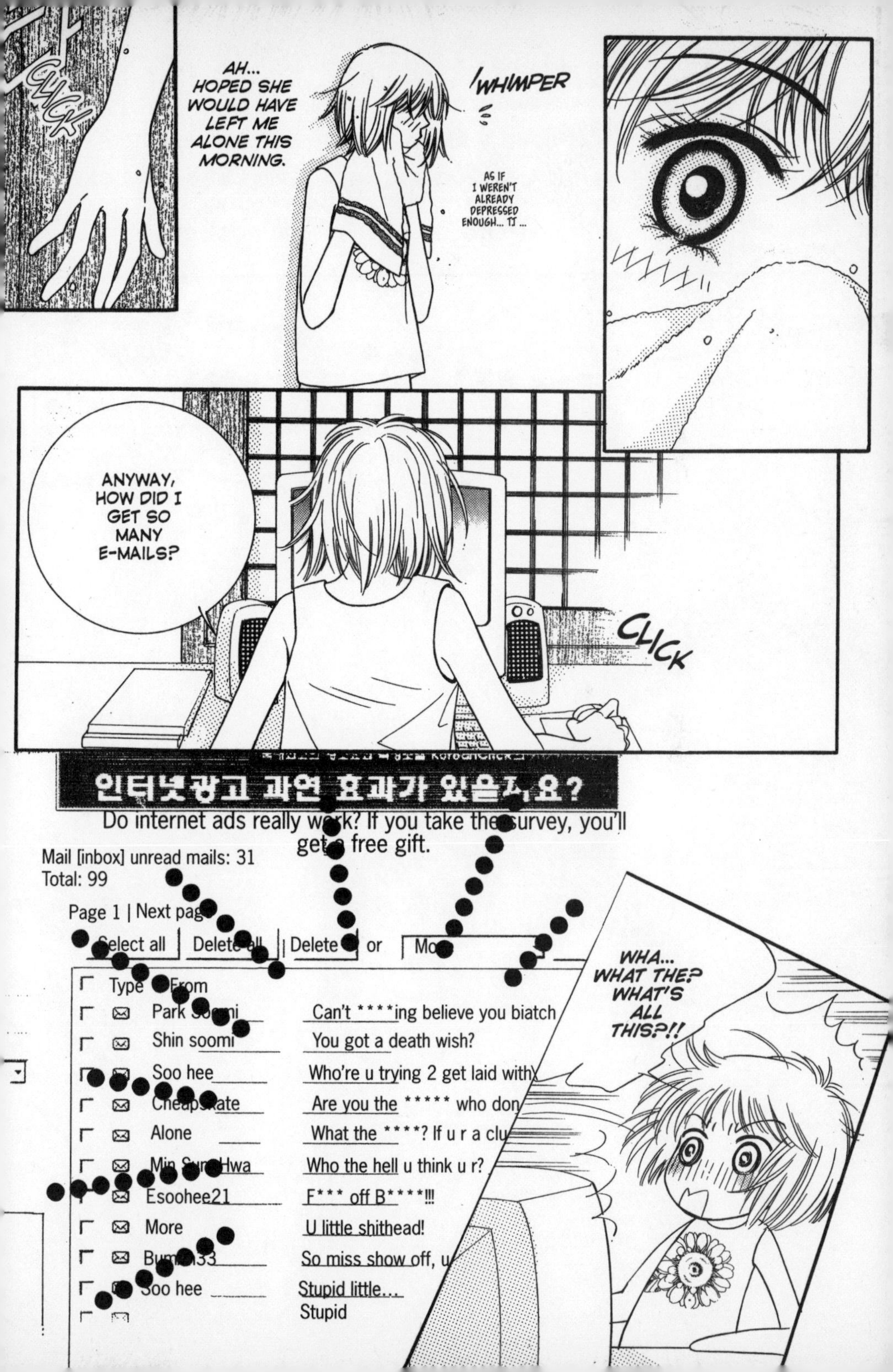
CLICK
AH... HOPED SHE WOULD HAVE LEFT ME ALONE THIS MORNING.
WHIMPER
AS IF I WEREN'T ALREADY DEPRESSED ENOUGH... TT ...
ANYWAY, HOW DID I GET SO MANY E-MAILS?
CLICK
인터넷광고 과연 효과가 있을지요?
Do internet ads really work? If you take the survey, you'll get a free gift.
Mail [inbox] unread mails: 31
Total: 99
Page 1 | Next page
Select all | Delete all | Delete or | More
Type From
Park Soomi Can't ****ing believe you biatch
Shin soomi You got a death wish?
Soo hee Who're u trying 2 get laid with
Cheapskate Are you the ***** who don
Alone What the ****? If u r a clu
Min Sung Hwa Who the hell u think u r?
Esoohee21 F*** off B****!!!
More U little shithead!
Bum33 So miss show off, u
Soo hee Stupid little...
Stupid
WHA... WHAT THE? WHAT'S ALL THIS?!!

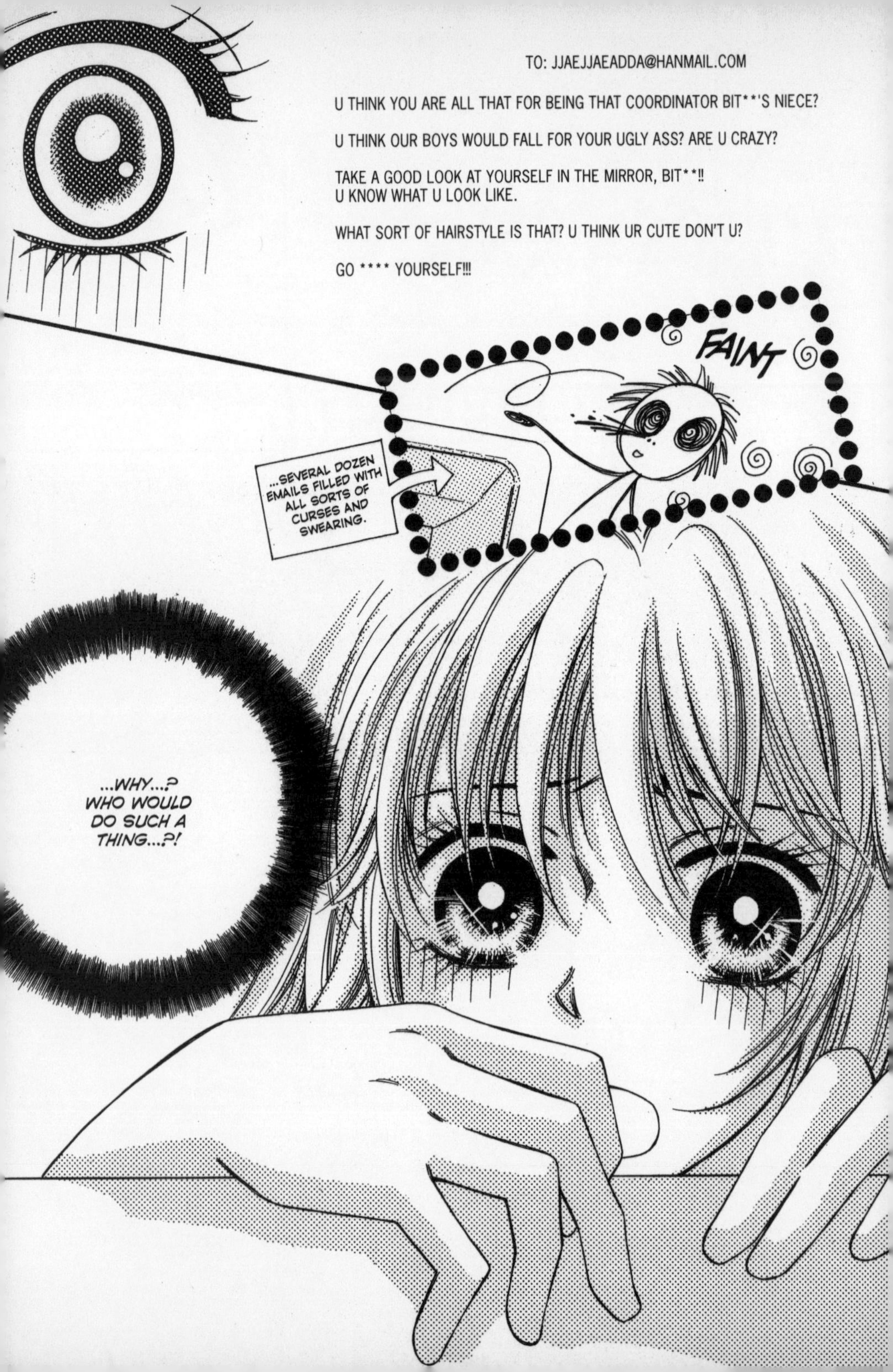
TO: JJAEJJAEADDA@HANMAIL.COM
U THINK YOU ARE ALL THAT FOR BEING THAT COORDINATOR BIT**'S NIECE?
U THINK OUR BOYS WOULD FALL FOR YOUR UGLY ASS? ARE U CRAZY?
TAKE A GOOD LOOK AT YOURSELF IN THE MIRROR, BIT**!! U KNOW WHAT U LOOK LIKE.
WHAT SORT OF HAIRSTYLE IS THAT? U THINK UR CUTE DON'T U?
GO **** YOURSELF!!!
...SEVERAL DOZEN EMAILS FILLED WITH ALL SORTS OF CURSES AND SWEARING.
FAINT
...WHY...? WHO WOULD DO SUCH A THING...?!

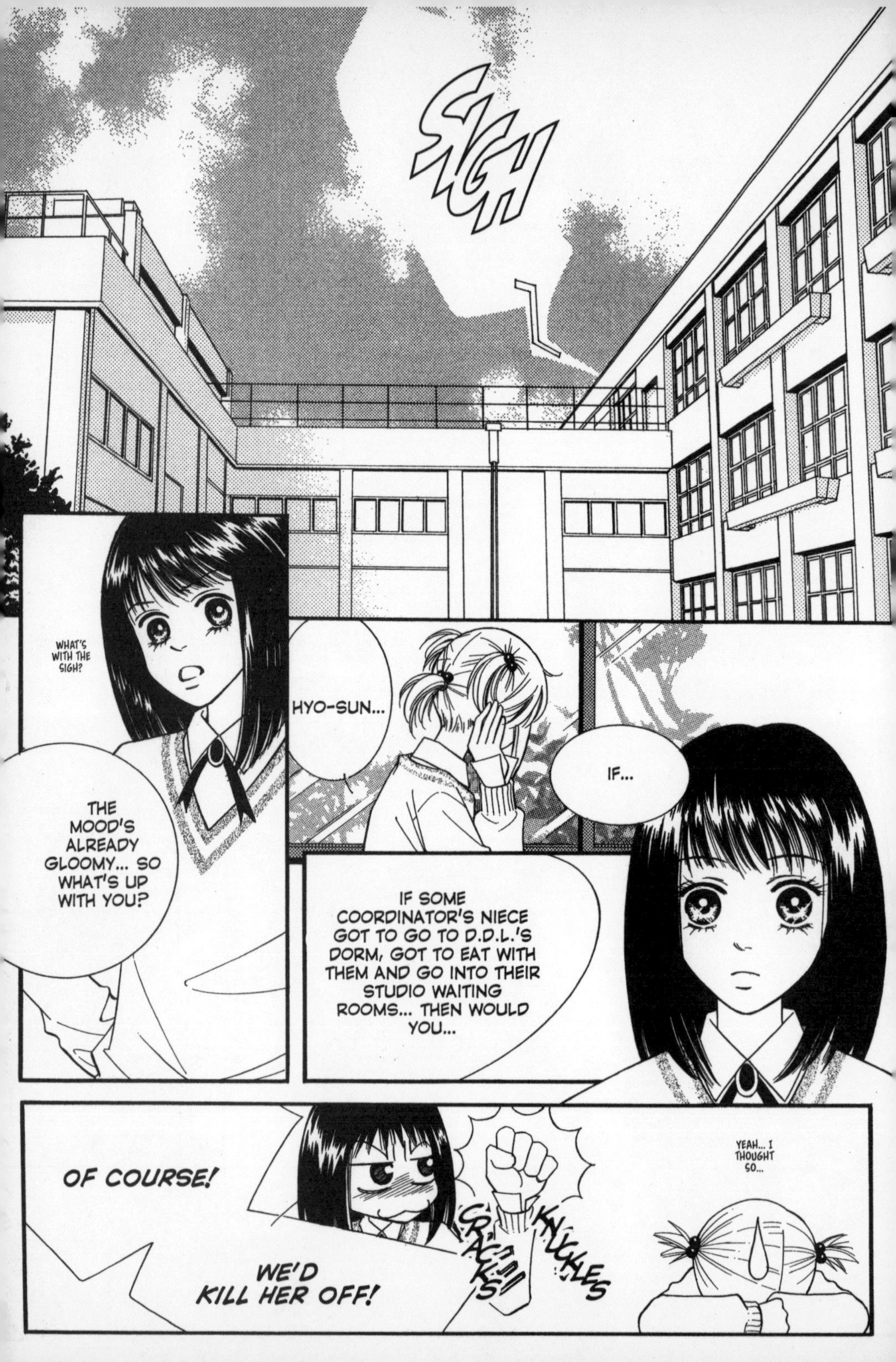
SIGH
WHAT'S WITH THE SIGH?
THE MOOD'S ALREADY GLOOMY... SO WHAT'S UP WITH YOU?
HYO-SUN...
IF...
IF SOME COORDINATOR'S NIECE GOT TO GO TO D.D.L.'S DORM, GOT TO EAT WITH THEM AND GO INTO THEIR STUDIO WAITING ROOMS... THEN WOULD YOU...
OF COURSE!
WE'D KILL HER OFF!
CRACKS!!
KNUCKLES
YEAH... I THOUGHT SO...

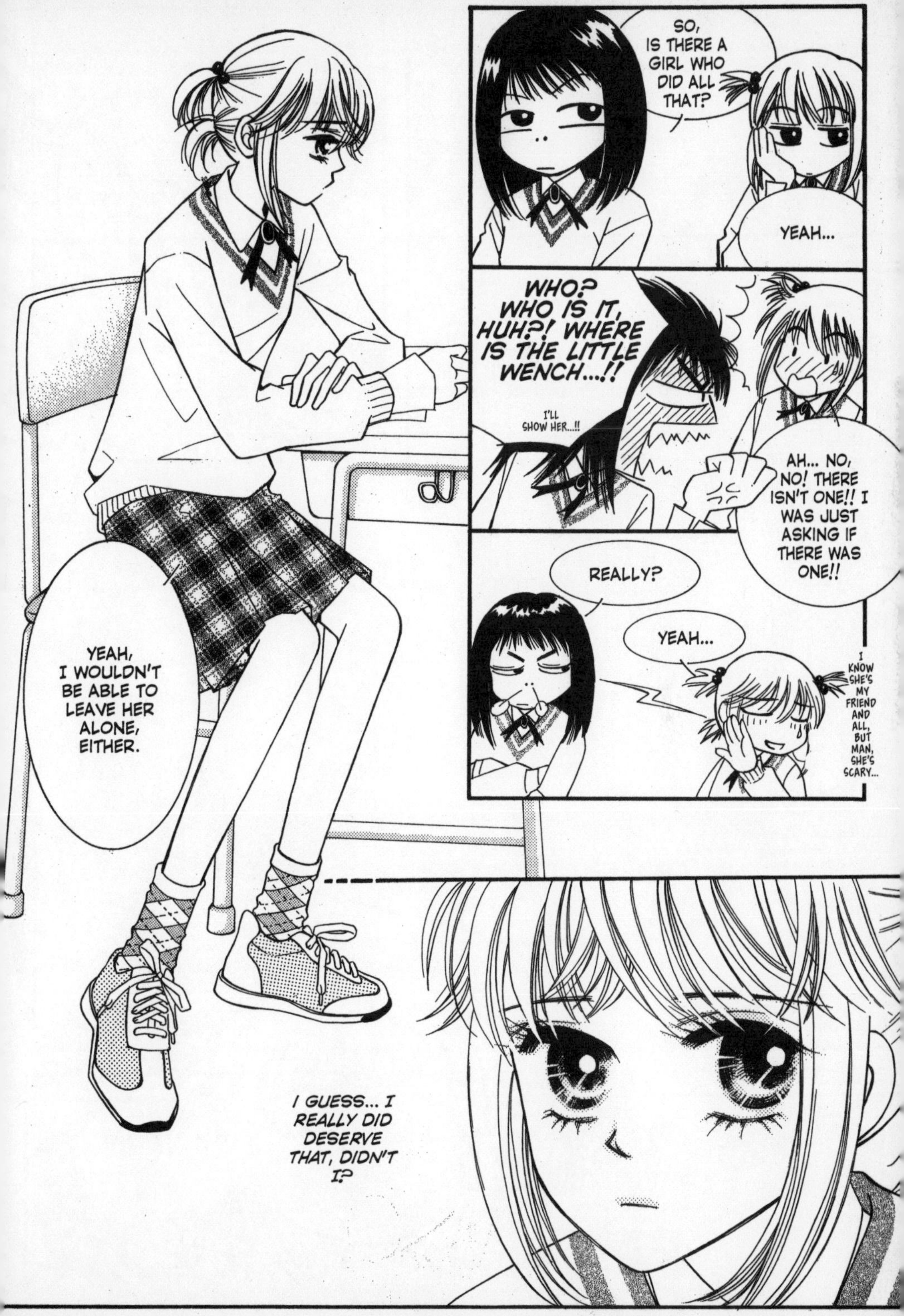
YEAH, I WOULDN'T BE ABLE TO LEAVE HER ALONE, EITHER.
SO, IS THERE A GIRL WHO DID ALL THAT?
YEAH...
WHO? WHO IS IT, HUH?! WHERE IS THE LITTLE WENCH...!!
I'LL SHOW HER...!!
AH... NO, NO! THERE ISN'T ONE!! I WAS JUST ASKING IF THERE WAS ONE!!
REALLY?
YEAH...
I KNOW SHE'S MY FRIEND AND ALL, BUT MAN, SHE'S SCARY...
I GUESS... I REALLY DID DESERVE THAT, DIDN'T I?

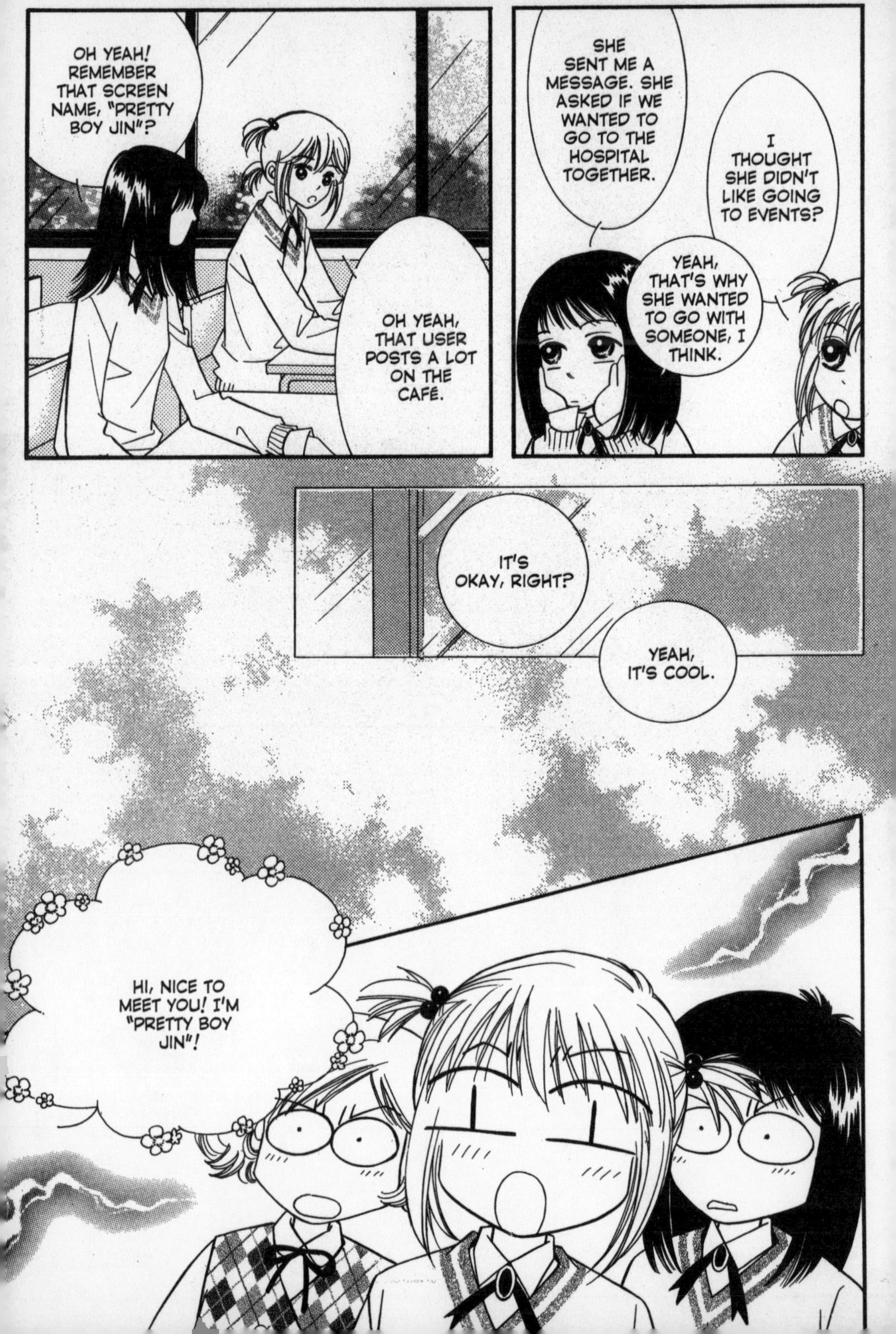
OH YEAH! REMEMBER THAT SCREEN NAME, "PRETTY BOY JIN"?
OH YEAH, THAT USER POSTS A LOT ON THE CAFÉ.
SHE SENT ME A MESSAGE. SHE ASKED IF WE WANTED TO GO TO THE HOSPITAL TOGETHER.
I THOUGHT SHE DIDN'T LIKE GOING TO EVENTS?
YEAH, THAT'S WHY SHE WANTED TO GO WITH SOMEONE, I THINK.
IT'S OKAY, RIGHT?
YEAH, IT'S COOL.
HI, NICE TO MEET YOU! I'M "PRETTY BOY JIN"!

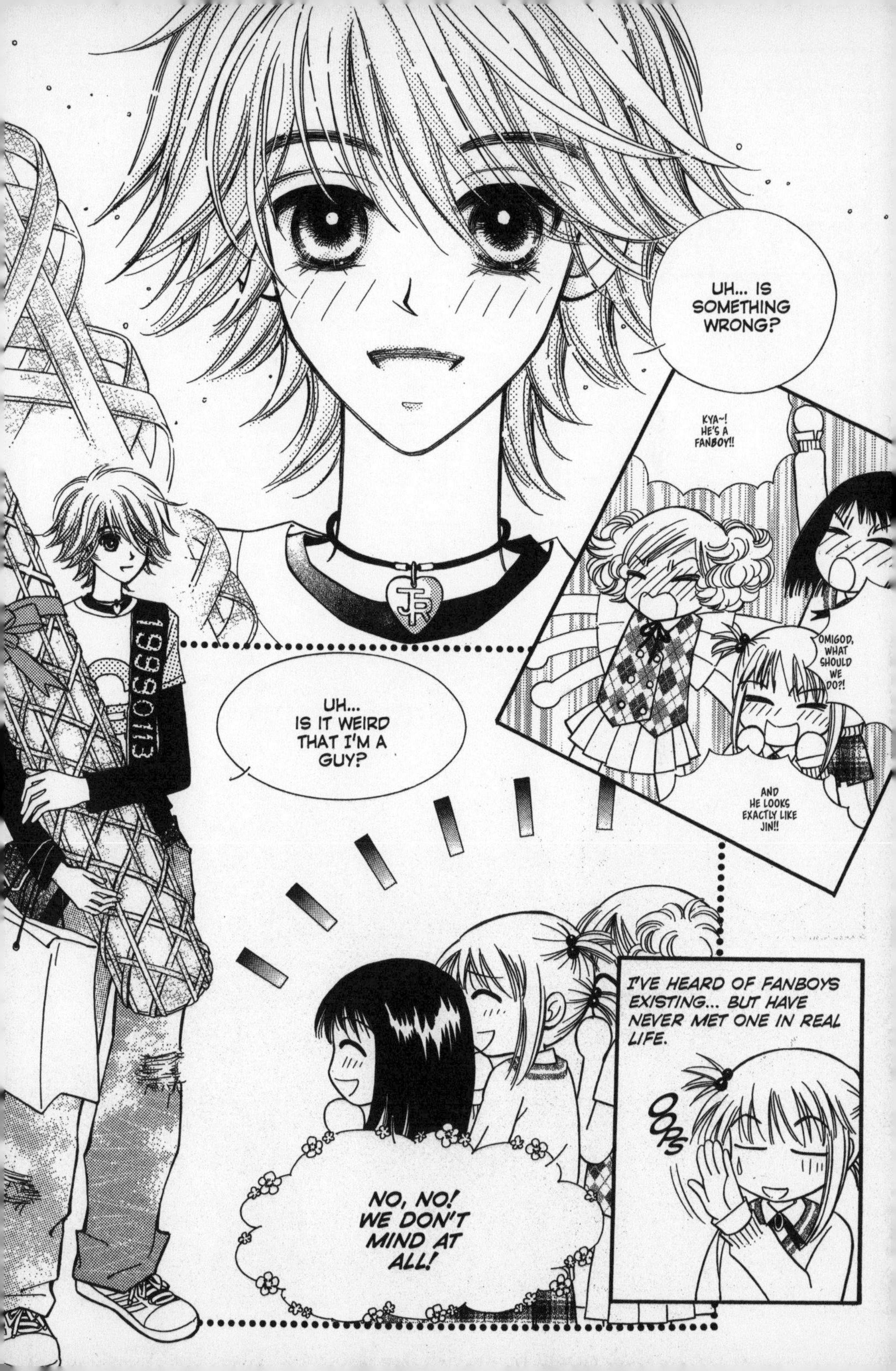
UH... IS SOMETHING WRONG?
KYA~! HE'S A FANBOY!!
OMIGOD, WHAT SHOULD WE DO?!
AND HE LOOKS EXACTLY LIKE JIN!!
UH... IS IT WEIRD THAT I'M A GUY?
NO, NO! WE DON'T MIND AT ALL!
I'VE HEARD OF FANBOYS EXISTING... BUT HAVE NEVER MET ONE IN REAL LIFE.
OOPS

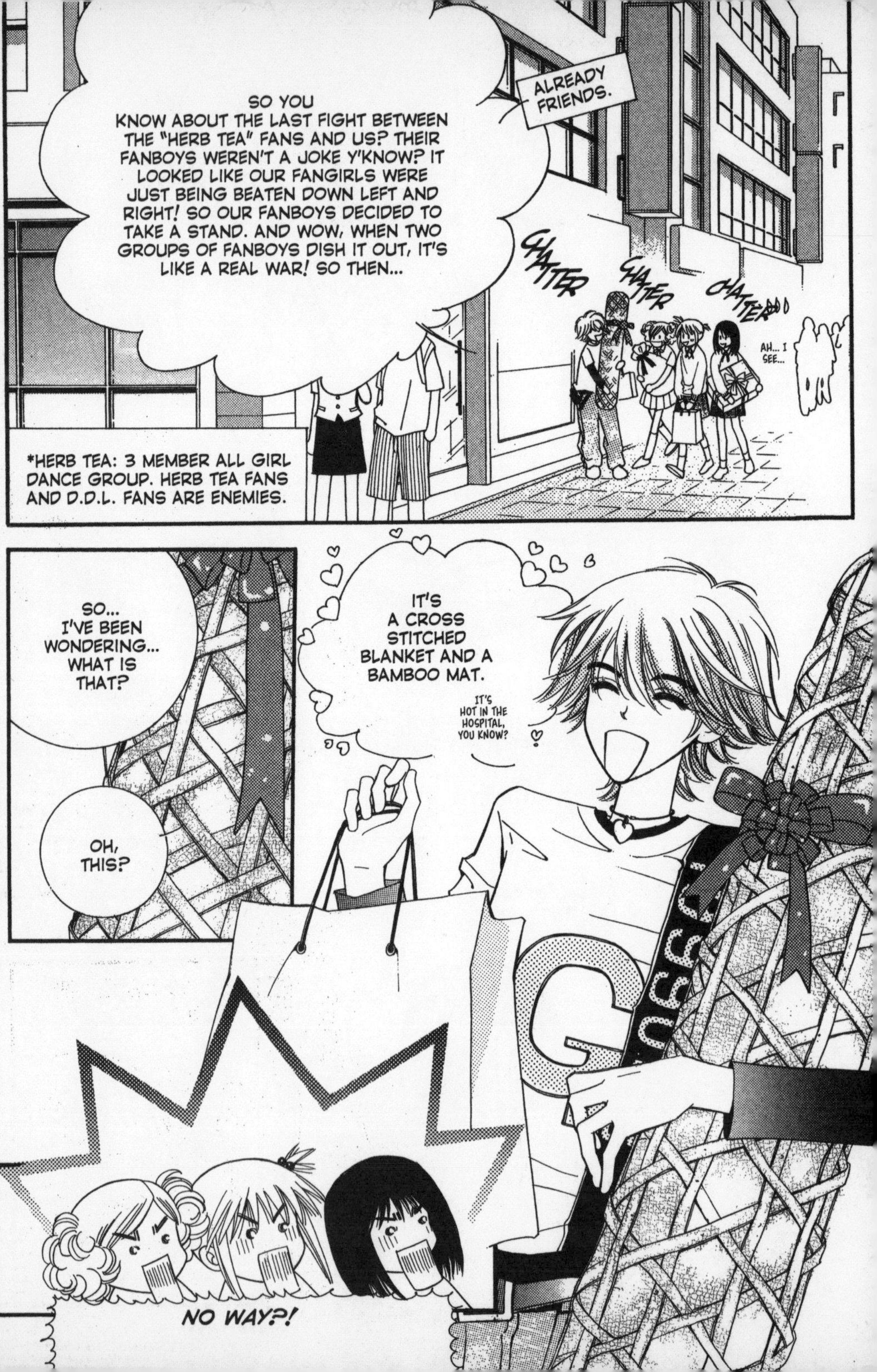
SO YOU KNOW ABOUT THE LAST FIGHT BETWEEN THE "HERB TEA" FANS AND US? THEIR FANBOYS WEREN'T A JOKE Y'KNOW? IT LOOKED LIKE OUR FANGIRLS WERE JUST BEING BEATEN DOWN LEFT AND RIGHT! SO OUR FANBOYS DECIDED TO TAKE A STAND. AND WOW, WHEN TWO GROUPS OF FANBOYS DISH IT OUT, IT'S LIKE A REAL WAR! SO THEN...
ALREADY FRIENDS.
CHATTER
CHATTER
CHATTER
AH... I SEE...
*HERB TEA: 3 MEMBER ALL GIRL DANCE GROUP. HERB TEA FANS AND D.D.L. FANS ARE ENEMIES.
SO... I'VE BEEN WONDERING... WHAT IS THAT?
OH, THIS?
IT'S A CROSS STITCHED BLANKET AND A BAMBOO MAT.
IT'S HOT IN THE HOSPITAL, YOU KNOW?
NO WAY?!

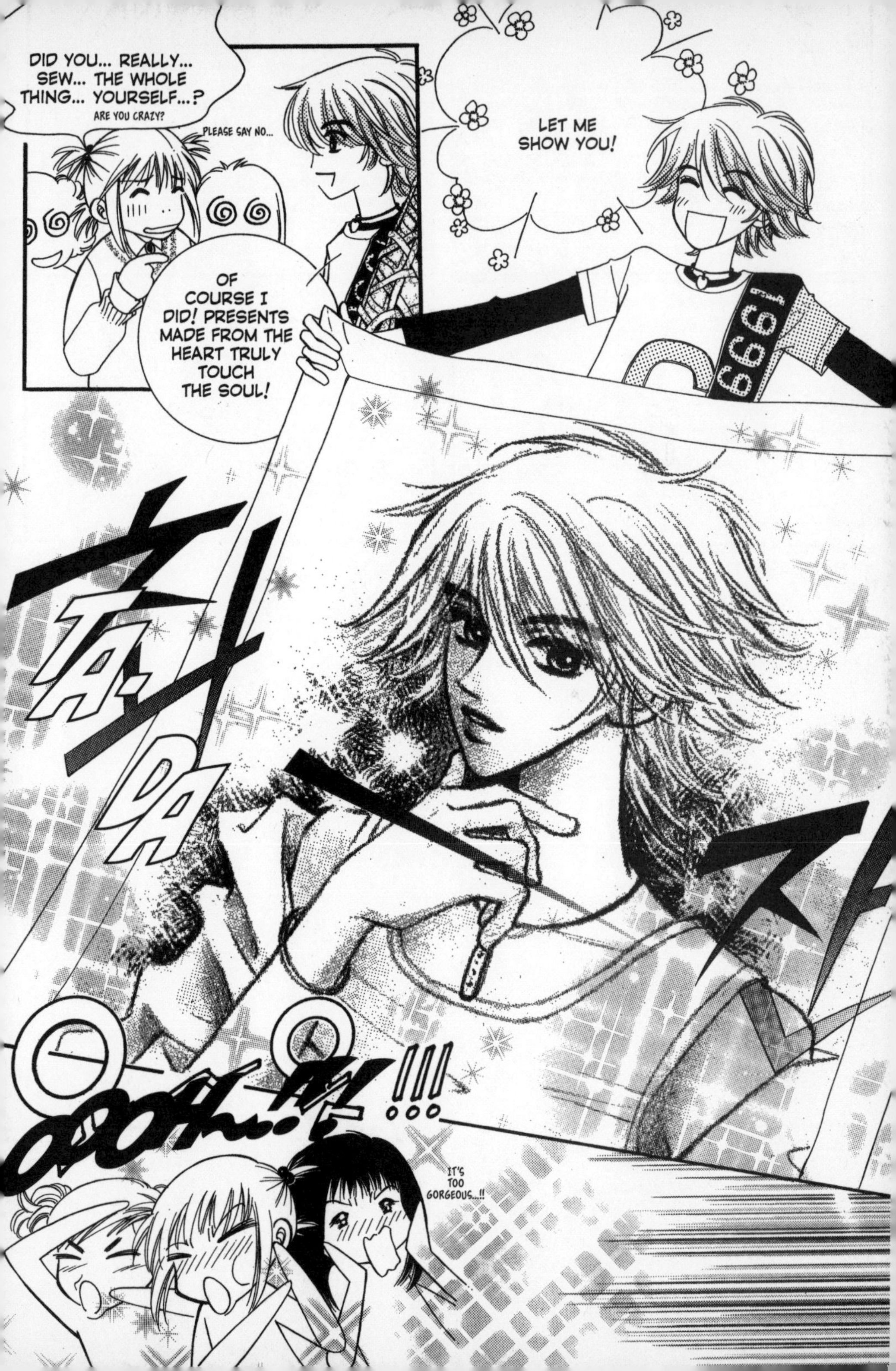
DID YOU... REALLY... SEW... THE WHOLE THING... YOURSELF...?
ARE YOU CRAZY?
PLEASE SAY NO...
OF COURSE I DID! PRESENTS MADE FROM THE HEART TRULY TOUCH THE SOUL!
LET ME SHOW YOU!
TA-DA
IT'S TOO GORGEOUS...!!

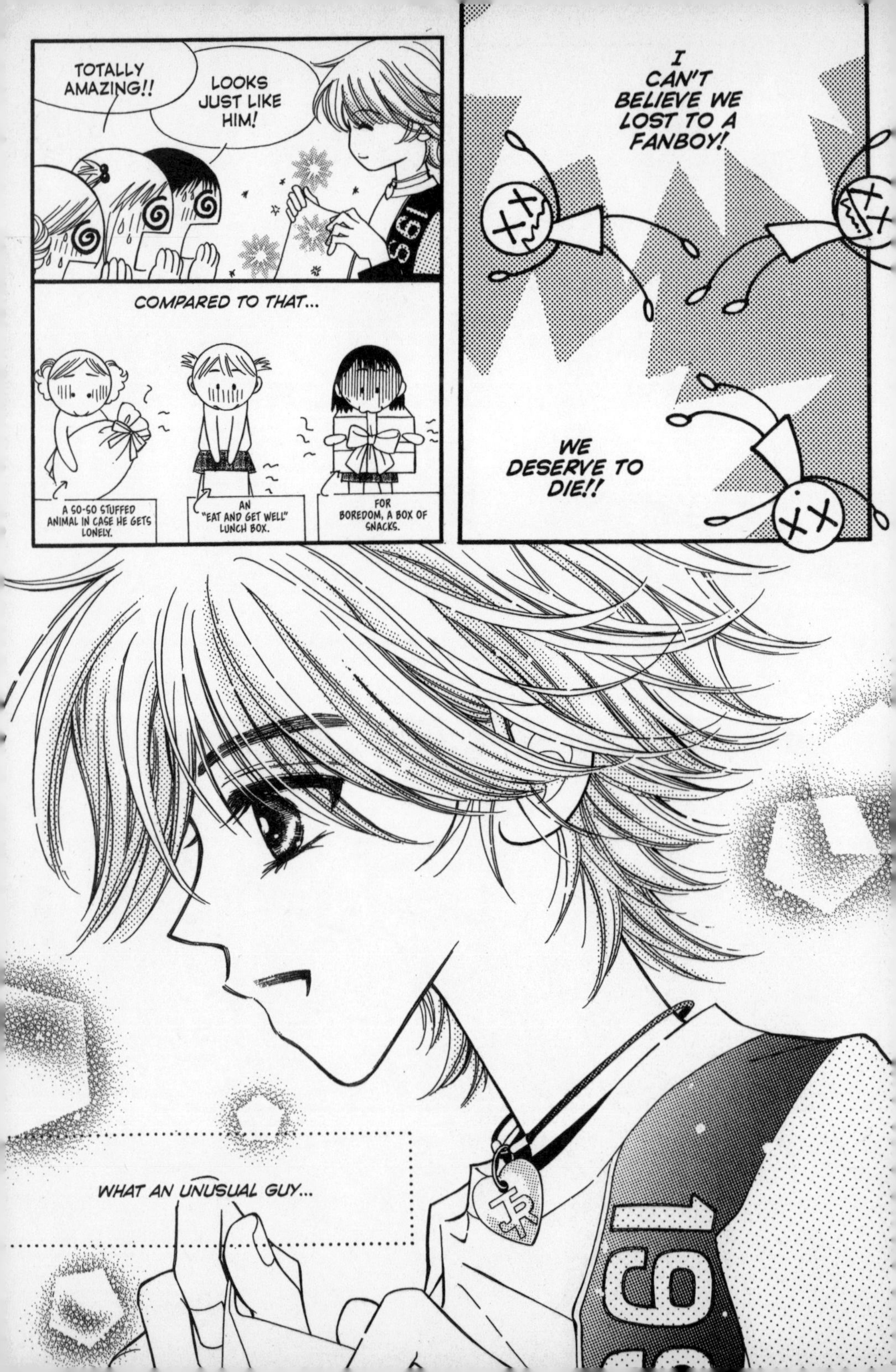
TOTALLY AMAZING!!
LOOKS JUST LIKE HIM!
COMPARED TO THAT...
A SO-SO STUFFED ANIMAL IN CASE HE GETS LONELY.
AN "EAT AND GET WELL" LUNCH BOX.
FOR BOREDOM, A BOX OF SNACKS.
I CAN'T BELIEVE WE LOST TO A FANBOY!
WE DESERVE TO DIE!!
WHAT AN UNUSUAL GUY...

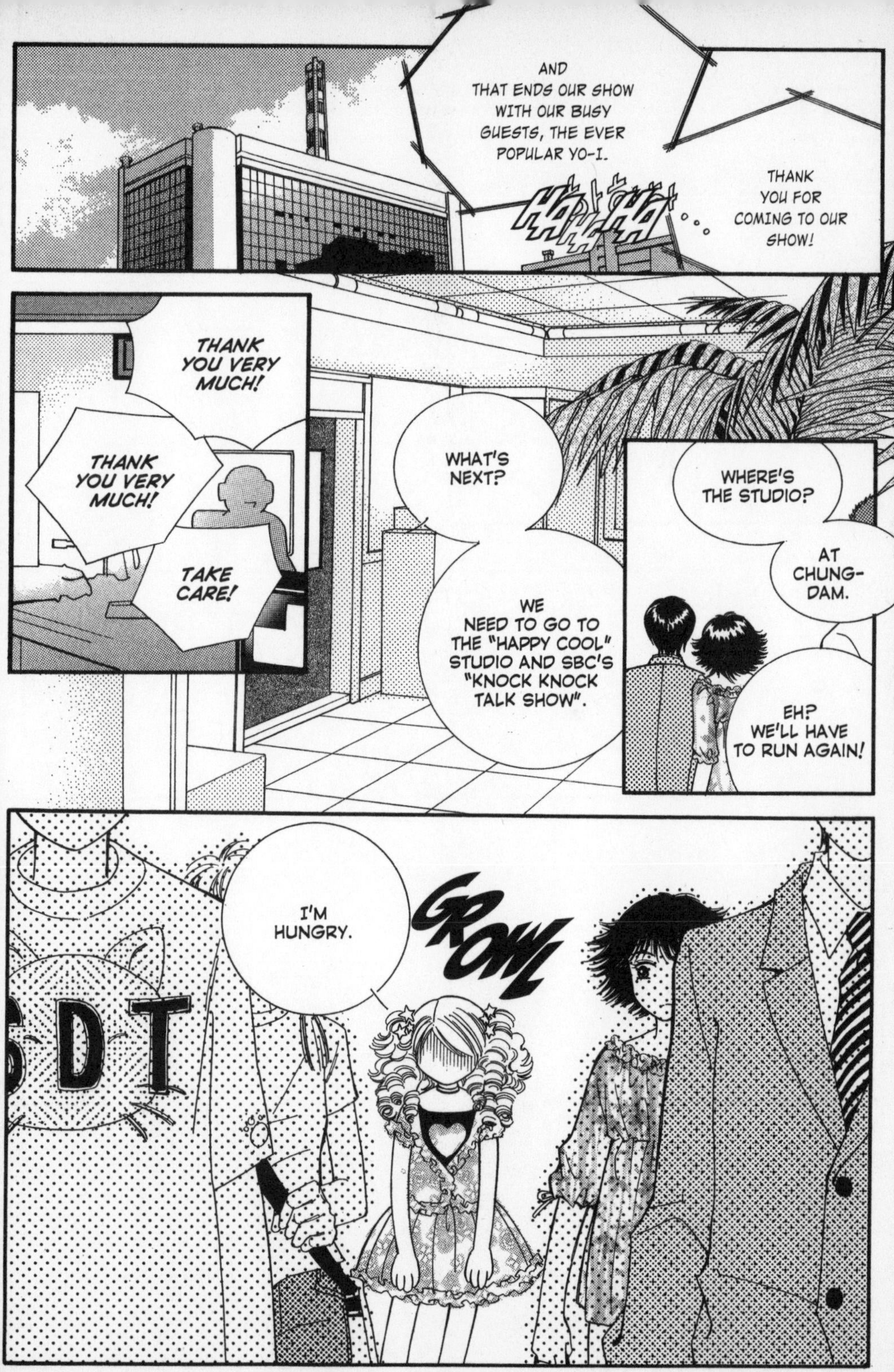
AND THAT ENDS OUR SHOW WITH OUR BUSY GUESTS, THE EVER POPULAR YO-I.
THANK YOU FOR COMING TO OUR SHOW!
THANK YOU VERY MUCH!
THANK YOU VERY MUCH!
TAKE CARE!
WHAT'S NEXT?
WE NEED TO GO TO THE "HAPPY COOL" STUDIO AND SBC'S "KNOCK KNOCK TALK SHOW".
WHERE'S THE STUDIO?
AT CHUNG-DAM.
EH? WE'LL HAVE TO RUN AGAIN!
I'M HUNGRY.
GROWL
SDT

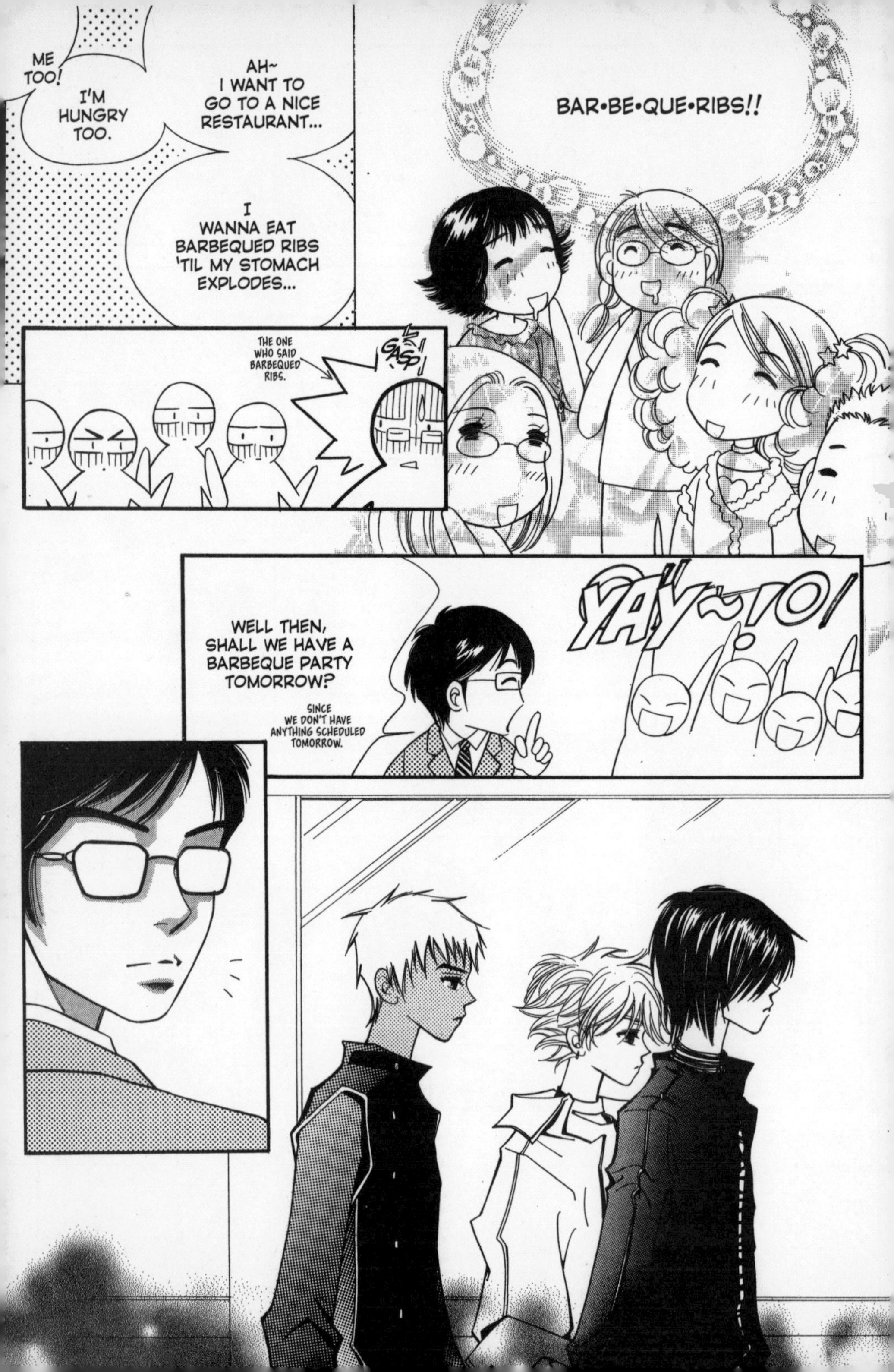

ME TOO!
I'M HUNGRY TOO.
AH~ I WANT TO GO TO A NICE RESTAURANT...
I WANNA EAT BARBEQUED RIBS 'TIL MY STOMACH EXPLODES...
BAR•BE•QUE•RIBS!!
THE ONE WHO SAID BARBEQUED RIBS.
GASP!
WELL THEN, SHALL WE HAVE A BARBEQUE PARTY TOMORROW?
SINCE WE DON'T HAVE ANYTHING SCHEDULED TOMORROW.
YAY~!♪!

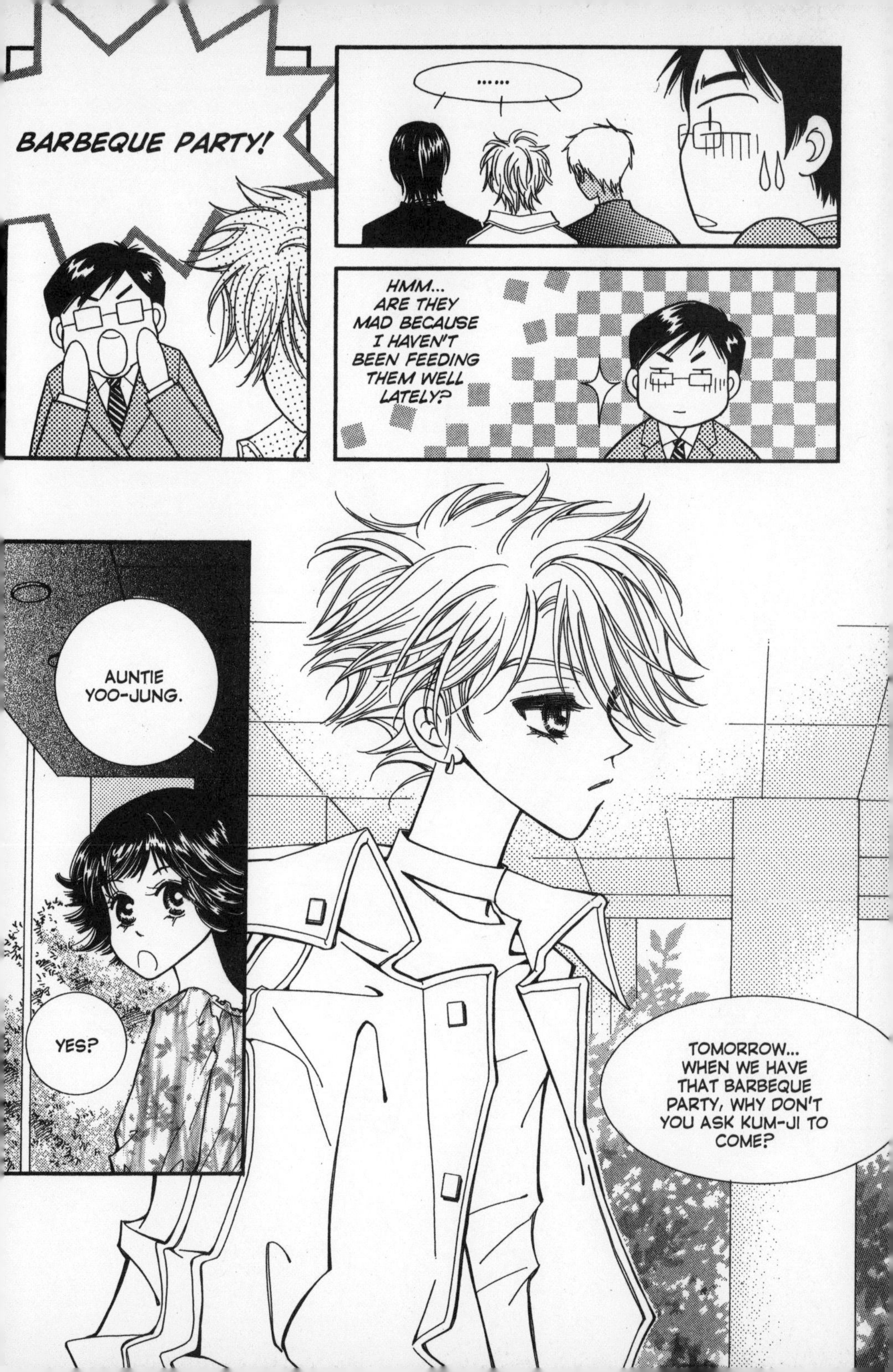
BARBEQUE PARTY!
......
HMM... ARE THEY MAD BECAUSE I HAVEN'T BEEN FEEDING THEM WELL LATELY?
AUNTIE YOO-JUNG.
YES?
TOMORROW... WHEN WE HAVE THAT BARBEQUE PARTY, WHY DON'T YOU ASK KUM-JI TO COME?

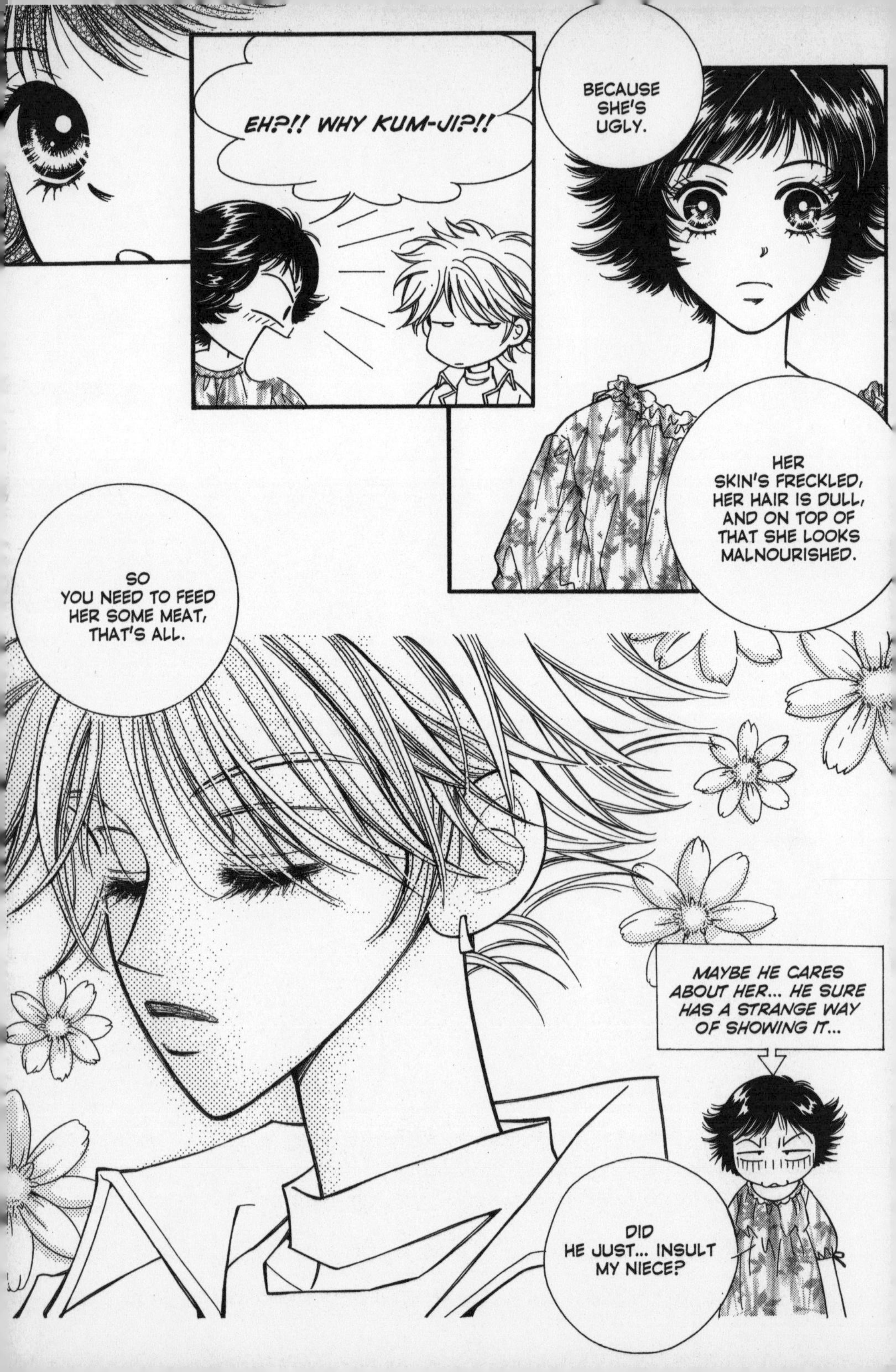
EH?!! WHY KUM-JI?!!
BECAUSE SHE'S UGLY.
HER SKIN'S FRECKLED, HER HAIR IS DULL, AND ON TOP OF THAT SHE LOOKS MALNOURISHED.
SO YOU NEED TO FEED HER SOME MEAT, THAT'S ALL.
MAYBE HE CARES ABOUT HER... HE SURE HAS A STRANGE WAY OF SHOWING IT...
DID HE JUST... INSULT MY NIECE?

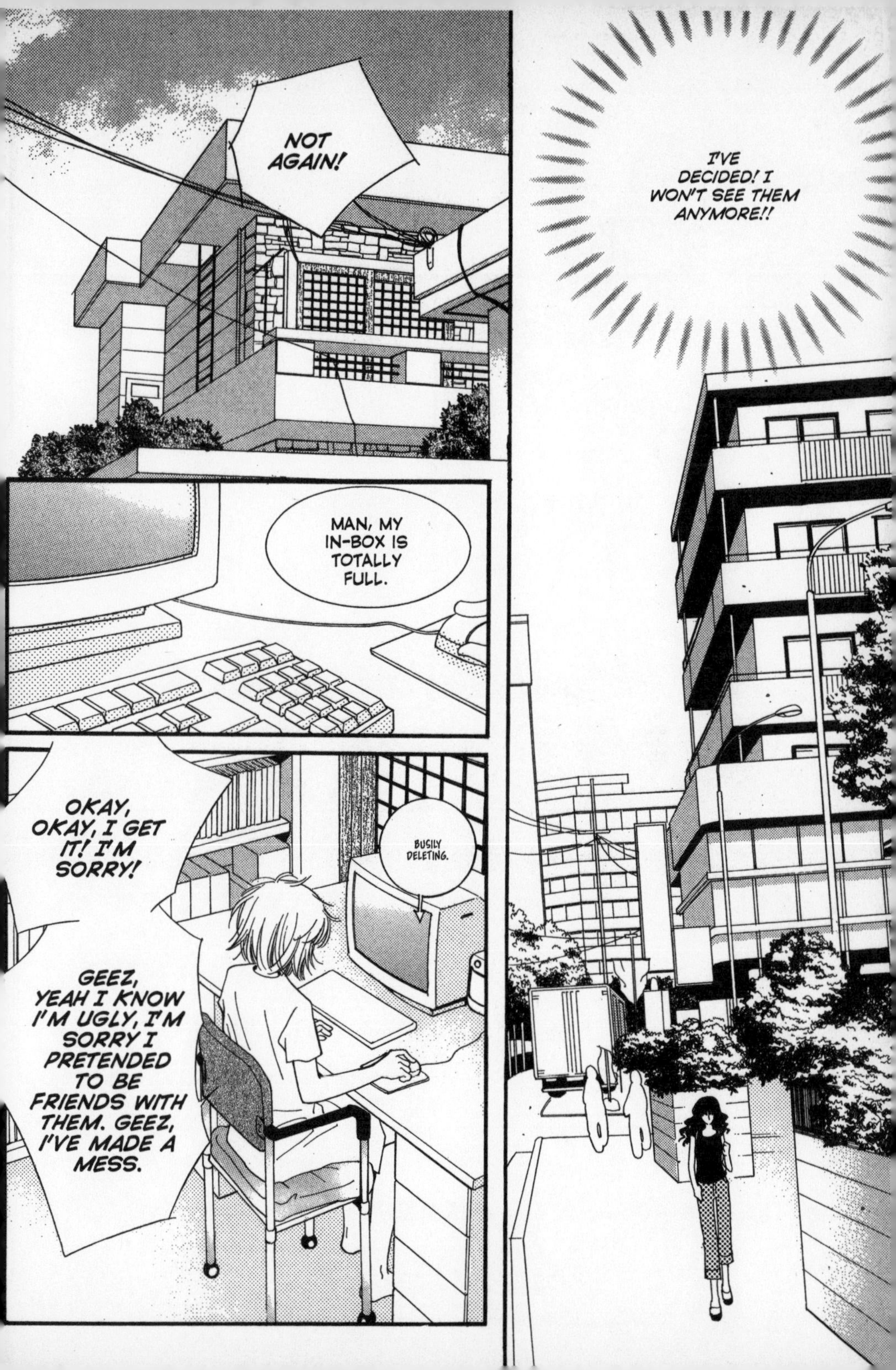
NOT AGAIN!
MAN, MY IN-BOX IS TOTALLY FULL.
OKAY, OKAY, I GET IT! I'M SORRY!
BUSILY DELETING.
GEEZ, YEAH I KNOW I'M UGLY, I'M SORRY I PRETENDED TO BE FRIENDS WITH THEM. GEEZ, I'VE MADE A MESS.
I'VE DECIDED! I WON'T SEE THEM ANYMORE!!

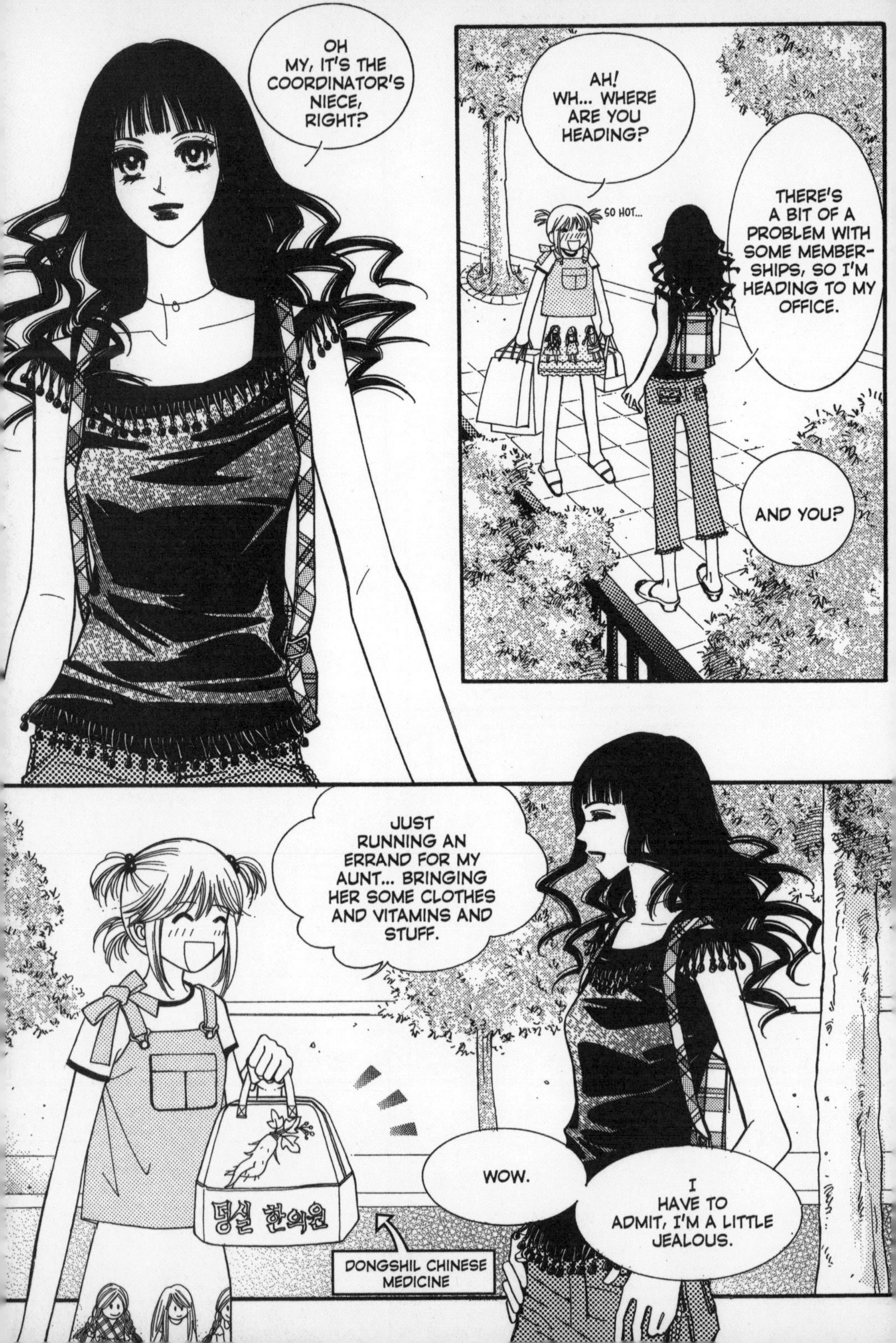
OH MY, IT'S THE COORDINATOR'S NIECE, RIGHT?
AH! WH... WHERE ARE YOU HEADING?
SO HOT...
THERE'S A BIT OF A PROBLEM WITH SOME MEMBERSHIPS, SO I'M HEADING TO MY OFFICE.
AND YOU?
JUST RUNNING AN ERRAND FOR MY AUNT... BRINGING HER SOME CLOTHES AND VITAMINS AND STUFF.
동실 한의원
DONGSHIL CHINESE MEDICINE
WOW.
I HAVE TO ADMIT, I'M A LITTLE JEALOUS.

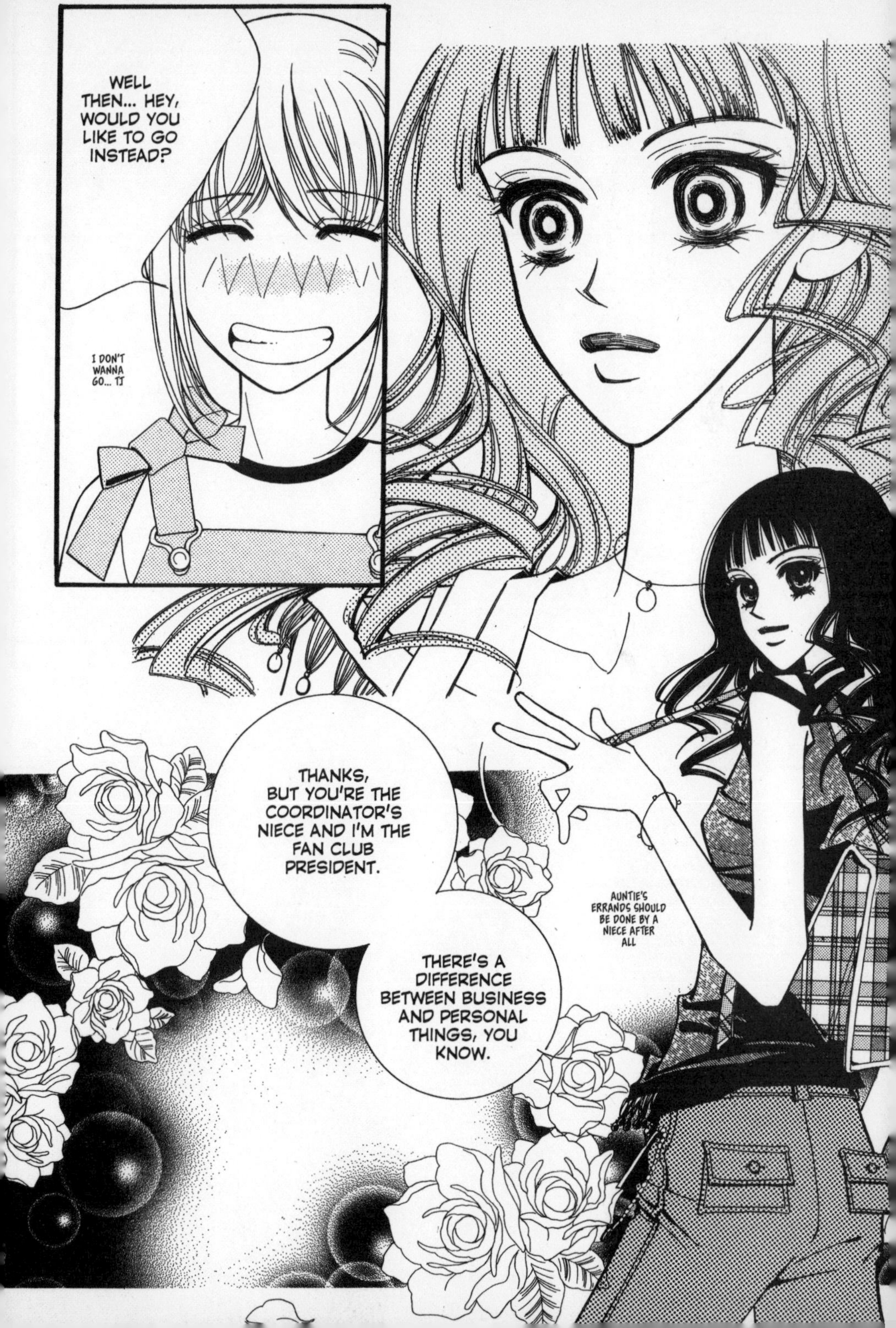
WELL THEN... HEY, WOULD YOU LIKE TO GO INSTEAD?
I DON'T WANNA GO... TT
THANKS, BUT YOU'RE THE COORDINATOR'S NIECE AND I'M THE FAN CLUB PRESIDENT.
THERE'S A DIFFERENCE BETWEEN BUSINESS AND PERSONAL THINGS, YOU KNOW.
AUNTIE'S ERRANDS SHOULD BE DONE BY A NIECE AFTER ALL

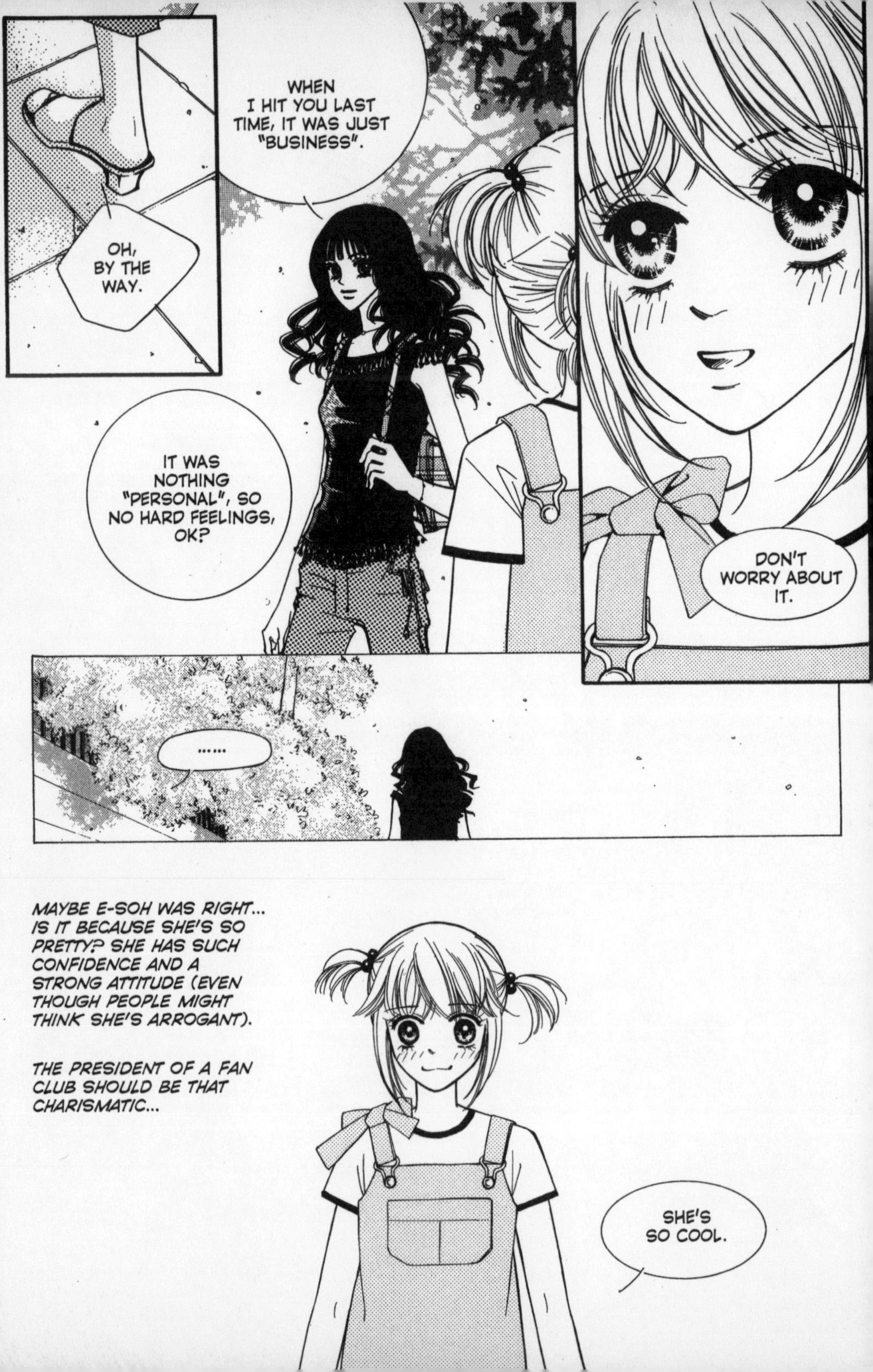
OH, BY THE WAY.
WHEN I HIT YOU LAST TIME, IT WAS JUST "BUSINESS".
IT WAS NOTHING "PERSONAL", SO NO HARD FEELINGS, OK?
DON'T WORRY ABOUT IT.
......
MAYBE E-SOH WAS RIGHT... IS IT BECAUSE SHE'S SO PRETTY? SHE HAS SUCH CONFIDENCE AND A STRONG ATTITUDE (EVEN THOUGH PEOPLE MIGHT THINK SHE'S ARROGANT).
THE PRESIDENT OF A FAN CLUB SHOULD BE THAT CHARISMATIC...
SHE'S SO COOL.

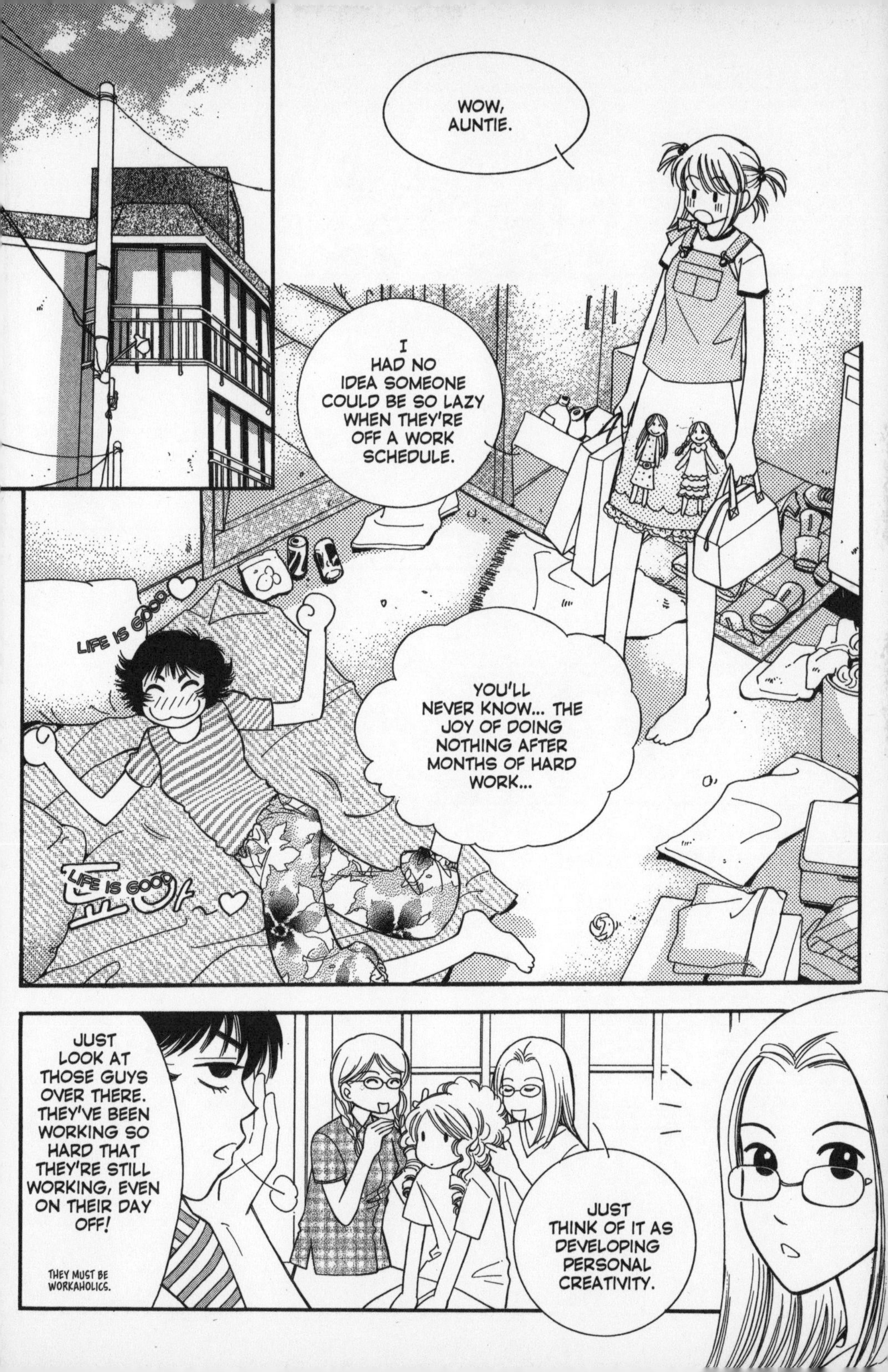
WOW, AUNTIE.
I HAD NO IDEA SOMEONE COULD BE SO LAZY WHEN THEY'RE OFF A WORK SCHEDULE.
LIFE IS GOOD
YOU'LL NEVER KNOW... THE JOY OF DOING NOTHING AFTER MONTHS OF HARD WORK...
LIFE IS GOOD
JUST LOOK AT THOSE GUYS OVER THERE. THEY'VE BEEN WORKING SO HARD THAT THEY'RE STILL WORKING, EVEN ON THEIR DAY OFF!
THEY MUST BE WORKAHOLICS.
JUST THINK OF IT AS DEVELOPING PERSONAL CREATIVITY.

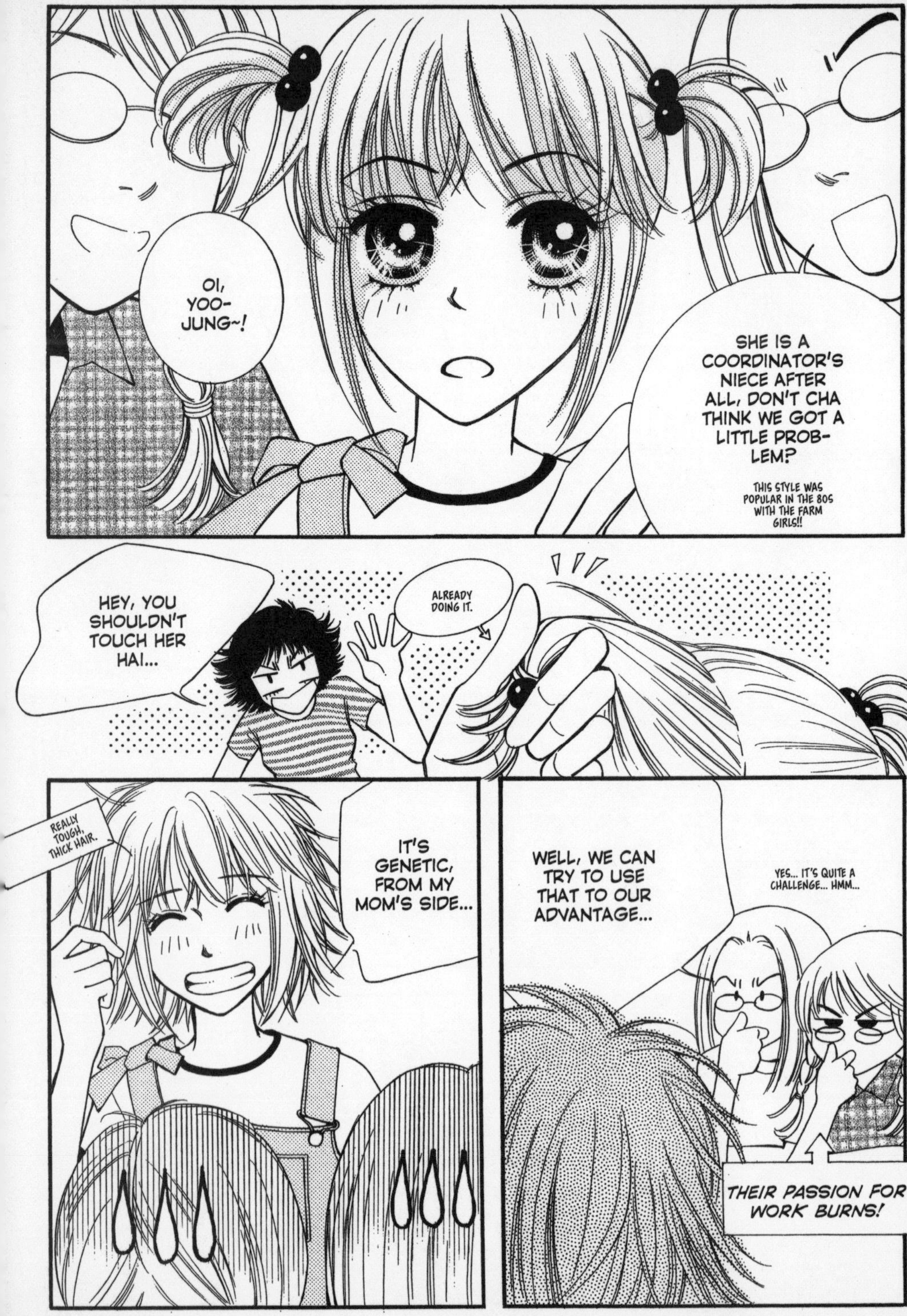
OI, YOO-JUNG~!
SHE IS A COORDINATOR'S NIECE AFTER ALL, DON'T CHA THINK WE GOT A LITTLE PROB-LEM?
THIS STYLE WAS POPULAR IN THE 80S WITH THE FARM GIRLS!!
HEY, YOU SHOULDN'T TOUCH HER HAI...
ALREADY DOING IT.
REALLY TOUGH, THICK HAIR.
IT'S GENETIC, FROM MY MOM'S SIDE...
WELL, WE CAN TRY TO USE THAT TO OUR ADVANTAGE...
YES... IT'S QUITE A CHALLENGE... HMM...
THEIR PASSION FOR WORK BURNS!

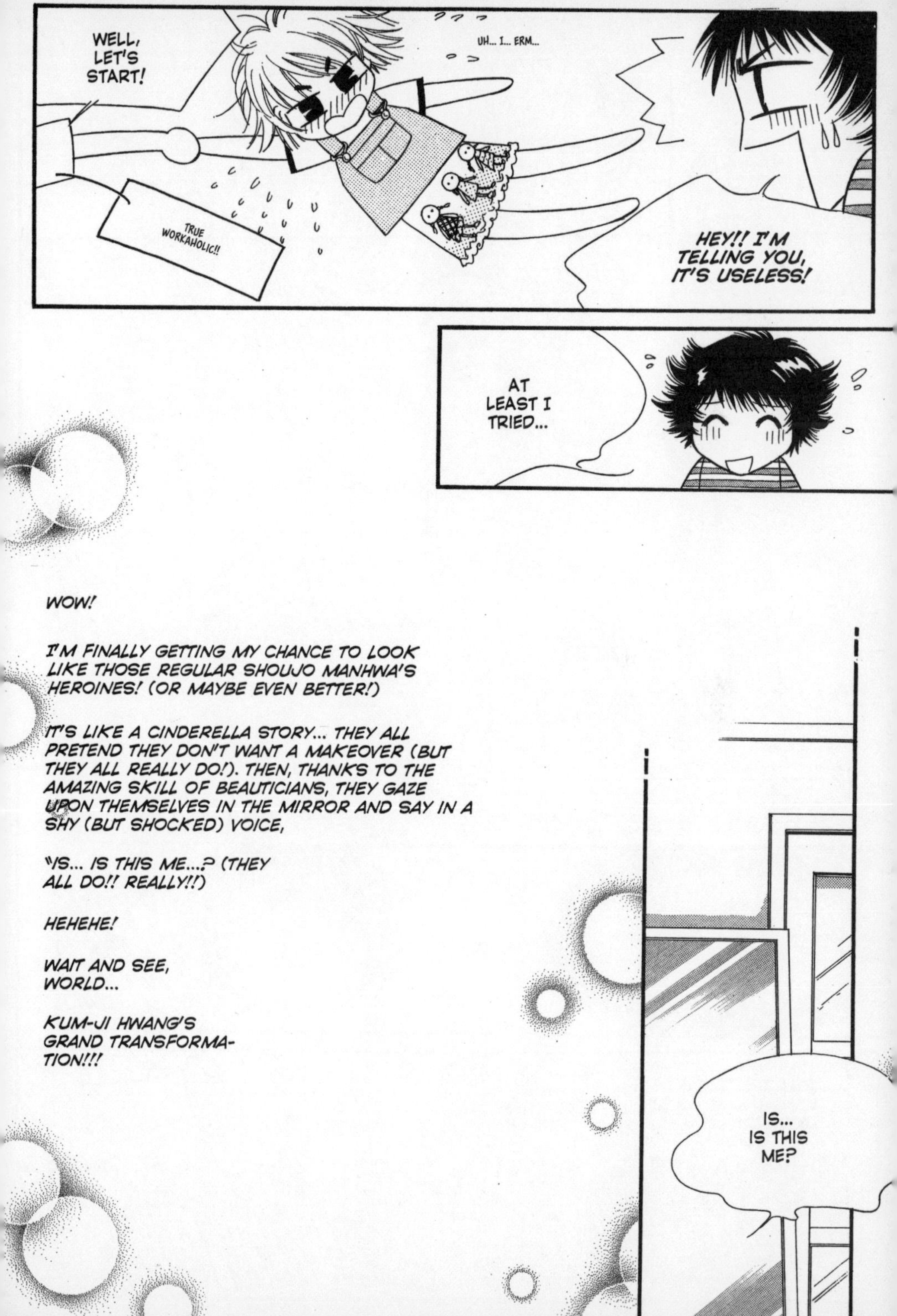
WELL, LET'S START!
UH... I... ERM...
TRUE WORKAHOLIC!!
HEY!! I'M TELLING YOU, IT'S USELESS!
AT LEAST I TRIED...
WOW!
I'M FINALLY GETTING MY CHANCE TO LOOK LIKE THOSE REGULAR SHOUJO MANHWA'S HEROINES! (OR MAYBE EVEN BETTER!)
IT'S LIKE A CINDERELLA STORY... THEY ALL PRETEND THEY DON'T WANT A MAKEOVER (BUT THEY ALL REALLY DO!). THEN, THANKS TO THE AMAZING SKILL OF BEAUTICIANS, THEY GAZE UPON THEMSELVES IN THE MIRROR AND SAY IN A SHY (BUT SHOCKED) VOICE,
"IS... IS THIS ME...? (THEY ALL DO!! REALLY!!)
HEHEHE!
WAIT AND SEE, WORLD...
KUM-JI HWANG'S GRAND TRANSFORMATION!!!
IS... IS THIS ME?

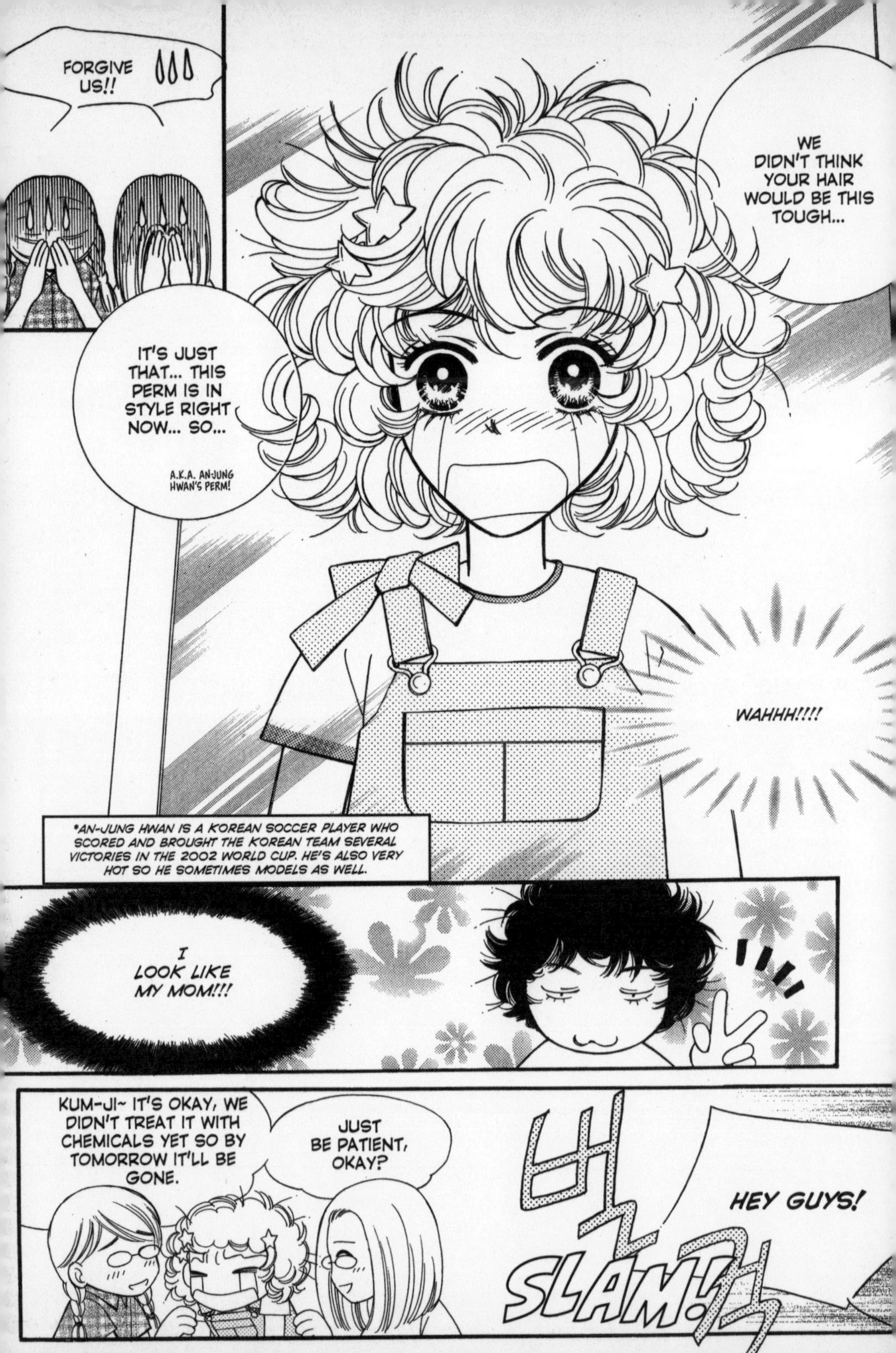
FORGIVE US!!
WE DIDN'T THINK YOUR HAIR WOULD BE THIS TOUGH...
IT'S JUST THAT... THIS PERM IS IN STYLE RIGHT NOW... SO...
A.K.A. AN-JUNG HWAN'S PERM!
WAHHH!!!!
*AN-JUNG HWAN IS A KOREAN SOCCER PLAYER WHO SCORED AND BROUGHT THE KOREAN TEAM SEVERAL VICTORIES IN THE 2002 WORLD CUP. HE'S ALSO VERY HOT SO HE SOMETIMES MODELS AS WELL.
I LOOK LIKE MY MOM!!!
KUM-JI~ IT'S OKAY, WE DIDN'T TREAT IT WITH CHEMICALS YET SO BY TOMORROW IT'LL BE GONE.
JUST BE PATIENT, OKAY?
HEY GUYS!
SLAM!

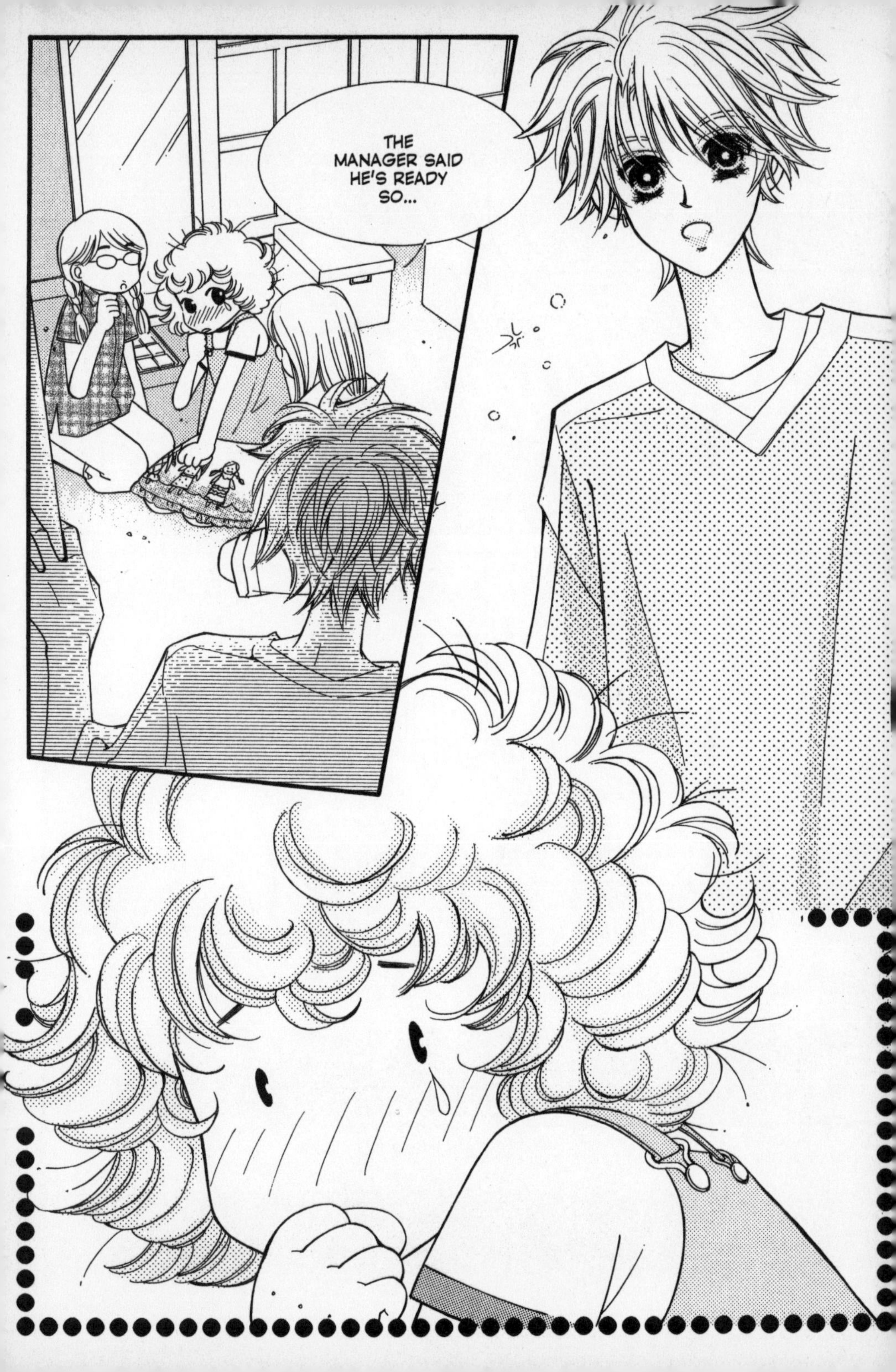
THE MANAGER SAID HE'S READY SO...

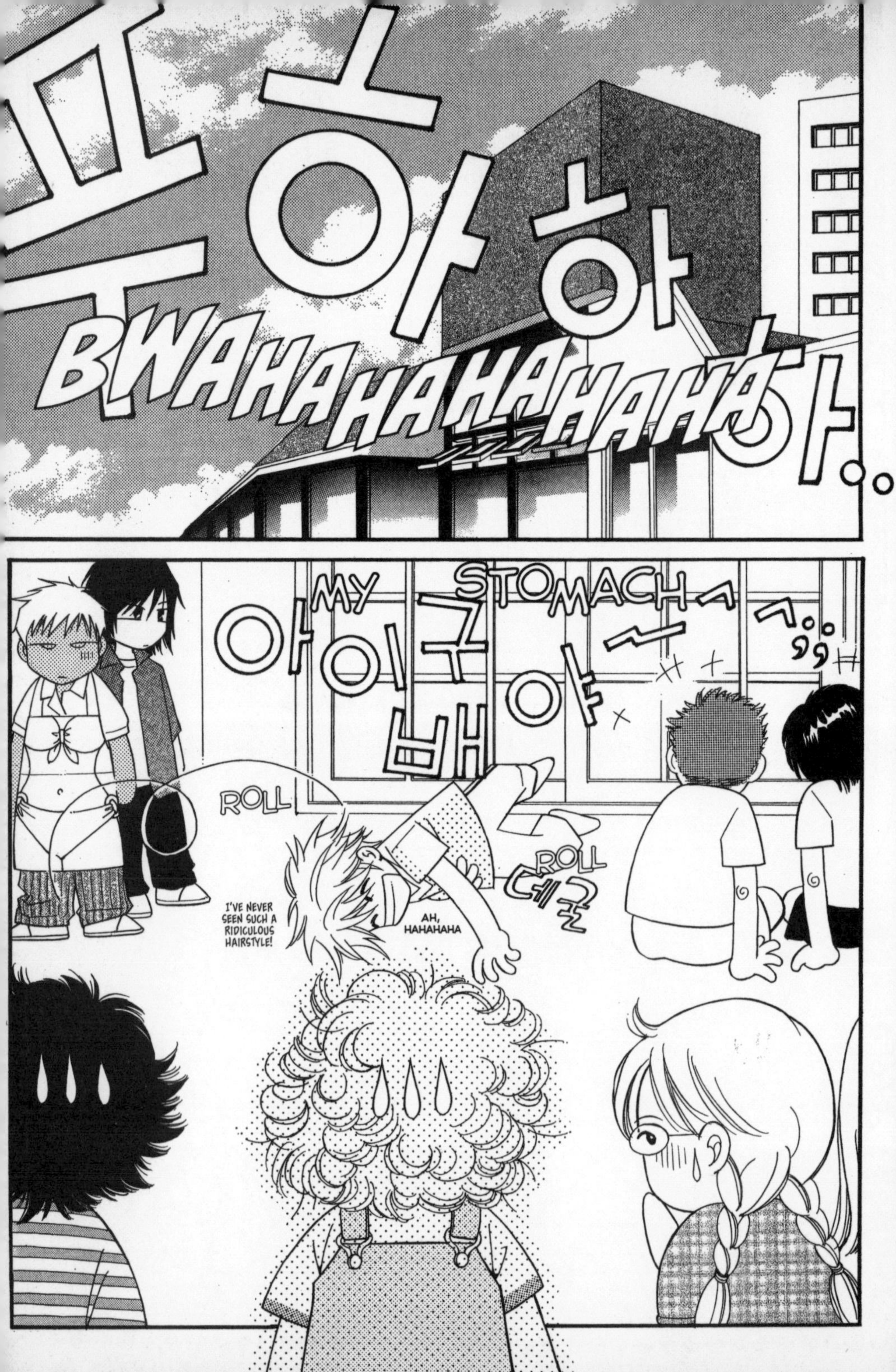
푸하하하…
BWAHAHAHAHAHA
MY STOMACH
아이구 배야~~
ROLL
ROLL
데굴
I'VE NEVER SEEN SUCH A RIDICULOUS HAIRSTYLE!
AH, HAHAHAHA

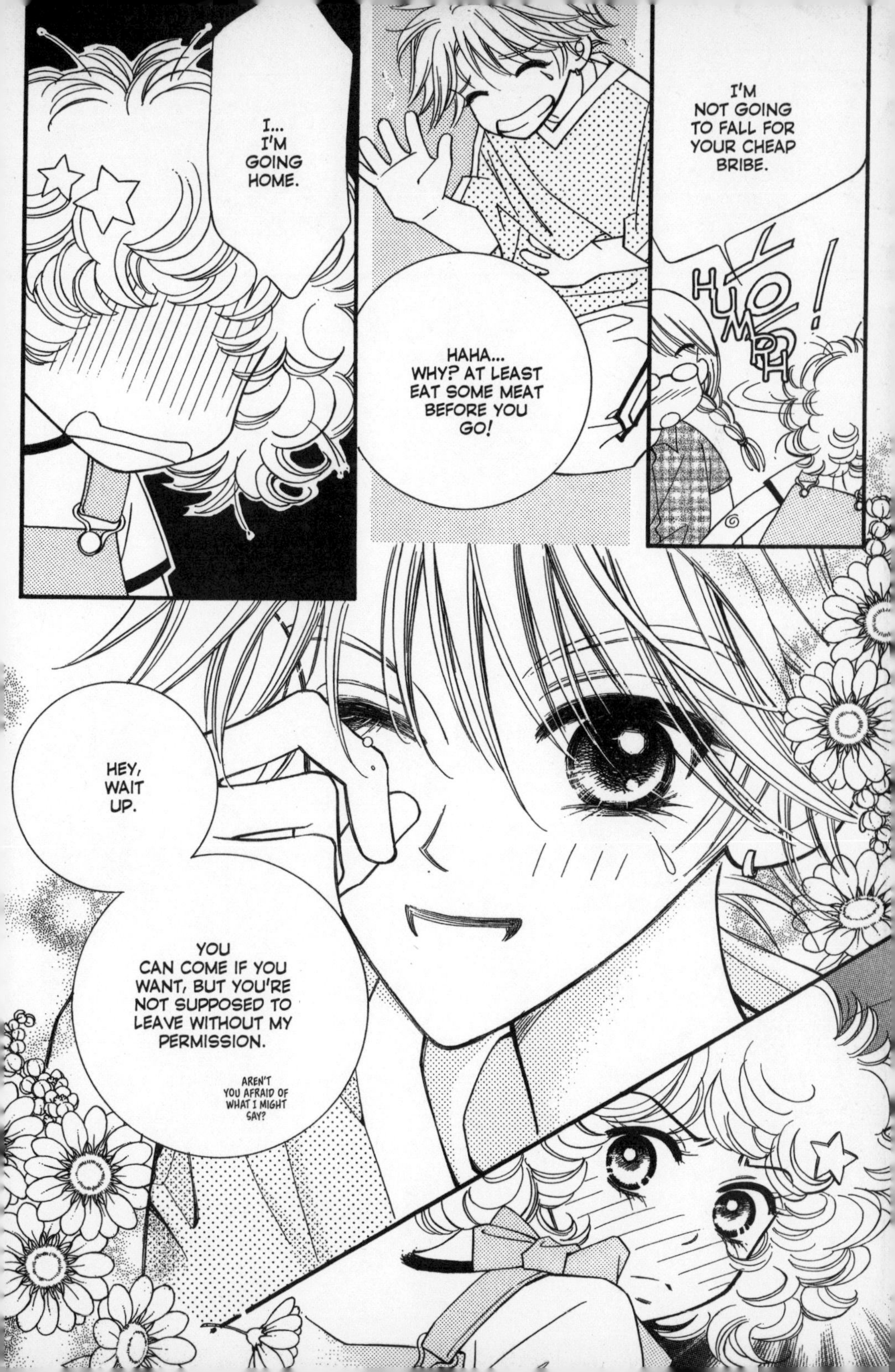
I... I'M GOING HOME.
HAHA... WHY? AT LEAST EAT SOME MEAT BEFORE YOU GO!
I'M NOT GOING TO FALL FOR YOUR CHEAP BRIBE.
HUMPH
HEY, WAIT UP.
YOU CAN COME IF YOU WANT, BUT YOU'RE NOT SUPPOSED TO LEAVE WITHOUT MY PERMISSION.
AREN'T YOU AFRAID OF WHAT I MIGHT SAY?

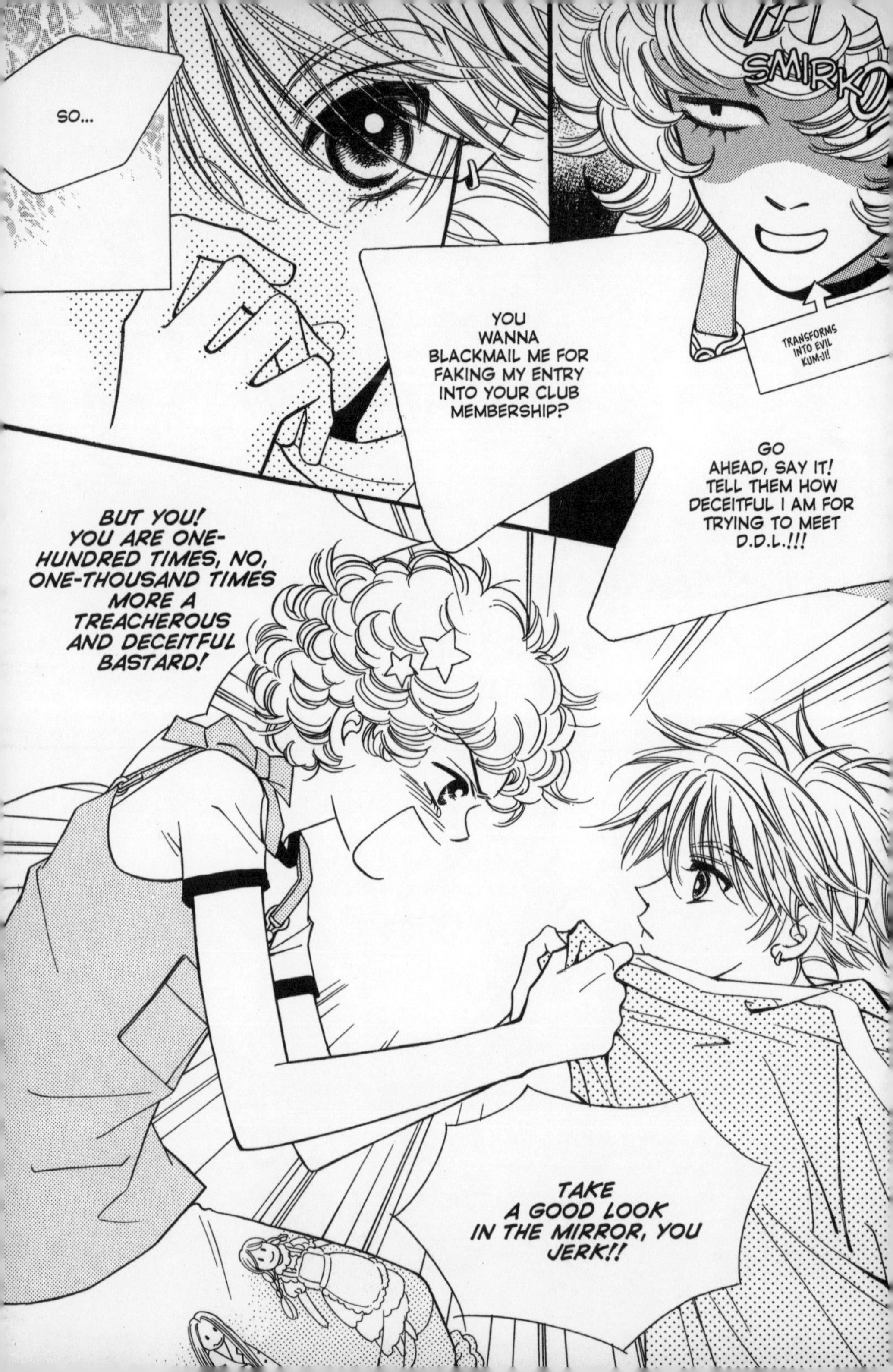
SO...
YOU WANNA BLACKMAIL ME FOR FAKING MY ENTRY INTO YOUR CLUB MEMBERSHIP?
SMIRK
TRANSFORMS INTO EVIL KUM-JI!
GO AHEAD, SAY IT! TELL THEM HOW DECEITFUL I AM FOR TRYING TO MEET D.D.L.!!!
BUT YOU! YOU ARE ONE-HUNDRED TIMES, NO, ONE-THOUSAND TIMES MORE A TREACHEROUS AND DECEITFUL BASTARD!
TAKE A GOOD LOOK IN THE MIRROR, YOU JERK!!

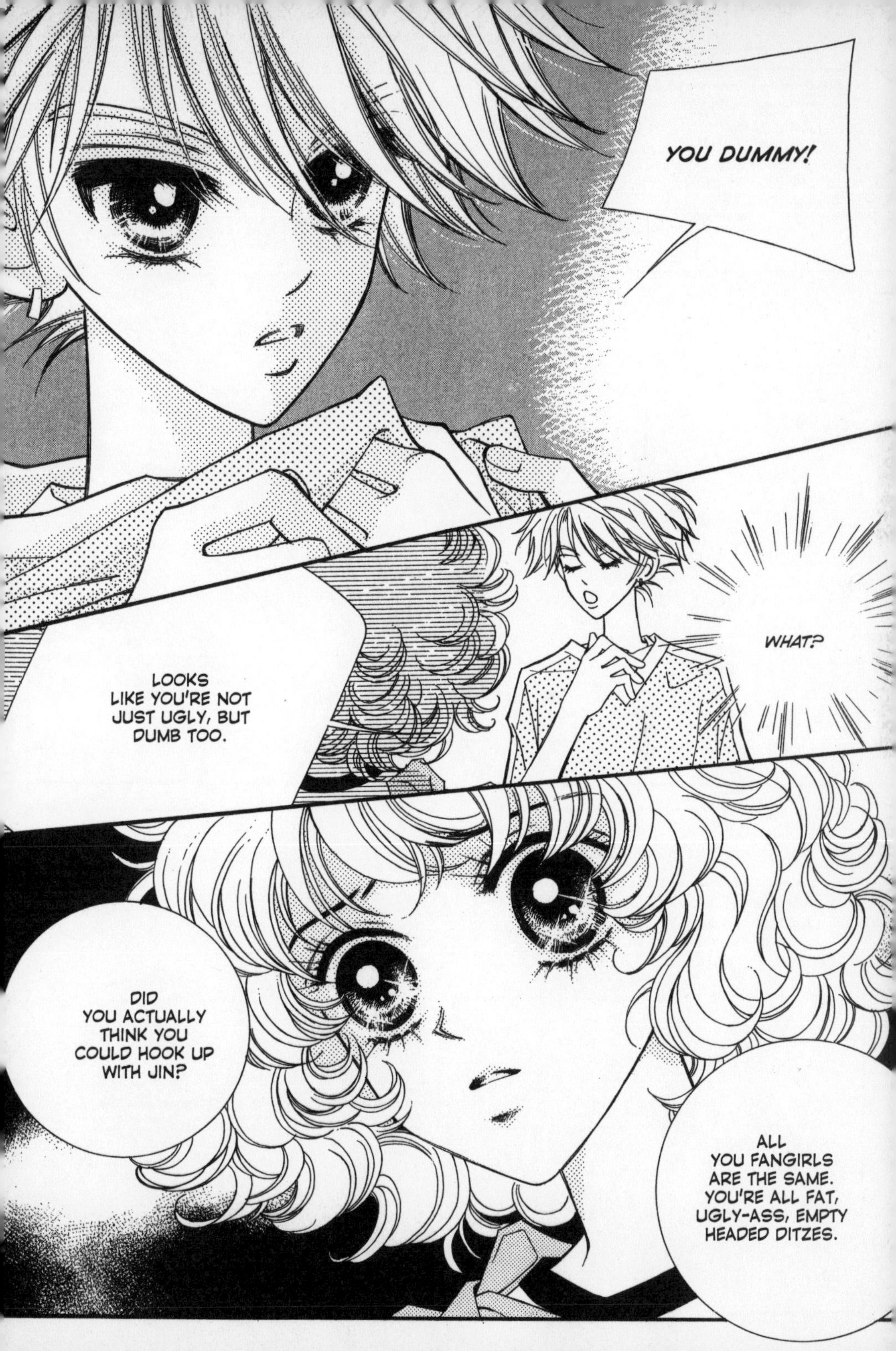
YOU DUMMY!
WHAT?
LOOKS LIKE YOU'RE NOT JUST UGLY, BUT DUMB TOO.
ALL YOU FANGIRLS ARE THE SAME. YOU'RE ALL FAT, UGLY-ASS, EMPTY HEADED DITZES.
DID YOU ACTUALLY THINK YOU COULD HOOK UP WITH JIN?

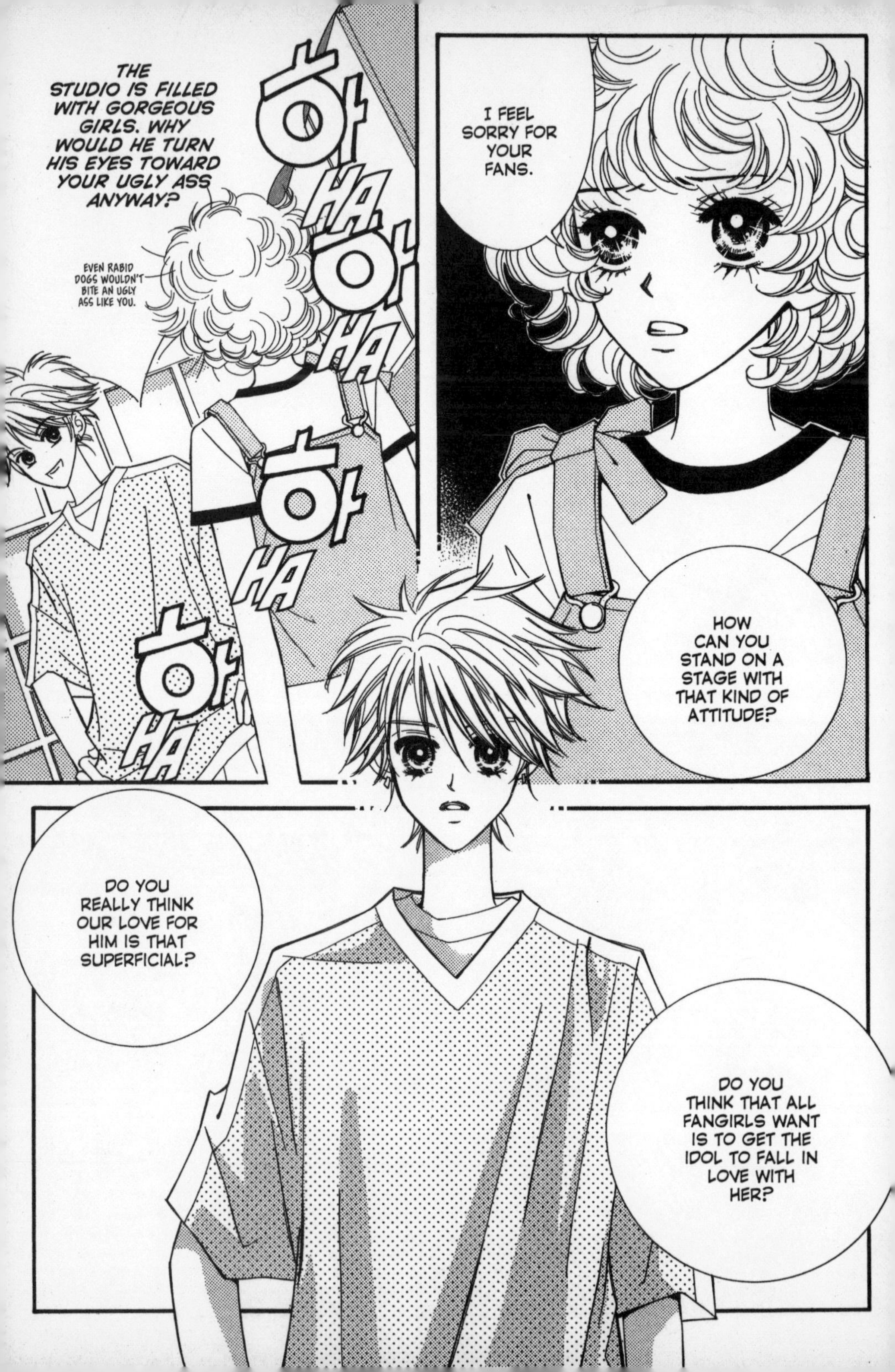
THE STUDIO IS FILLED WITH GORGEOUS GIRLS. WHY WOULD HE TURN HIS EYES TOWARD YOUR UGLY ASS ANYWAY?
EVEN RABID DOGS WOULDN'T BITE AN UGLY ASS LIKE YOU.
하 HA 아 HA 하 HA 하 HA
I FEEL SORRY FOR YOUR FANS.
HOW CAN YOU STAND ON A STAGE WITH THAT KIND OF ATTITUDE?
DO YOU REALLY THINK OUR LOVE FOR HIM IS THAT SUPERFICIAL?
DO YOU THINK THAT ALL FANGIRLS WANT IS TO GET THE IDOL TO FALL IN LOVE WITH HER?

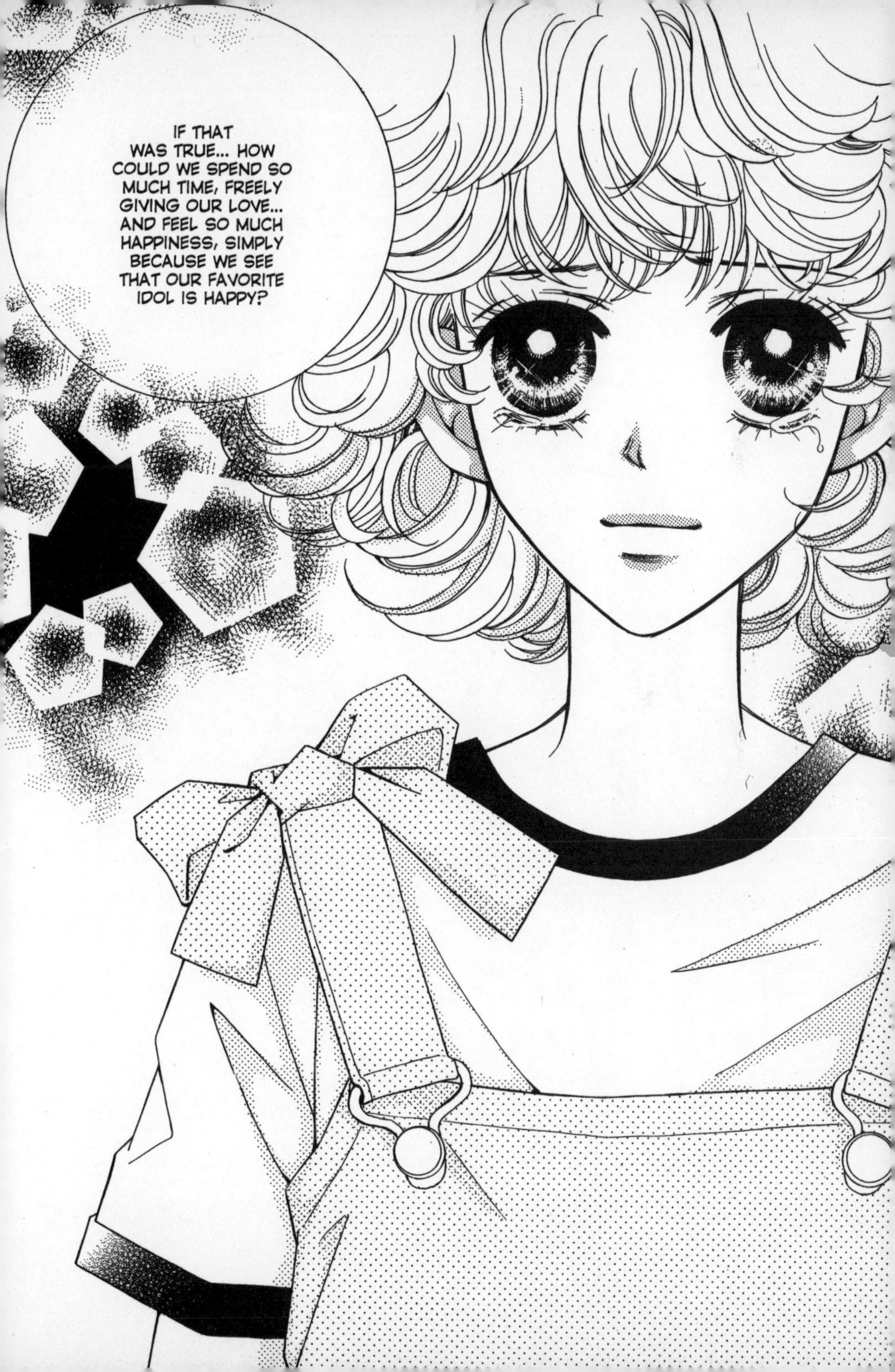
IF THAT WAS TRUE... HOW COULD WE SPEND SO MUCH TIME, FREELY GIVING OUR LOVE... AND FEEL SO MUCH HAPPINESS, SIMPLY BECAUSE WE SEE THAT OUR FAVORITE IDOL IS HAPPY?

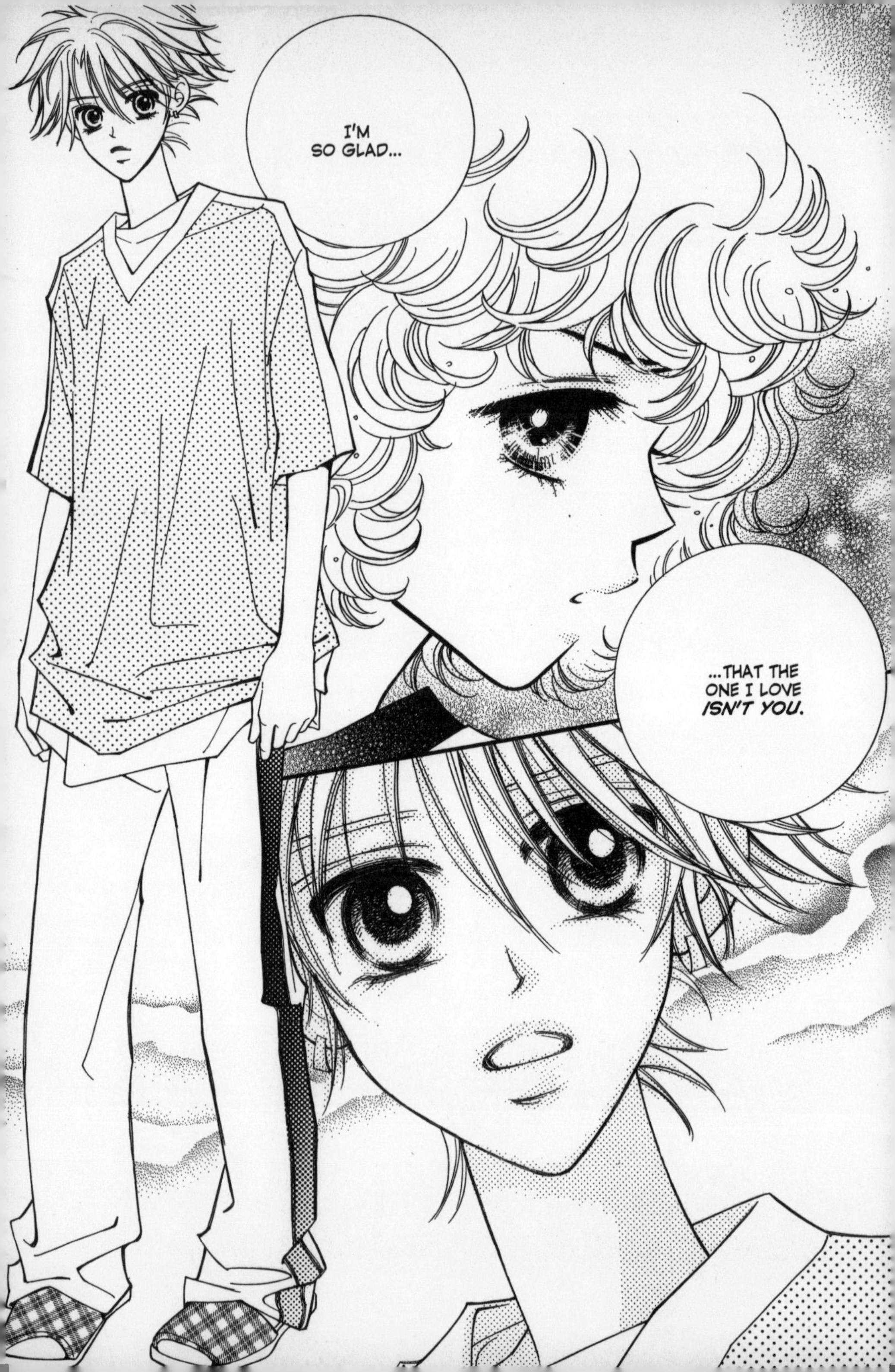
I'M SO GLAD...
...THAT THE ONE I LOVE *ISN'T YOU.*

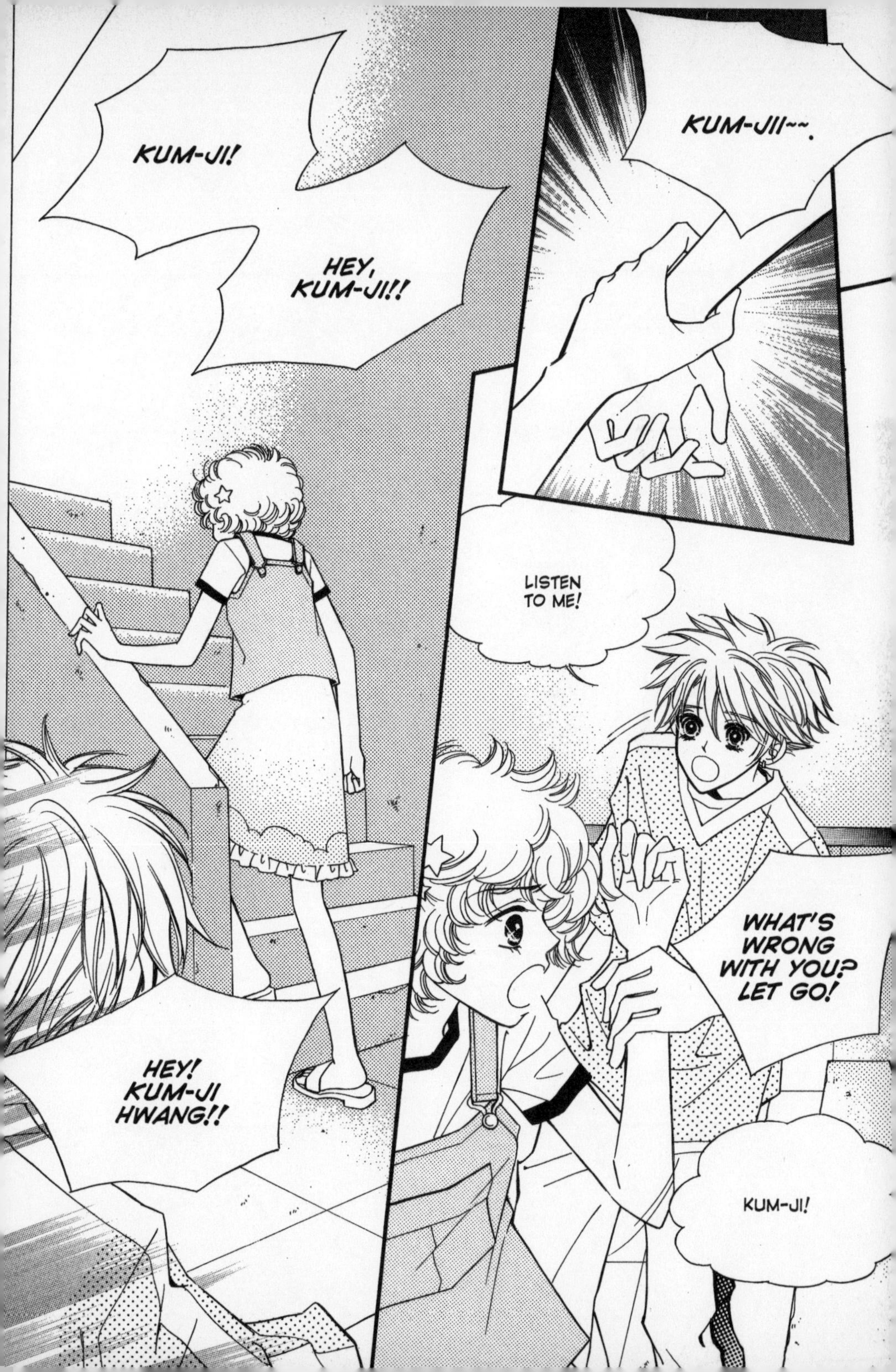
KUM-JI!
HEY, KUM-JI!!
HEY! KUM-JI HWANG!!
KUM-JII~~.
LISTEN TO ME!
WHAT'S WRONG WITH YOU? LET GO!
KUM-JI!

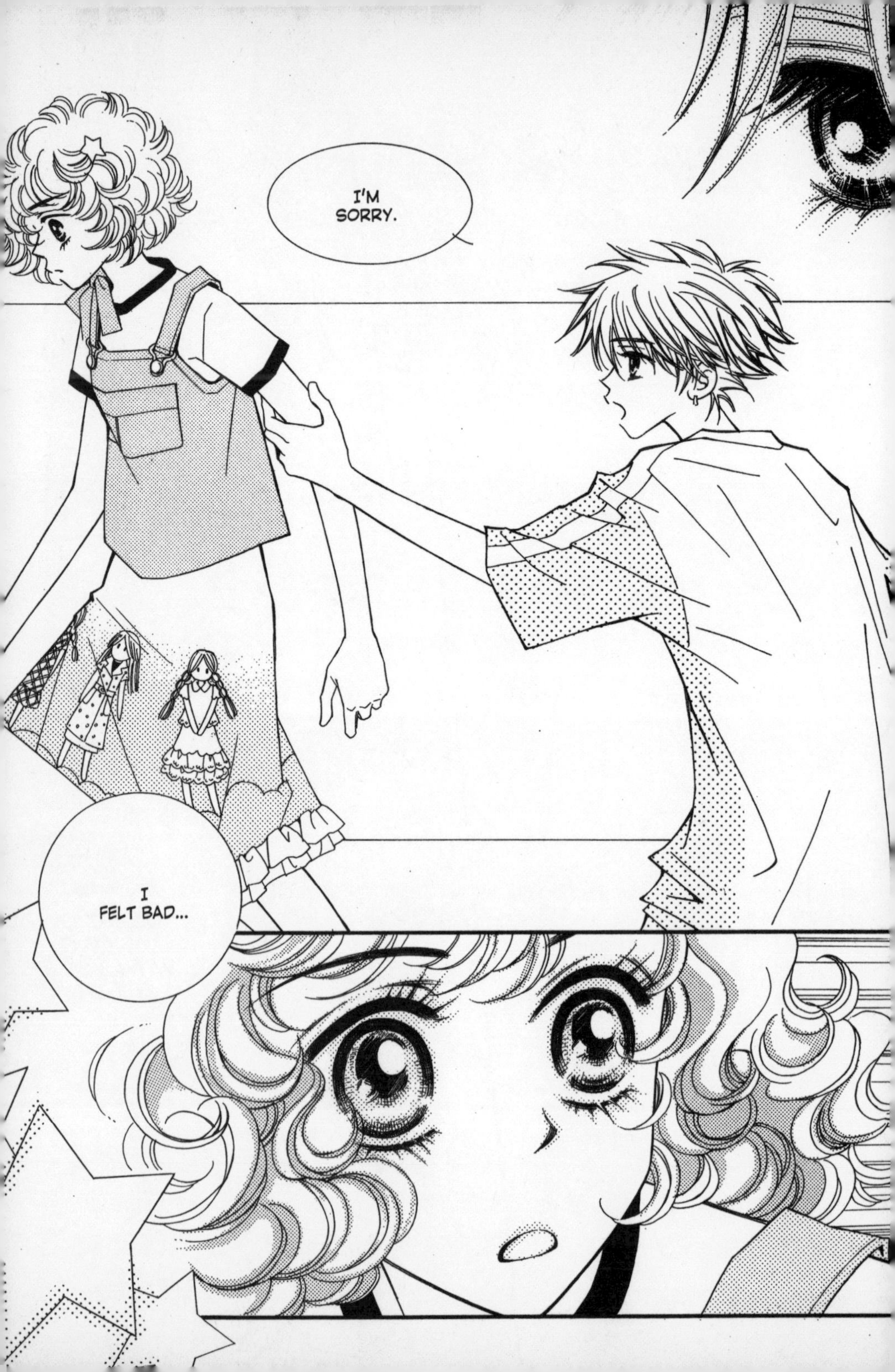
I'M SORRY.
I FELT BAD...

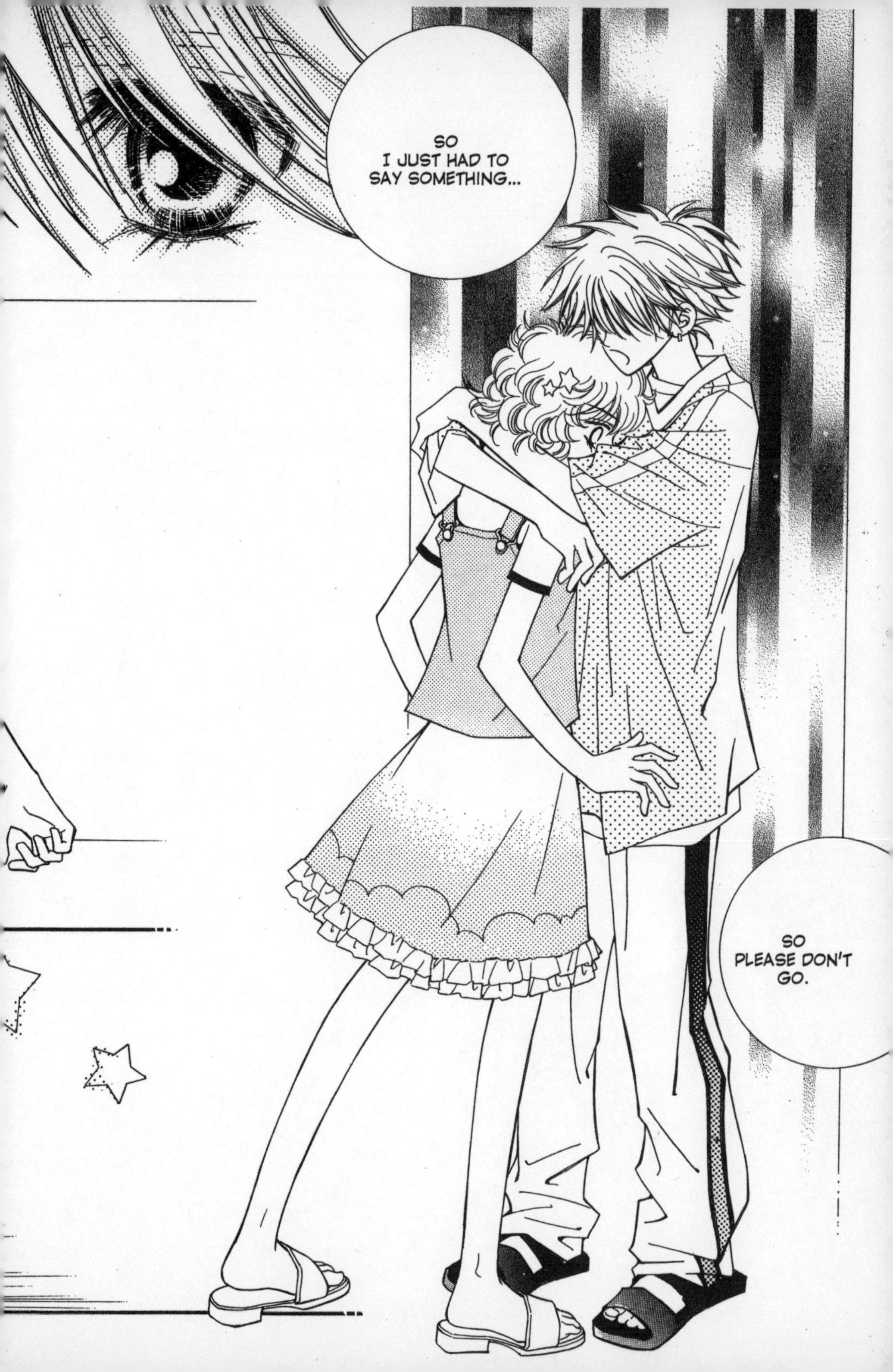
SO I JUST HAD TO SAY SOMETHING...
SO PLEASE DON'T GO.

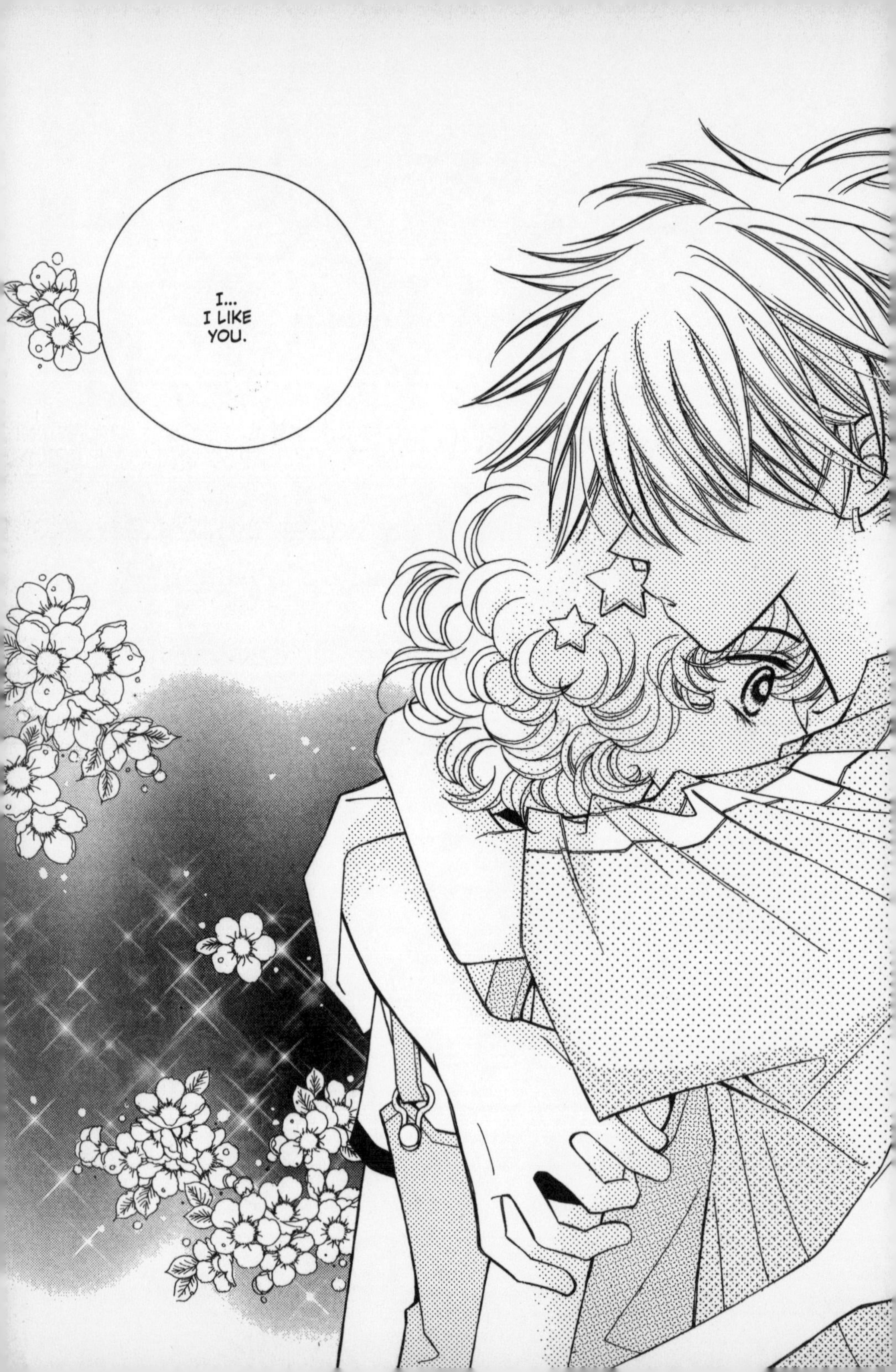
I... I LIKE YOU.

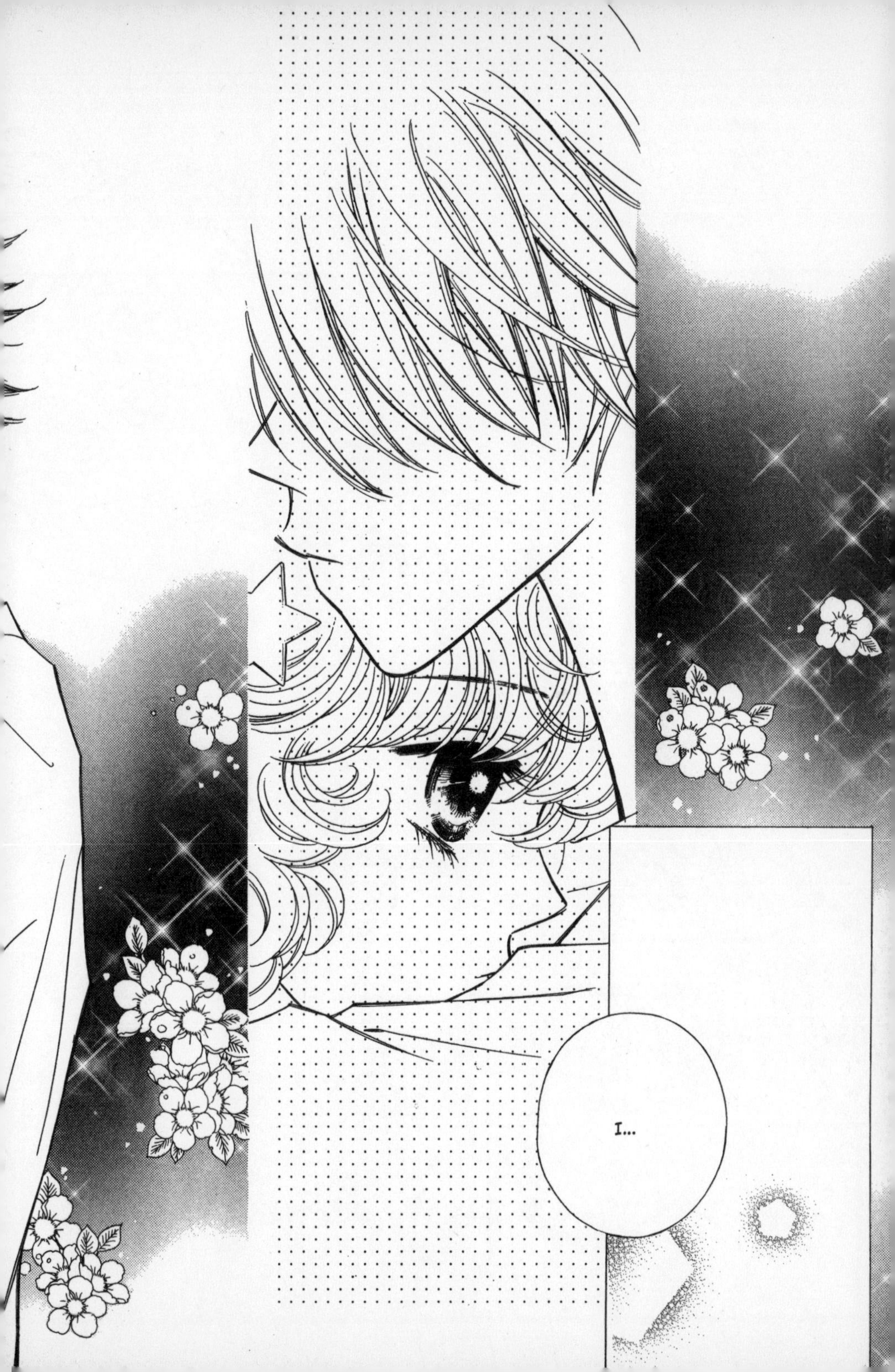
I...

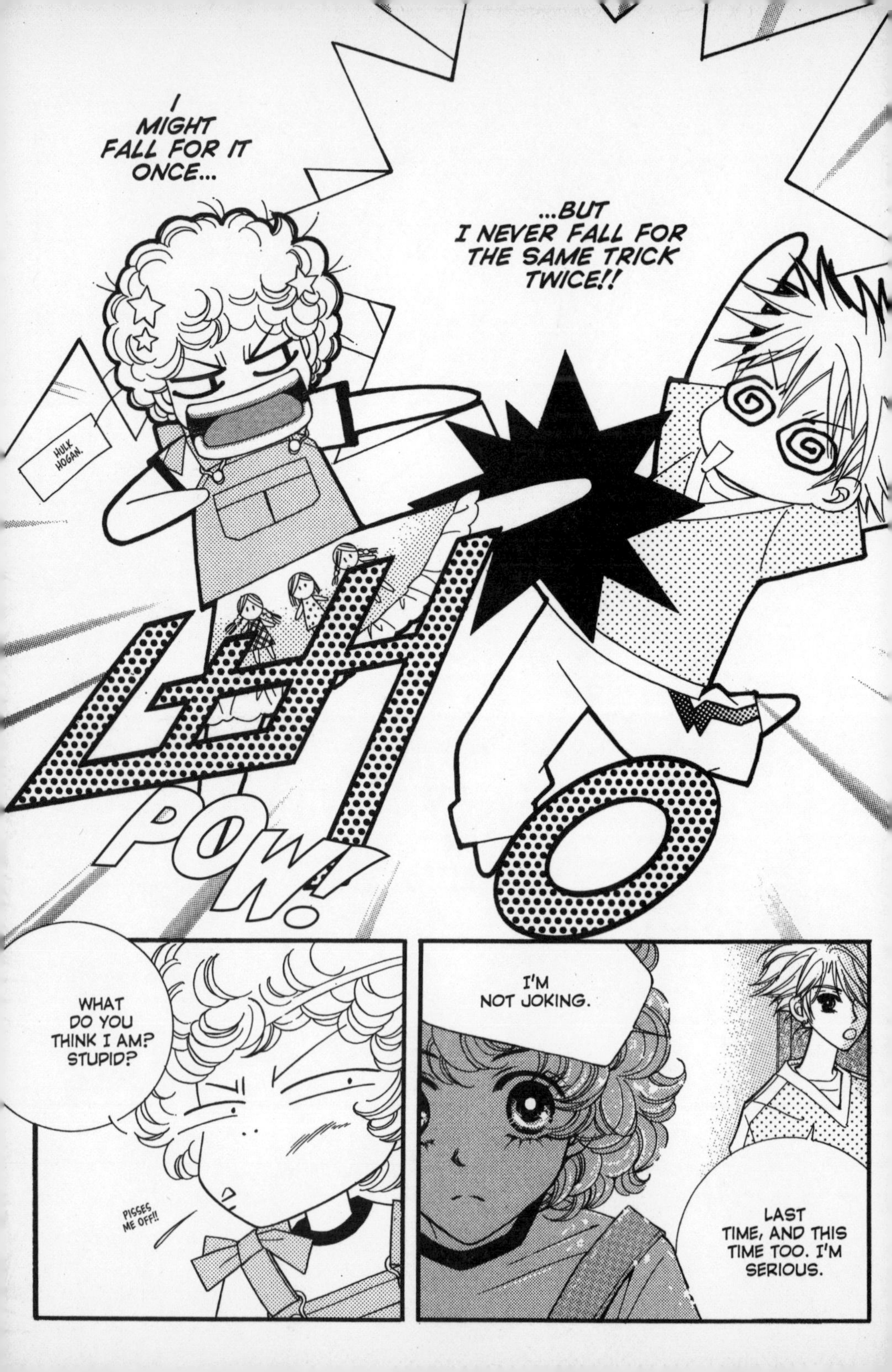
I MIGHT FALL FOR IT ONCE...
HULK HOGAN.
...BUT I NEVER FALL FOR THE SAME TRICK TWICE!!
POW!
WHAT DO YOU THINK I AM? STUPID?
PISSES ME OFF!!
I'M NOT JOKING.
LAST TIME, AND THIS TIME TOO. I'M SERIOUS.

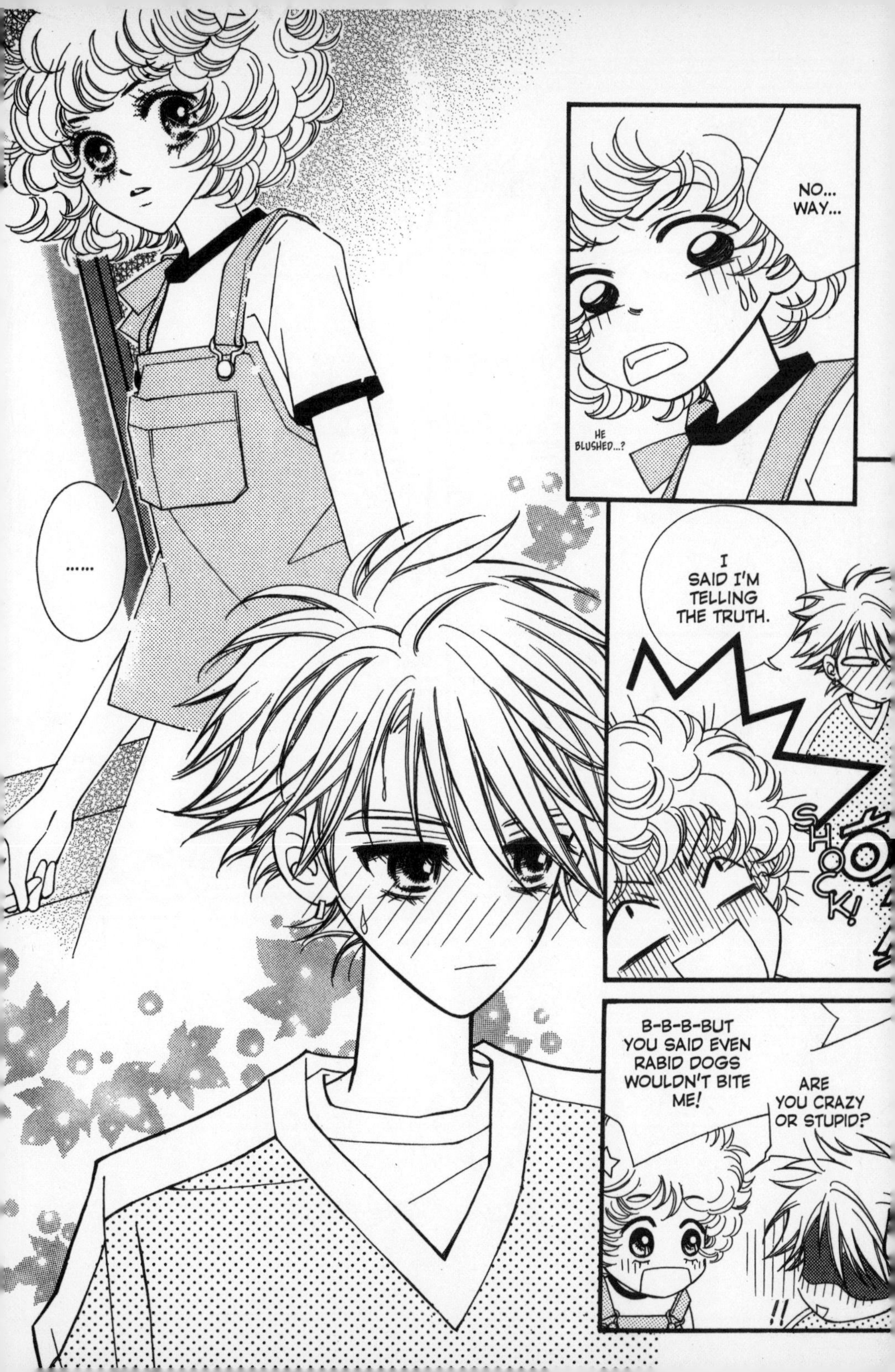
......
NO... WAY...
HE BLUSHED...?
I SAID I'M TELLING THE TRUTH.
SHOCK!
B-B-B-BUT YOU SAID EVEN RABID DOGS WOULDN'T BITE ME!
ARE YOU CRAZY OR STUPID?
!!

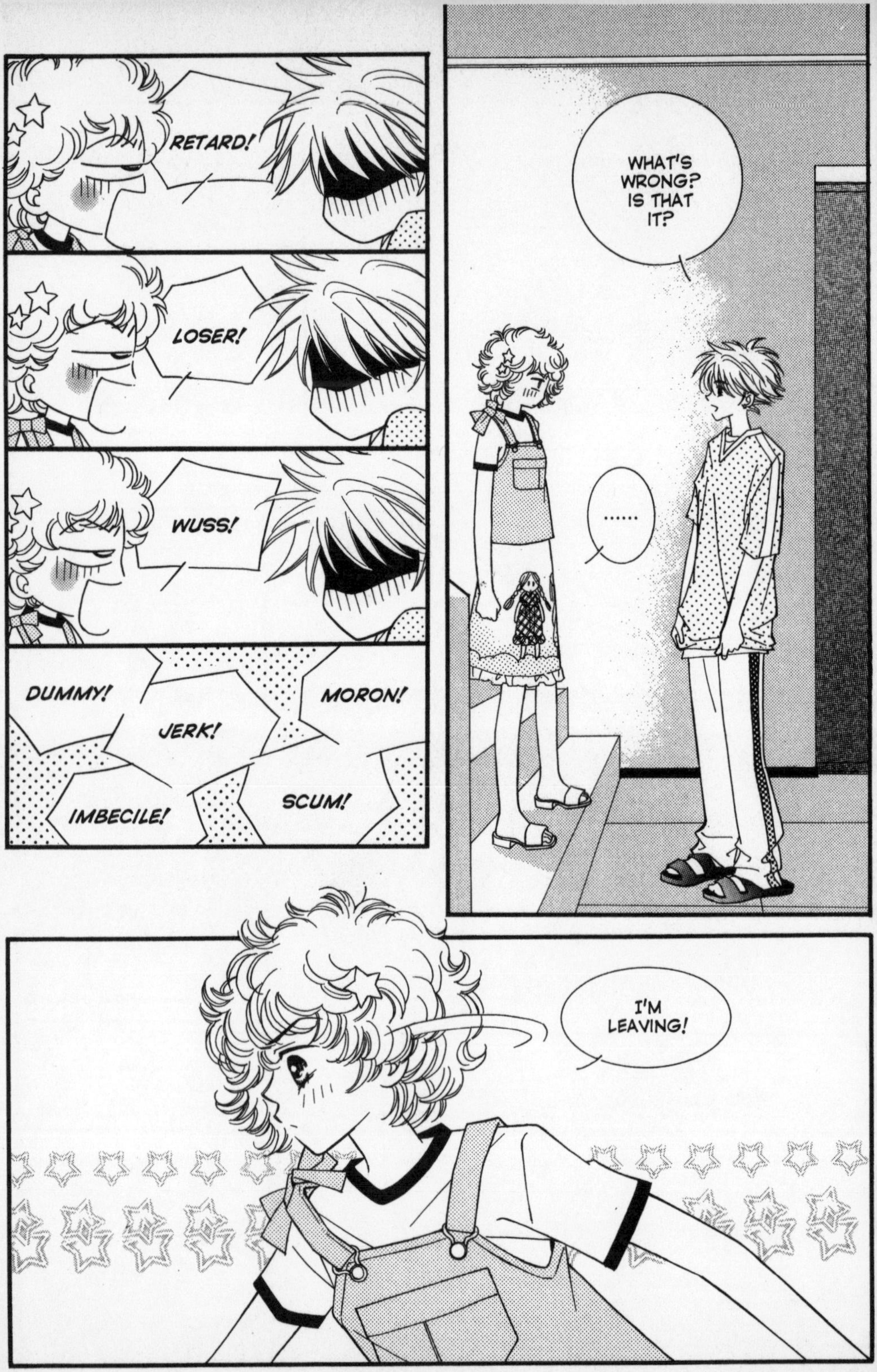
RETARD!
LOSER!
WUSS!
DUMMY!
JERK!
MORON!
IMBECILE!
SCUM!
WHAT'S WRONG? IS THAT IT?
......
I'M LEAVING!

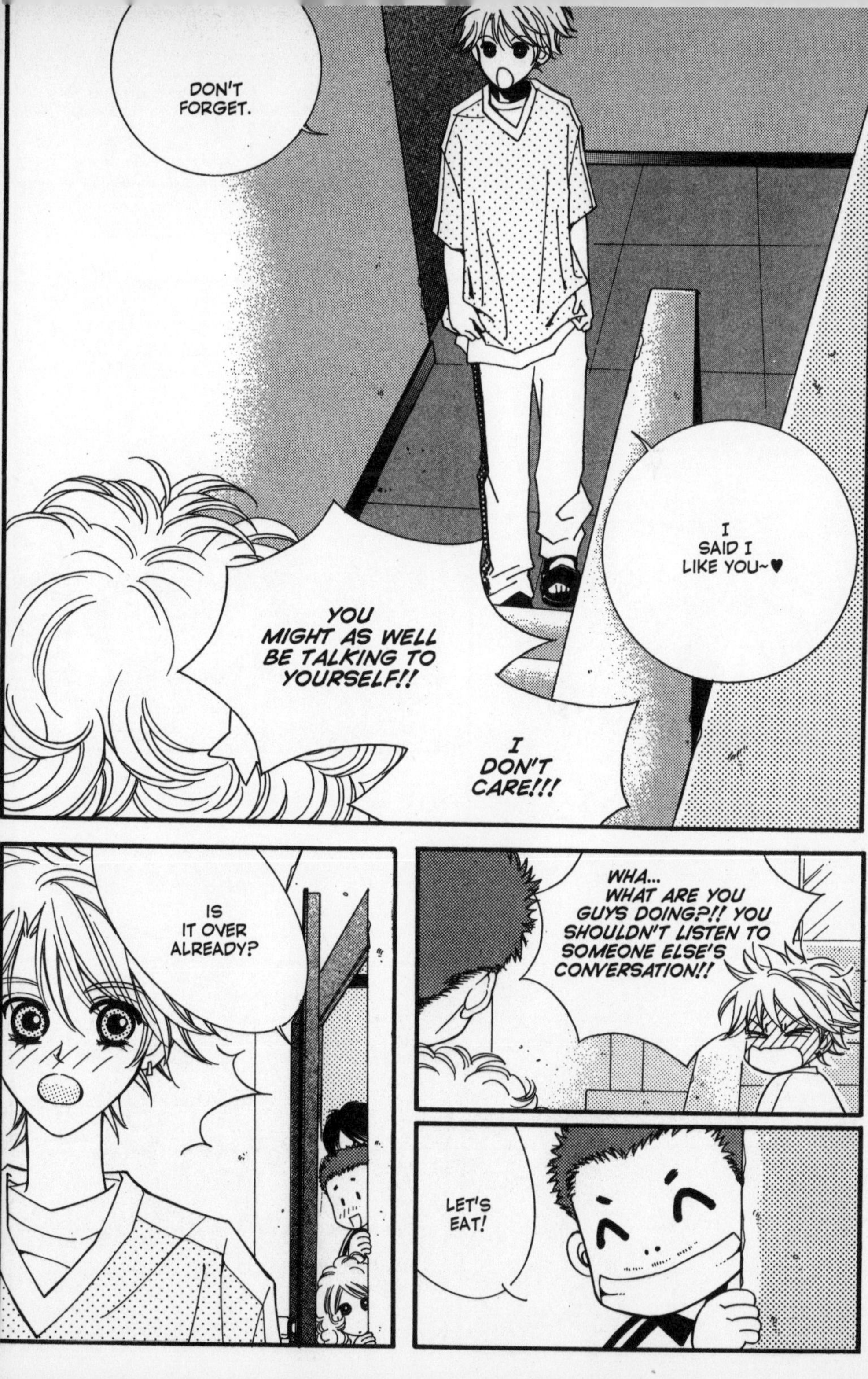
DON'T FORGET.
I SAID I LIKE YOU~♥
YOU MIGHT AS WELL BE TALKING TO YOURSELF!!
I DON'T CARE!!!
IS IT OVER ALREADY?
WHA... WHAT ARE YOU GUYS DOING?!! YOU SHOULDN'T LISTEN TO SOMEONE ELSE'S CONVERSATION!!
LET'S EAT!

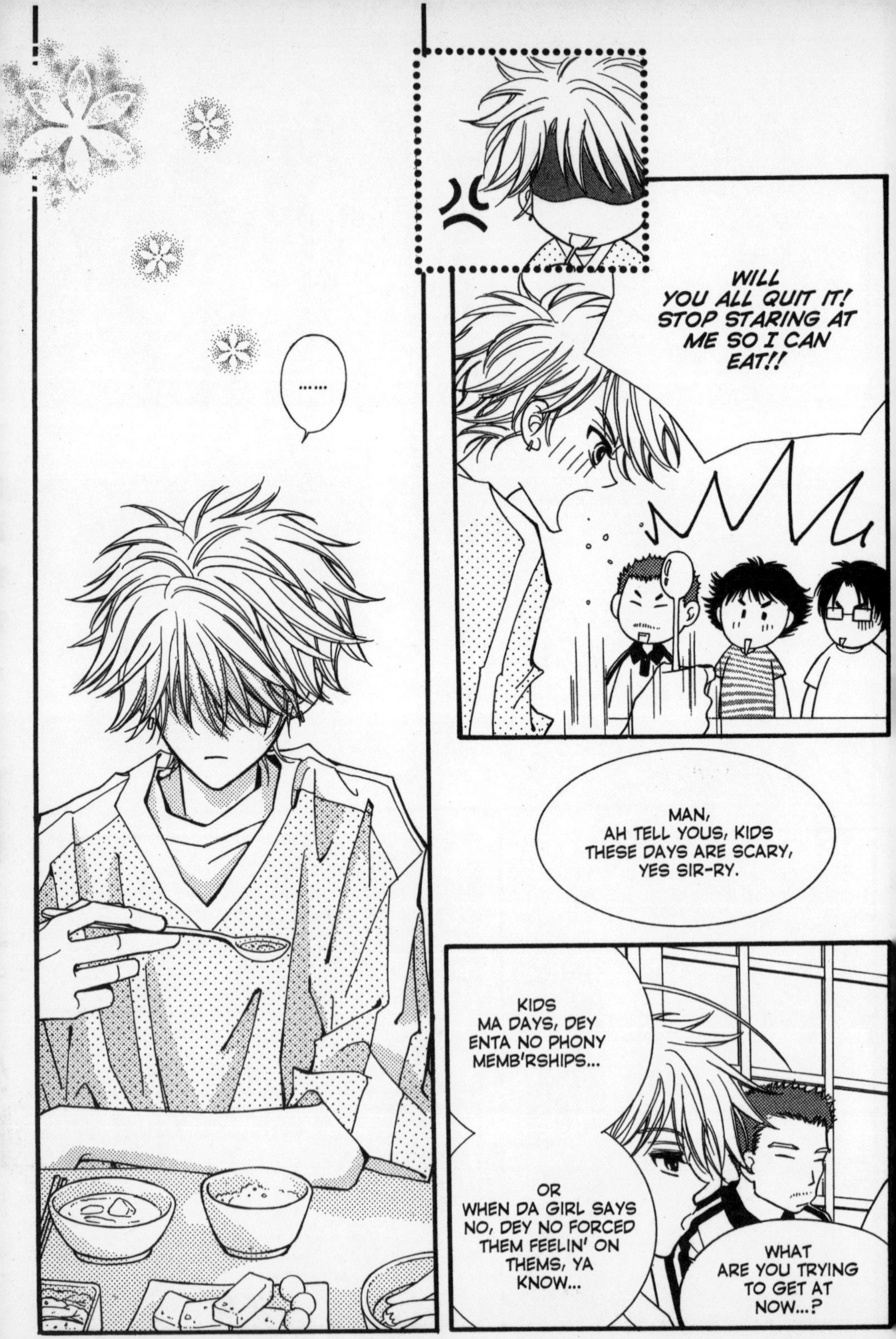
......
WILL YOU ALL QUIT IT! STOP STARING AT ME SO I CAN EAT!!
MAN, AH TELL YOUS, KIDS THESE DAYS ARE SCARY, YES SIR-RY.
KIDS MA DAYS, DEY ENTA NO PHONY MEMB'RSHIPS...
OR WHEN DA GIRL SAYS NO, DEY NO FORCED THEM FEELIN' ON THEMS, YA KNOW...
WHAT ARE YOU TRYING TO GET AT NOW...?

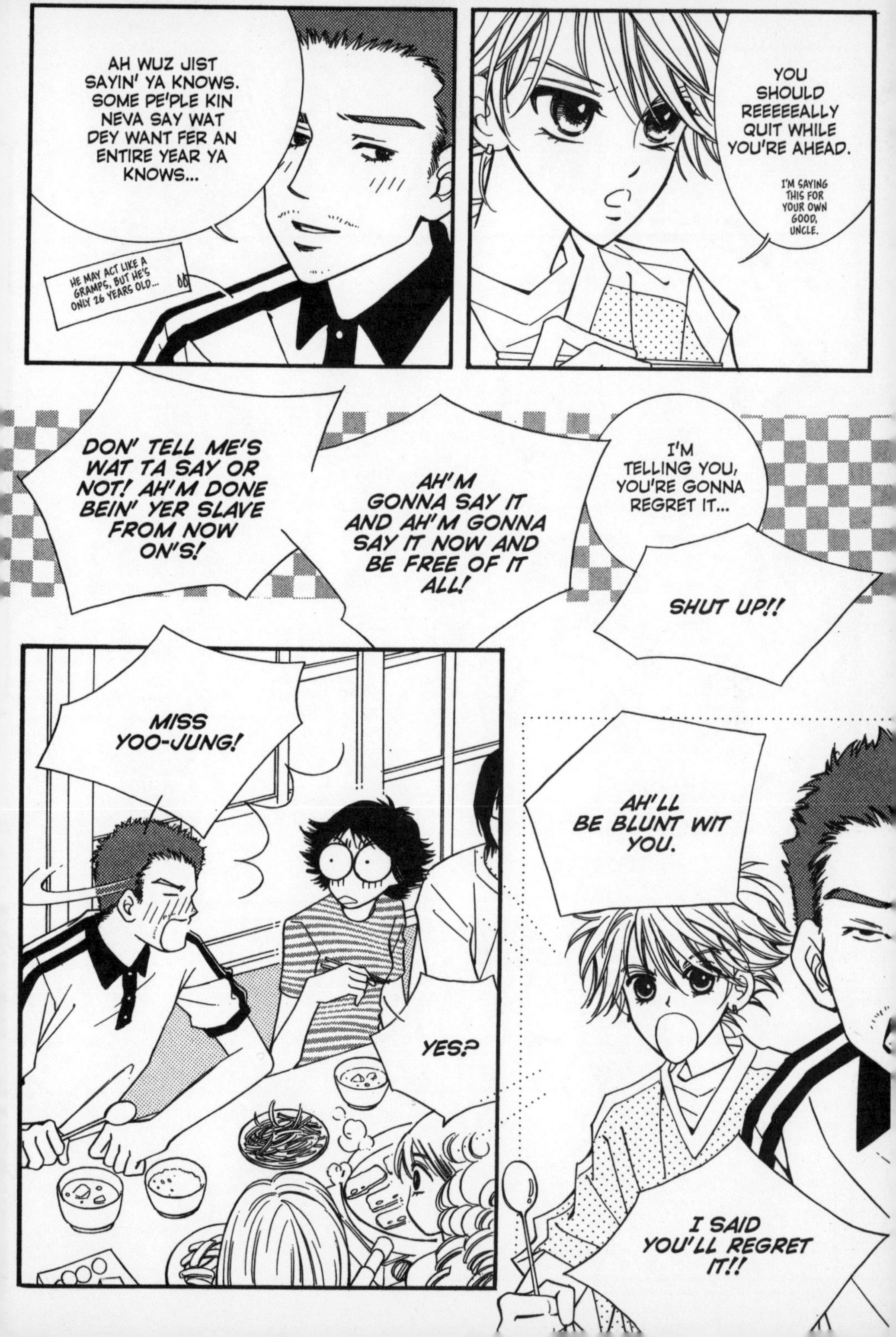
AH WUZ JIST SAYIN' YA KNOWS. SOME PE'PLE KIN NEVA SAY WAT DEY WANT FER AN ENTIRE YEAR YA KNOWS...
HE MAY ACT LIKE A GRAMPS, BUT HE'S ONLY 26 YEARS OLD...
YOU SHOULD REEEEEALLY QUIT WHILE YOU'RE AHEAD.
I'M SAYING THIS FOR YOUR OWN GOOD, UNCLE.
DON' TELL ME'S WAT TA SAY OR NOT! AH'M DONE BEIN' YER SLAVE FROM NOW ON'S!
AH'M GONNA SAY IT AND AH'M GONNA SAY IT NOW AND BE FREE OF IT ALL!
I'M TELLING YOU, YOU'RE GONNA REGRET IT...
SHUT UP!!
MISS YOO-JUNG!
YES?
AH'LL BE BLUNT WIT YOU.
I SAID YOU'LL REGRET IT!!

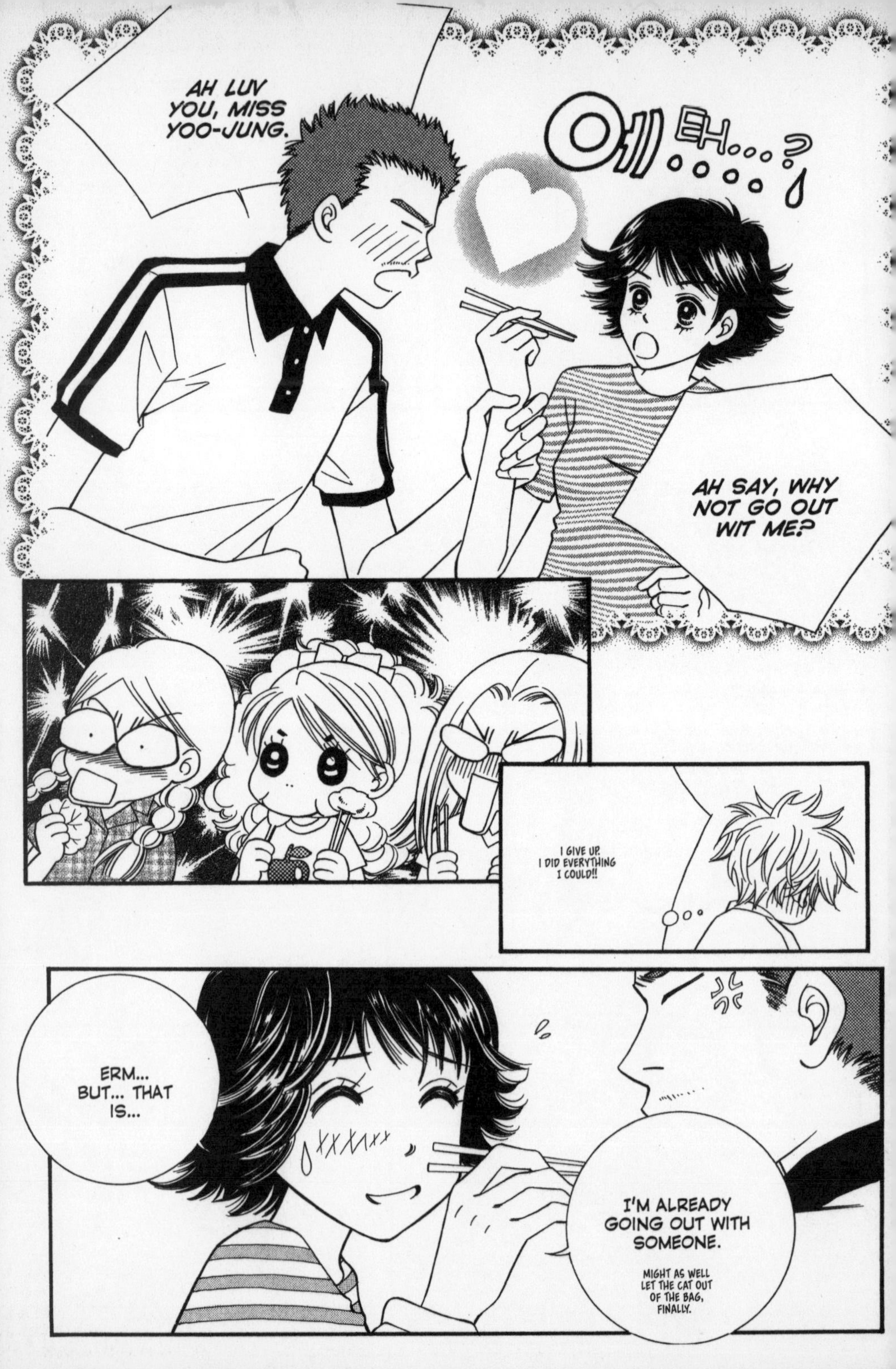
AH LUV YOU, MISS YOO-JUNG.
EH...?
AH SAY, WHY NOT GO OUT WIT ME?
I GIVE UP. I DID EVERYTHING I COULD!!
ERM... BUT... THAT IS...
I'M ALREADY GOING OUT WITH SOMEONE.
MIGHT AS WELL LET THE CAT OUT OF THE BAG, FINALLY.

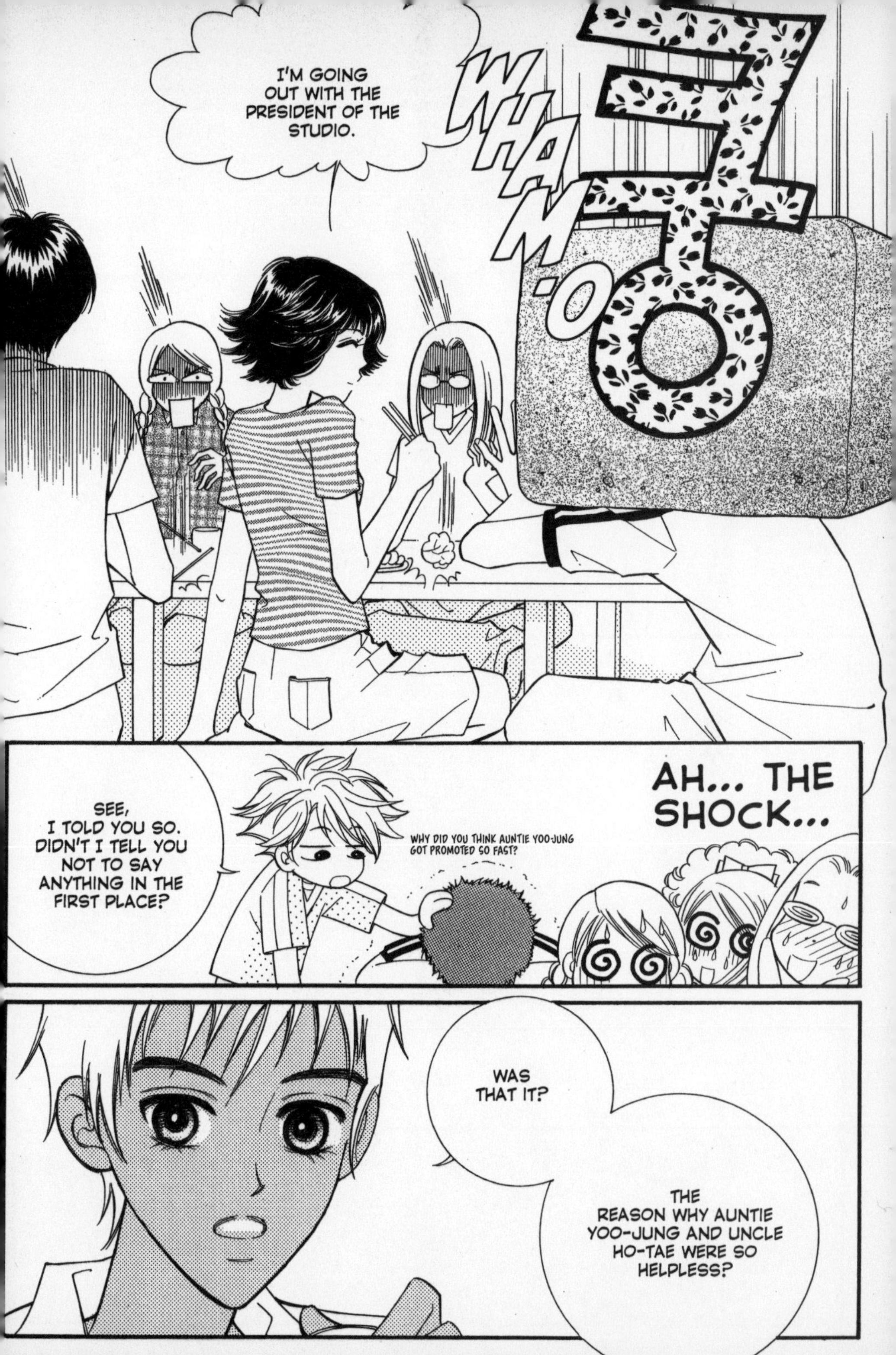
I'M GOING OUT WITH THE PRESIDENT OF THE STUDIO.
WHAM-O
SEE, I TOLD YOU SO. DIDN'T I TELL YOU NOT TO SAY ANYTHING IN THE FIRST PLACE?
WHY DID YOU THINK AUNTIE YOO-JUNG GOT PROMOTED SO FAST?
AH... THE SHOCK...
WAS THAT IT?
THE REASON WHY AUNTIE YOO-JUNG AND UNCLE HO-TAE WERE SO HELPLESS?

SO, HOW DID YOU END UP DATING THE PRESIDENT?

HE LOOKS LIKE SOME BURGLAR...

OH, BACK WHEN THE PRESIDENT WAS JUST A MANAGER FOR D-BOYZ,

I HAPPENED TO BE A HARDCORE D-BOYZ FANGIRL.

BUT THEN... INSTEAD OF SEEING D-BOYZ, I BUMPED INTO THE MANAGER MORE OFTEN... AND THEN... YOU KNOW, THINGS HAP-PENED...

WOW, THEY REALLY HAPPEN! THOSE STORIES OF MANAGERS STEALING FANS!

WELL, HE ISN'T THE SORT OF A FACE YOU'D BE STOLEN TO...

WHAT DID YOU JUST SAY?!

UM... IS TODAY A DAY OF FORGIVENESS?

I... I CAN BE FREE FROM E-SOH TOO?

I DRANK ALCOHOL!

AND TWO BOTTLES OF IT TOO!

PUUUH!

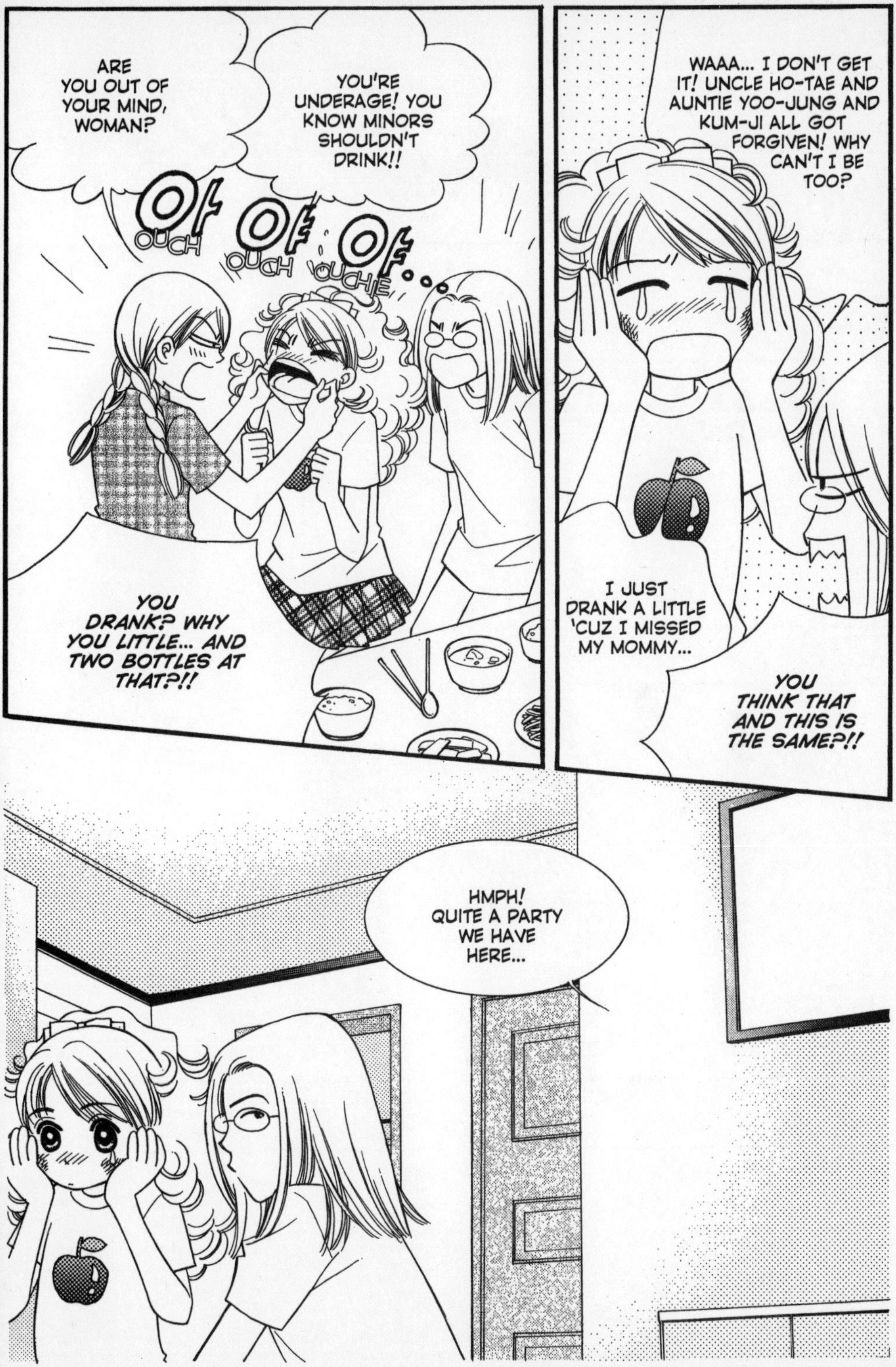
ARE YOU OUT OF YOUR MIND, WOMAN?
YOU'RE UNDERAGE! YOU KNOW MINORS SHOULDN'T DRINK!!
OUCH OUCH OUCHIE...
YOU DRANK? WHY YOU LITTLE... AND TWO BOTTLES AT THAT?!!
WAAA... I DON'T GET IT! UNCLE HO-TAE AND AUNTIE YOO-JUNG AND KUM-JI ALL GOT FORGIVEN! WHY CAN'T I BE TOO?
I JUST DRANK A LITTLE 'CUZ I MISSED MY MOMMY...
YOU THINK THAT AND THIS IS THE SAME?!!
HMPH! QUITE A PARTY WE HAVE HERE...

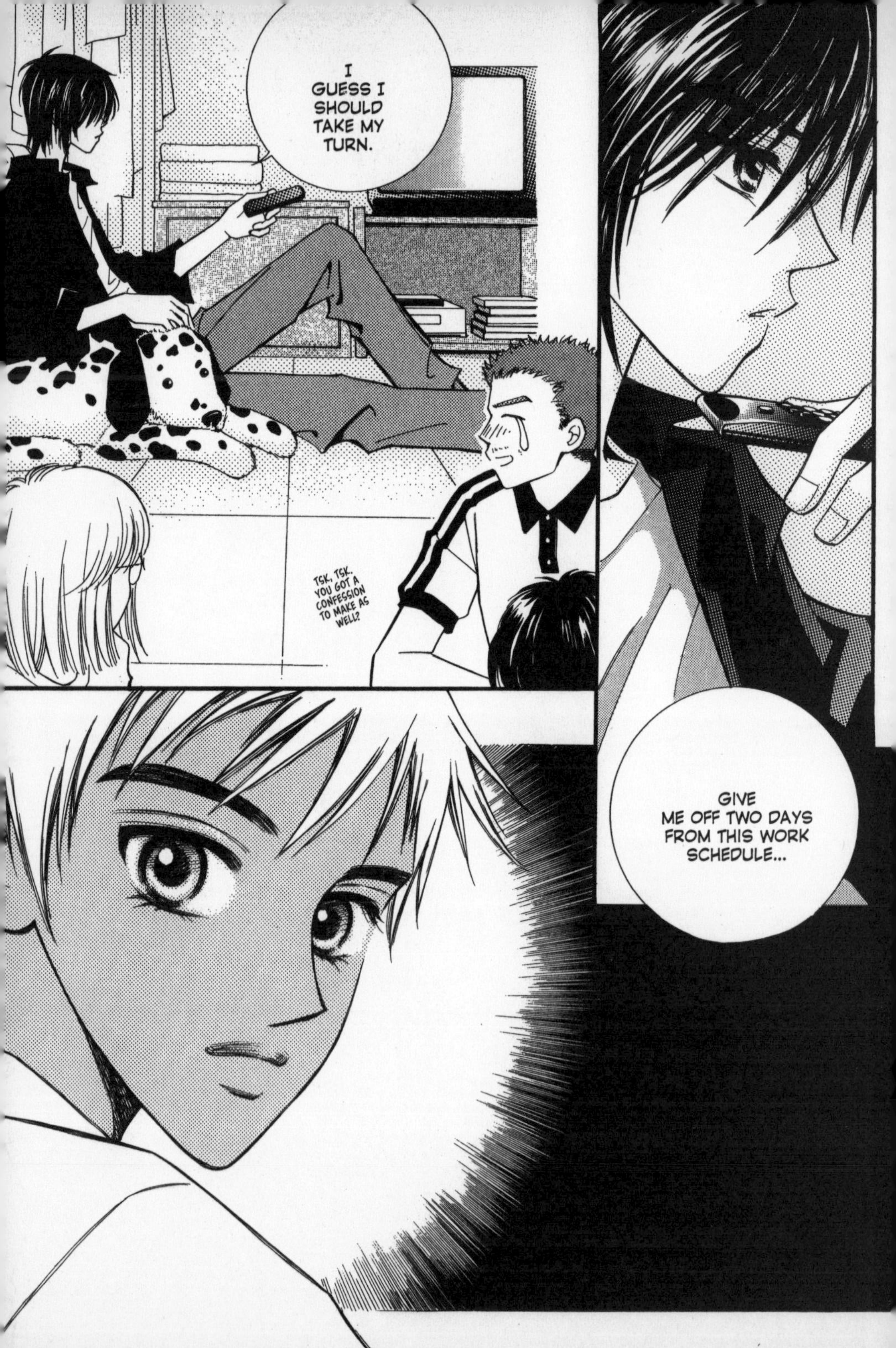
I GUESS I SHOULD TAKE MY TURN.
TSK, TSK. YOU GOT A CONFESSION TO MAKE AS WELL?
GIVE ME OFF TWO DAYS FROM THIS WORK SCHEDULE...

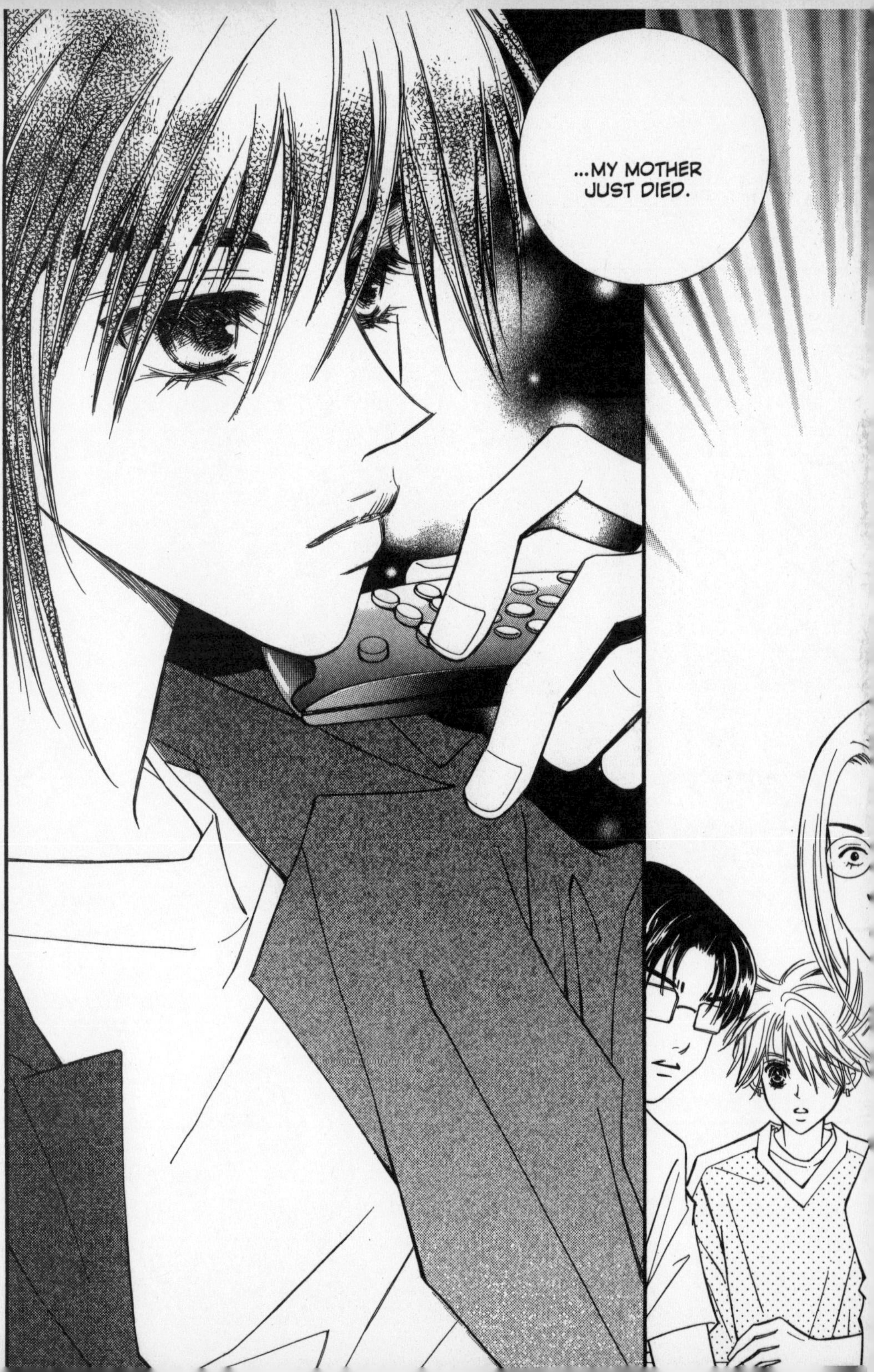
...MY MOTHER JUST DIED.

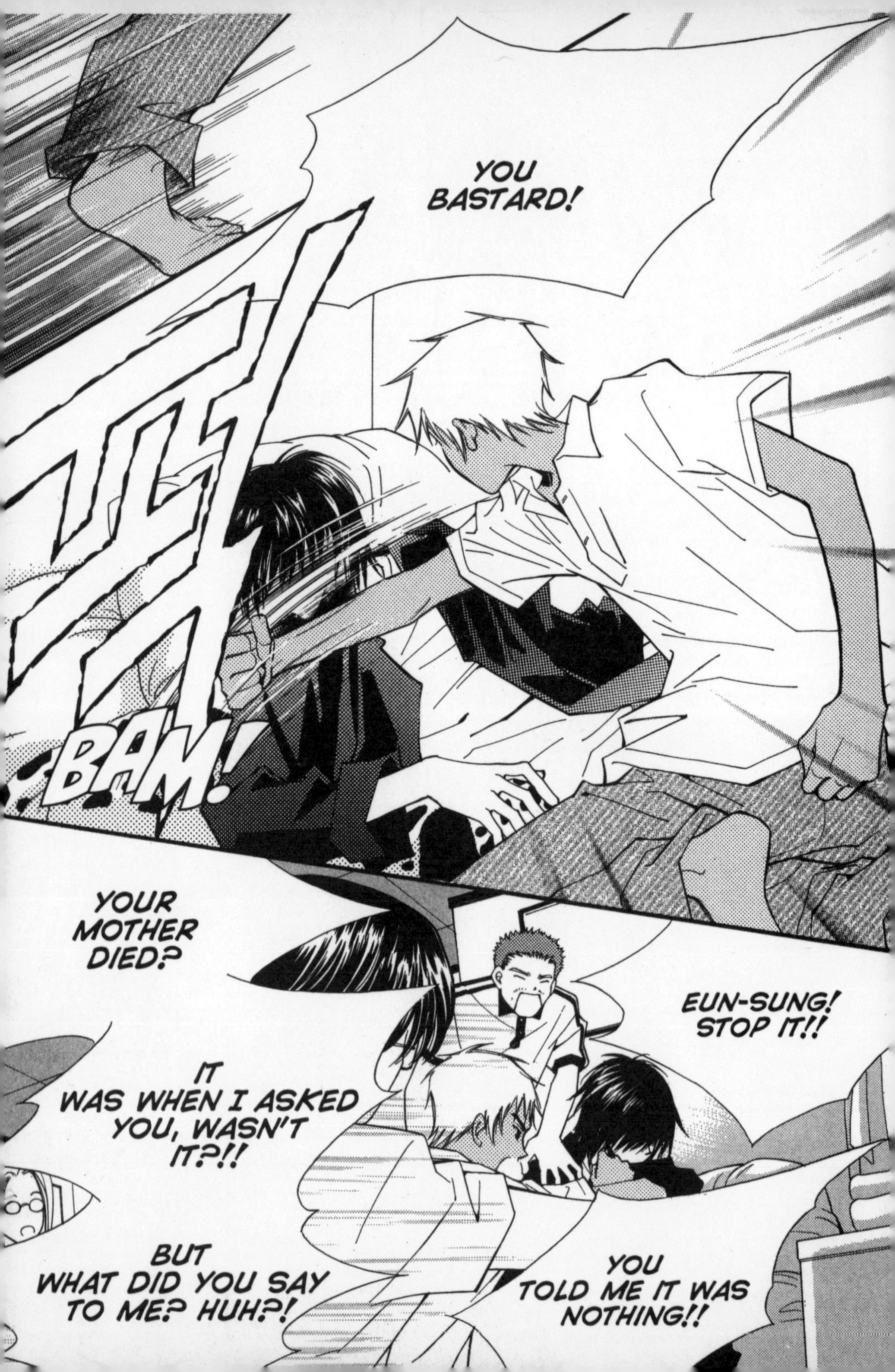
YOU BASTARD!
BAM!
YOUR MOTHER DIED?
IT WAS WHEN I ASKED YOU, WASN'T IT?!!
EUN-SUNG! STOP IT!!
BUT WHAT DID YOU SAY TO ME? HUH?!
YOU TOLD ME IT WAS NOTHING!!

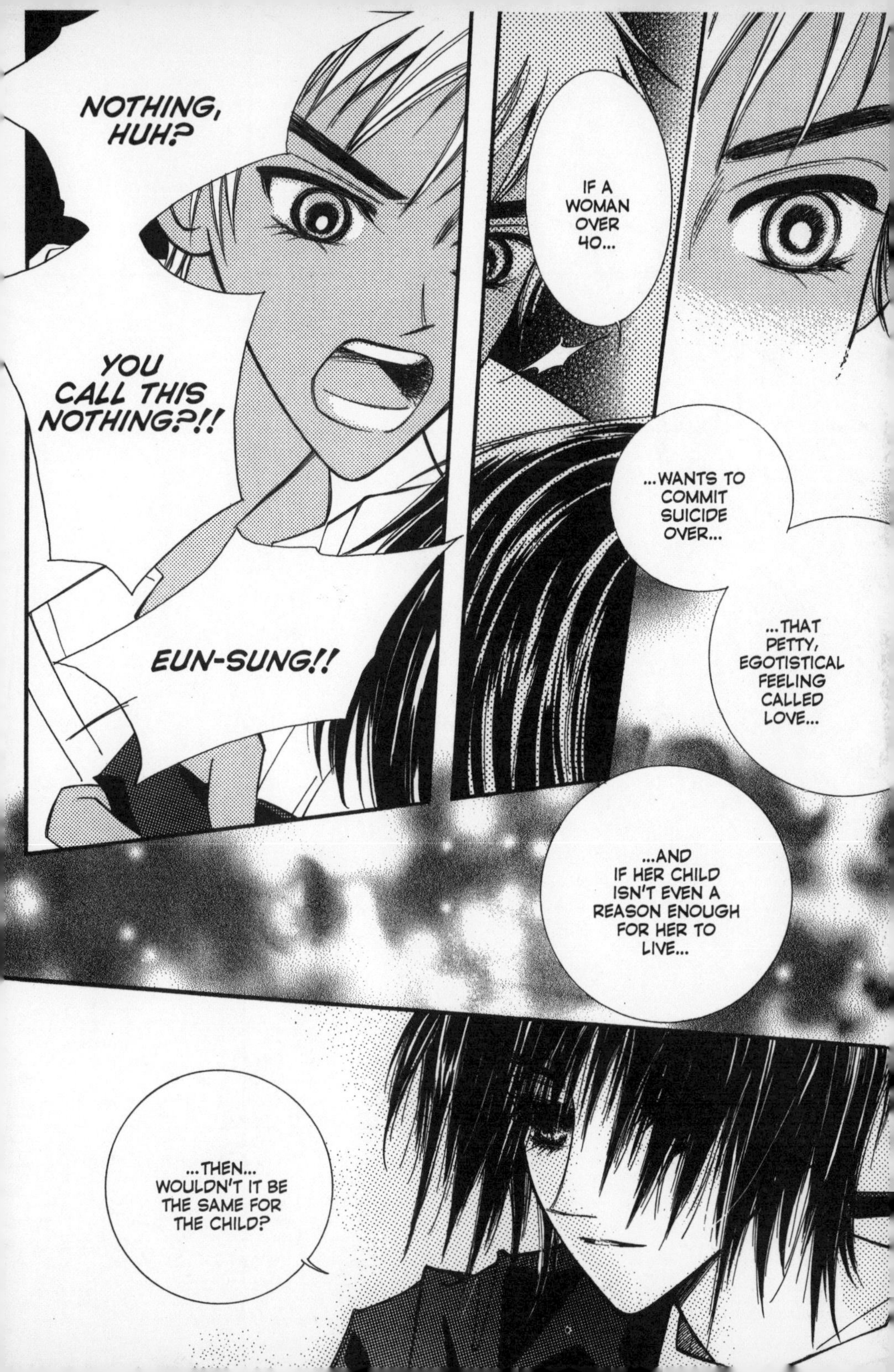
NOTHING, HUH?
YOU CALL THIS NOTHING?!!
EUN-SUNG!!
IF A WOMAN OVER 40...
...WANTS TO COMMIT SUICIDE OVER...
...THAT PETTY, EGOTISTICAL FEELING CALLED LOVE...
...AND IF HER CHILD ISN'T EVEN A REASON ENOUGH FOR HER TO LIVE...
...THEN... WOULDN'T IT BE THE SAME FOR THE CHILD?

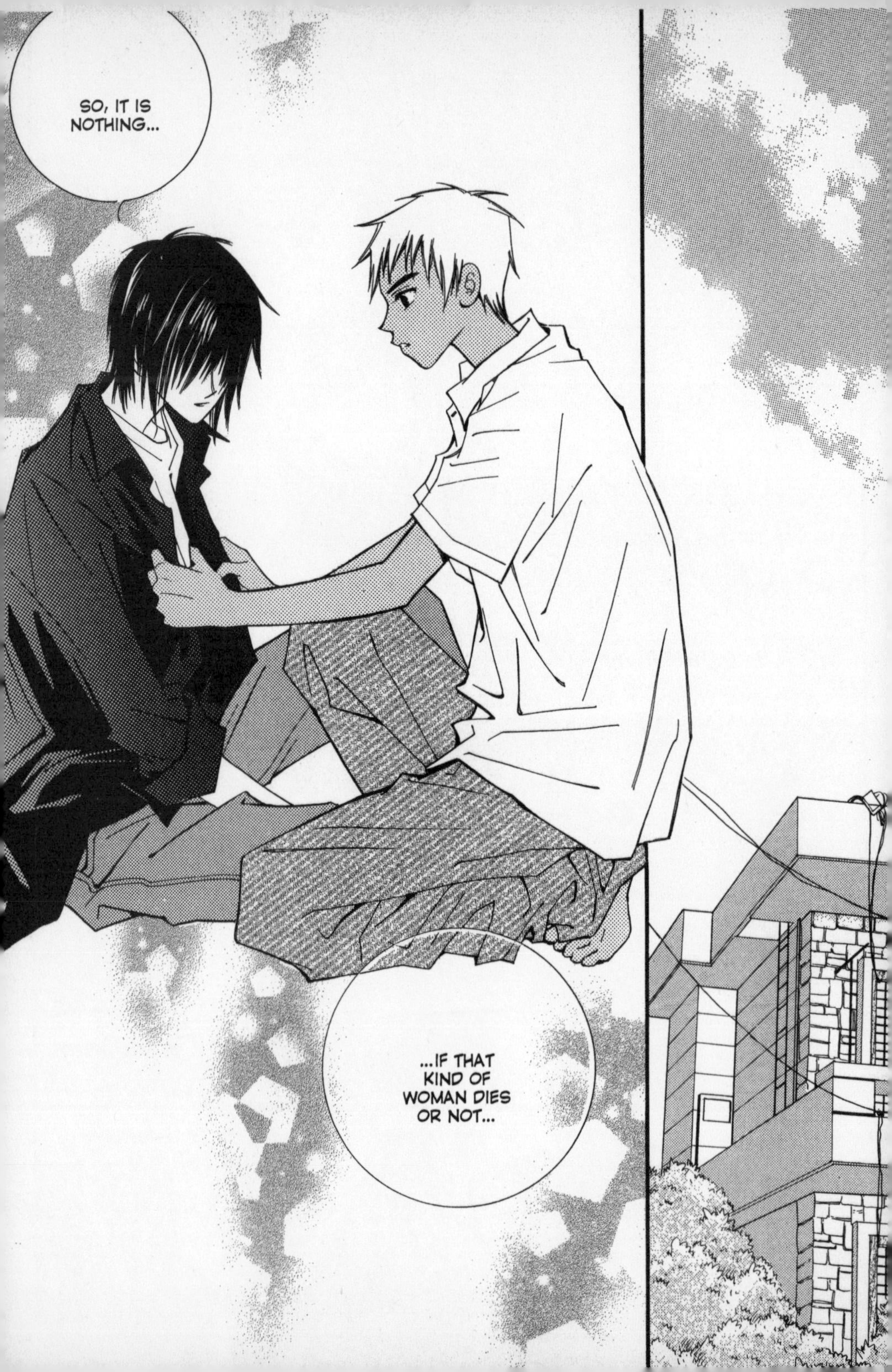
SO, IT IS NOTHING...
...IF THAT KIND OF WOMAN DIES OR NOT...

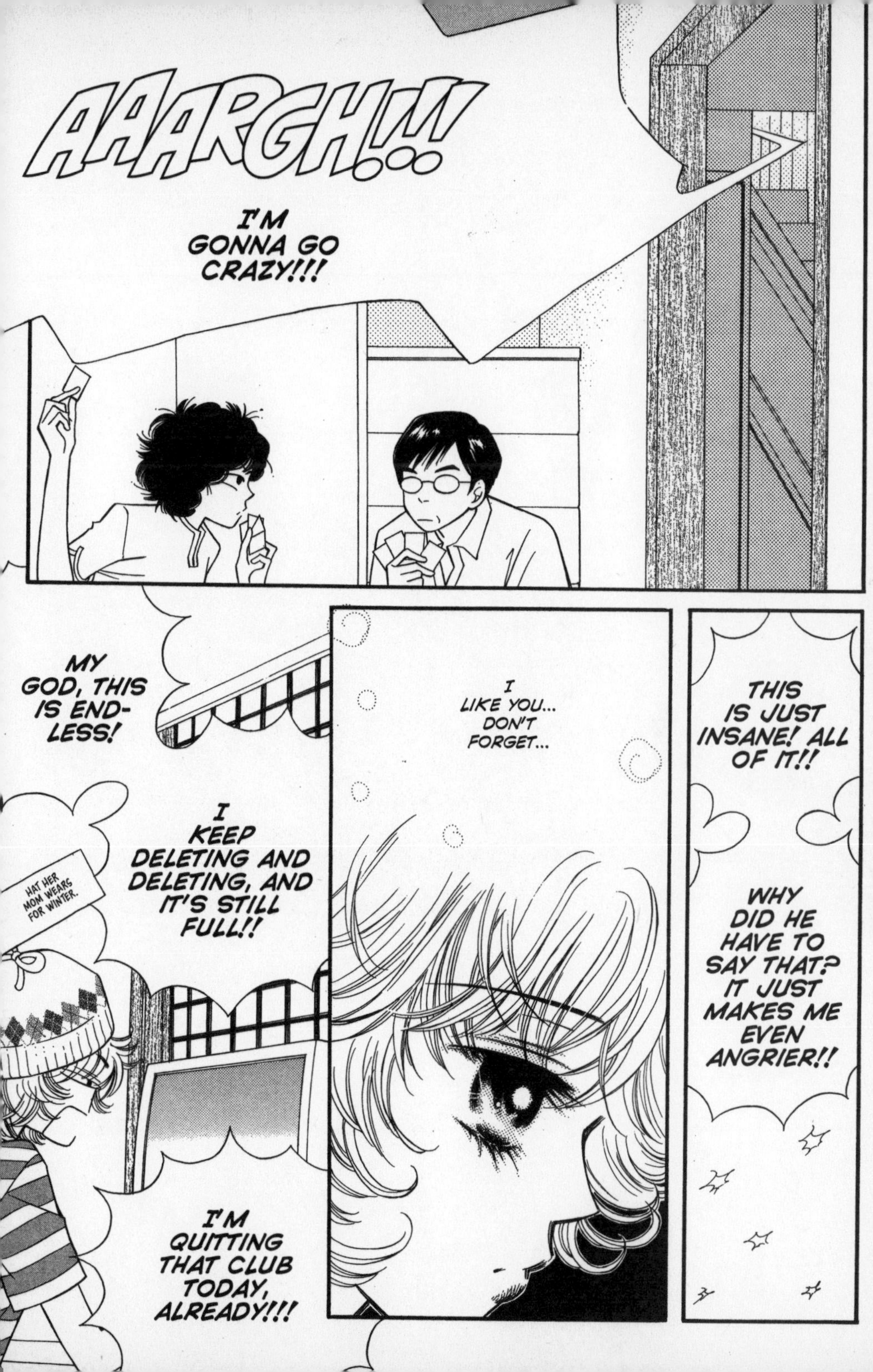
AAARGH!!!
I'M GONNA GO CRAZY!!!
MY GOD, THIS IS END-LESS!
I KEEP DELETING AND DELETING, AND IT'S STILL FULL!!
HAT HER MOM WEARS FOR WINTER.
I'M QUITTING THAT CLUB TODAY, ALREADY!!!
I LIKE YOU... DON'T FORGET...
THIS IS JUST INSANE! ALL OF IT!!
WHY DID HE HAVE TO SAY THAT? IT JUST MAKES ME EVEN ANGRIER!!

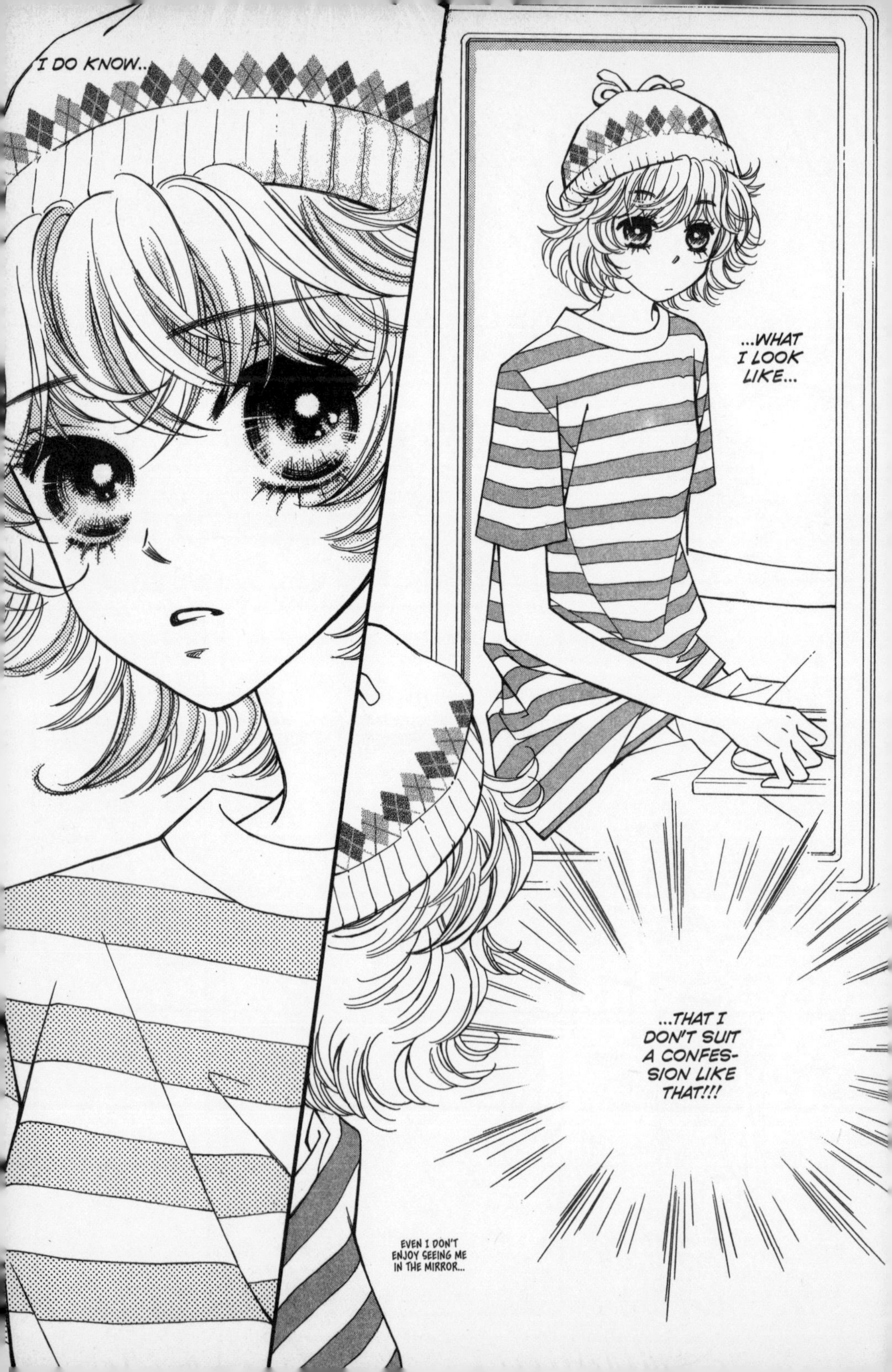
I DO KNOW...
...WHAT I LOOK LIKE...
...THAT I DON'T SUIT A CONFES-SION LIKE THAT!!!
EVEN I DON'T ENJOY SEEING ME IN THE MIRROR...

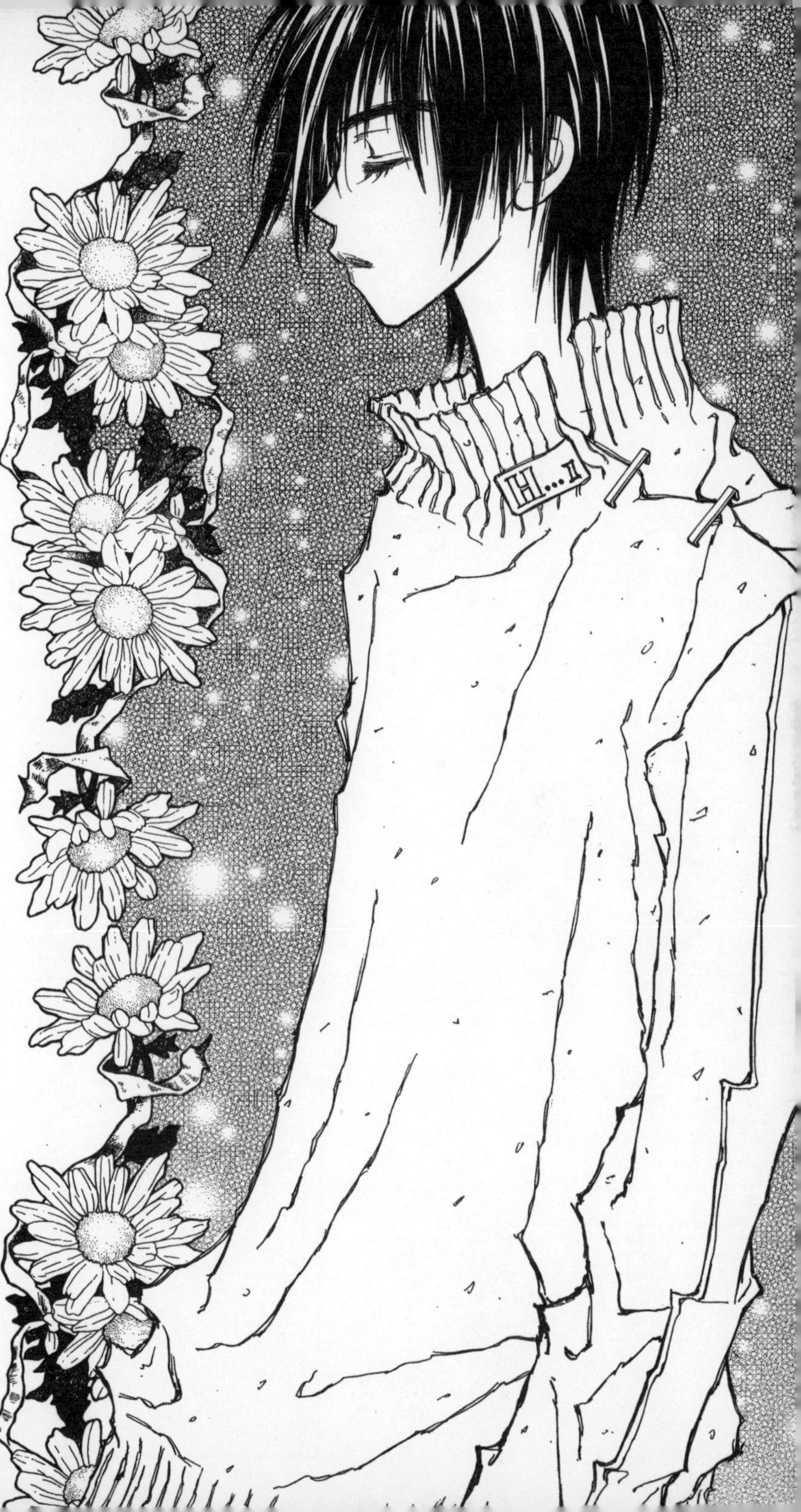

AW-- MAN, WHY ME?!!
STOP WHINING AND GO!
AH~
I DON'T WANNA...
THERE'S NO TIME, SO GO QUICKLY. REMEMBER, IT'S THE FRONT ENTRANCE OF DONGNAM HOSPITAL, OKAY?
ADDA
AUNTIE??
YES, I'M ON MY WAY.

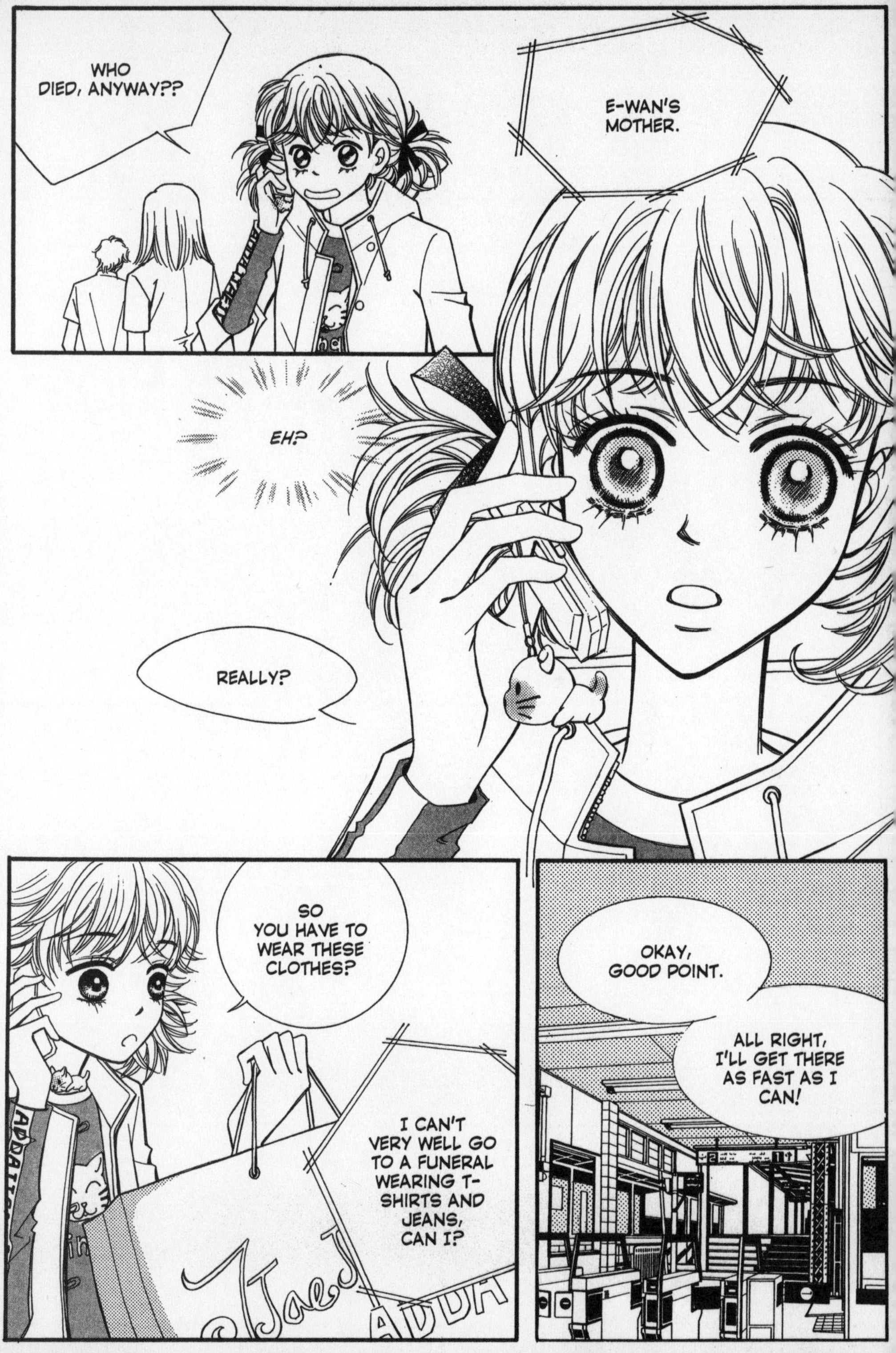
WHO DIED, ANYWAY??
E-WAN'S MOTHER.
EH?
REALLY?
SO YOU HAVE TO WEAR THESE CLOTHES?
I CAN'T VERY WELL GO TO A FUNERAL WEARING T-SHIRTS AND JEANS, CAN I?
OKAY, GOOD POINT.
ALL RIGHT, I'LL GET THERE AS FAST AS I CAN!

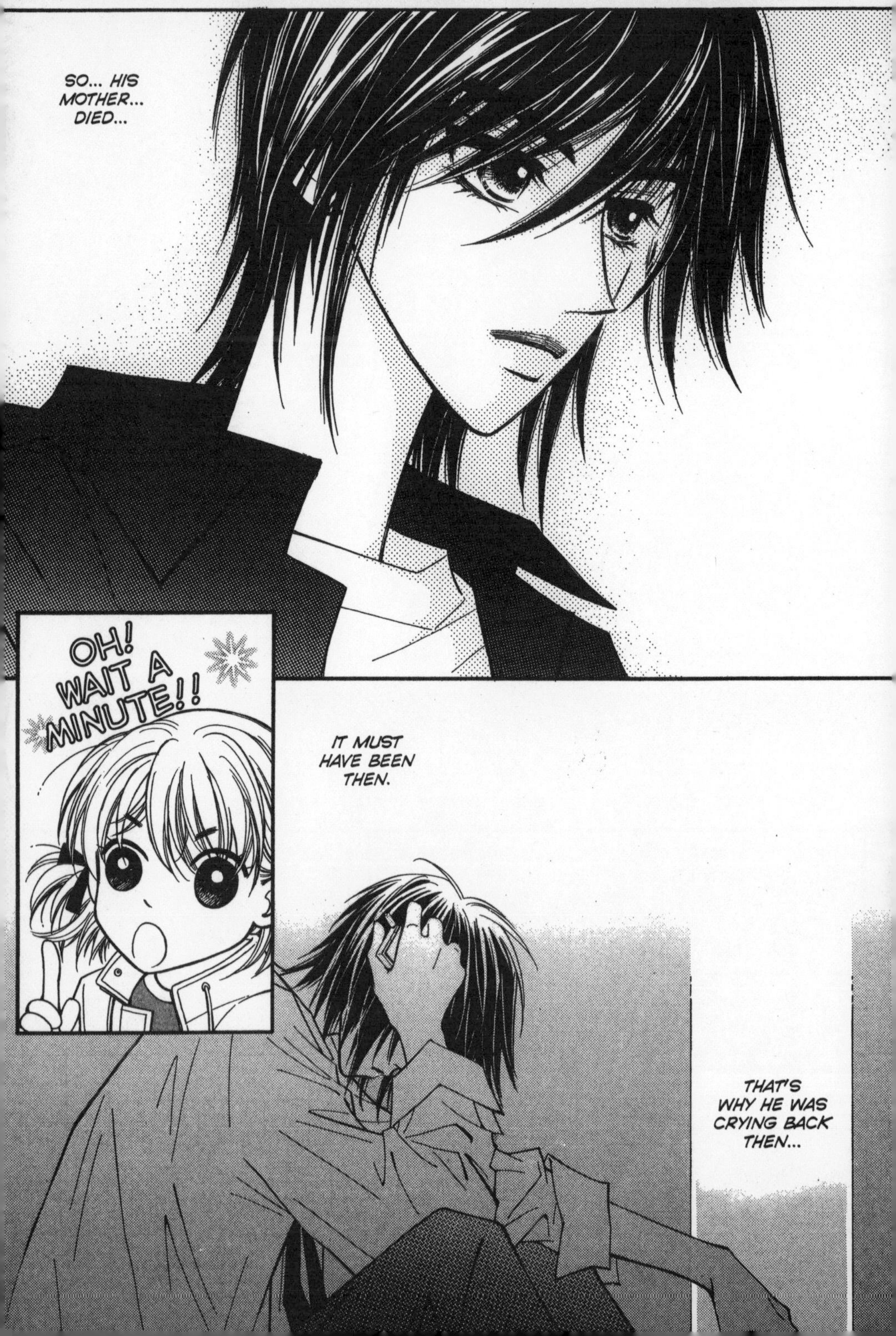
SO... HIS MOTHER... DIED...
OH! WAIT A MINUTE!!
IT MUST HAVE BEEN THEN.
THAT'S WHY HE WAS CRYING BACK THEN...

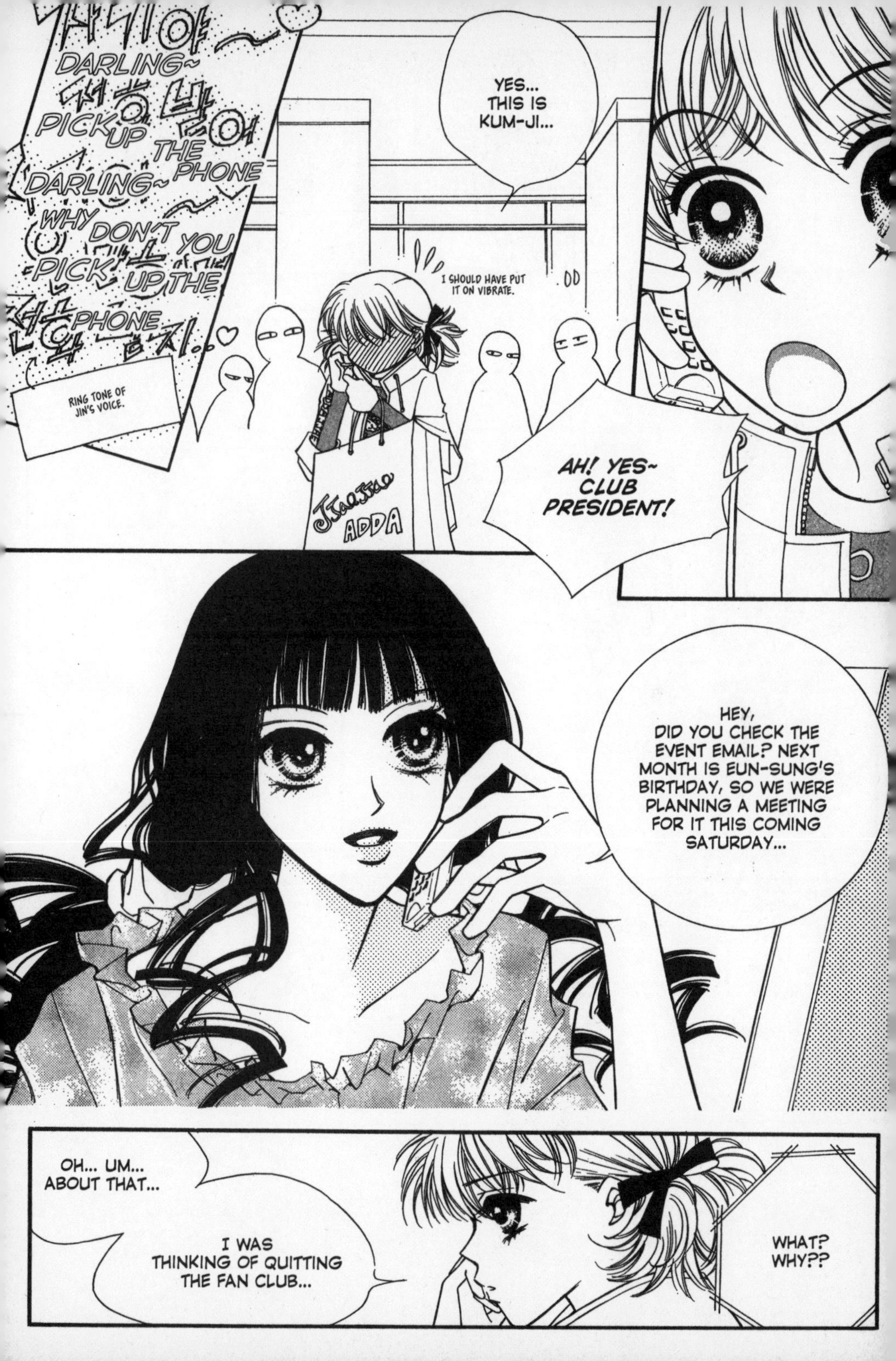
DARLING~
PICK UP THE PHONE
DARLING~
WHY DON'T YOU PICK UP THE PHONE
RING TONE OF JIN'S VOICE.
YES... THIS IS KUM-JI...
I SHOULD HAVE PUT IT ON VIBRATE.
JJAEJJAE ADDA
AH! YES~ CLUB PRESIDENT!
HEY, DID YOU CHECK THE EVENT EMAIL? NEXT MONTH IS EUN-SUNG'S BIRTHDAY, SO WE WERE PLANNING A MEETING FOR IT THIS COMING SATURDAY...
OH... UM... ABOUT THAT...
I WAS THINKING OF QUITTING THE FAN CLUB...
WHAT? WHY??

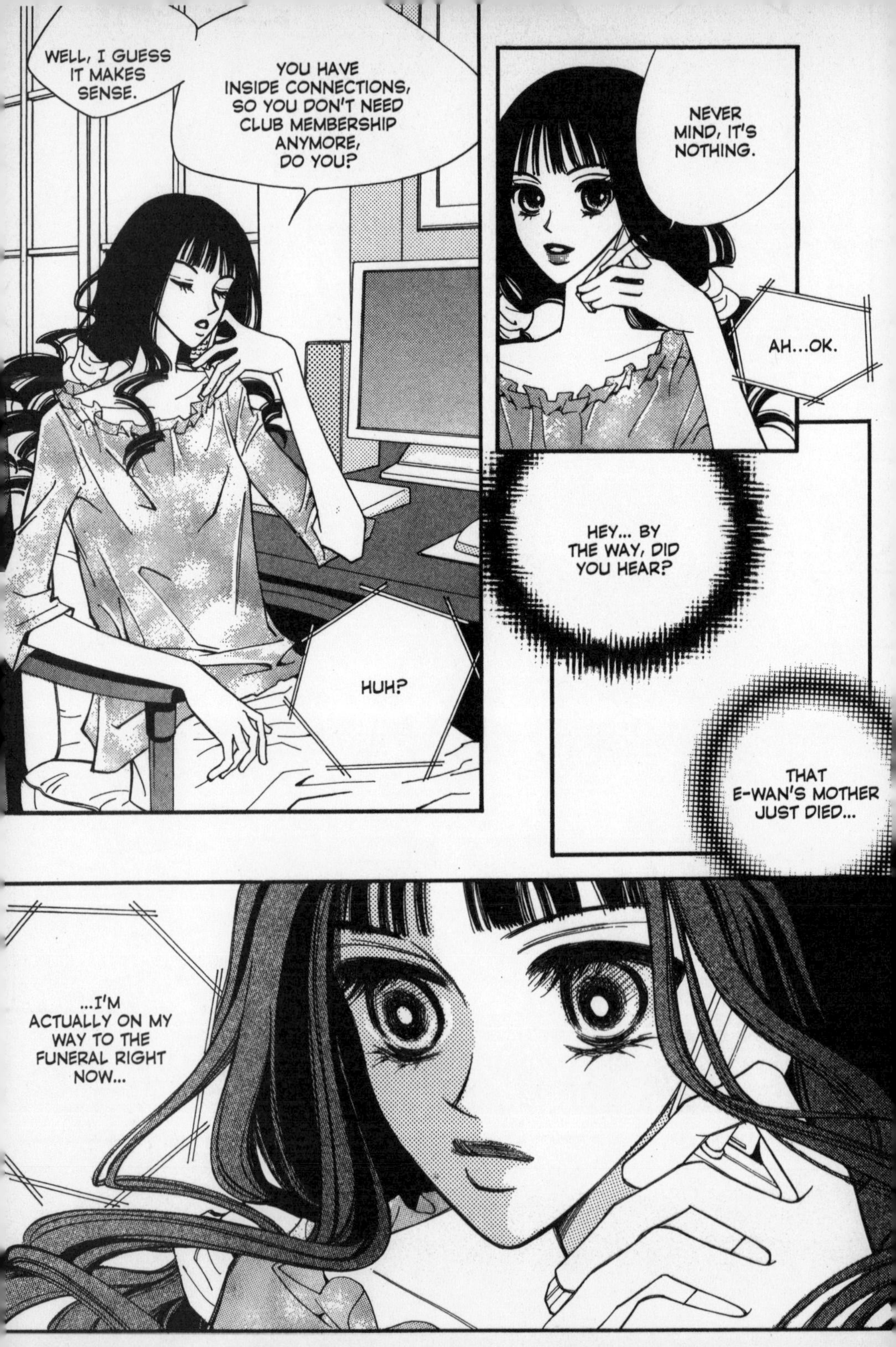
WELL, I GUESS IT MAKES SENSE.
YOU HAVE INSIDE CONNECTIONS, SO YOU DON'T NEED CLUB MEMBERSHIP ANYMORE, DO YOU?
HUH?
NEVER MIND, IT'S NOTHING.
AH...OK.
HEY... BY THE WAY, DID YOU HEAR?
THAT E-WAN'S MOTHER JUST DIED...
...I'M ACTUALLY ON MY WAY TO THE FUNERAL RIGHT NOW...

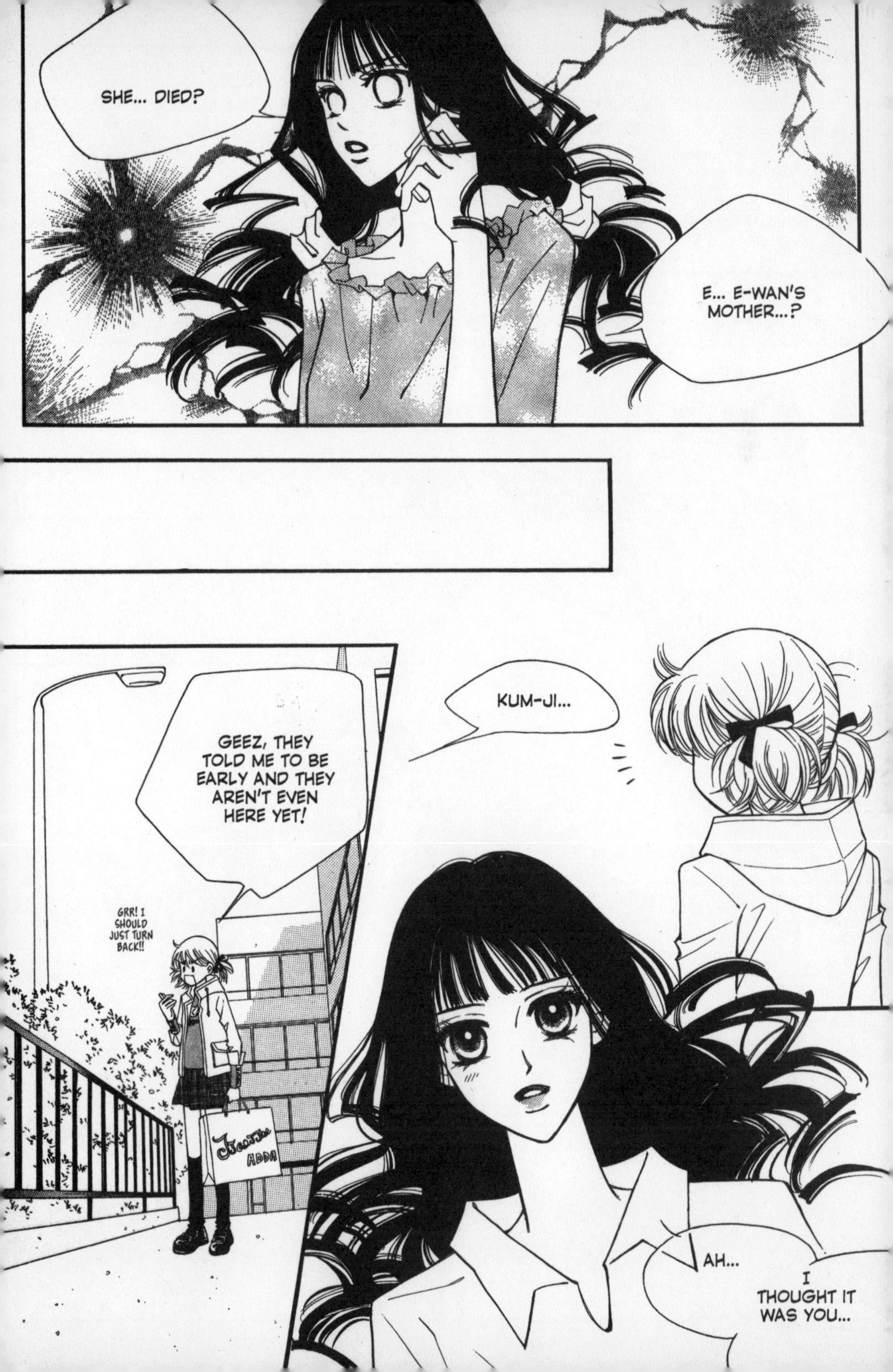
SHE... DIED?
E... E-WAN'S MOTHER...?
GEEZ, THEY TOLD ME TO BE EARLY AND THEY AREN'T EVEN HERE YET!
GRR! I SHOULD JUST TURN BACK!!
KUM-JI...
AH...
I THOUGHT IT WAS YOU...

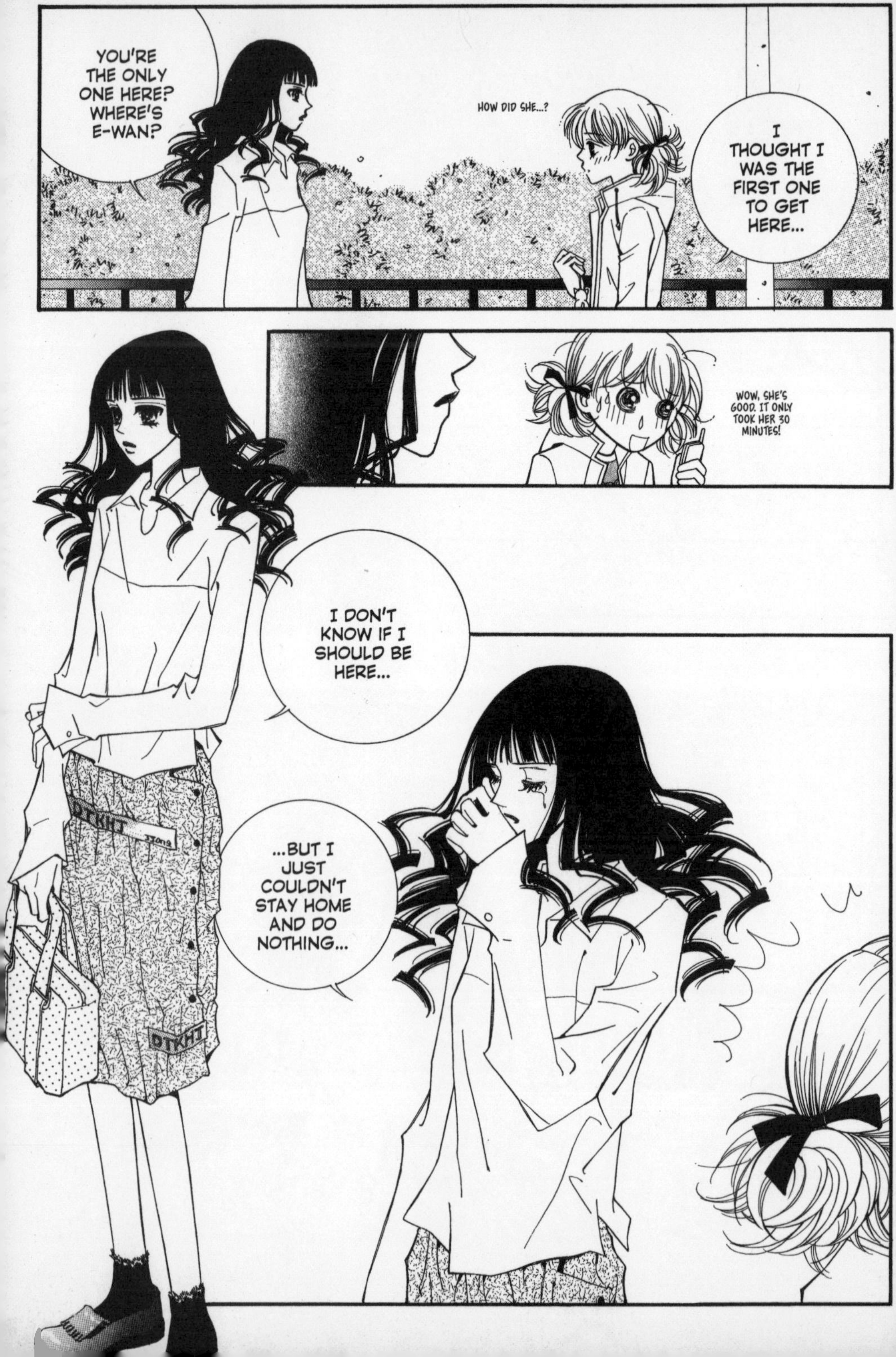
YOU'RE THE ONLY ONE HERE? WHERE'S E-WAN?
HOW DID SHE...?
I THOUGHT I WAS THE FIRST ONE TO GET HERE...
WOW, SHE'S GOOD. IT ONLY TOOK HER 30 MINUTES!
I DON'T KNOW IF I SHOULD BE HERE...
...BUT I JUST COULDN'T STAY HOME AND DO NOTHING...

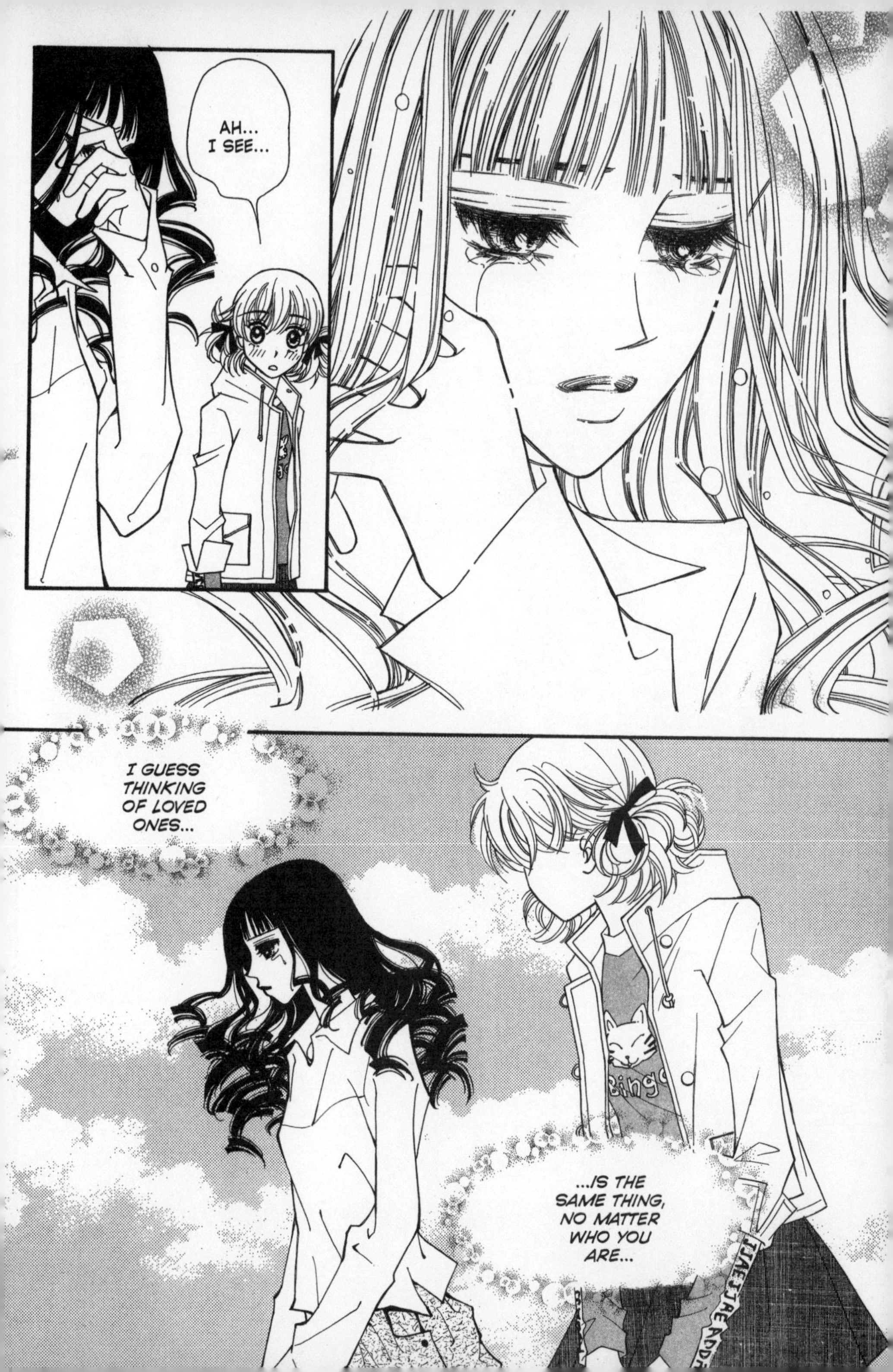
AH... I SEE...
I GUESS THINKING OF LOVED ONES...
...IS THE SAME THING, NO MATTER WHO YOU ARE...

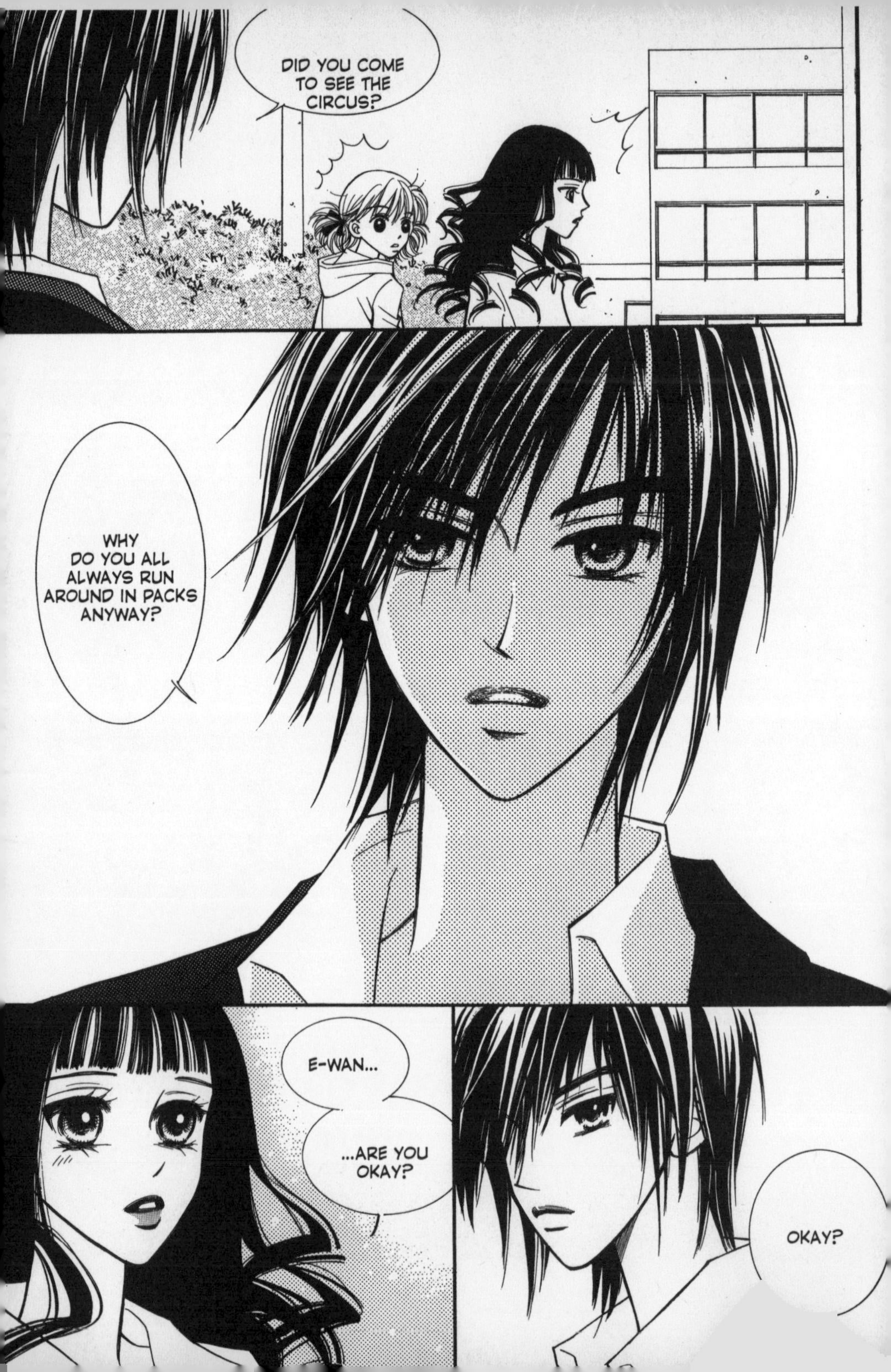
DID YOU COME TO SEE THE CIRCUS?
WHY DO YOU ALL ALWAYS RUN AROUND IN PACKS ANYWAY?
E-WAN...
...ARE YOU OKAY?
OKAY?

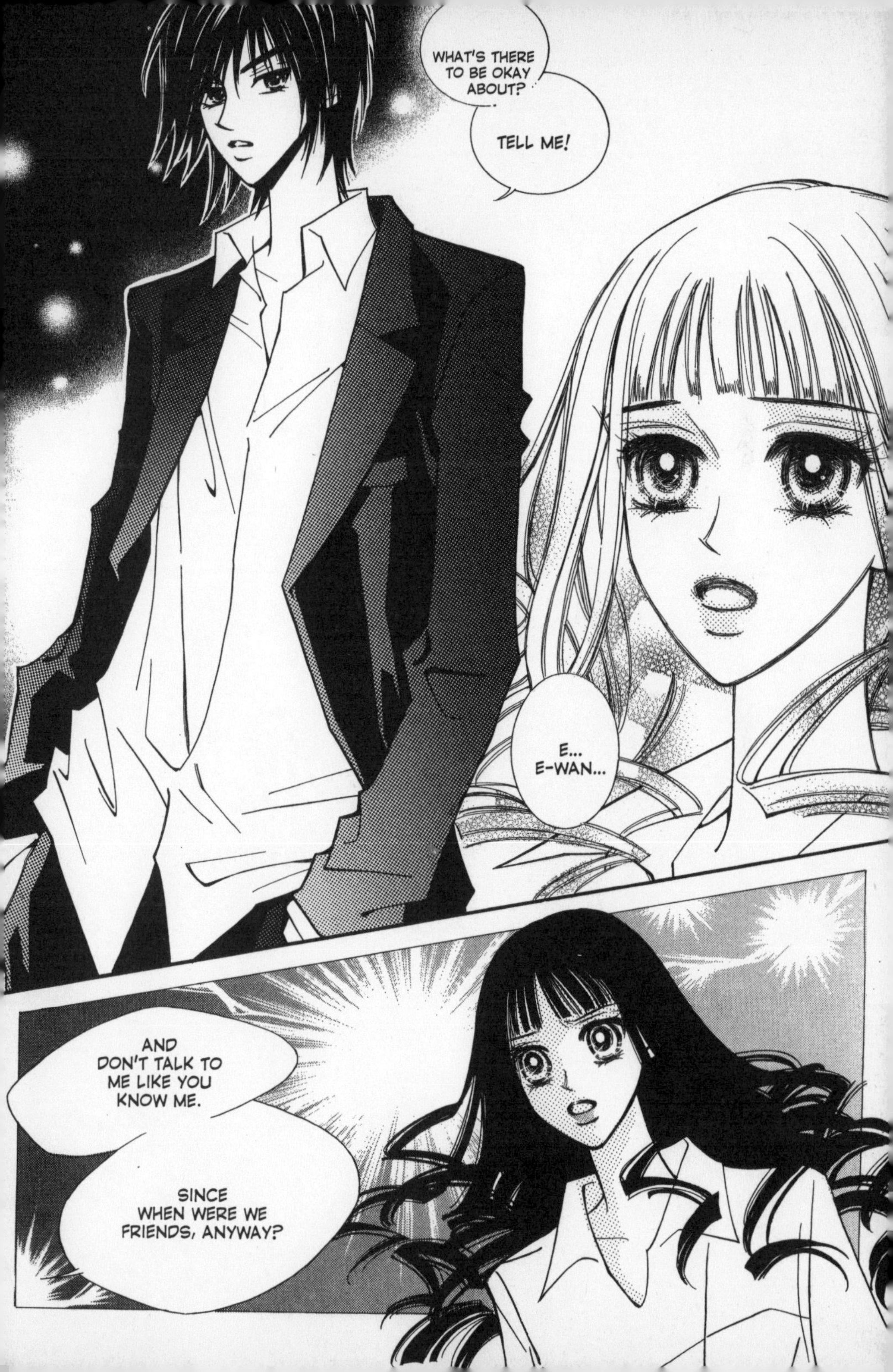
WHAT'S THERE TO BE OKAY ABOUT?
TELL ME!
E... E-WAN...
AND DON'T TALK TO ME LIKE YOU KNOW ME.
SINCE WHEN WERE WE FRIENDS, ANYWAY?

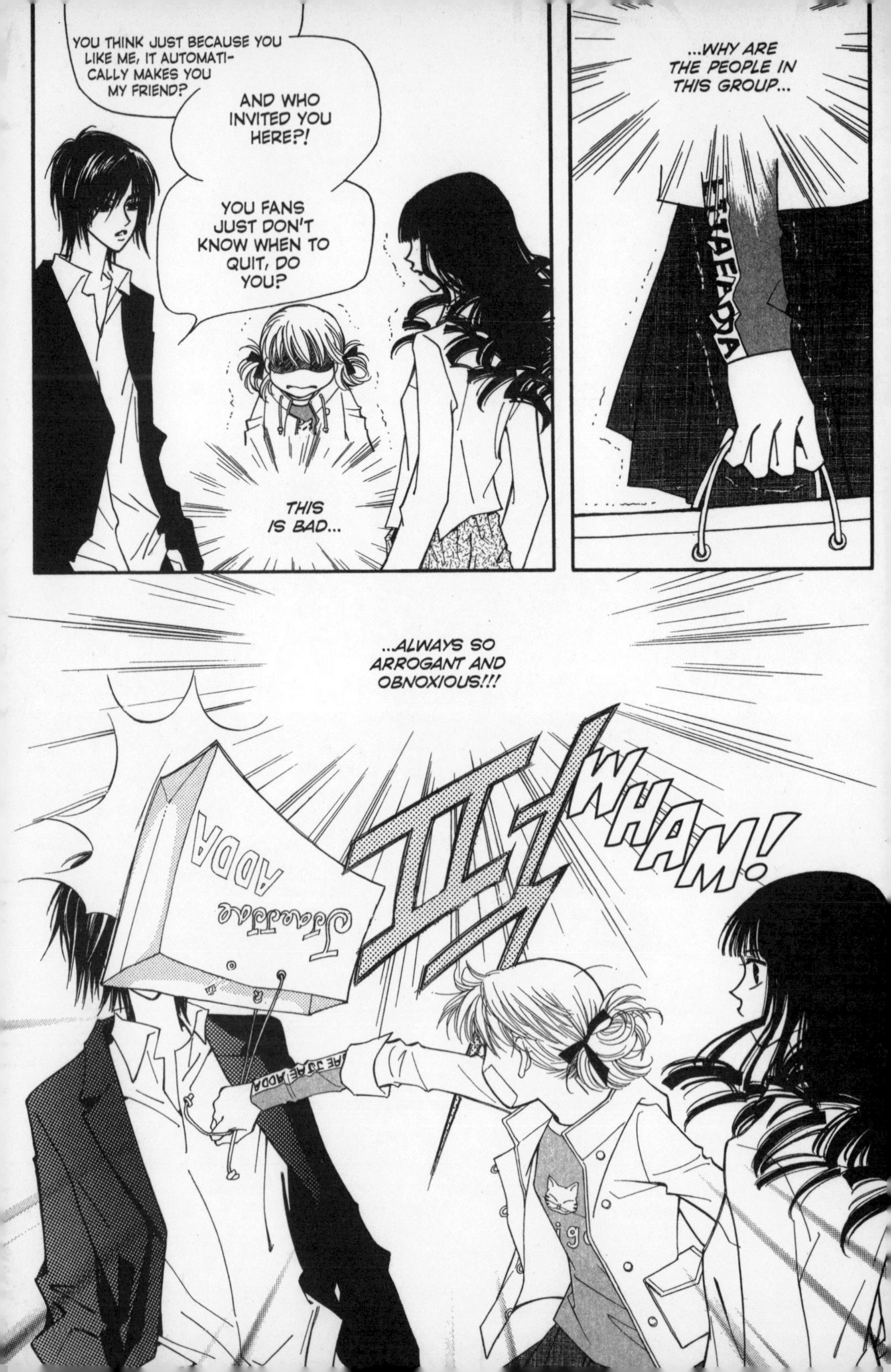
YOU THINK JUST BECAUSE YOU LIKE ME, IT AUTOMATICALLY MAKES YOU MY FRIEND?
AND WHO INVITED YOU HERE?!
YOU FANS JUST DON'T KNOW WHEN TO QUIT, DO YOU?
THIS IS BAD...
...WHY ARE THE PEOPLE IN THIS GROUP...
...ALWAYS SO ARROGANT AND OBNOXIOUS!!!
WHAM!

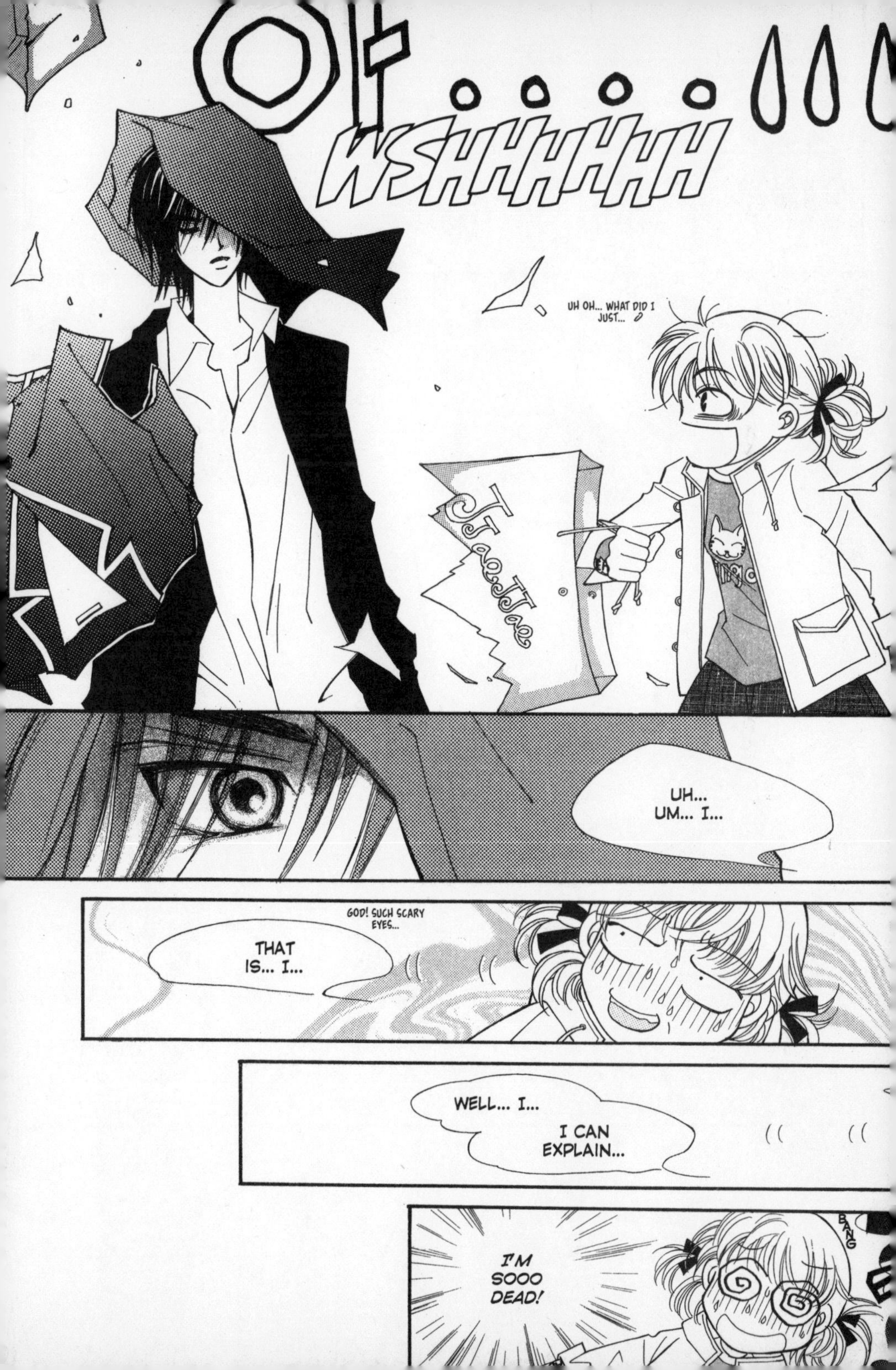
OH.....
WSHHHHHHH
UH OH... WHAT DID I JUST...
UH... UM... I...
GOD! SUCH SCARY EYES...
THAT IS... I...
WELL... I... I CAN EXPLAIN...
I'M SOOO DEAD!
BANG

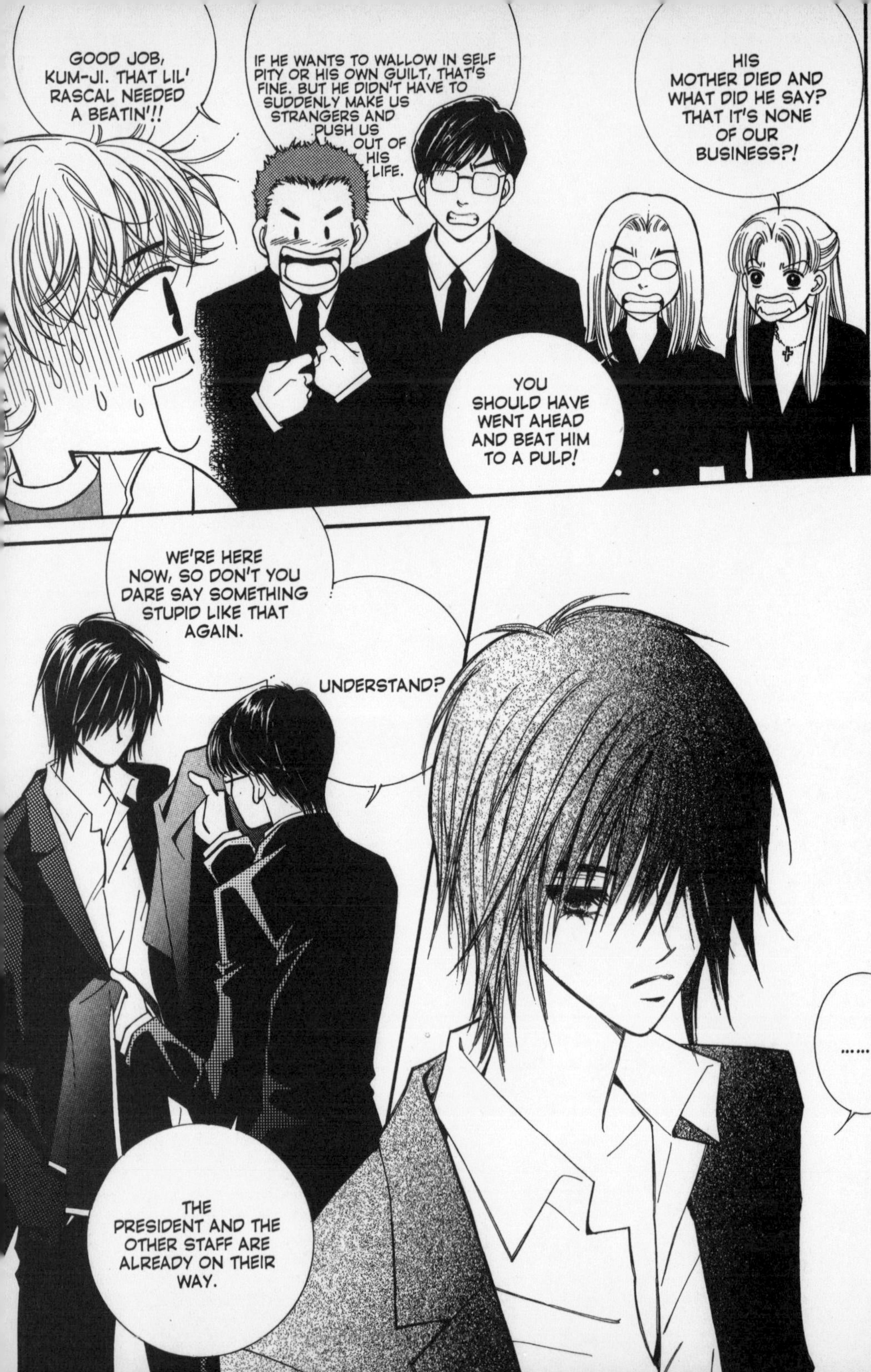
GOOD JOB, KUM-JI. THAT LIL' RASCAL NEEDED A BEATIN'!!
IF HE WANTS TO WALLOW IN SELF PITY OR HIS OWN GUILT, THAT'S FINE. BUT HE DIDN'T HAVE TO SUDDENLY MAKE US STRANGERS AND PUSH US OUT OF HIS LIFE.
HIS MOTHER DIED AND WHAT DID HE SAY? THAT IT'S NONE OF OUR BUSINESS?!
YOU SHOULD HAVE WENT AHEAD AND BEAT HIM TO A PULP!
WE'RE HERE NOW, SO DON'T YOU DARE SAY SOMETHING STUPID LIKE THAT AGAIN.
UNDERSTAND?
THE PRESIDENT AND THE OTHER STAFF ARE ALREADY ON THEIR WAY.
......

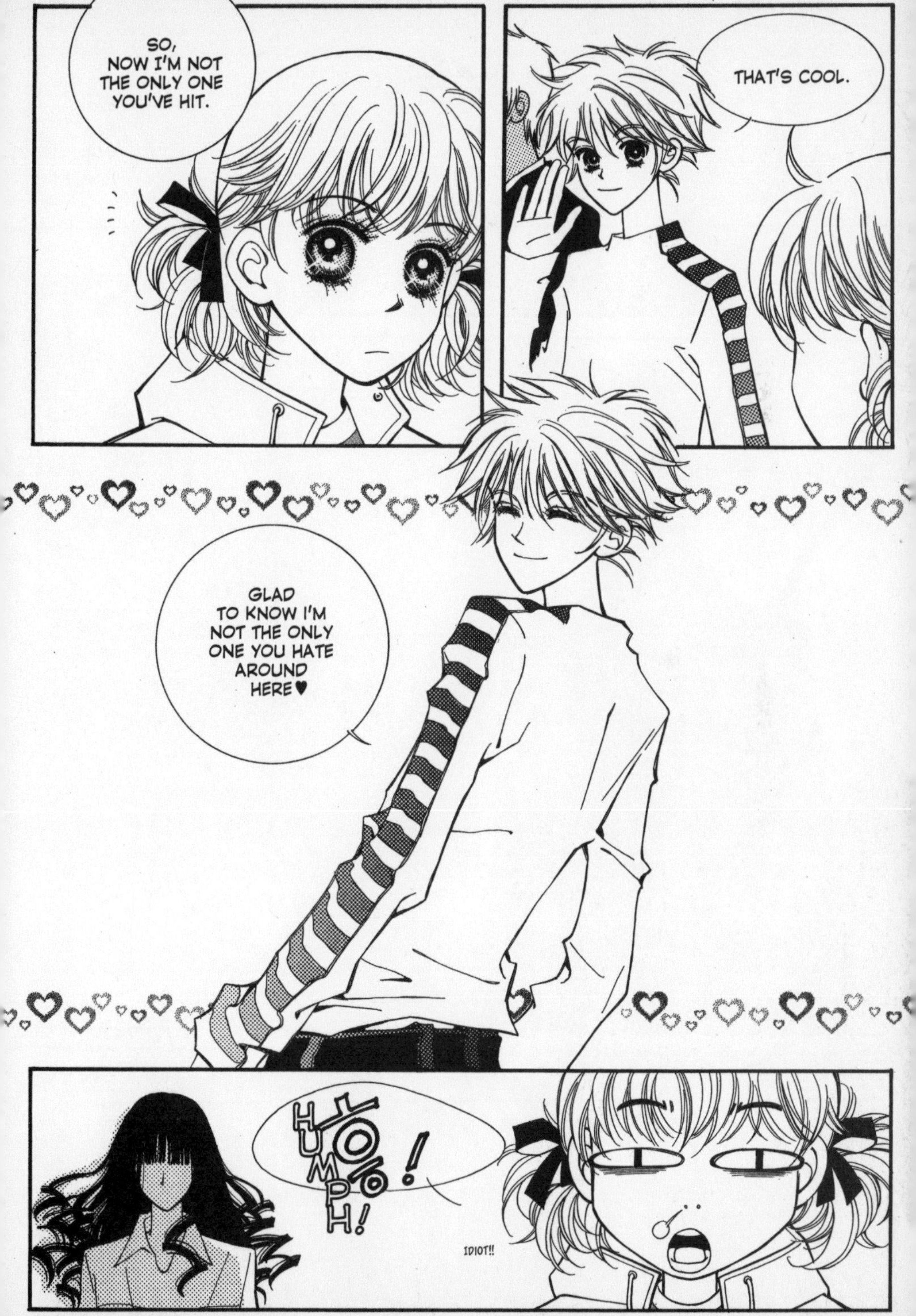
SO, NOW I'M NOT THE ONLY ONE YOU'VE HIT.
THAT'S COOL.
GLAD TO KNOW I'M NOT THE ONLY ONE YOU HATE AROUND HERE♥
HUMPH!
IDIOT!!

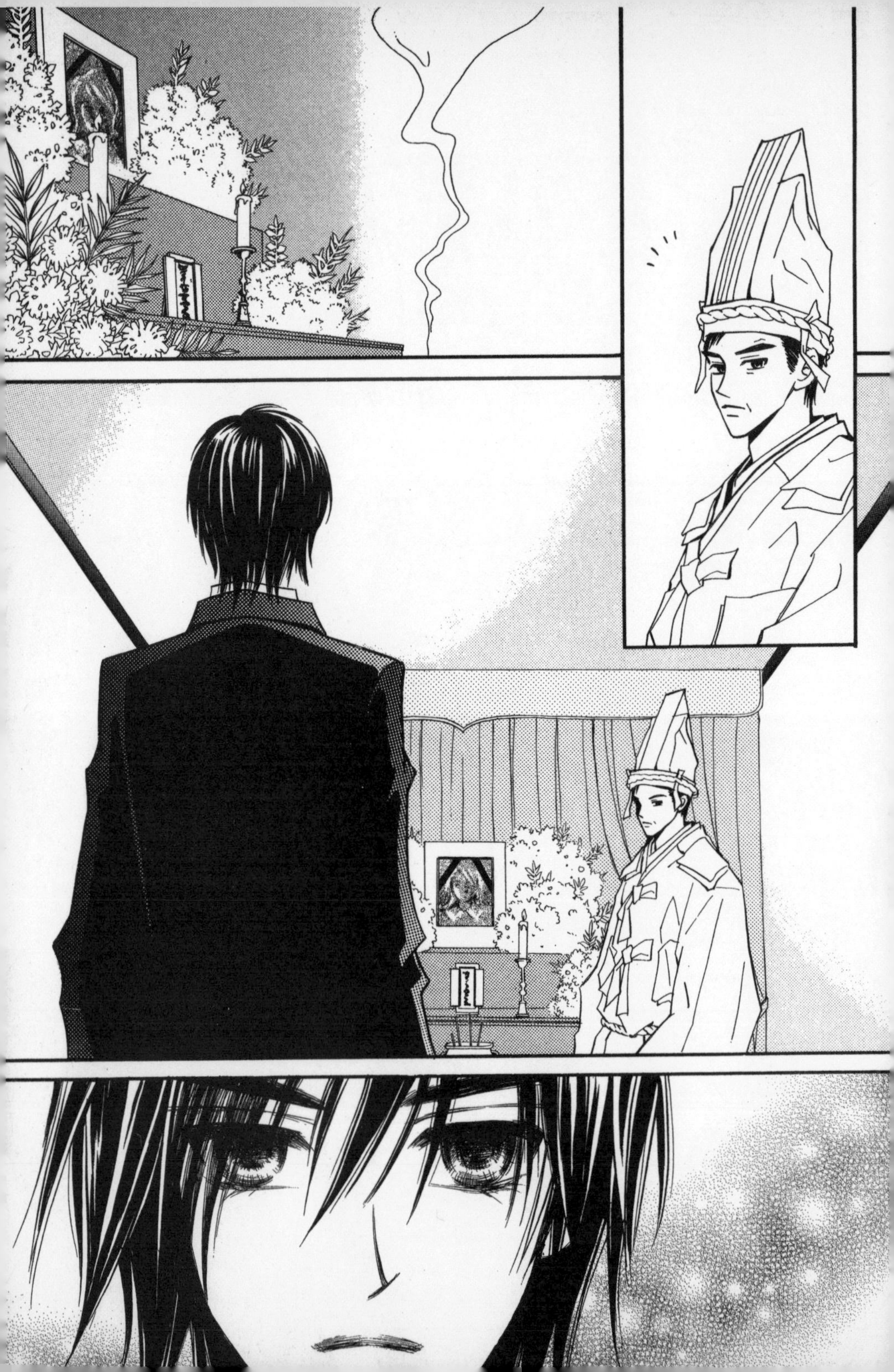

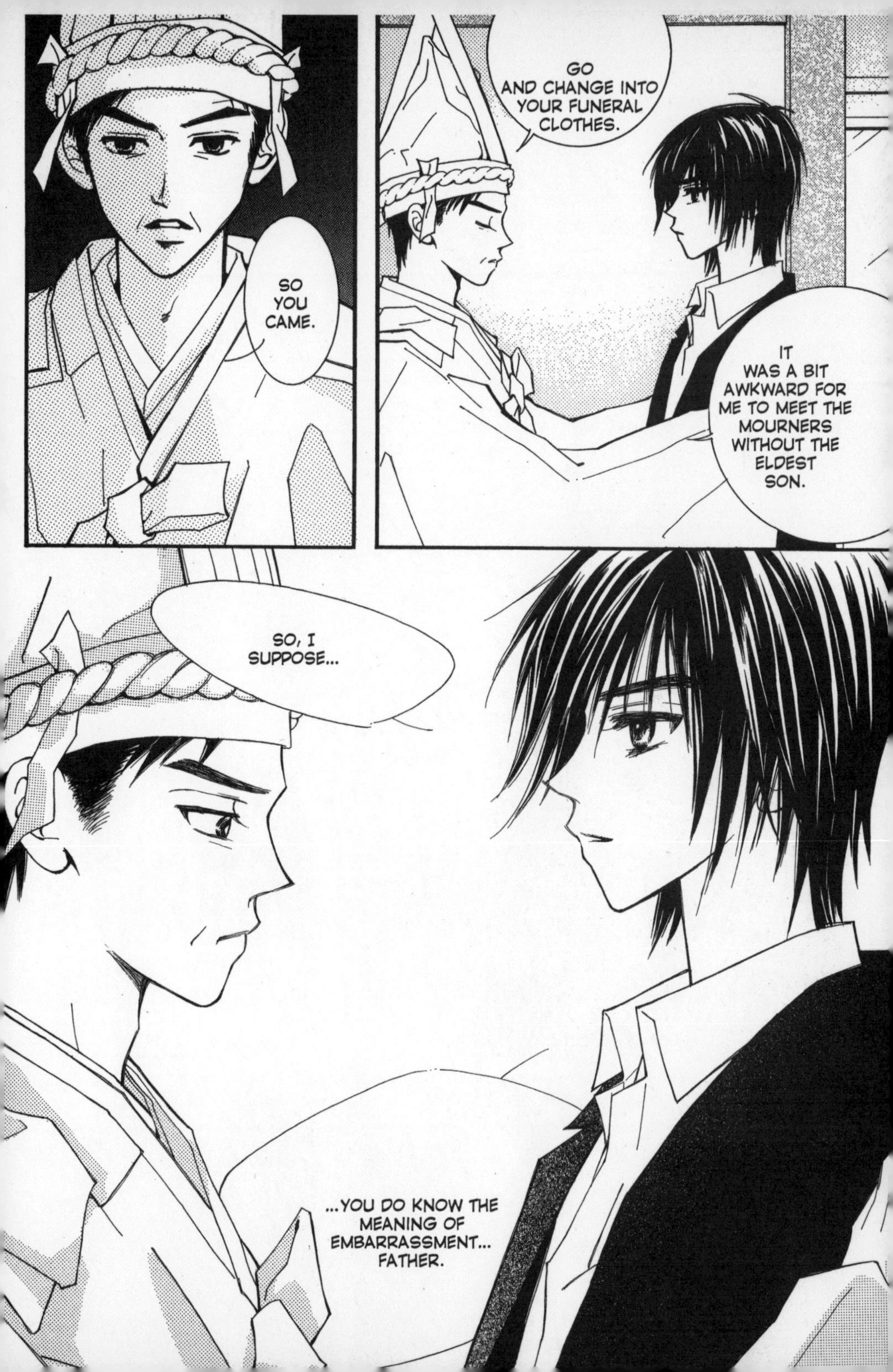
SO YOU CAME.
GO AND CHANGE INTO YOUR FUNERAL CLOTHES.
IT WAS A BIT AWKWARD FOR ME TO MEET THE MOURNERS WITHOUT THE ELDEST SON.
SO, I SUPPOSE...
...YOU DO KNOW THE MEANING OF EMBARRASSMENT... FATHER.

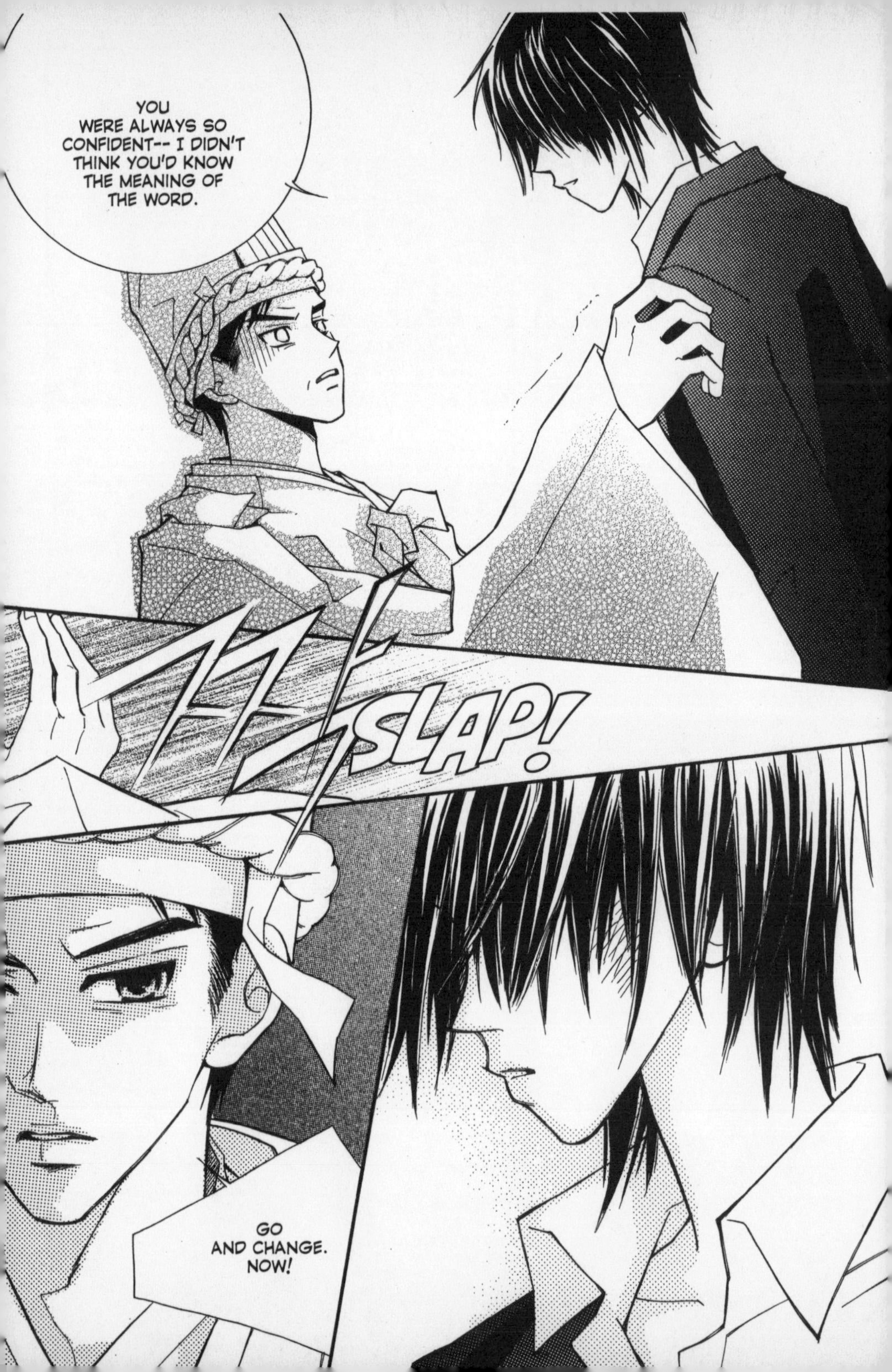
YOU WERE ALWAYS SO CONFIDENT-- I DIDN'T THINK YOU'D KNOW THE MEANING OF THE WORD.
SLAP!
GO AND CHANGE. NOW!

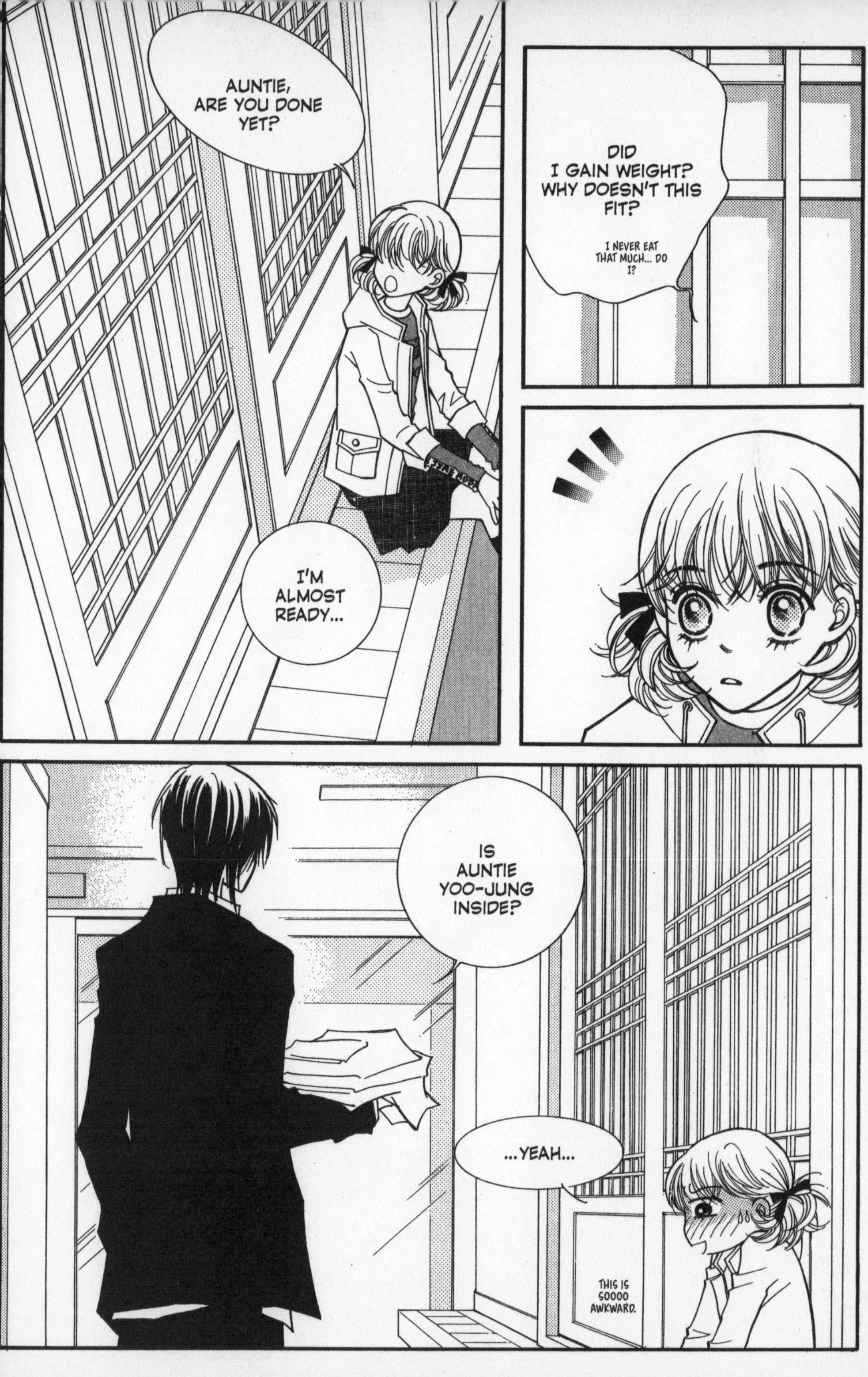
AUNTIE, ARE YOU DONE YET?
I'M ALMOST READY...
DID I GAIN WEIGHT? WHY DOESN'T THIS FIT?
I NEVER EAT THAT MUCH... DO I?
IS AUNTIE YOO-JUNG INSIDE?
...YEAH...
THIS IS SOOOO AWKWARD.

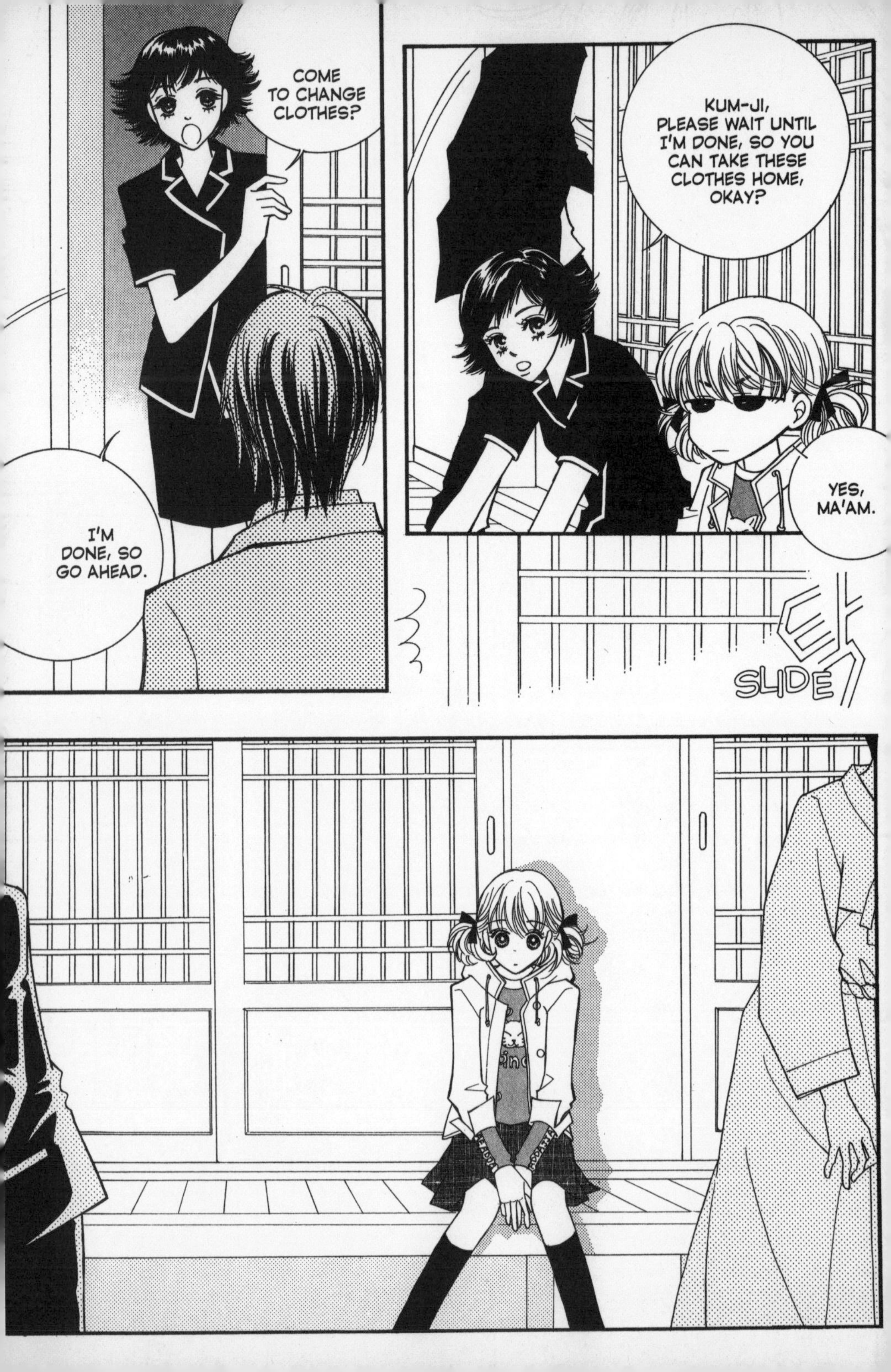
COME TO CHANGE CLOTHES?
I'M DONE, SO GO AHEAD.
KUM-JI, PLEASE WAIT UNTIL I'M DONE, SO YOU CAN TAKE THESE CLOTHES HOME, OKAY?
YES, MA'AM.
SLIDE

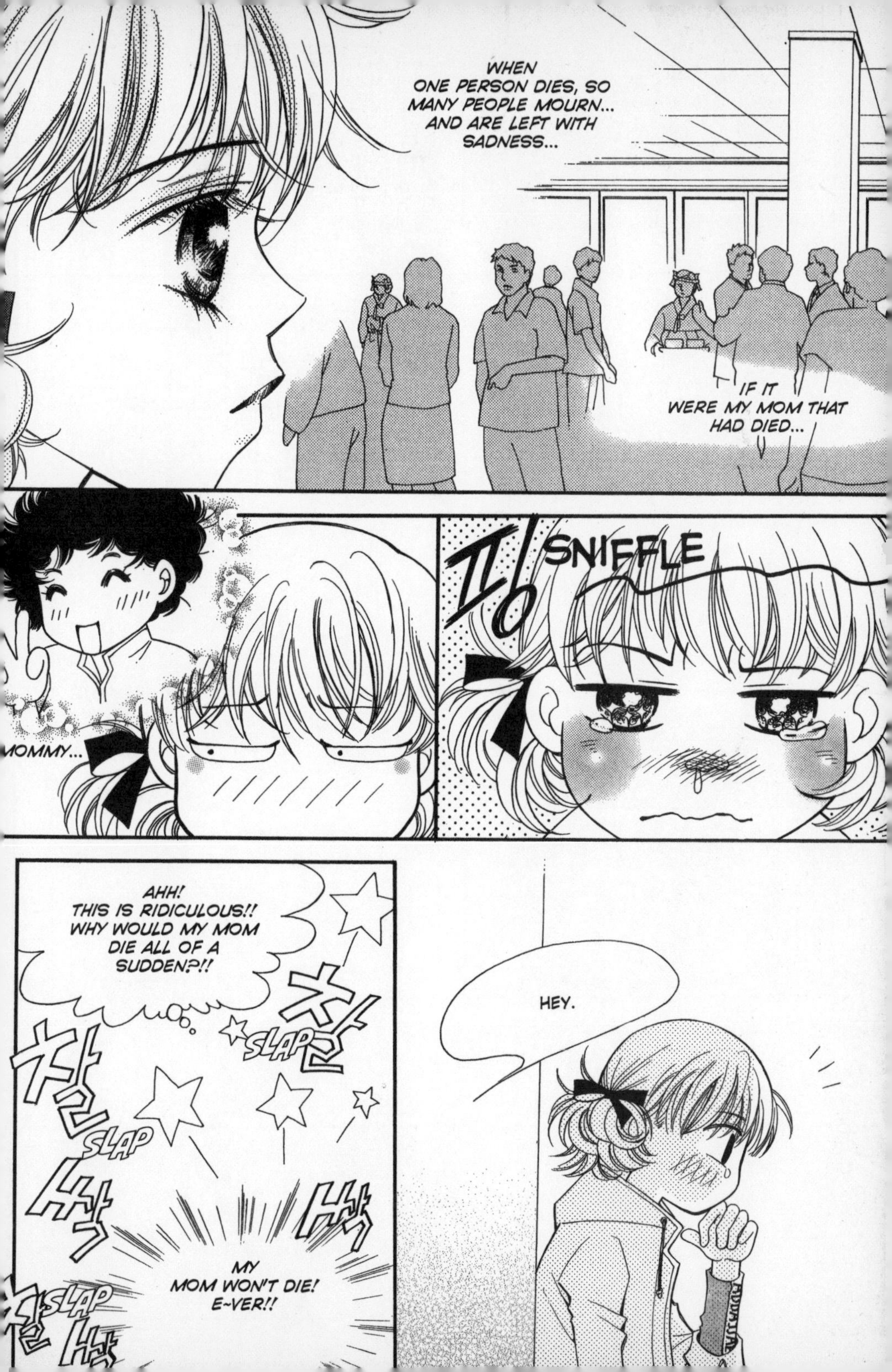
WHEN ONE PERSON DIES, SO MANY PEOPLE MOURN... AND ARE LEFT WITH SADNESS...
IF IT WERE MY MOM THAT HAD DIED...
MOMMY...
SNIFFLE
AHH! THIS IS RIDICULOUS!! WHY WOULD MY MOM DIE ALL OF A SUDDEN?!!
SLAP
SLAP
MY MOM WON'T DIE! E~VER!!
SLAP
HEY.

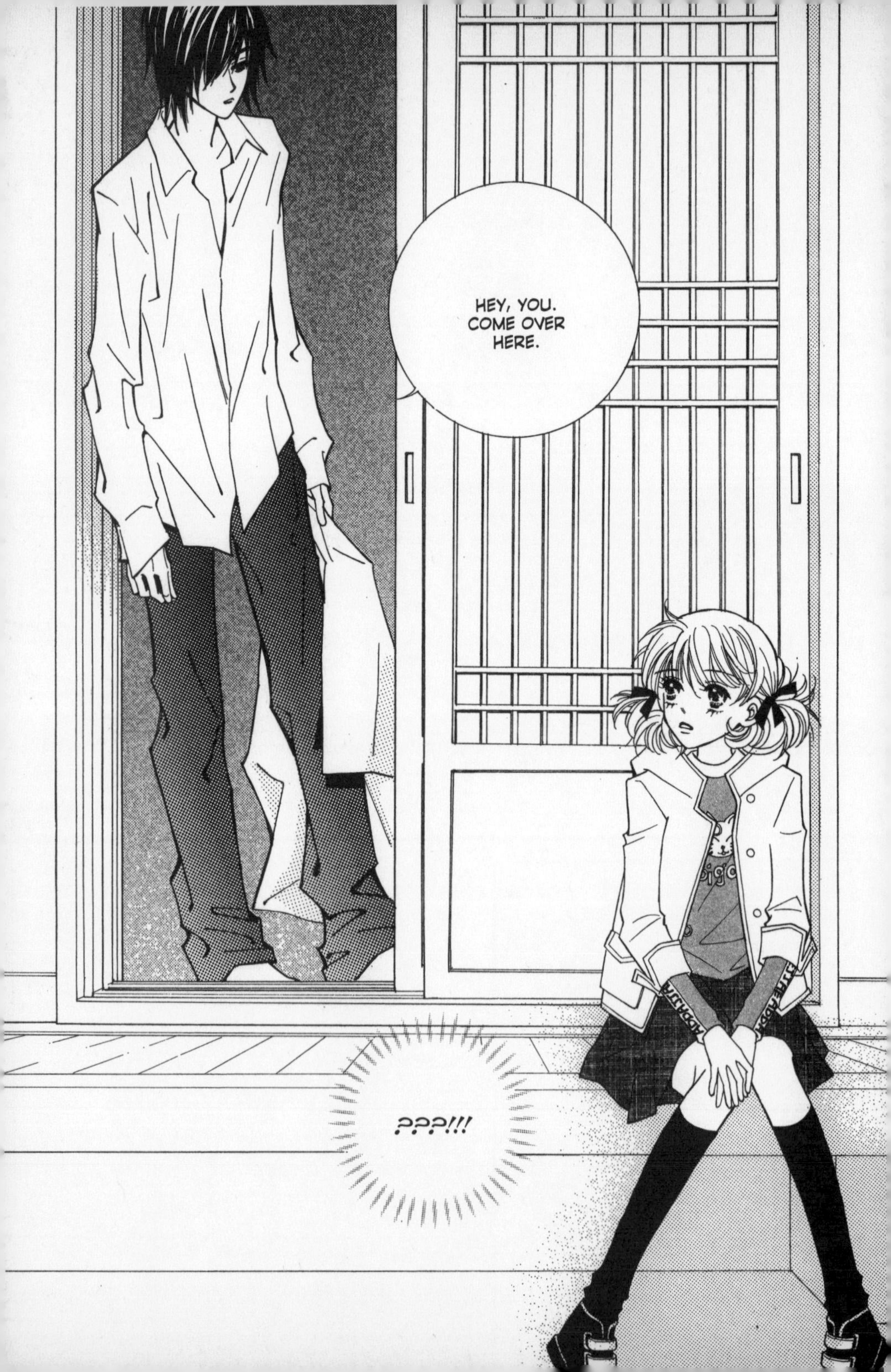
HEY, YOU. COME OVER HERE.
???!!!

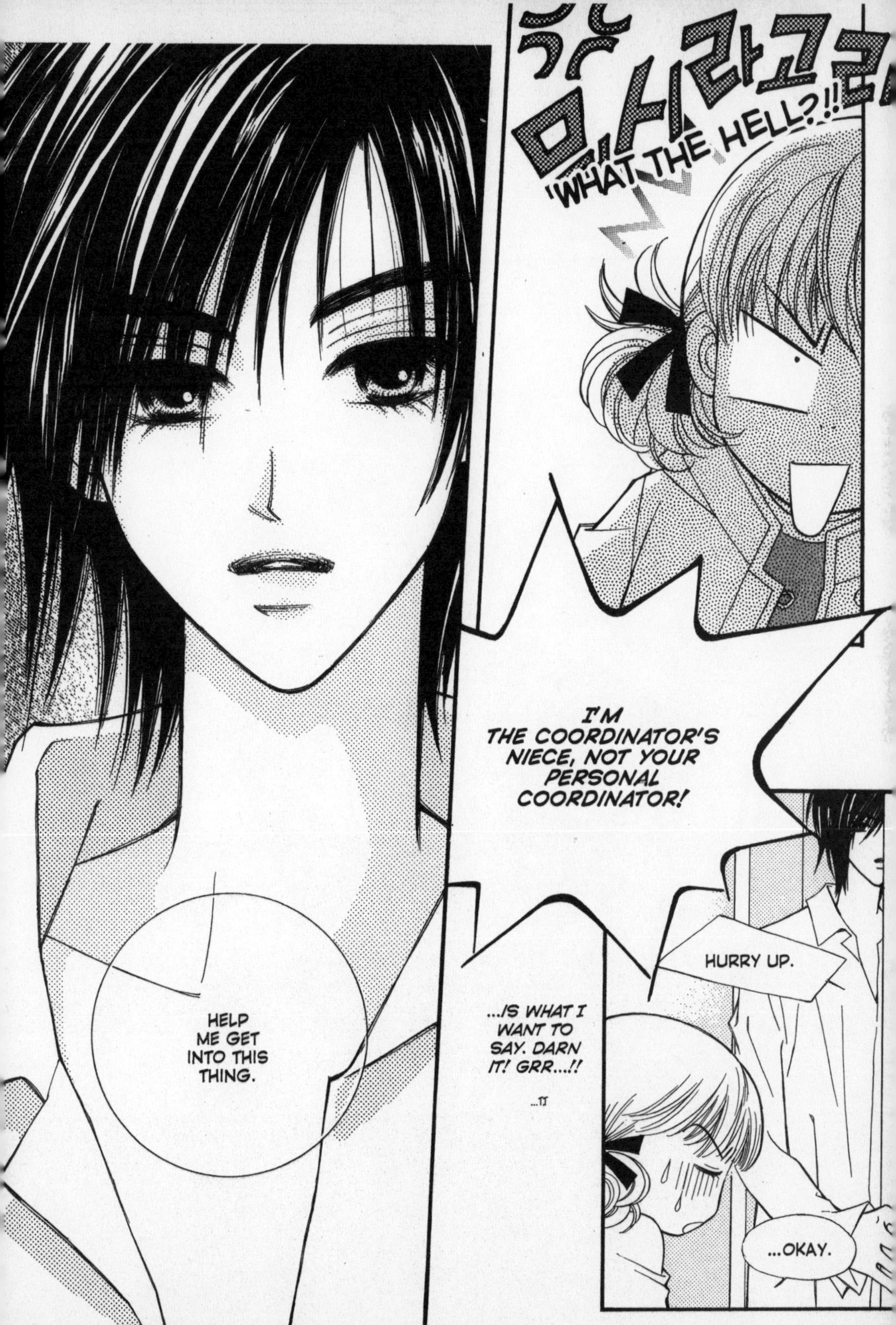
HELP ME GET INTO THIS THING.
WHAT THE HELL?!!
I'M THE COORDINATOR'S NIECE, NOT YOUR PERSONAL COORDINATOR!
...IS WHAT I WANT TO SAY. DARN IT! GRR...!!
HURRY UP.
...OKAY.

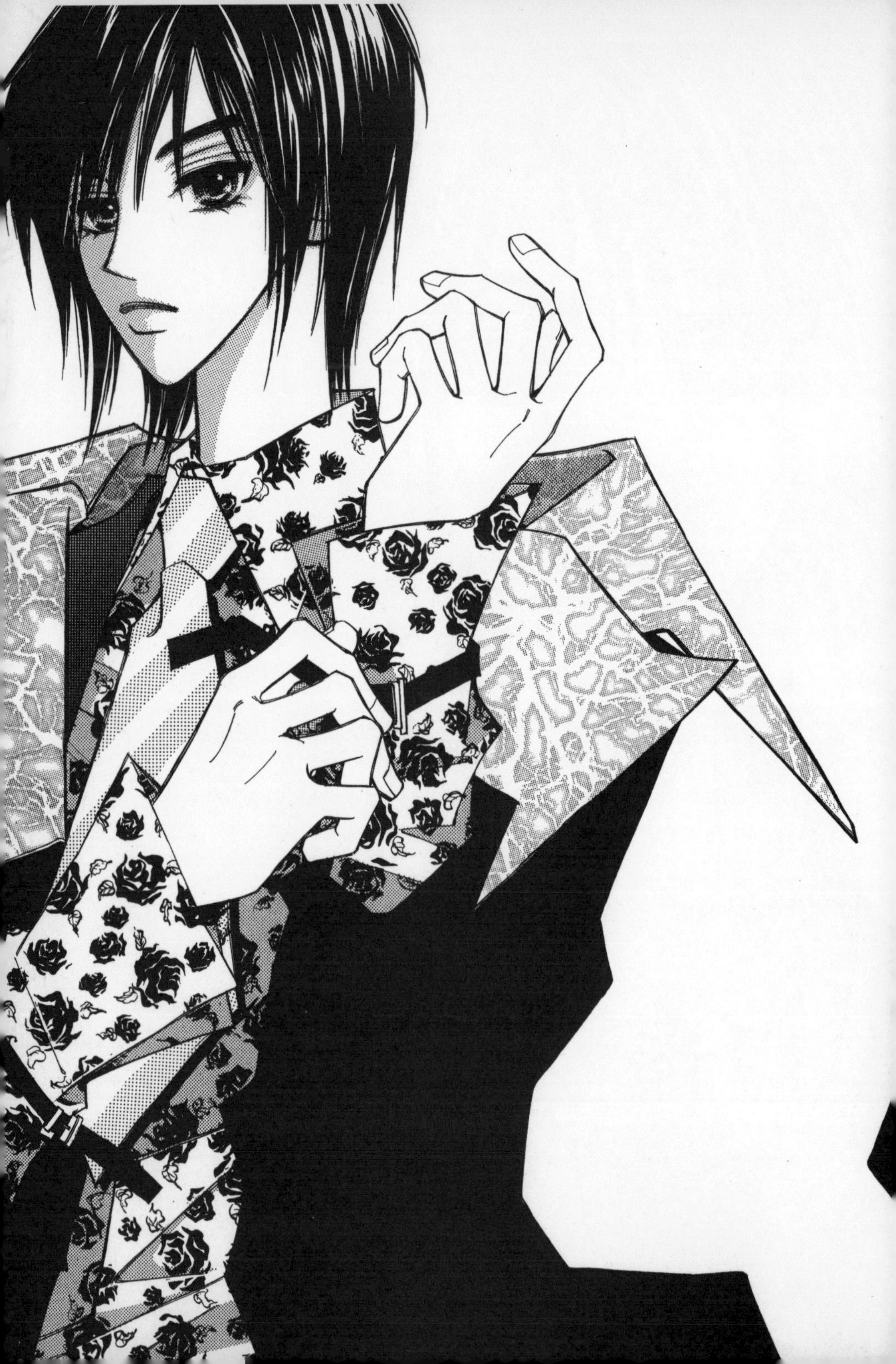

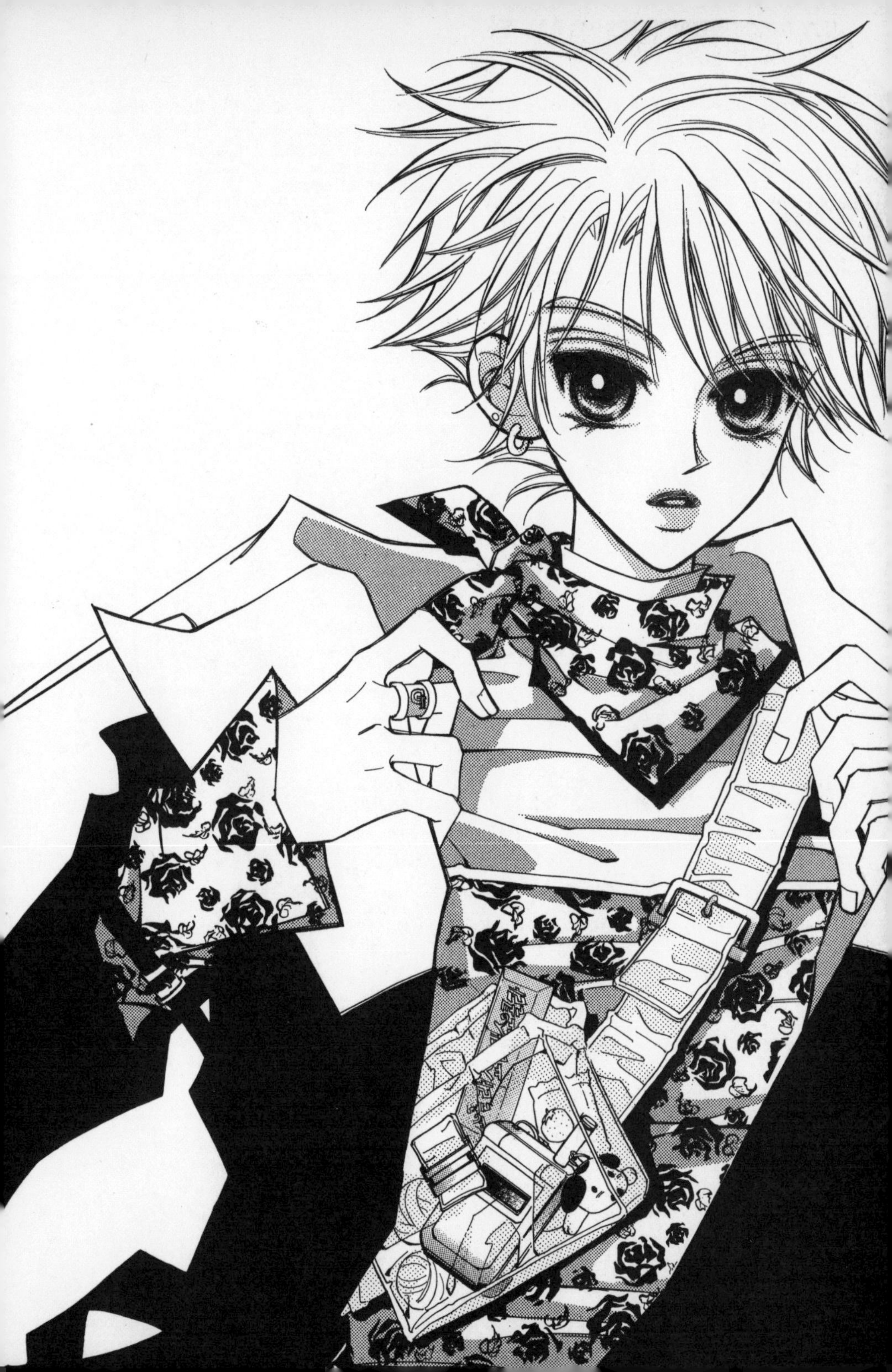

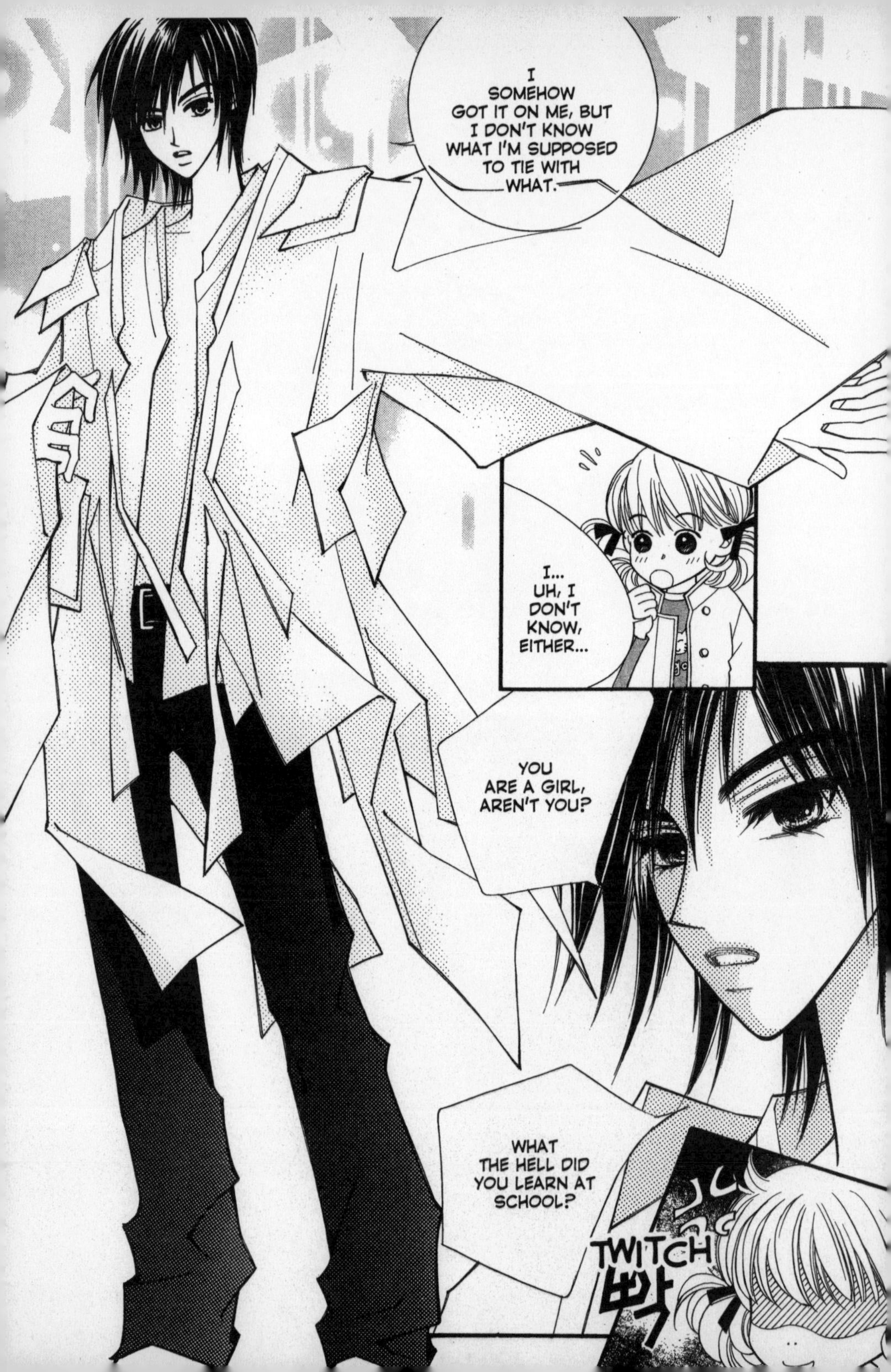
I SOMEHOW GOT IT ON ME, BUT I DON'T KNOW WHAT I'M SUPPOSED TO TIE WITH WHAT.
I... UH, I DON'T KNOW, EITHER...
YOU ARE A GIRL, AREN'T YOU?
WHAT THE HELL DID YOU LEARN AT SCHOOL?
TWITCH

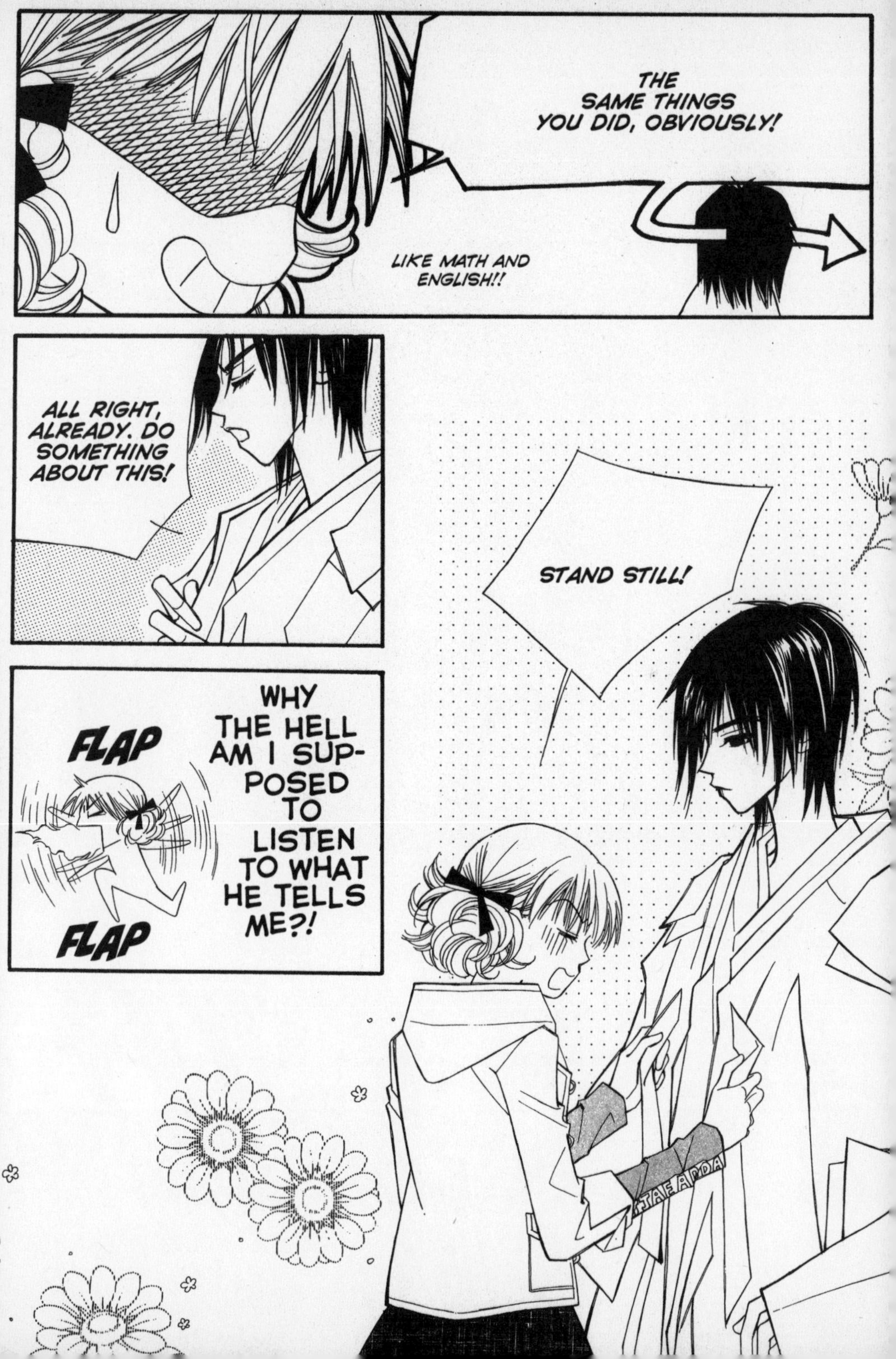
THE SAME THINGS YOU DID, OBVIOUSLY!
LIKE MATH AND ENGLISH!!
ALL RIGHT, ALREADY. DO SOMETHING ABOUT THIS!
STAND STILL!
FLAP
WHY THE HELL AM I SUP-POSED TO LISTEN TO WHAT HE TELLS ME?!
FLAP

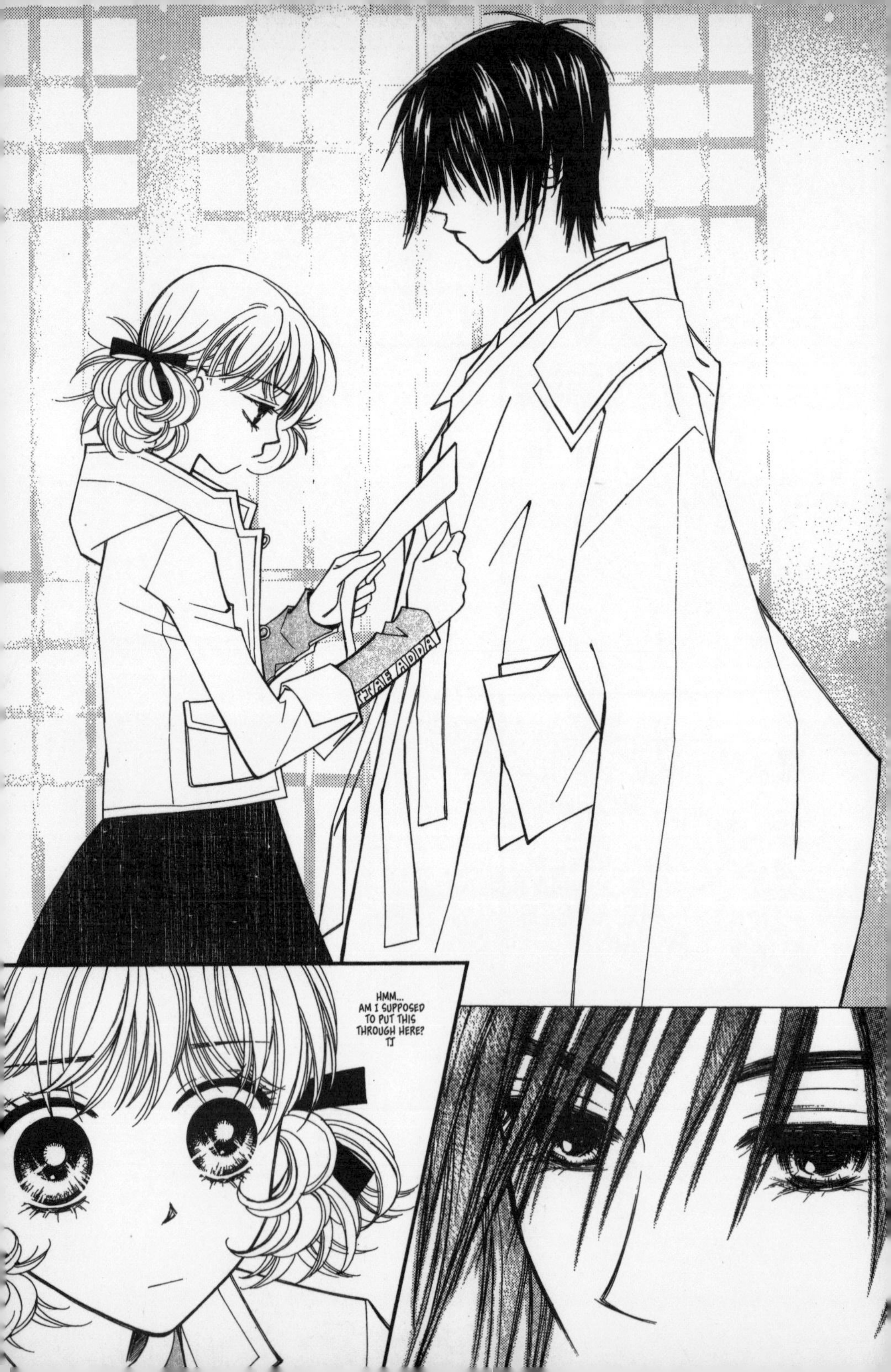
HMM... AM I SUPPOSED TO PUT THIS THROUGH HERE?
TJ

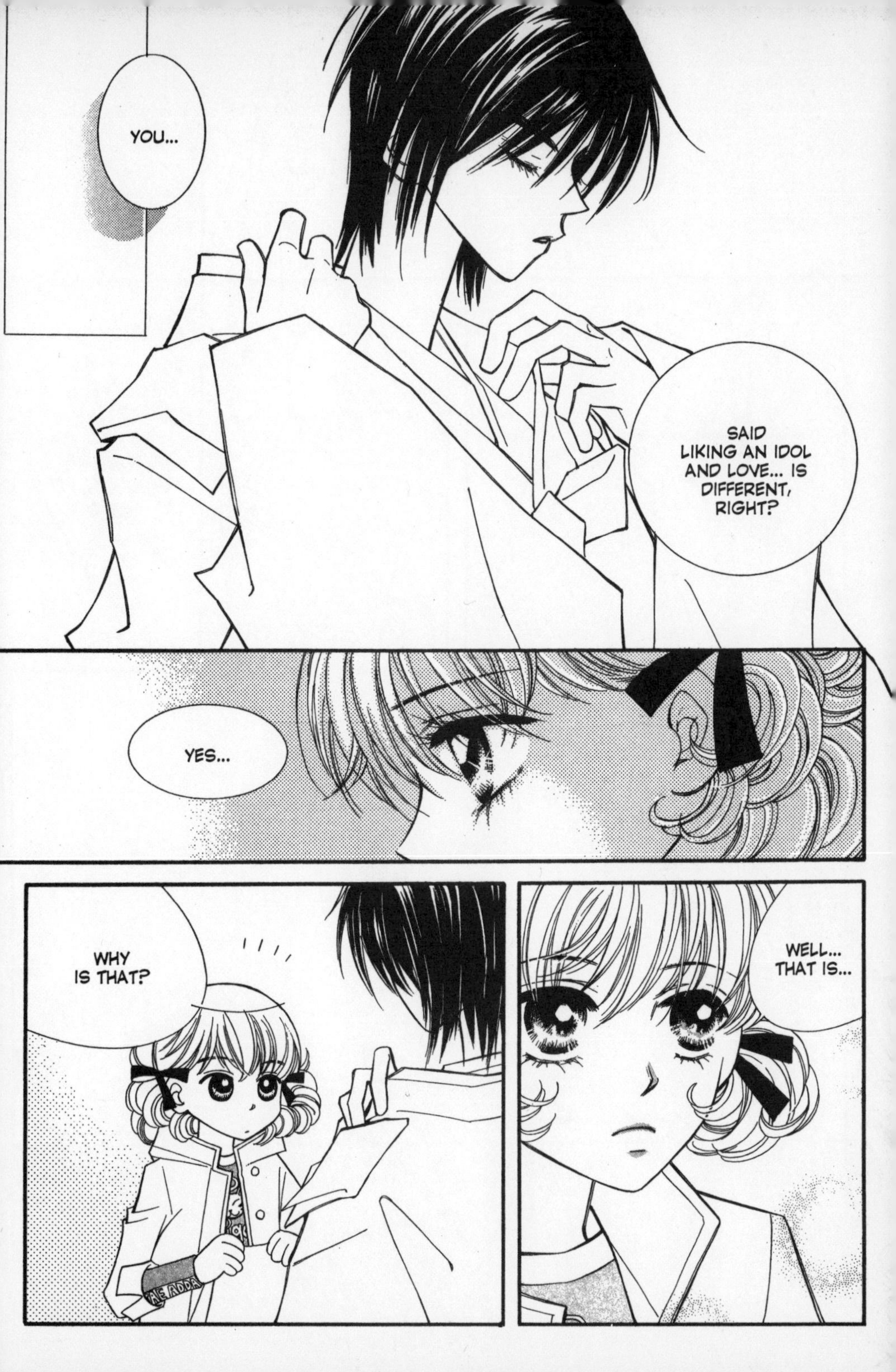
YOU...
SAID LIKING AN IDOL AND LOVE... IS DIFFERENT, RIGHT?
YES...
WHY IS THAT?
WELL... THAT IS...

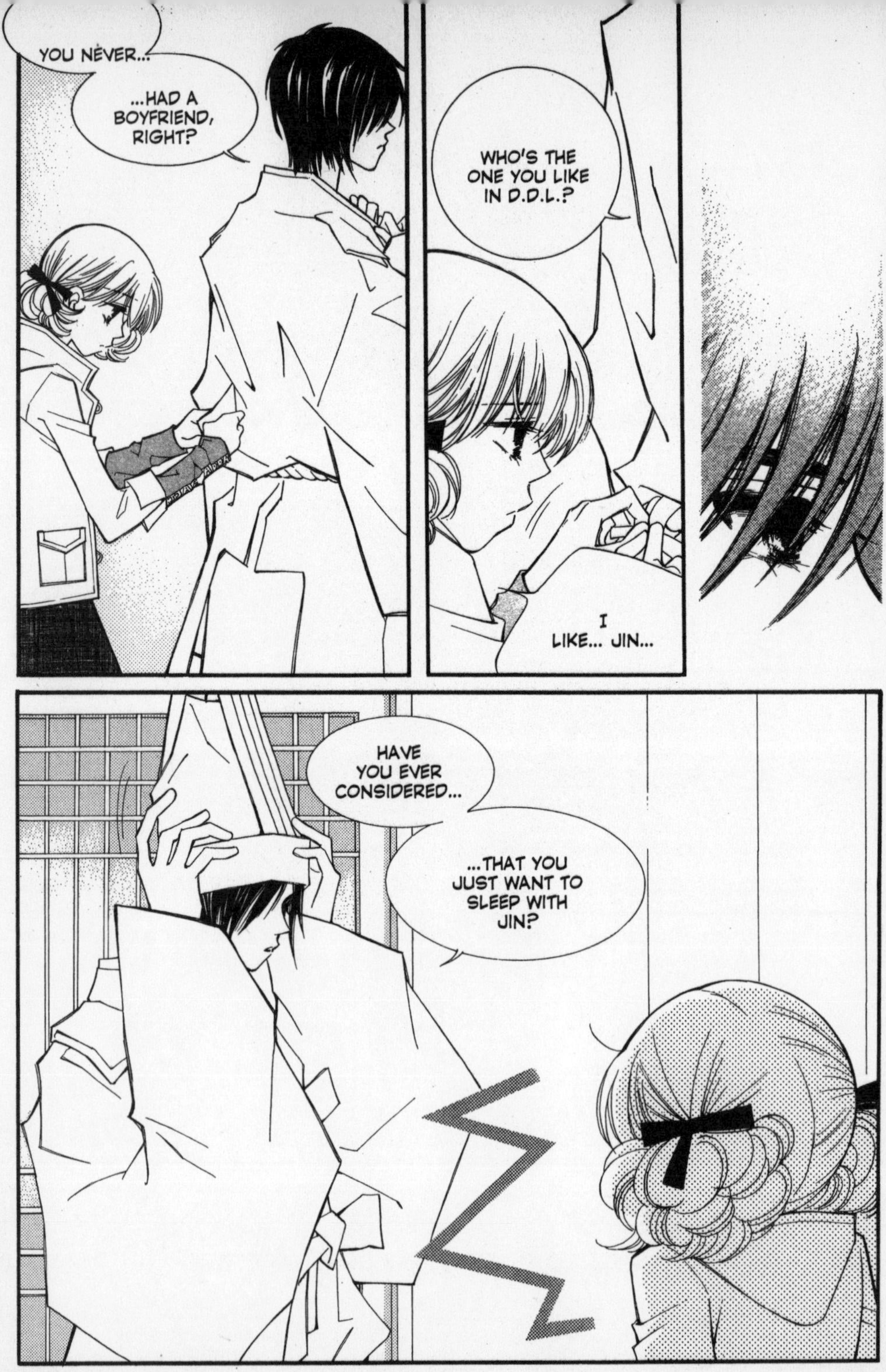
YOU NEVER...
...HAD A BOYFRIEND, RIGHT?
WHO'S THE ONE YOU LIKE IN D.D.L.?
I LIKE... JIN...
HAVE YOU EVER CONSIDERED...
...THAT YOU JUST WANT TO SLEEP WITH JIN?

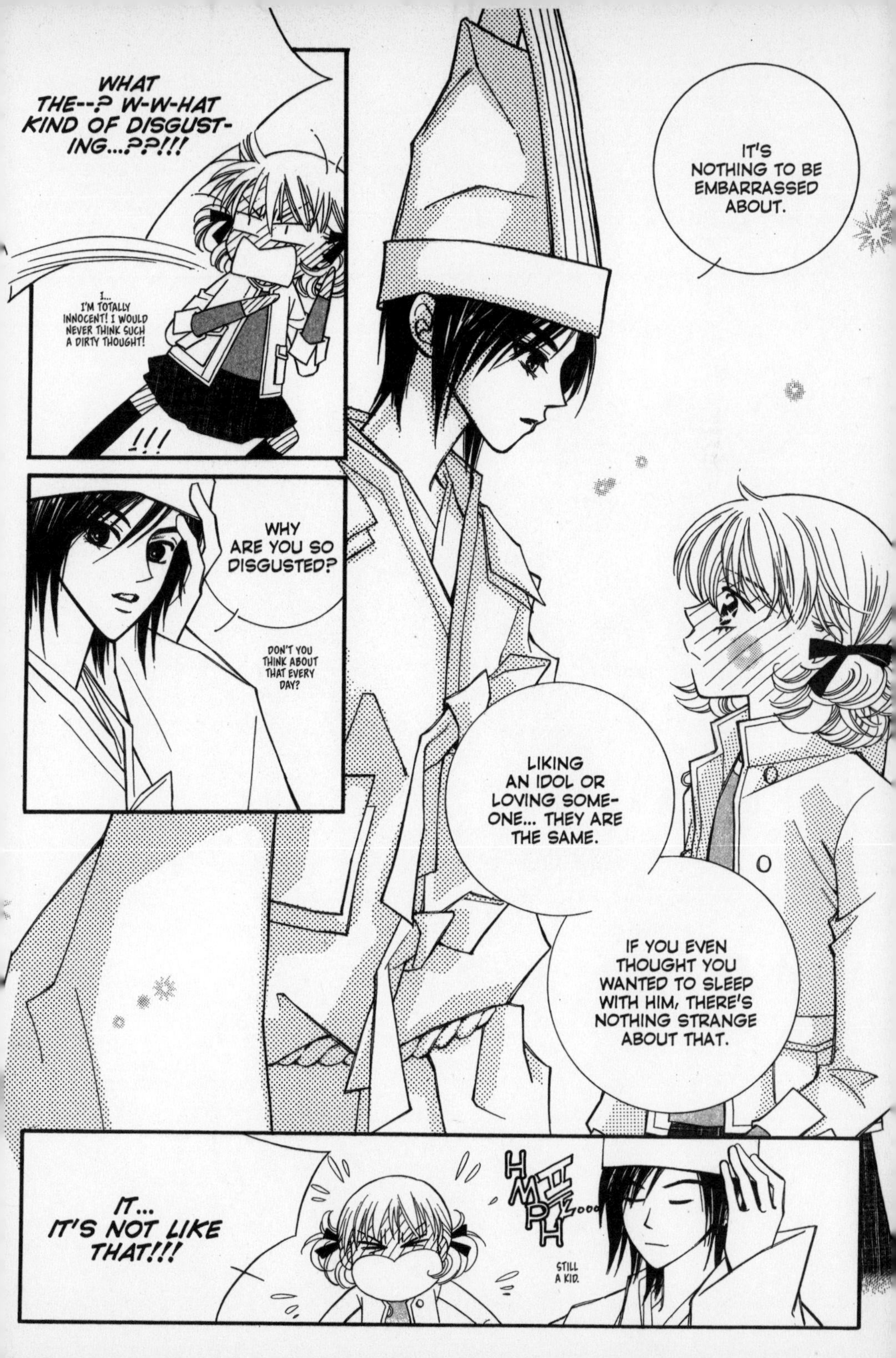
WHAT THE--? W-W-HAT KIND OF DISGUSTING...??!!!
I... I'M TOTALLY INNOCENT! I WOULD NEVER THINK SUCH A DIRTY THOUGHT!
!!!
WHY ARE YOU SO DISGUSTED?
DON'T YOU THINK ABOUT THAT EVERY DAY?
IT'S NOTHING TO BE EMBARRASSED ABOUT.
LIKING AN IDOL OR LOVING SOMEONE... THEY ARE THE SAME.
IF YOU EVEN THOUGHT YOU WANTED TO SLEEP WITH HIM, THERE'S NOTHING STRANGE ABOUT THAT.
IT... IT'S NOT LIKE THAT!!!
HMPH...
STILL A KID.

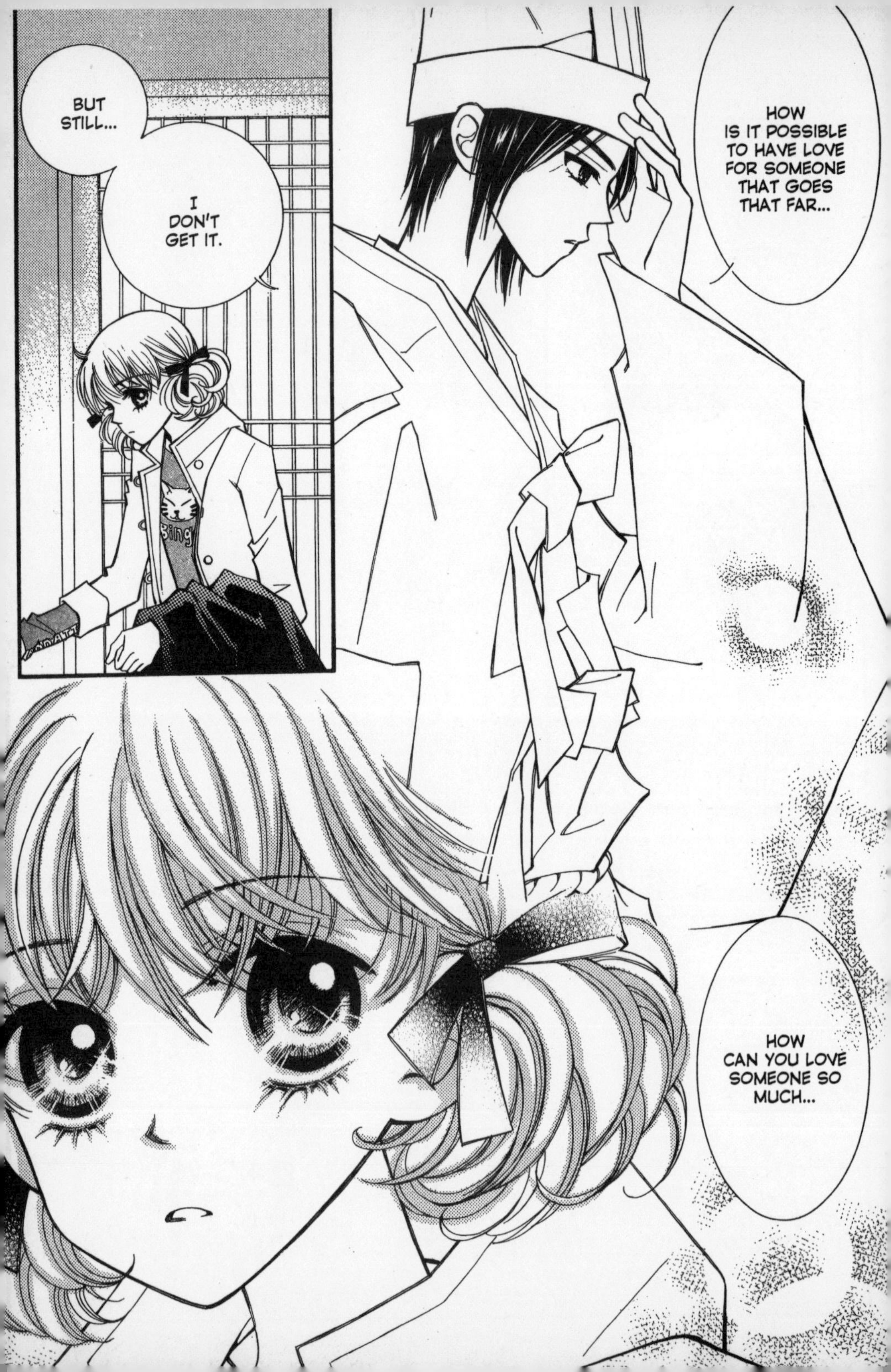
BUT STILL...
I DON'T GET IT.
HOW IS IT POSSIBLE TO HAVE LOVE FOR SOMEONE THAT GOES THAT FAR...
HOW CAN YOU LOVE SOMEONE SO MUCH...

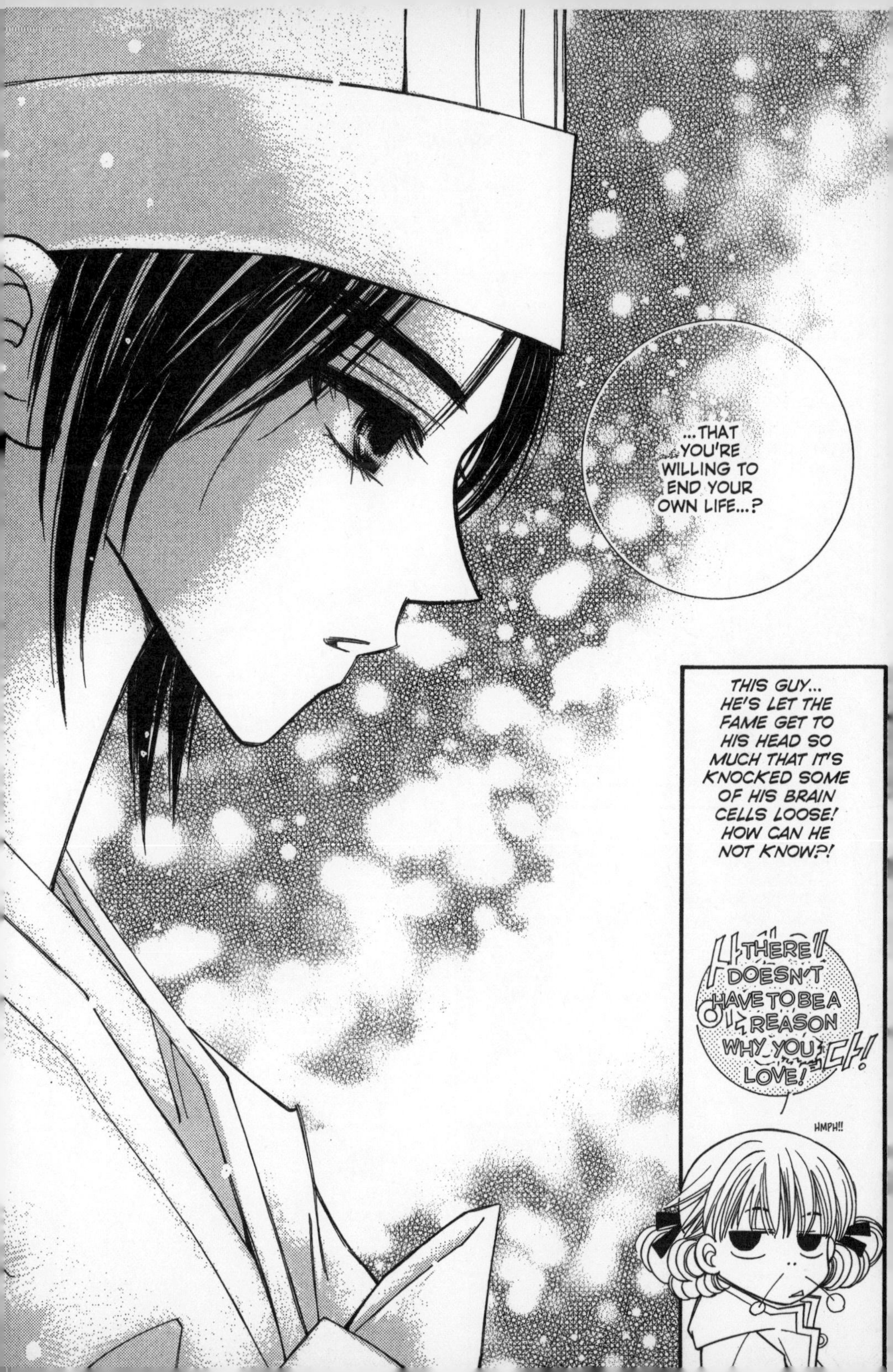
...THAT YOU'RE WILLING TO END YOUR OWN LIFE...?
THIS GUY... HE'S LET THE FAME GET TO HIS HEAD SO MUCH THAT IT'S KNOCKED SOME OF HIS BRAIN CELLS LOOSE! HOW CAN HE NOT KNOW?!
THERE DOESN'T HAVE TO BE A REASON WHY YOU LOVE!
HMPH!!

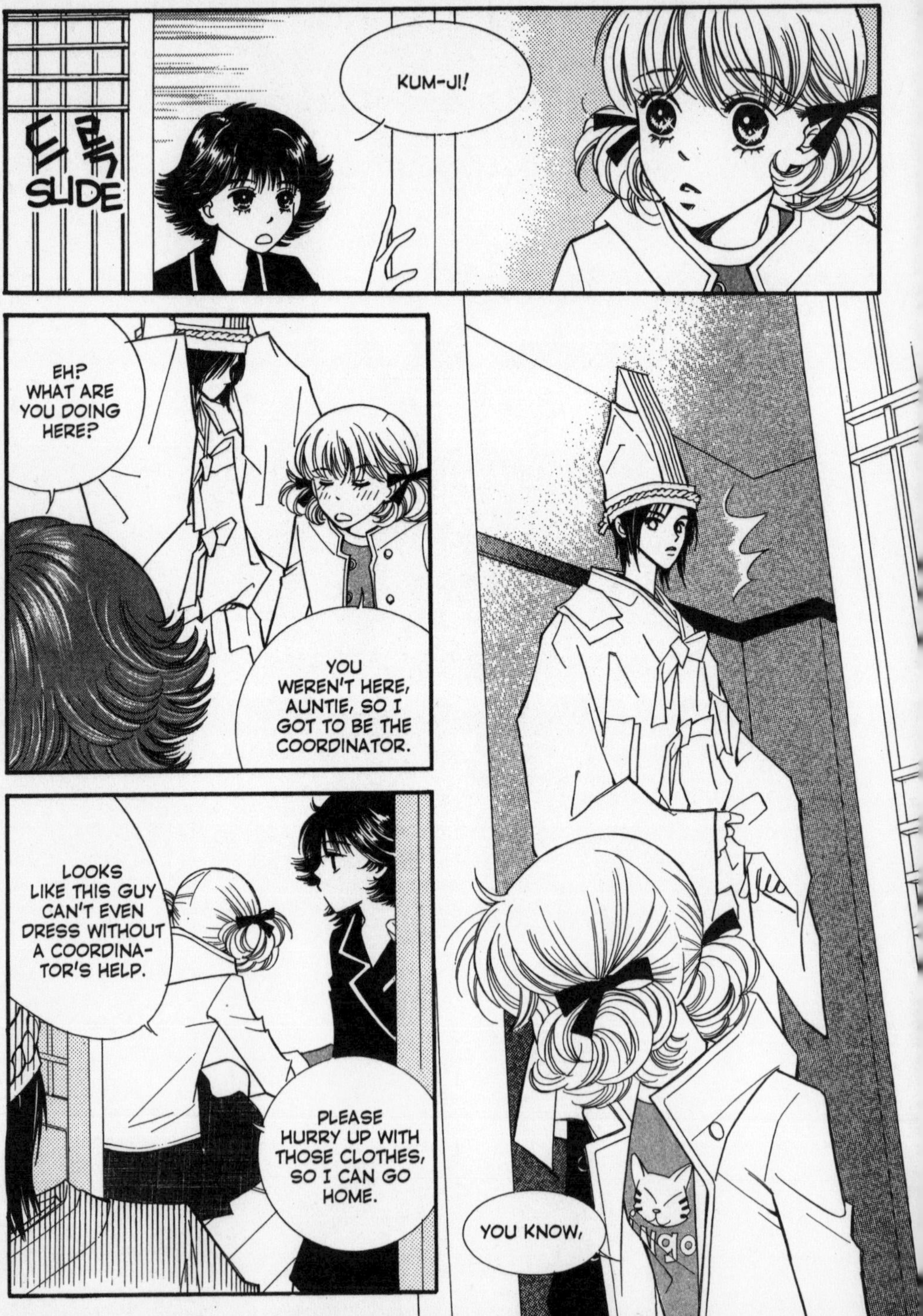
SLIDE
KUM-JI!
EH? WHAT ARE YOU DOING HERE?
YOU WEREN'T HERE, AUNTIE, SO I GOT TO BE THE COORDINATOR.
LOOKS LIKE THIS GUY CAN'T EVEN DRESS WITHOUT A COORDINATOR'S HELP.
PLEASE HURRY UP WITH THOSE CLOTHES, SO I CAN GO HOME.
YOU KNOW,

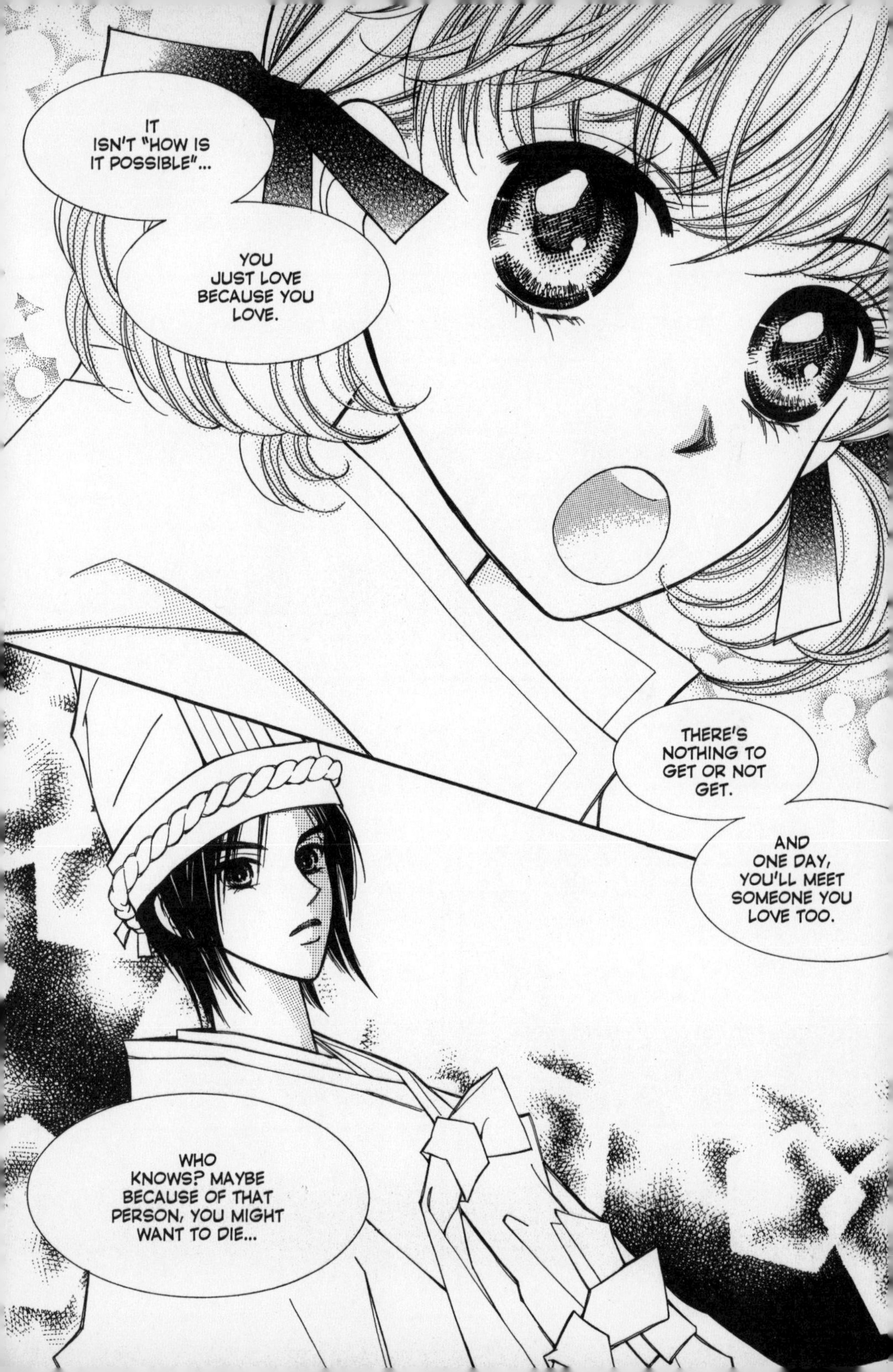
IT ISN'T "HOW IS IT POSSIBLE"...
YOU JUST LOVE BECAUSE YOU LOVE.
THERE'S NOTHING TO GET OR NOT GET.
AND ONE DAY, YOU'LL MEET SOMEONE YOU LOVE TOO.
WHO KNOWS? MAYBE BECAUSE OF THAT PERSON, YOU MIGHT WANT TO DIE...

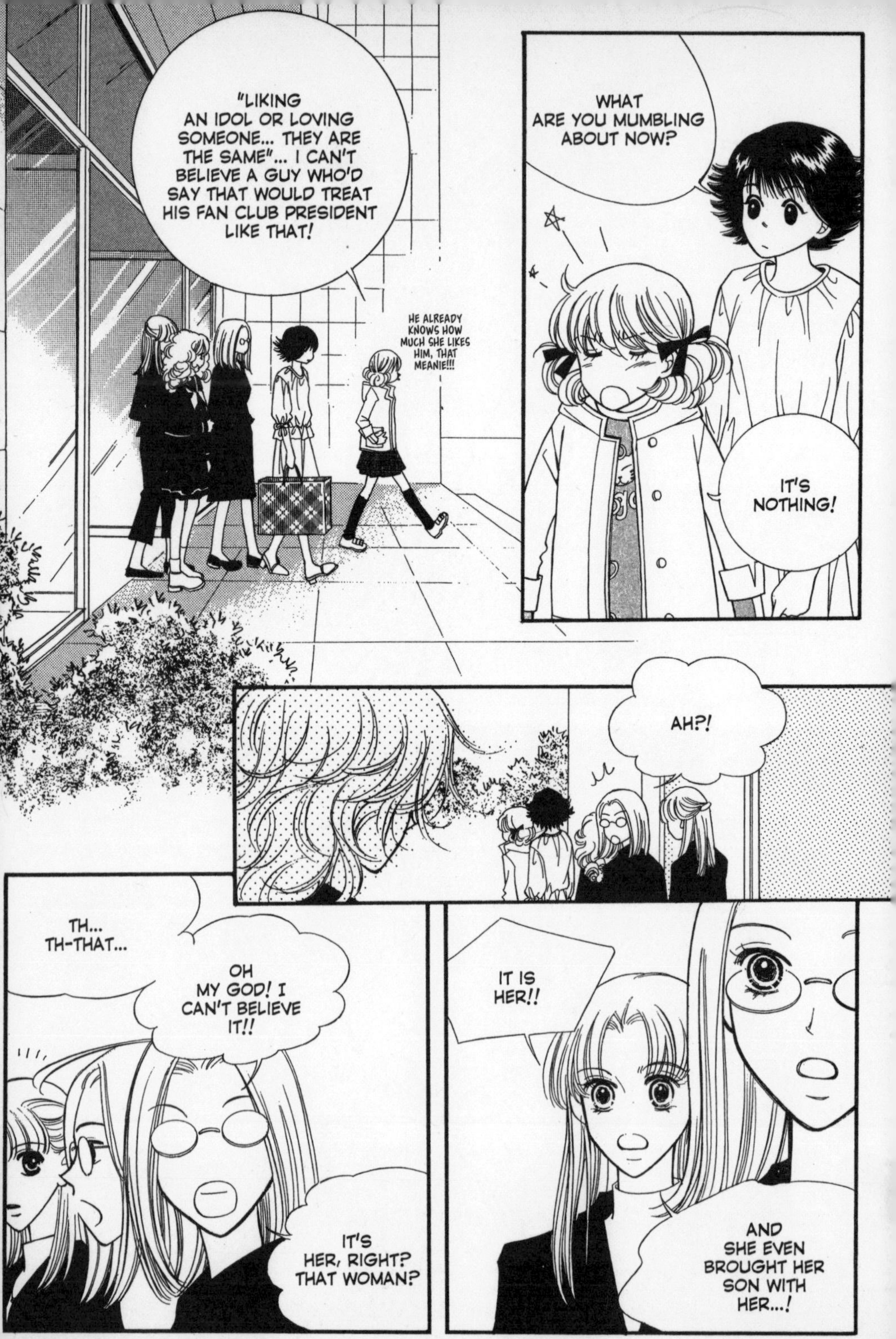
"LIKING AN IDOL OR LOVING SOMEONE... THEY ARE THE SAME"... I CAN'T BELIEVE A GUY WHO'D SAY THAT WOULD TREAT HIS FAN CLUB PRESIDENT LIKE THAT!
HE ALREADY KNOWS HOW MUCH SHE LIKES HIM, THAT MEANIE!!!
WHAT ARE YOU MUMBLING ABOUT NOW?
IT'S NOTHING!
AH?!
TH... TH-THAT...
OH MY GOD! I CAN'T BELIEVE IT!!
IT'S HER, RIGHT? THAT WOMAN?
IT IS HER!!
AND SHE EVEN BROUGHT HER SON WITH HER...!

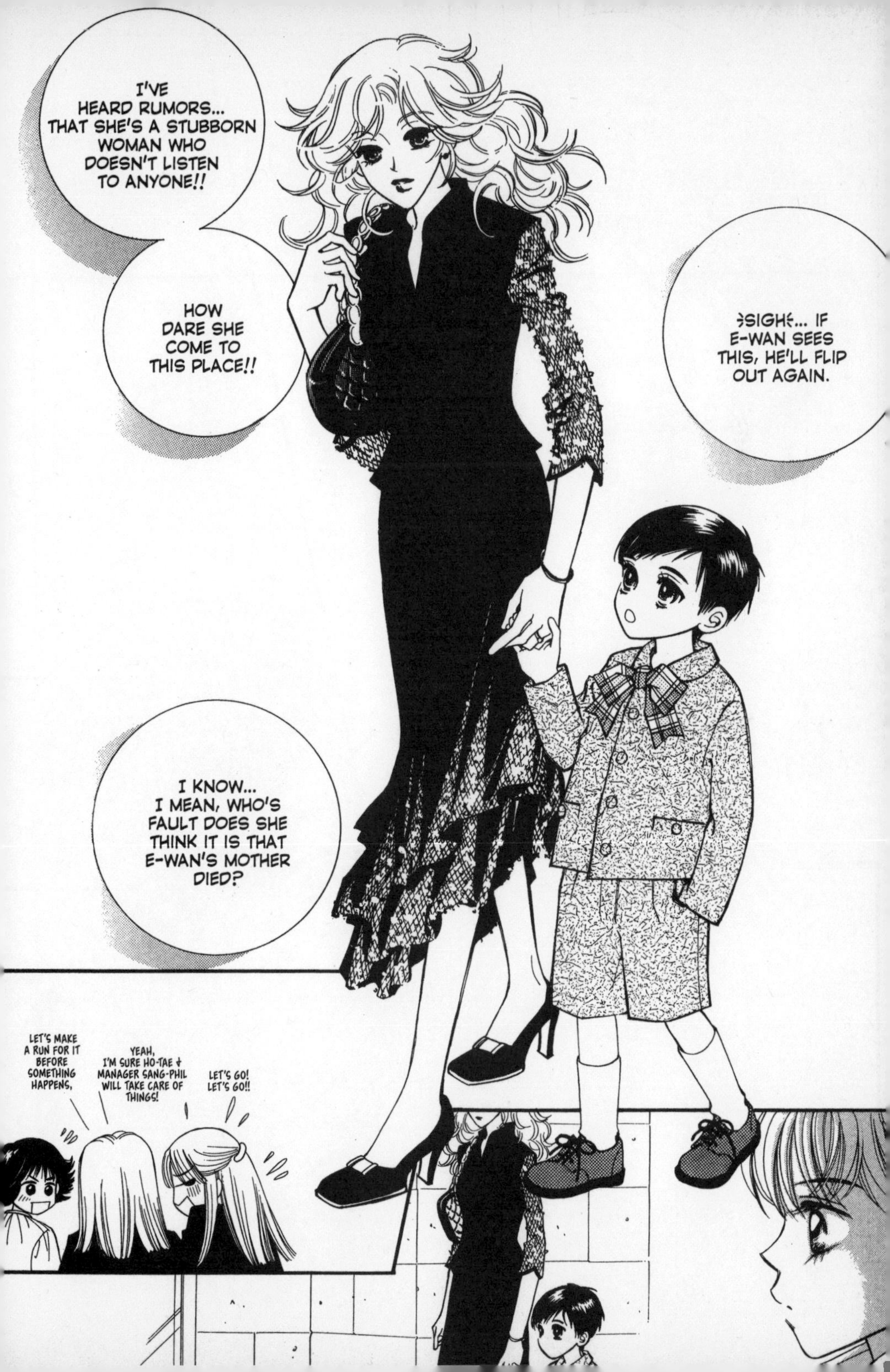
I'VE HEARD RUMORS... THAT SHE'S A STUBBORN WOMAN WHO DOESN'T LISTEN TO ANYONE!!
HOW DARE SHE COME TO THIS PLACE!!
SIGH... IF E-WAN SEES THIS, HE'LL FLIP OUT AGAIN.
I KNOW... I MEAN, WHO'S FAULT DOES SHE THINK IT IS THAT E-WAN'S MOTHER DIED?
LET'S MAKE A RUN FOR IT BEFORE SOMETHING HAPPENS,
YEAH, I'M SURE HO-TAE & MANAGER SANG-PHIL WILL TAKE CARE OF THINGS!
LET'S GO! LET'S GO!!

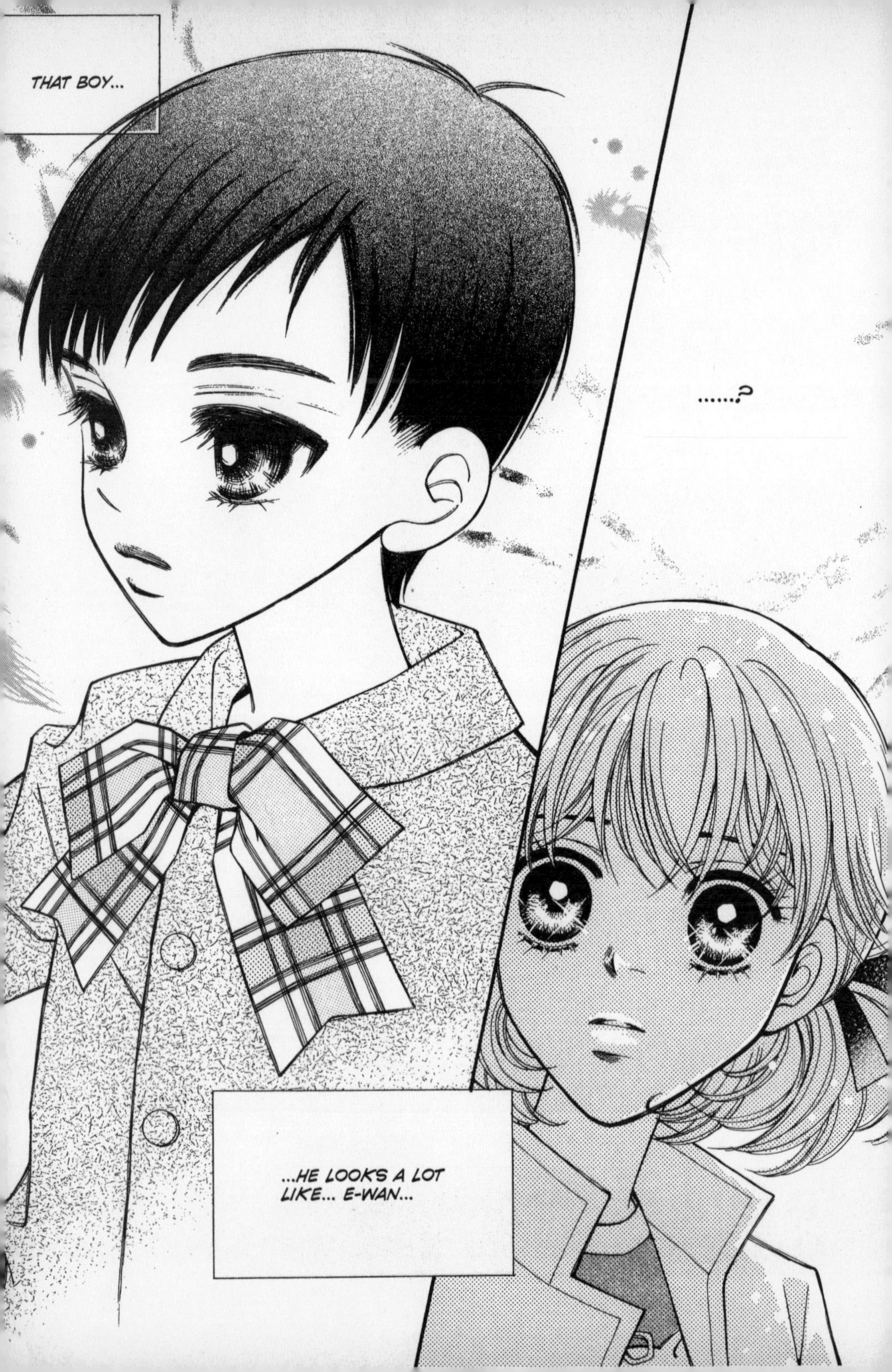
THAT BOY...
......?
...HE LOOKS A LOT LIKE... E-WAN...

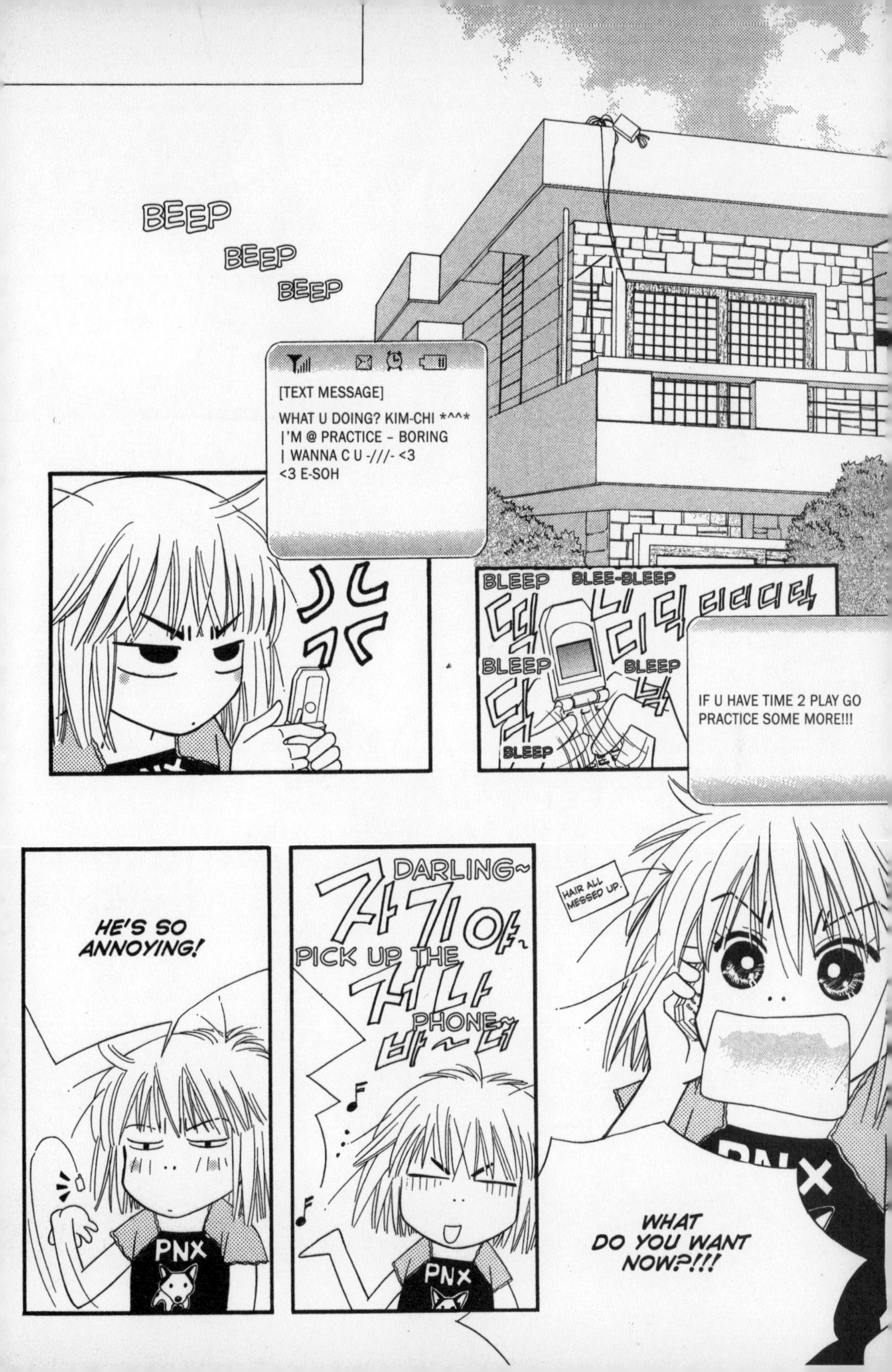
BEEP
BEEP
BEEP
[TEXT MESSAGE]
WHAT U DOING? KIM-CHI *^^*
I'M @ PRACTICE - BORING
I WANNA C U -///- <3
<3 E-SOH
BLEEP
BLEE-BLEEP
BLEEP
BLEEP
BLEEP
IF U HAVE TIME 2 PLAY GO PRACTICE SOME MORE!!!
HE'S SO ANNOYING!
DARLING~
PICK UP THE
PHONE~
HAIR ALL MESSED UP.
WHAT DO YOU WANT NOW?!!!

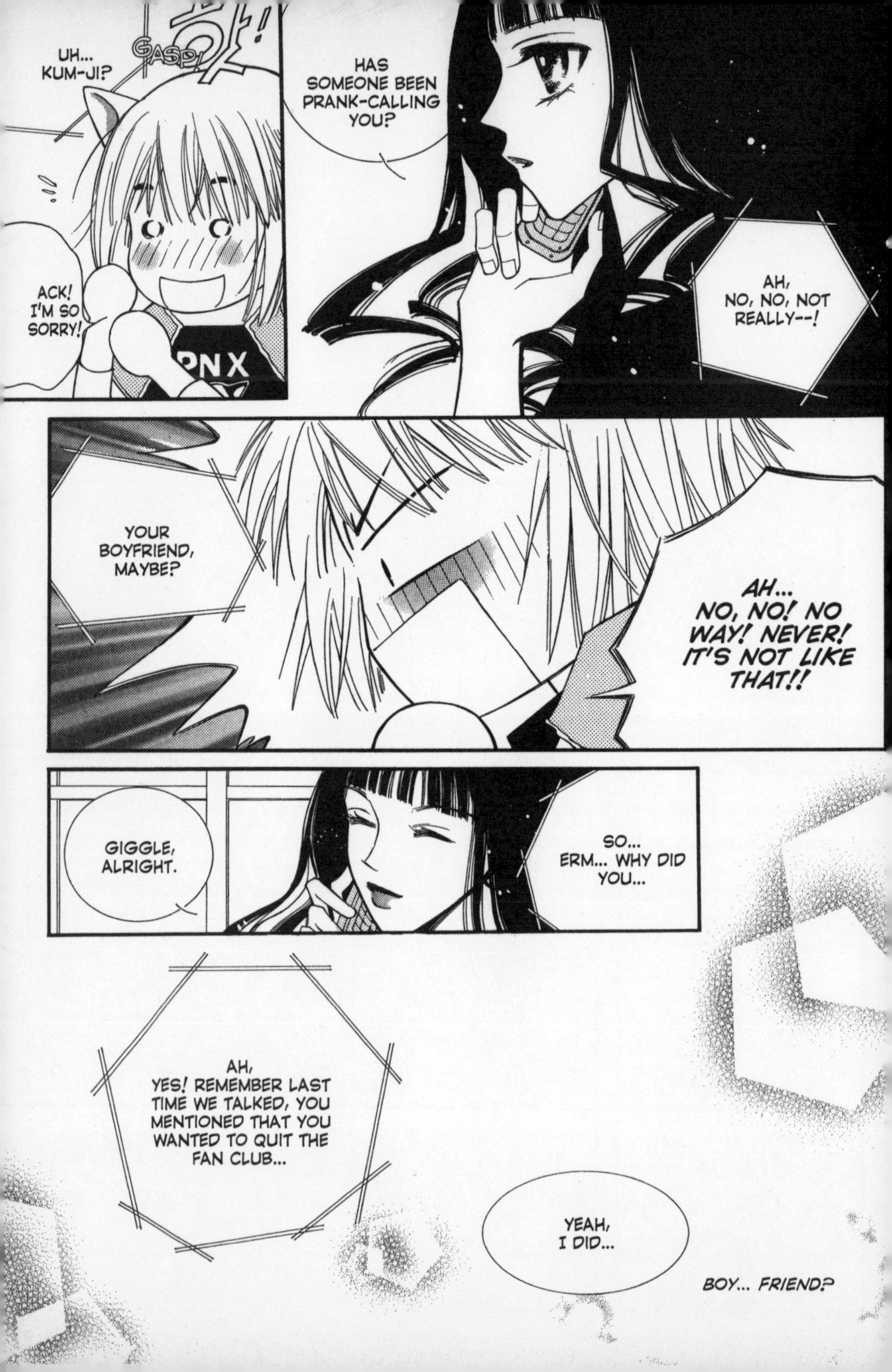
UH... KUM-JI?
GASP!
ACK! I'M SO SORRY!
HAS SOMEONE BEEN PRANK-CALLING YOU?
AH, NO, NO, NOT REALLY--!
YOUR BOYFRIEND, MAYBE?
AH... NO, NO! NO WAY! NEVER! IT'S NOT LIKE THAT!!
GIGGLE, ALRIGHT.
SO... ERM... WHY DID YOU...
AH, YES! REMEMBER LAST TIME WE TALKED, YOU MENTIONED THAT YOU WANTED TO QUIT THE FAN CLUB...
YEAH, I DID...
BOY... FRIEND?

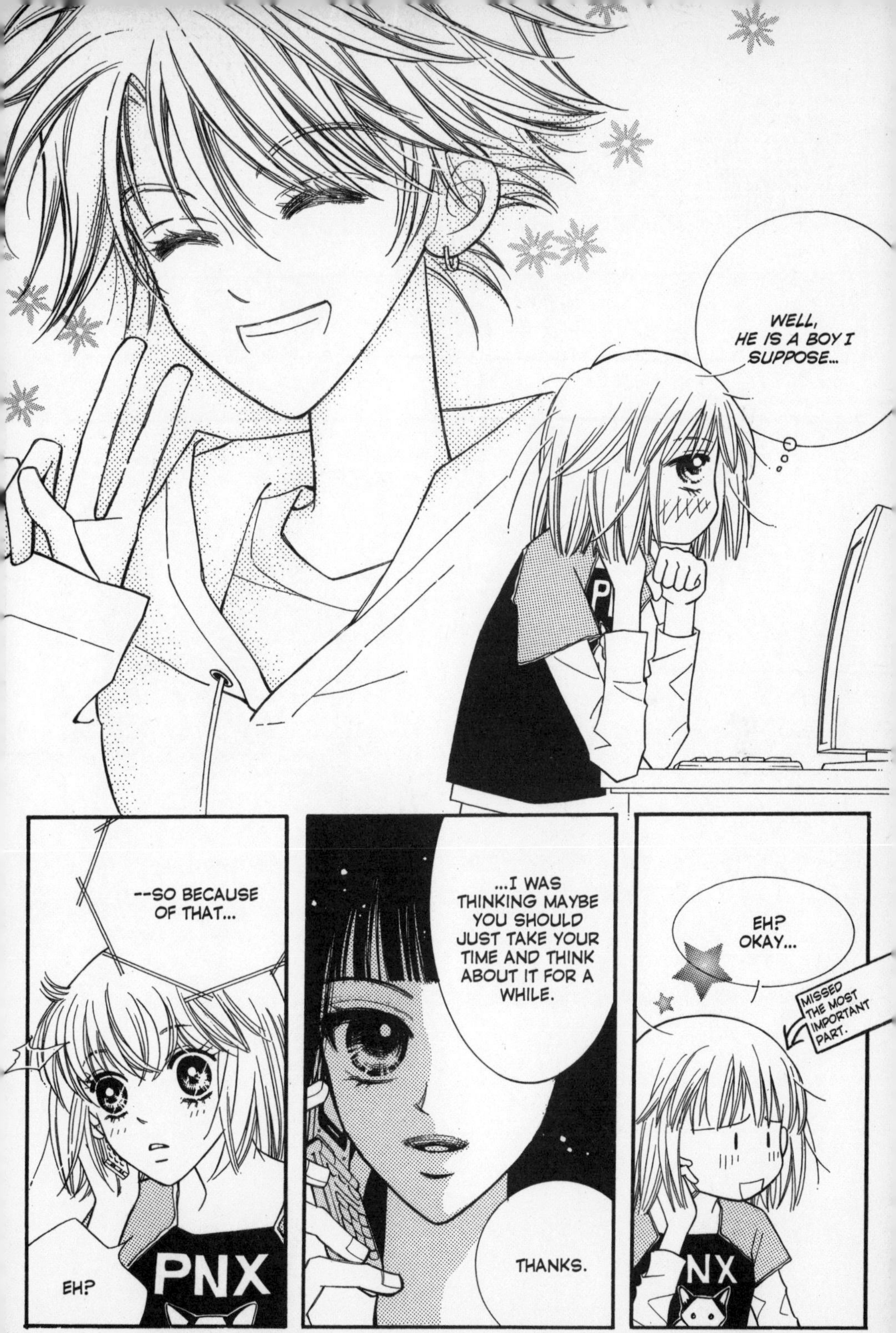
WELL, HE IS A BOY I SUPPOSE...
--SO BECAUSE OF THAT...
EH?
...I WAS THINKING MAYBE YOU SHOULD JUST TAKE YOUR TIME AND THINK ABOUT IT FOR A WHILE.
THANKS.
EH? OKAY...
MISSED THE MOST IMPORTANT PART.

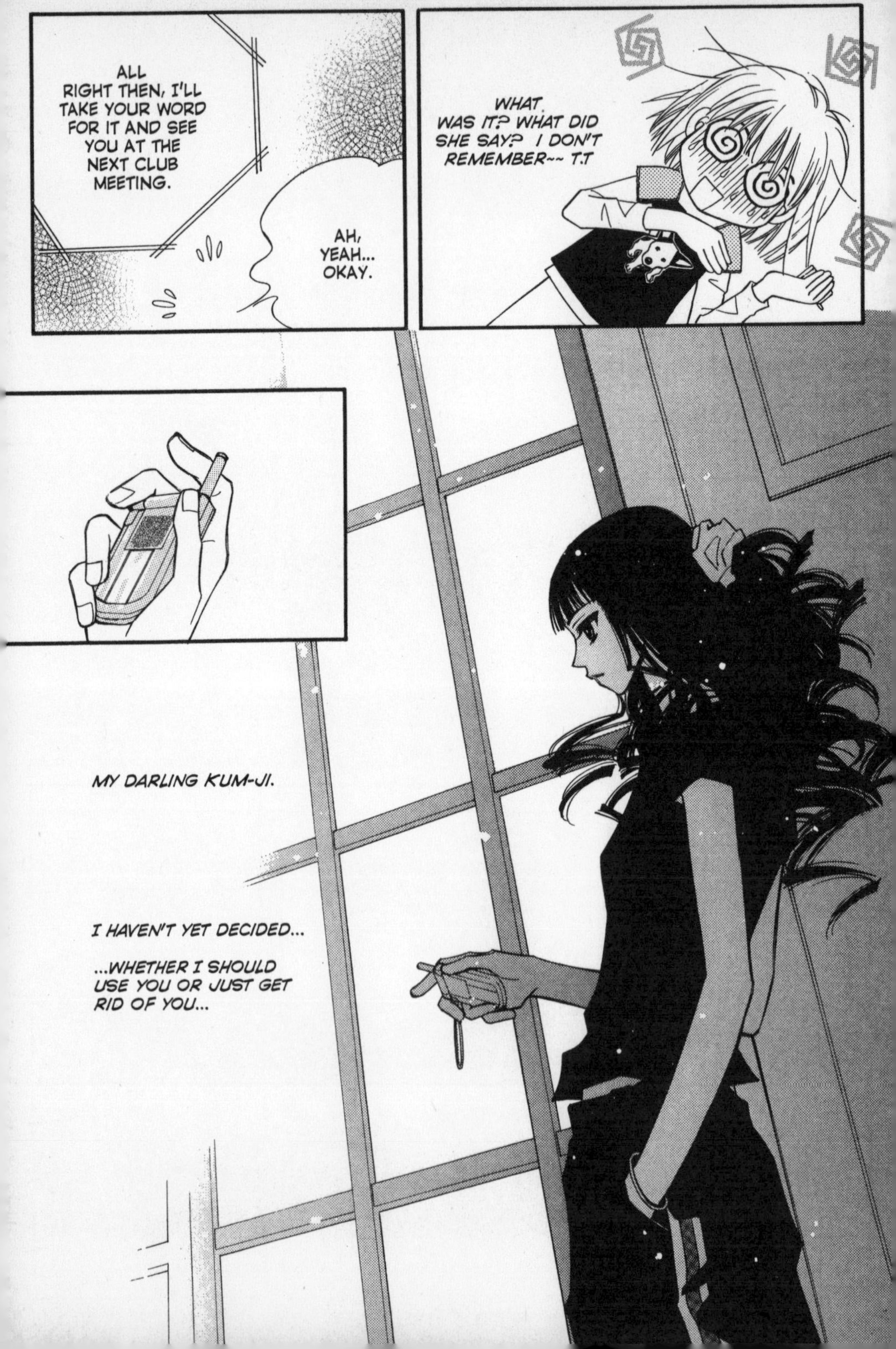
ALL RIGHT THEN, I'LL TAKE YOUR WORD FOR IT AND SEE YOU AT THE NEXT CLUB MEETING.
AH, YEAH... OKAY.
WHAT WAS IT? WHAT DID SHE SAY? I DON'T REMEMBER~~ T.T
MY DARLING KUM-JI.
I HAVEN'T YET DECIDED...
...WHETHER I SHOULD USE YOU OR JUST GET RID OF YOU...

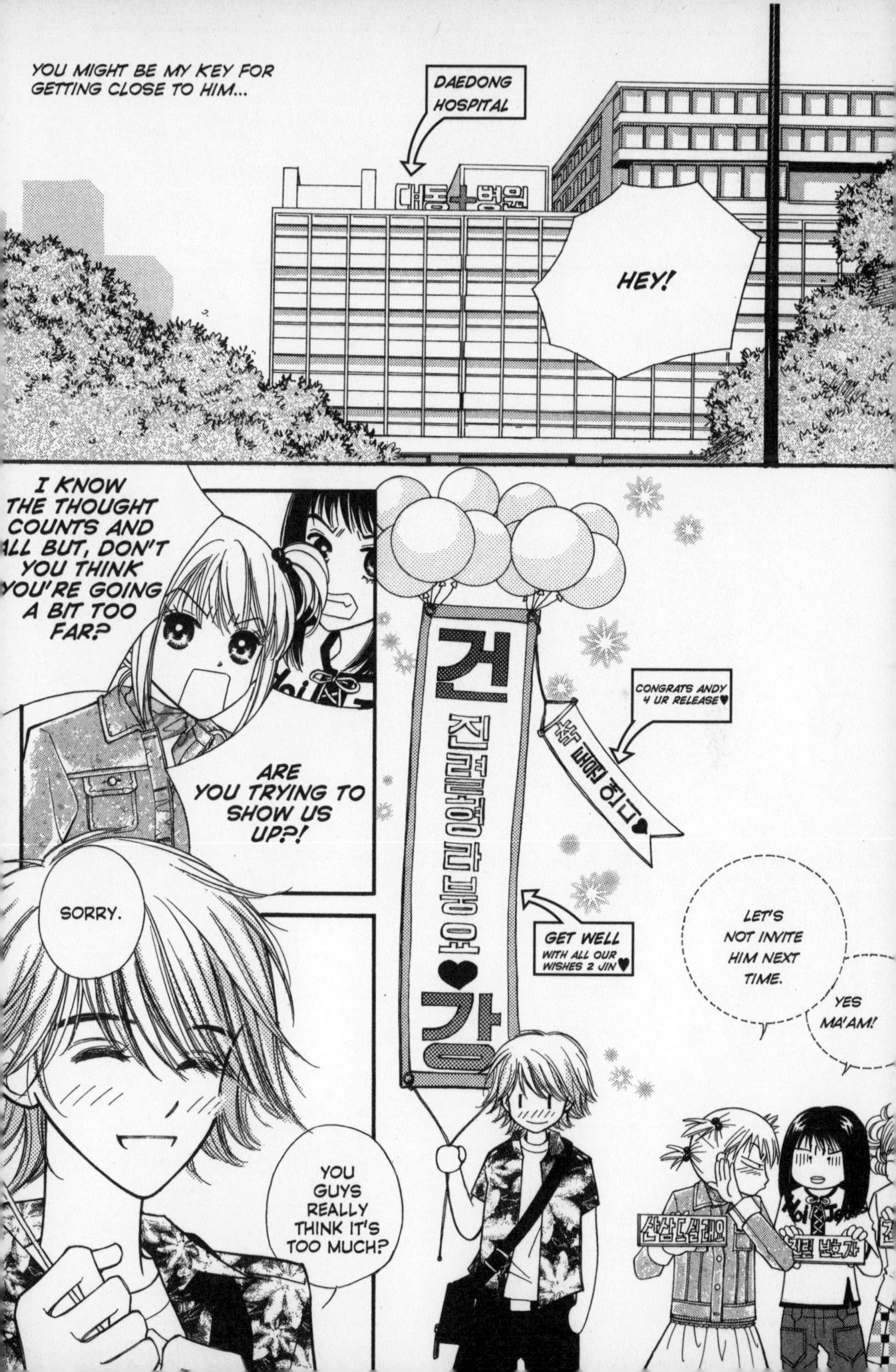
YOU MIGHT BE MY KEY FOR GETTING CLOSE TO HIM...
DAEDONG HOSPITAL
HEY!
I KNOW THE THOUGHT COUNTS AND ALL BUT, DON'T YOU THINK YOU'RE GOING A BIT TOO FAR?
ARE YOU TRYING TO SHOW US UP?!
SORRY.
YOU GUYS REALLY THINK IT'S TOO MUCH?
CONGRATS ANDY 4 UR RELEASE♥
GET WELL WITH ALL OUR WISHES 2 JIN♥
LET'S NOT INVITE HIM NEXT TIME.
YES MA'AM!

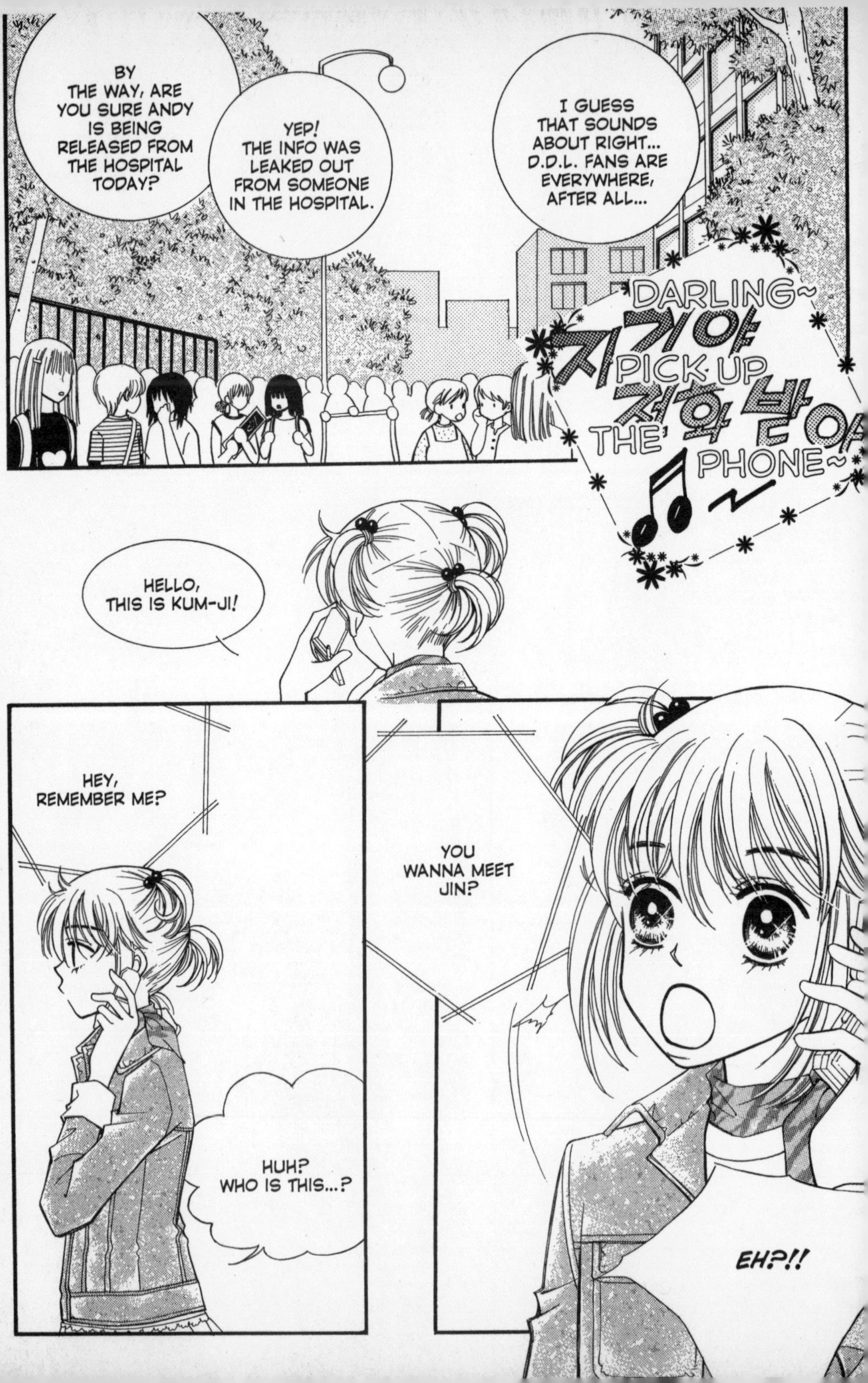
BY THE WAY, ARE YOU SURE ANDY IS BEING RELEASED FROM THE HOSPITAL TODAY?
YEP! THE INFO WAS LEAKED OUT FROM SOMEONE IN THE HOSPITAL.
I GUESS THAT SOUNDS ABOUT RIGHT... D.D.L. FANS ARE EVERYWHERE, AFTER ALL...
자기야 전화 받아
DARLING~ PICK UP THE PHONE~
HELLO, THIS IS KUM-JI!
HEY, REMEMBER ME?
YOU WANNA MEET JIN?
HUH? WHO IS THIS...?
EH?!!

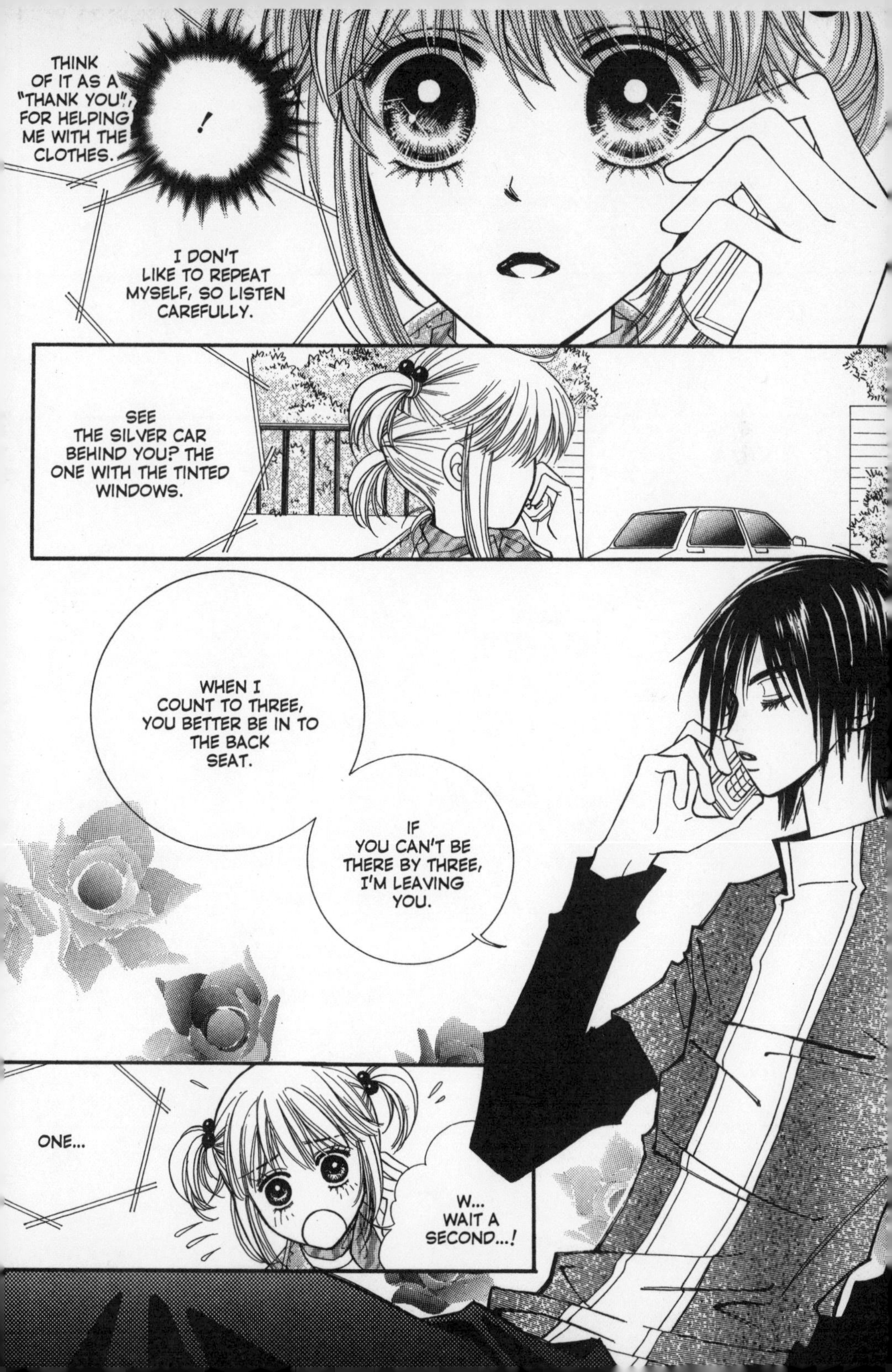
THINK OF IT AS A "THANK YOU", FOR HELPING ME WITH THE CLOTHES.
!
I DON'T LIKE TO REPEAT MYSELF, SO LISTEN CAREFULLY.
SEE THE SILVER CAR BEHIND YOU? THE ONE WITH THE TINTED WINDOWS.
WHEN I COUNT TO THREE, YOU BETTER BE IN TO THE BACK SEAT.
IF YOU CAN'T BE THERE BY THREE, I'M LEAVING YOU.
ONE...
W... WAIT A SECOND...!

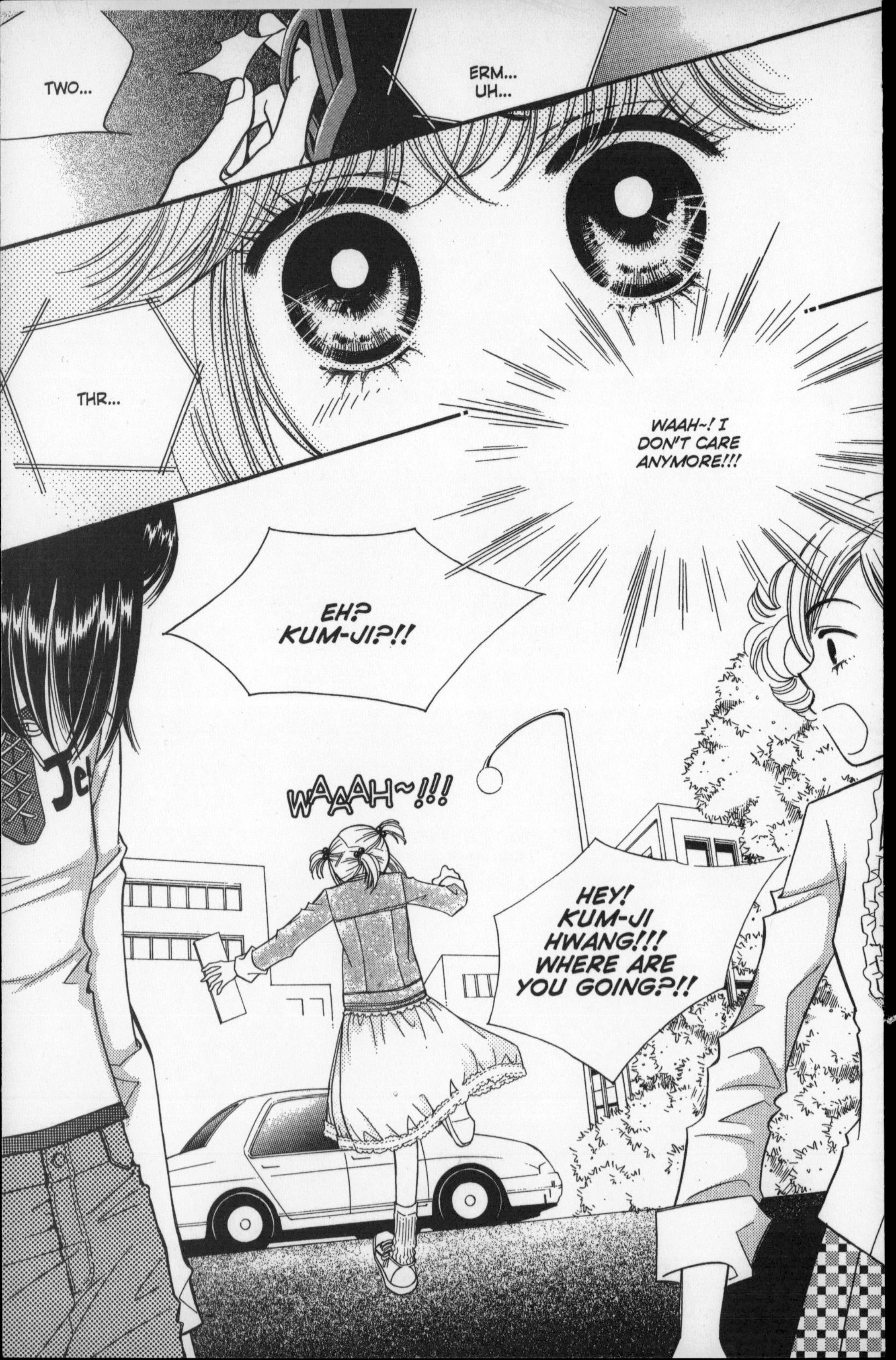
TWO...
ERM...
UH...
THR...
WAAH~! I
DON'T CARE
ANYMORE!!!
EH?
KUM-JI?!!
WAAAH~!!!
HEY!
KUM-JI
HWANG!!!
WHERE ARE
YOU GOING?!!

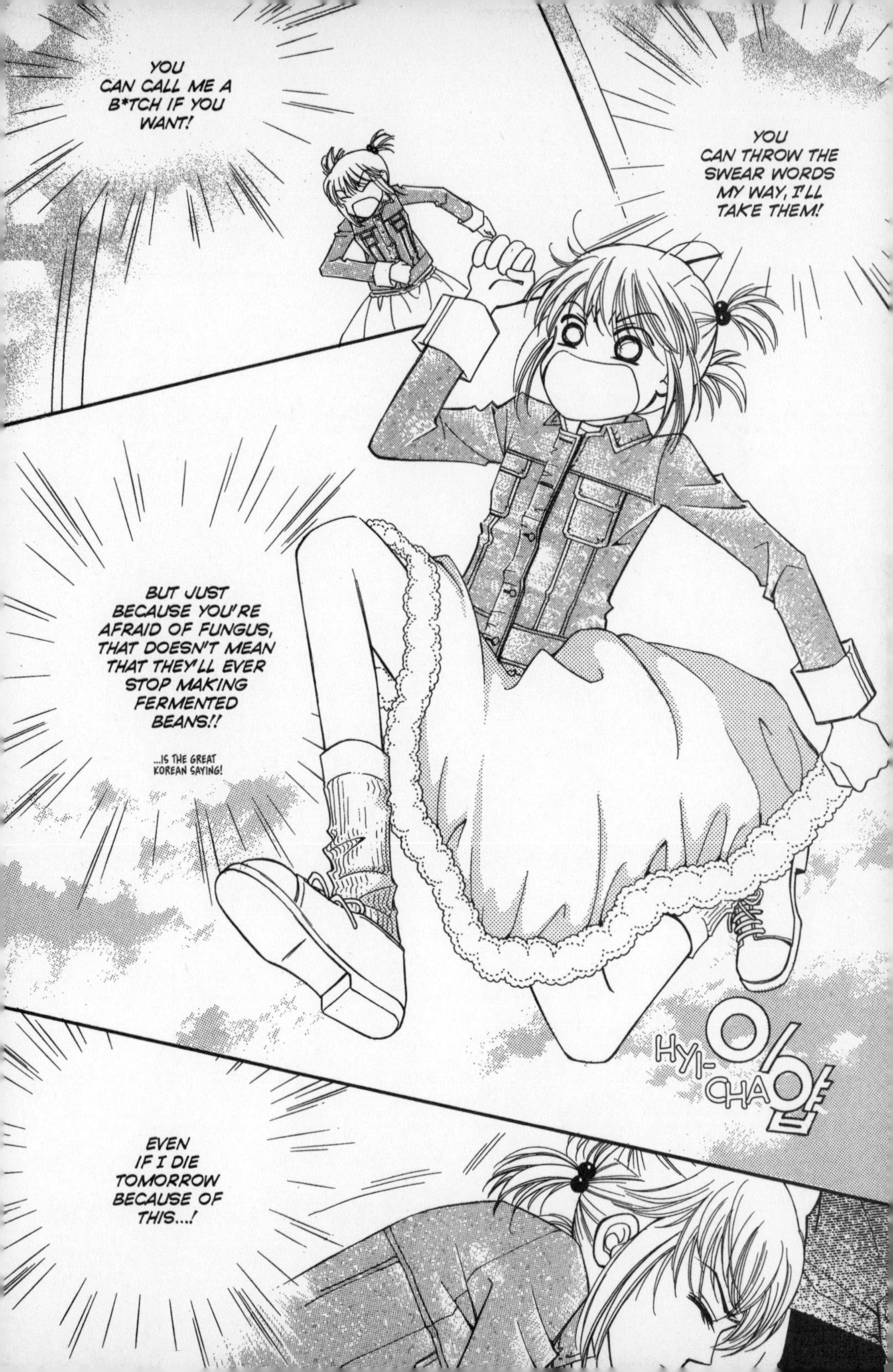
YOU CAN CALL ME A B*TCH IF YOU WANT!
YOU CAN THROW THE SWEAR WORDS MY WAY, I'LL TAKE THEM!
BUT JUST BECAUSE YOU'RE AFRAID OF FUNGUS, THAT DOESN'T MEAN THAT THEY'LL EVER STOP MAKING FERMENTED BEANS!!
...IS THE GREAT KOREAN SAYING!
HYI-CHA
EVEN IF I DIE TOMORROW BECAUSE OF THIS...!

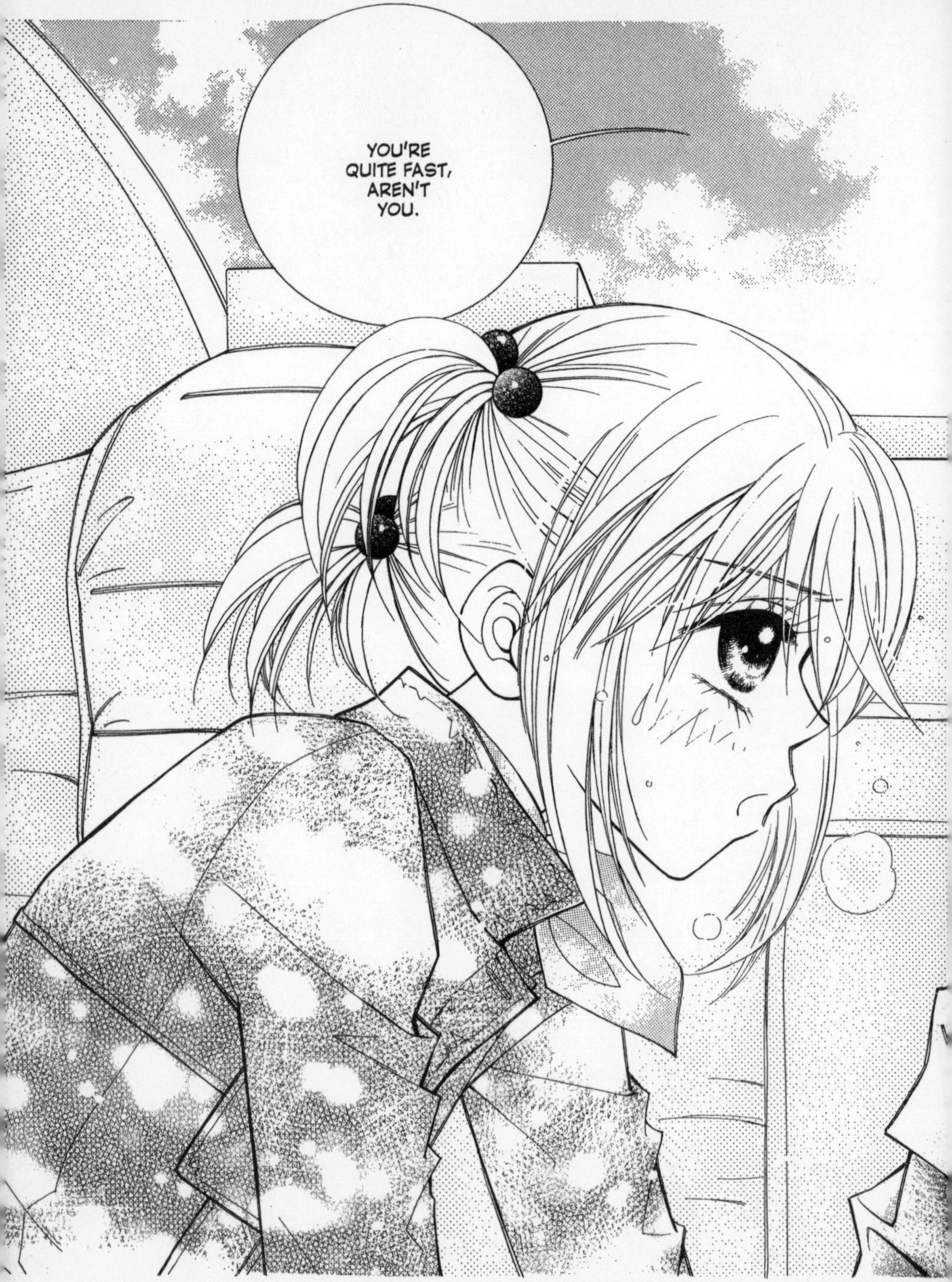
YOU'RE QUITE FAST, AREN'T YOU.

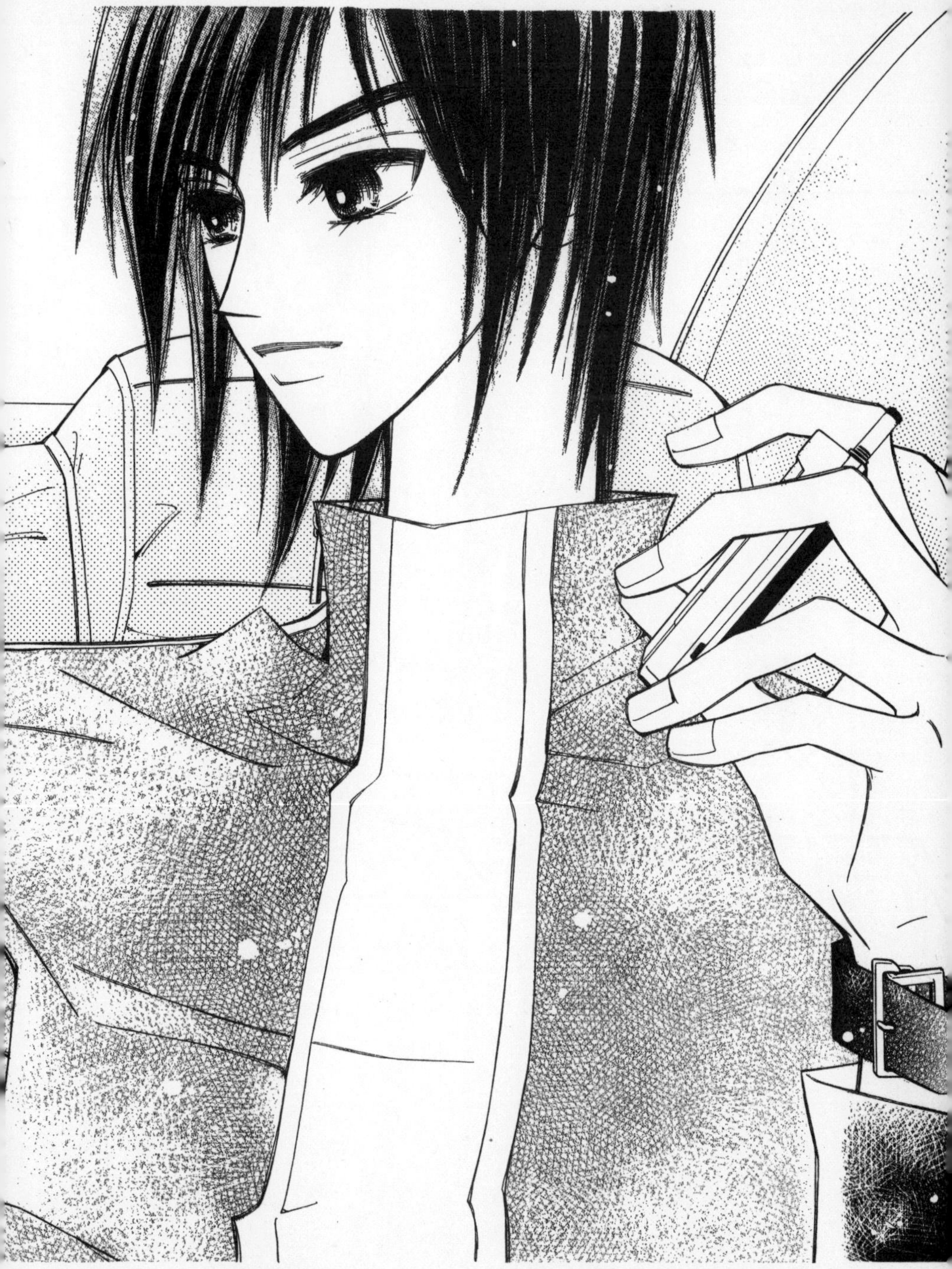

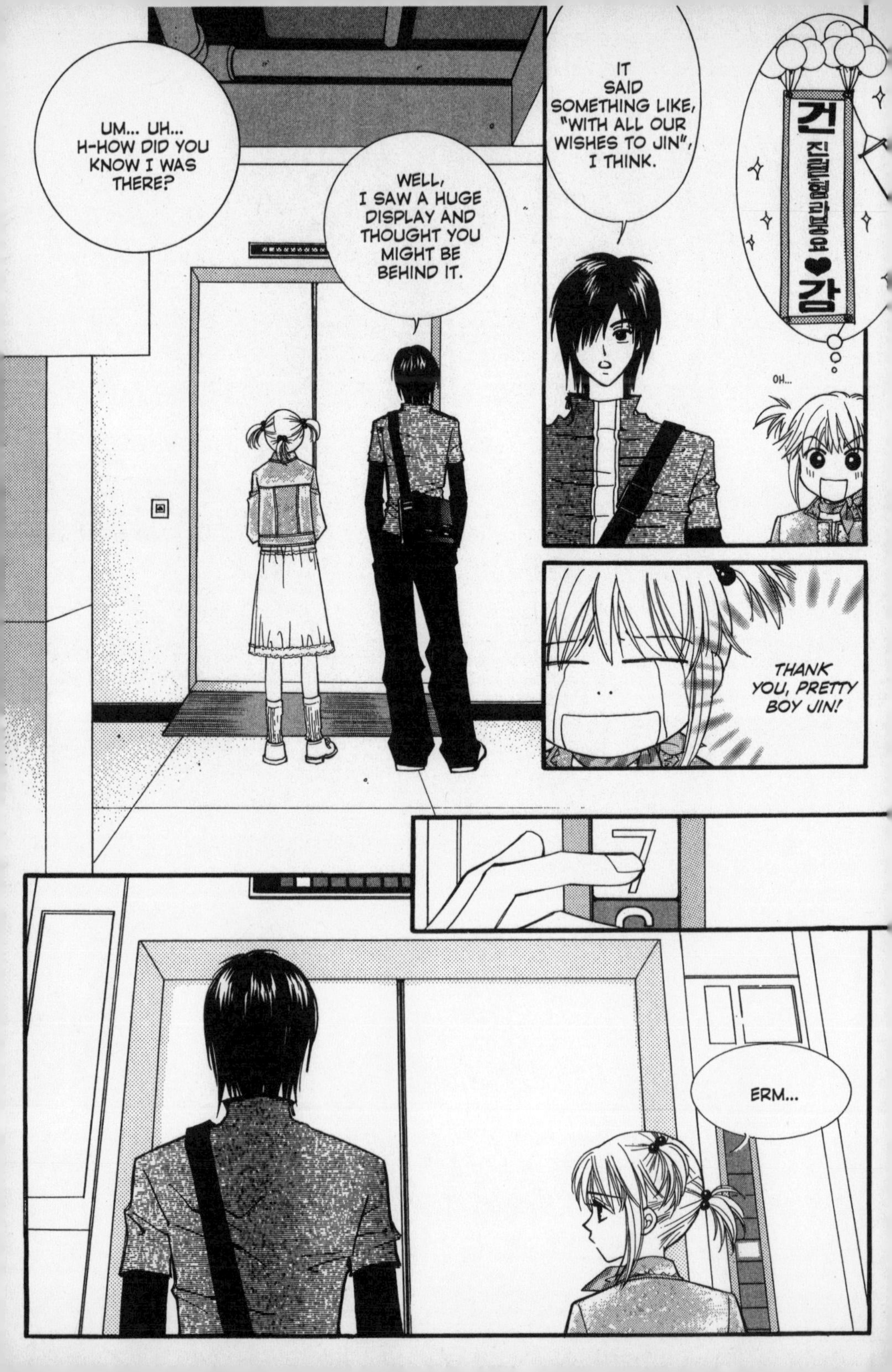
UM... UH... H-HOW DID YOU KNOW I WAS THERE?
WELL, I SAW A HUGE DISPLAY AND THOUGHT YOU MIGHT BE BEHIND IT.
IT SAID SOMETHING LIKE, "WITH ALL OUR WISHES TO JIN", I THINK.
OH...
THANK YOU, PRETTY BOY JIN!
7
ERM...

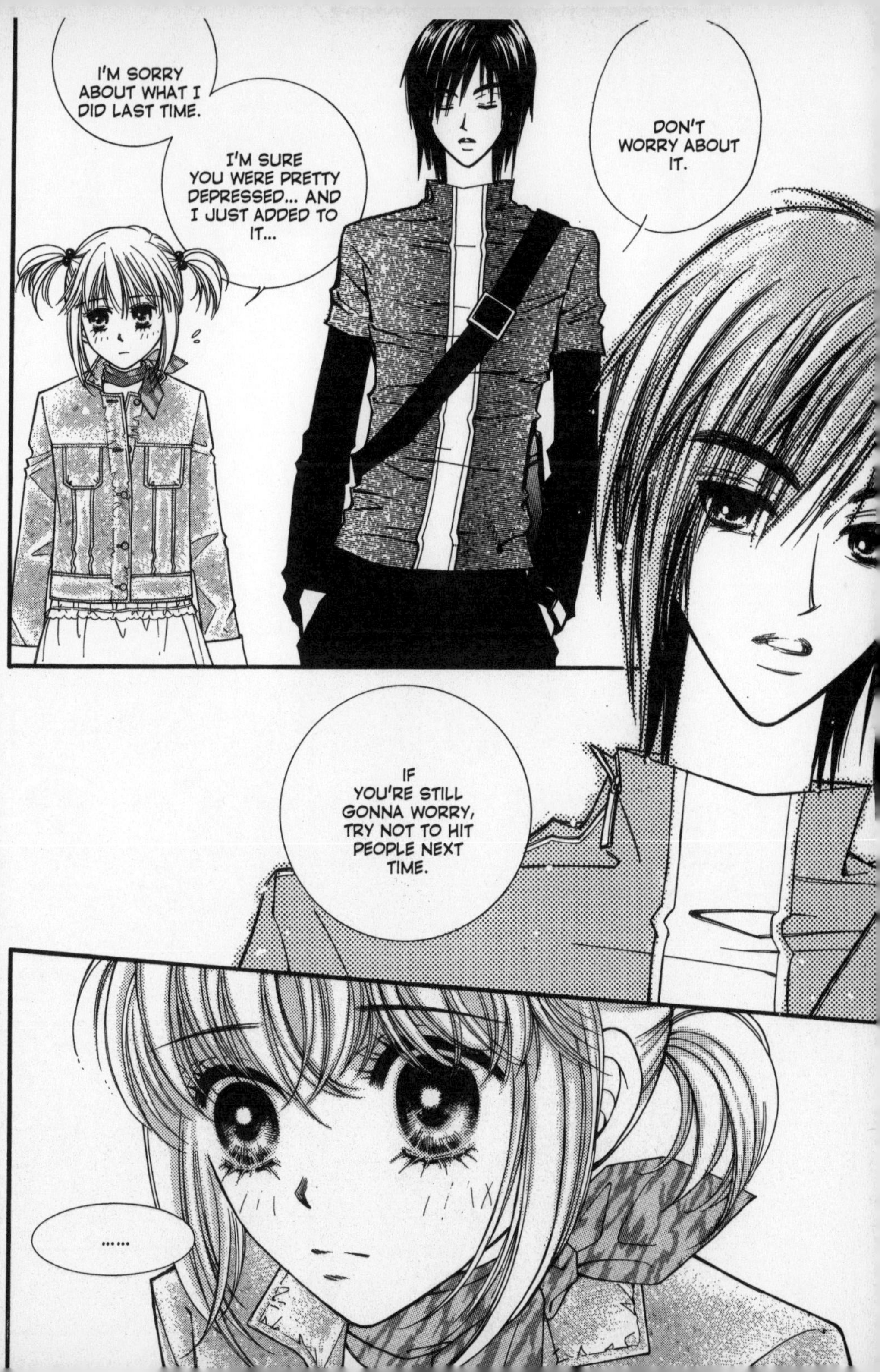
I'M SORRY ABOUT WHAT I DID LAST TIME.
I'M SURE YOU WERE PRETTY DEPRESSED... AND I JUST ADDED TO IT...
DON'T WORRY ABOUT IT.
IF YOU'RE STILL GONNA WORRY, TRY NOT TO HIT PEOPLE NEXT TIME.
......

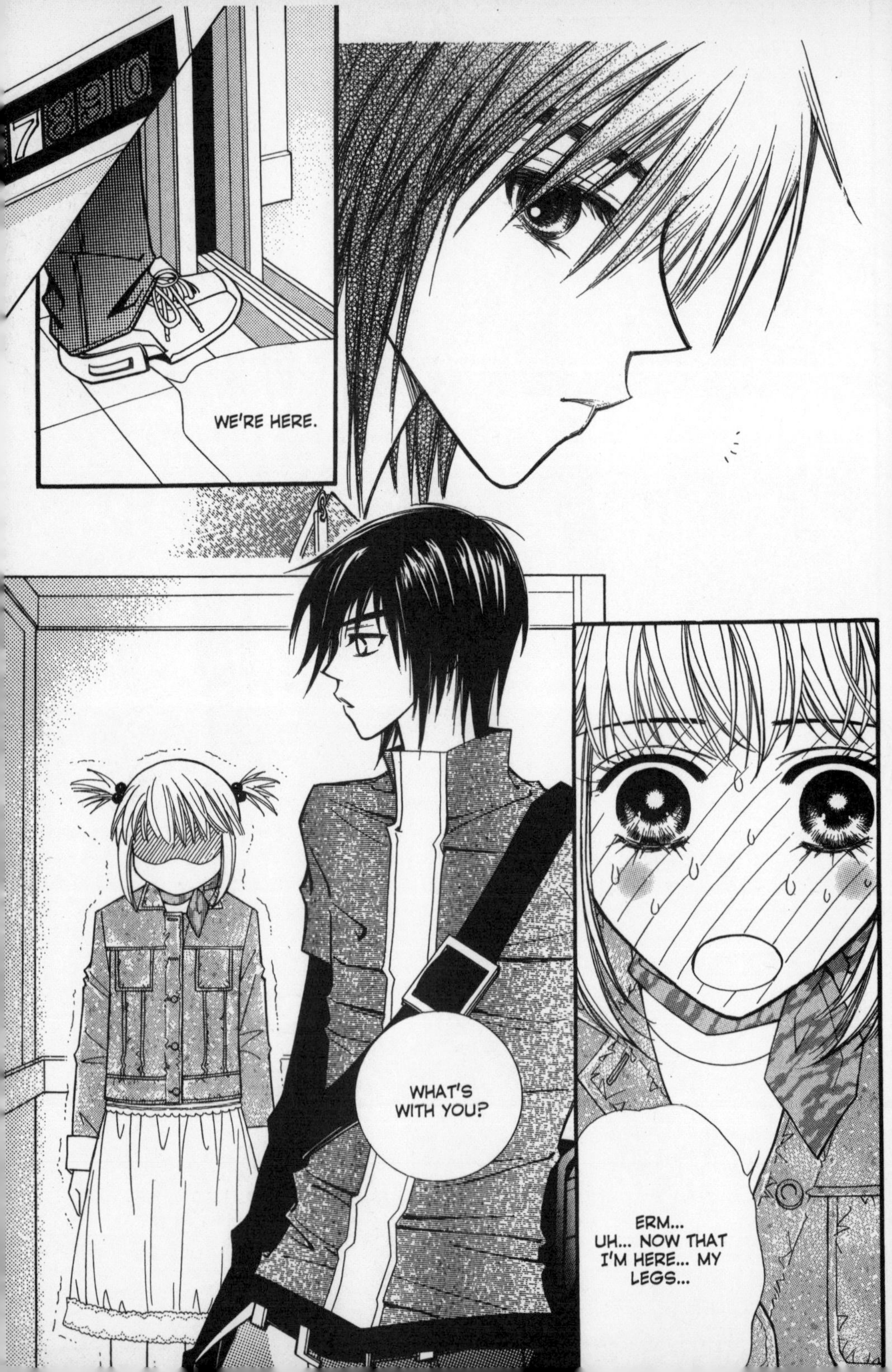
WE'RE HERE.
WHAT'S WITH YOU?
ERM... UH... NOW THAT I'M HERE... MY LEGS...

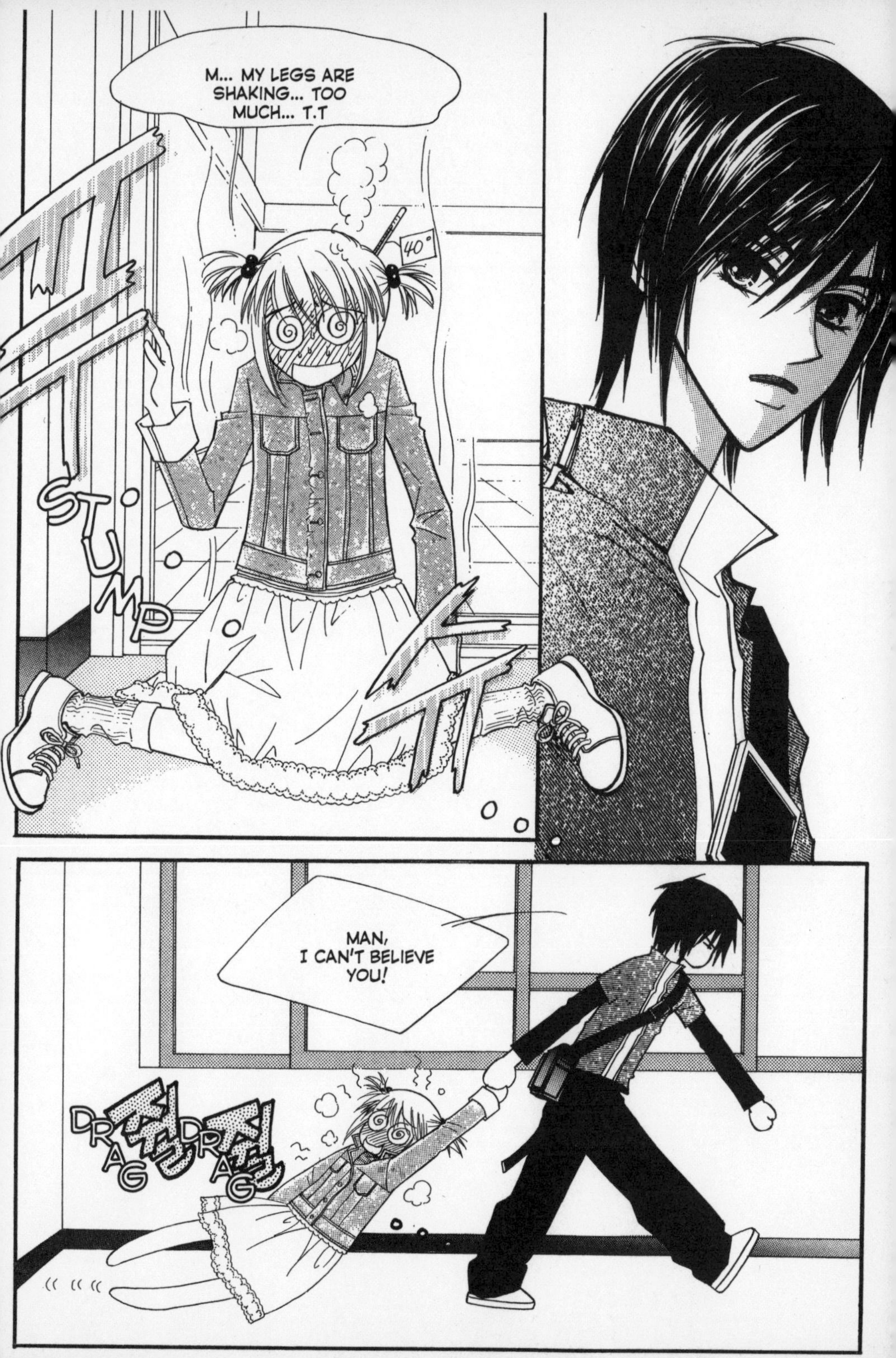
M... MY LEGS ARE SHAKING... TOO MUCH... T.T
40°
STUMP
MAN, I CAN'T BELIEVE YOU!
DRAG DRAG

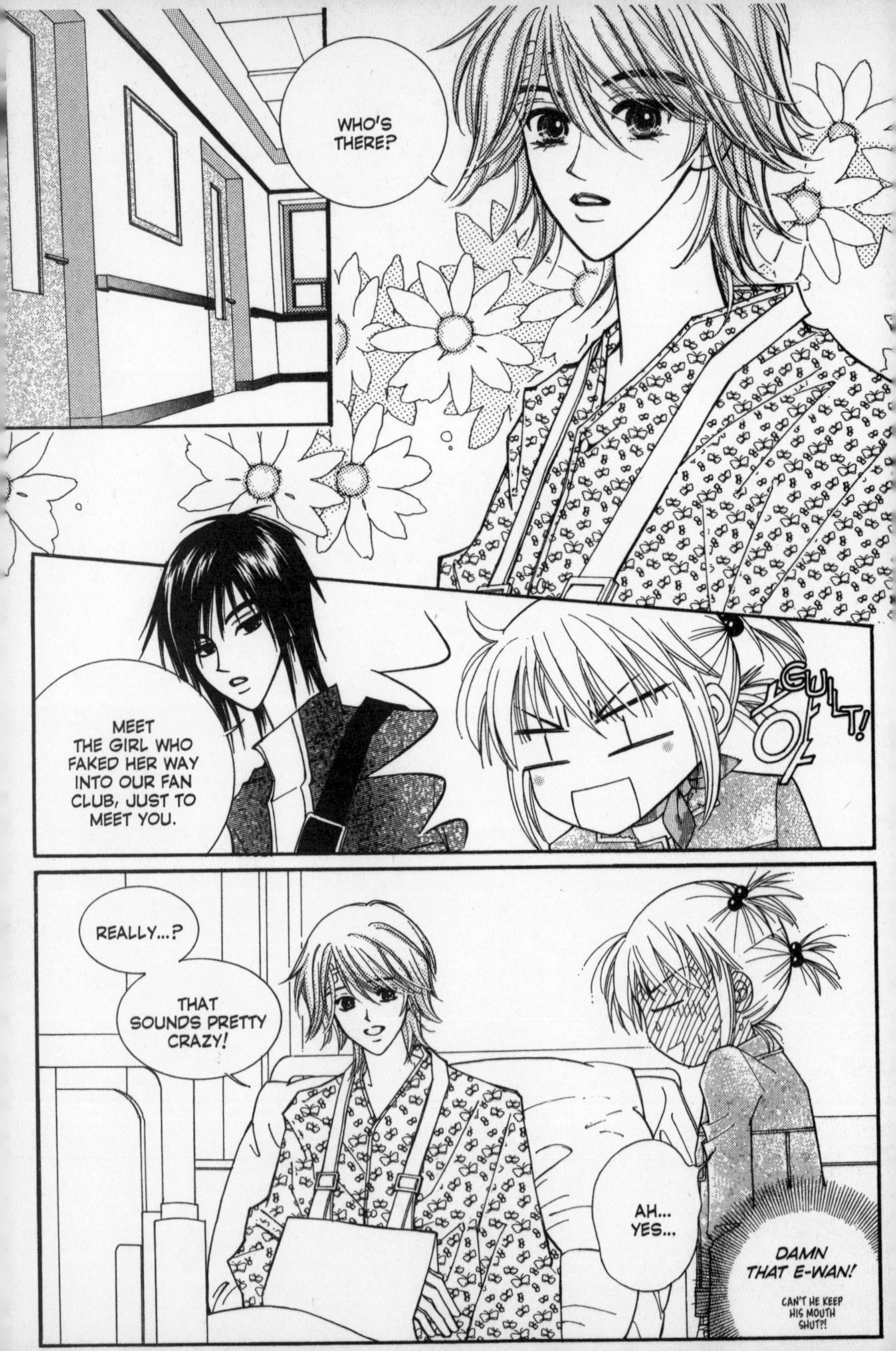
WHO'S THERE?
MEET THE GIRL WHO FAKED HER WAY INTO OUR FAN CLUB, JUST TO MEET YOU.
GUILT!
REALLY...?
THAT SOUNDS PRETTY CRAZY!
AH... YES...
DAMN THAT E-WAN!
CAN'T HE KEEP HIS MOUTH SHUT?!

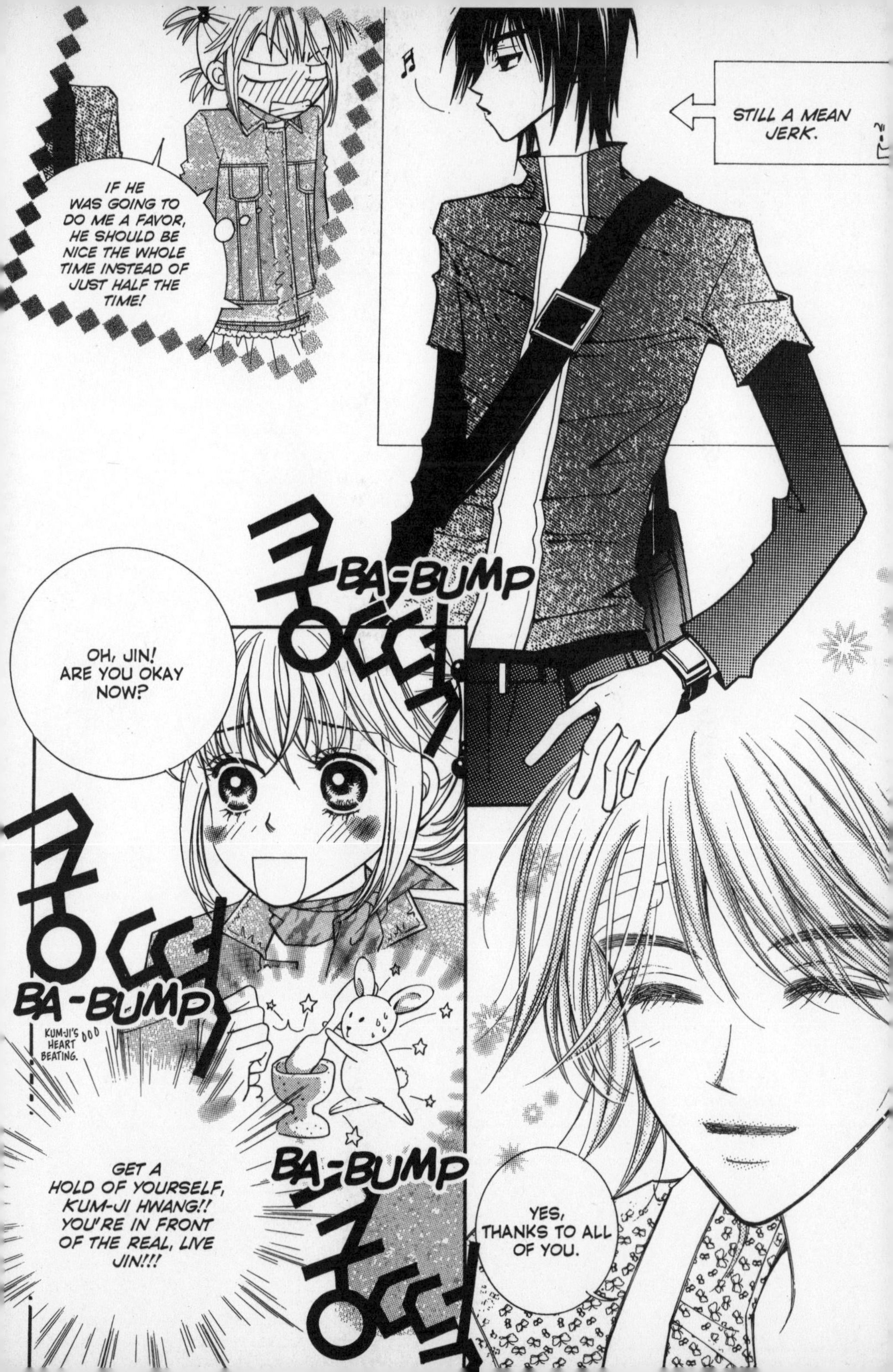
IF HE WAS GOING TO DO ME A FAVOR, HE SHOULD BE NICE THE WHOLE TIME INSTEAD OF JUST HALF THE TIME!
STILL A MEAN JERK.
BA-BUMP
OH, JIN! ARE YOU OKAY NOW?
BA-BUMP
KUM-JI'S HEART BEATING.
GET A HOLD OF YOURSELF, KUM-JI HWANG!! YOU'RE IN FRONT OF THE REAL, LIVE JIN!!!
BA-BUMP
YES, THANKS TO ALL OF YOU.

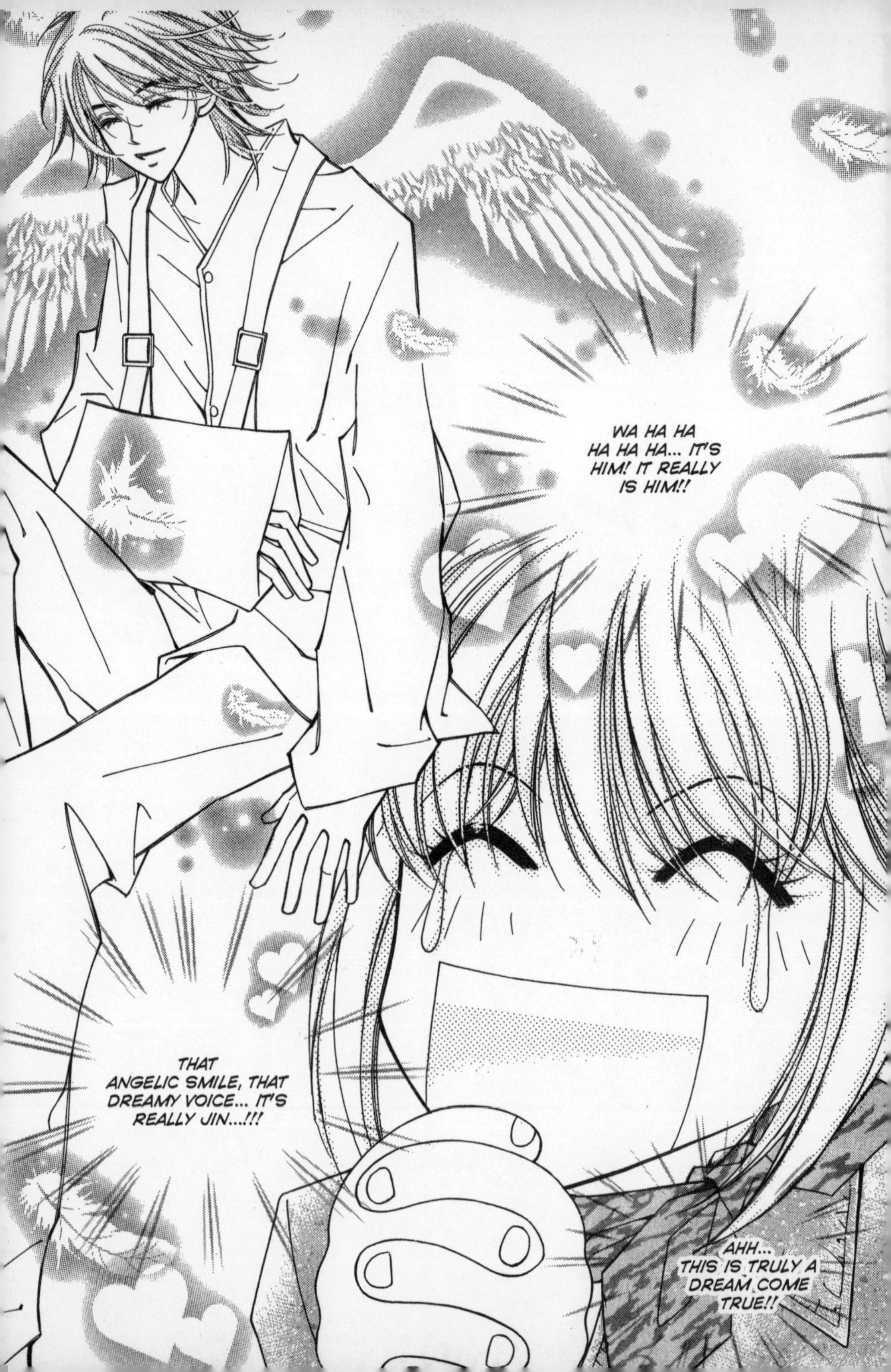
WA HA HA HA HA HA... IT'S HIM! IT REALLY IS HIM!!
THAT ANGELIC SMILE, THAT DREAMY VOICE... IT'S REALLY JIN...!!!
AHH... THIS IS TRULY A DREAM COME TRUE!!

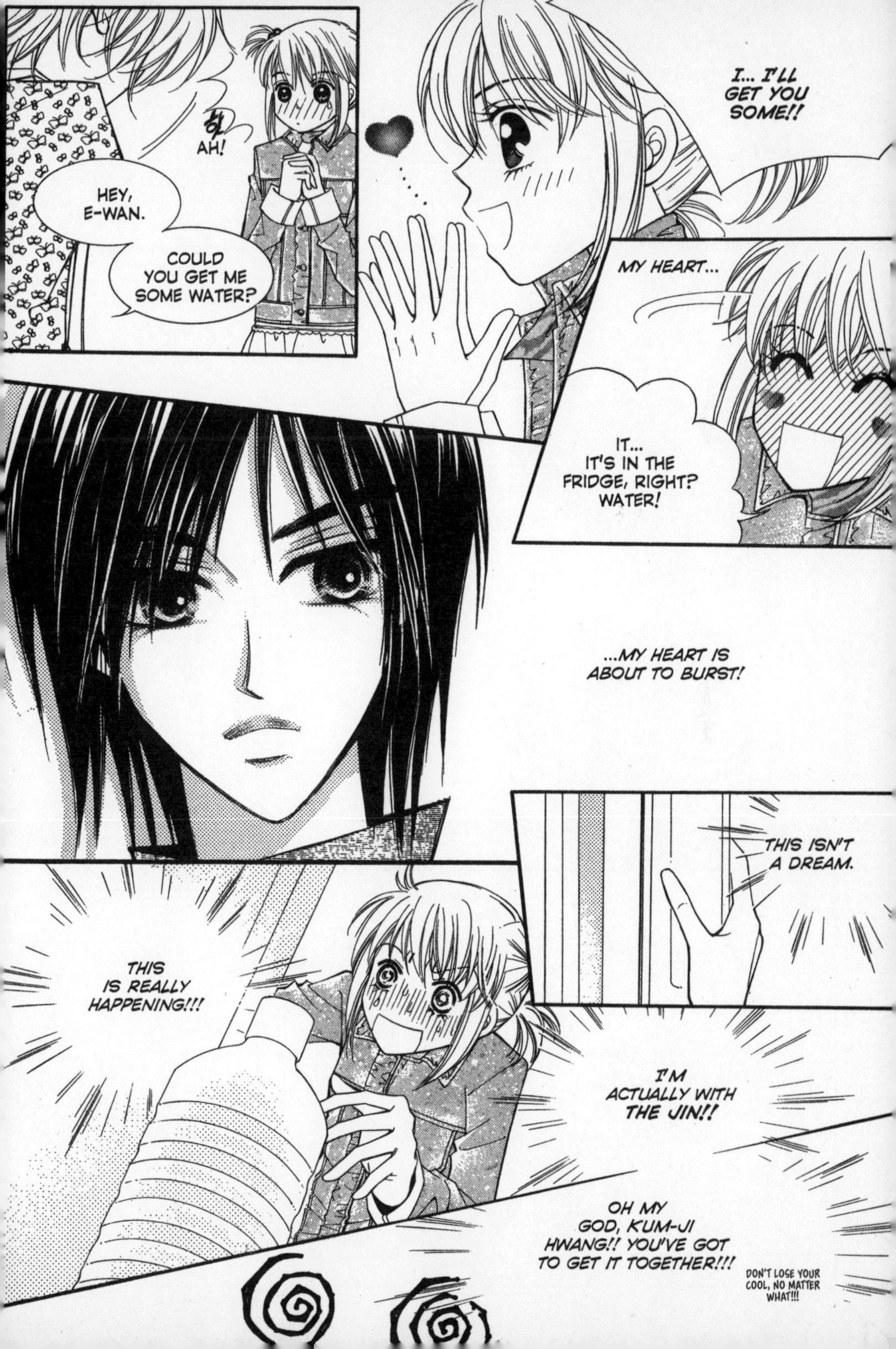
AH!
HEY, E-WAN.
COULD YOU GET ME SOME WATER?
I... I'LL GET YOU SOME!!
MY HEART...
IT... IT'S IN THE FRIDGE, RIGHT? WATER!
...MY HEART IS ABOUT TO BURST!
THIS ISN'T A DREAM.
THIS IS REALLY HAPPENING!!!
I'M ACTUALLY WITH THE JIN!!
OH MY GOD, KUM-JI HWANG!! YOU'VE GOT TO GET IT TOGETHER!!!
DON'T LOSE YOUR COOL, NO MATTER WHAT!!!

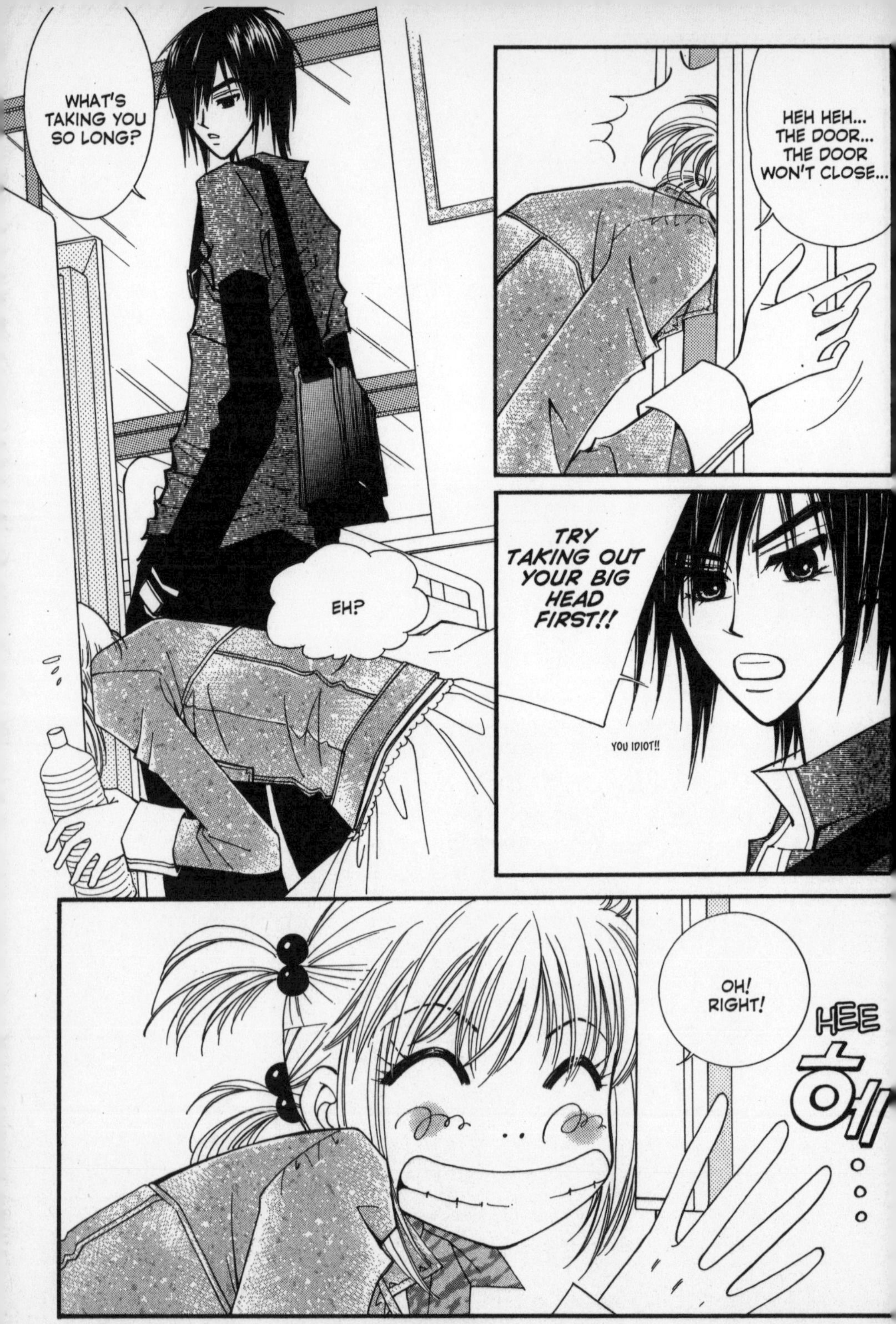
WHAT'S TAKING YOU SO LONG?
EH?
HEH HEH... THE DOOR... THE DOOR WON'T CLOSE...
TRY TAKING OUT YOUR BIG HEAD FIRST!!
YOU IDIOT!!
OH! RIGHT!
HEE
헤...

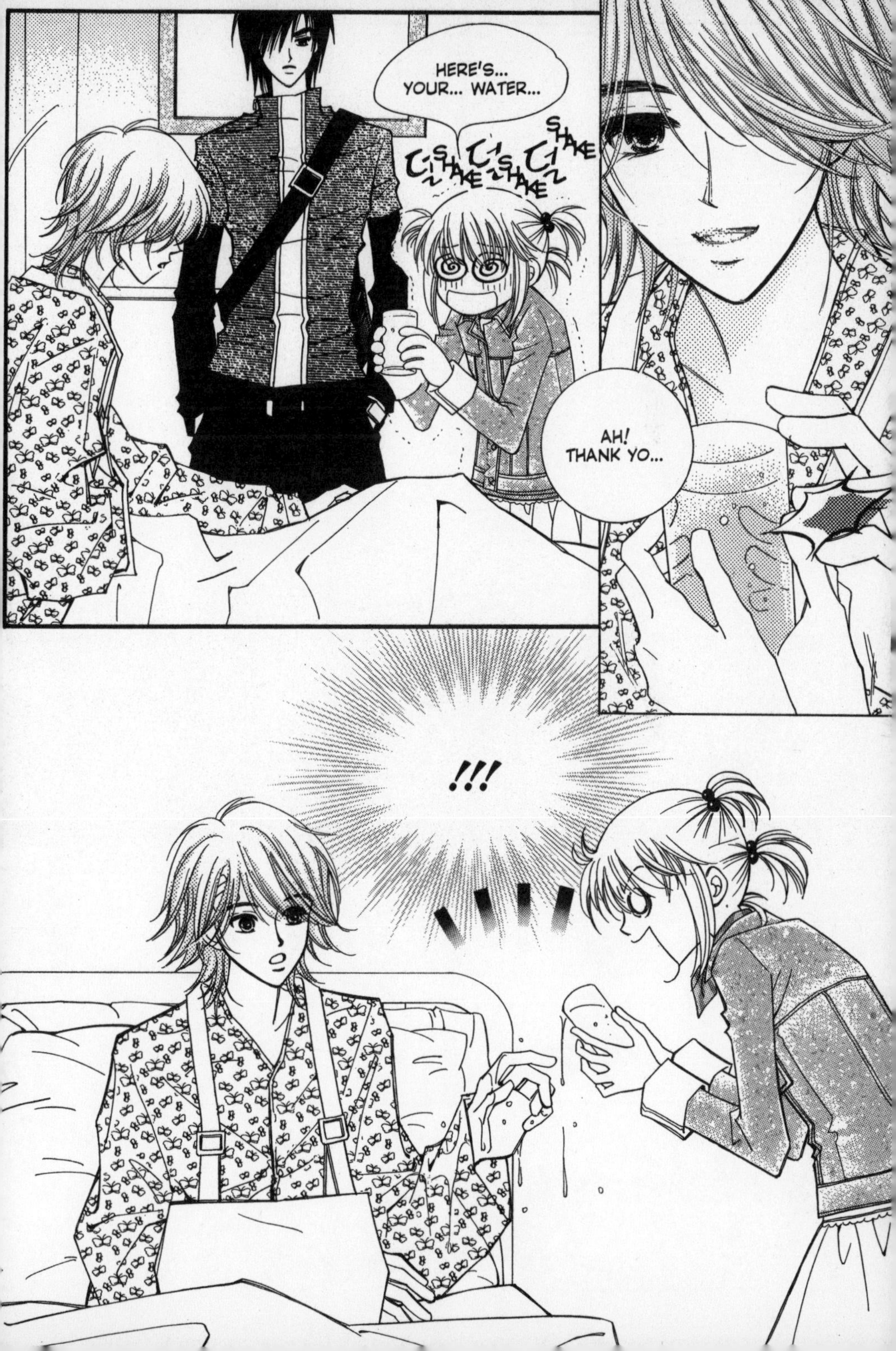
HERE'S... YOUR... WATER...
SHAKE SHAKE SHAKE
AH! THANK YO...
!!!

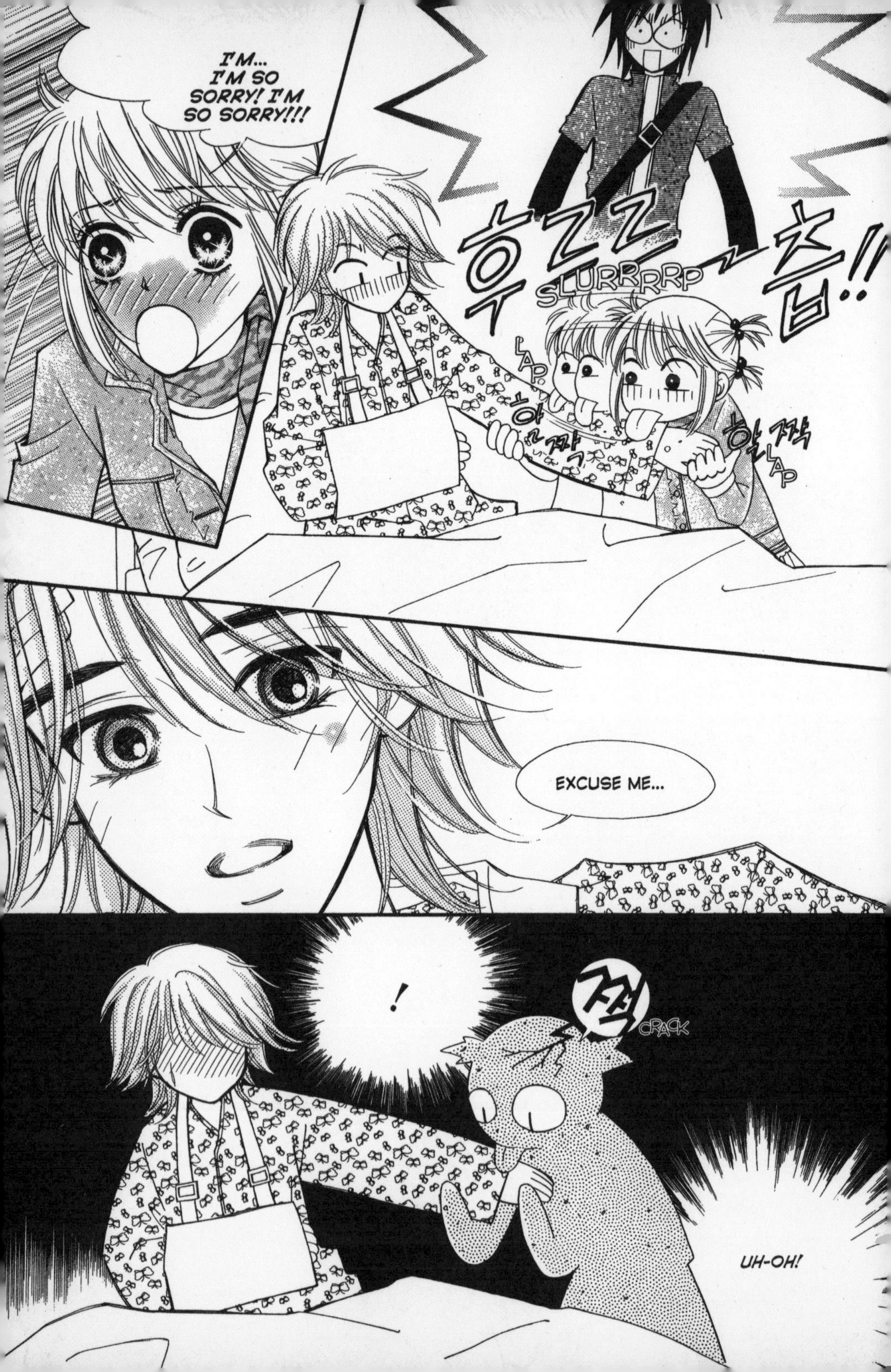
I'M... I'M SO SORRY! I'M SO SORRY!!!
SLURRRRP
LAP
할짝
LAP
EXCUSE ME...
!
CRACK
UH-OH!

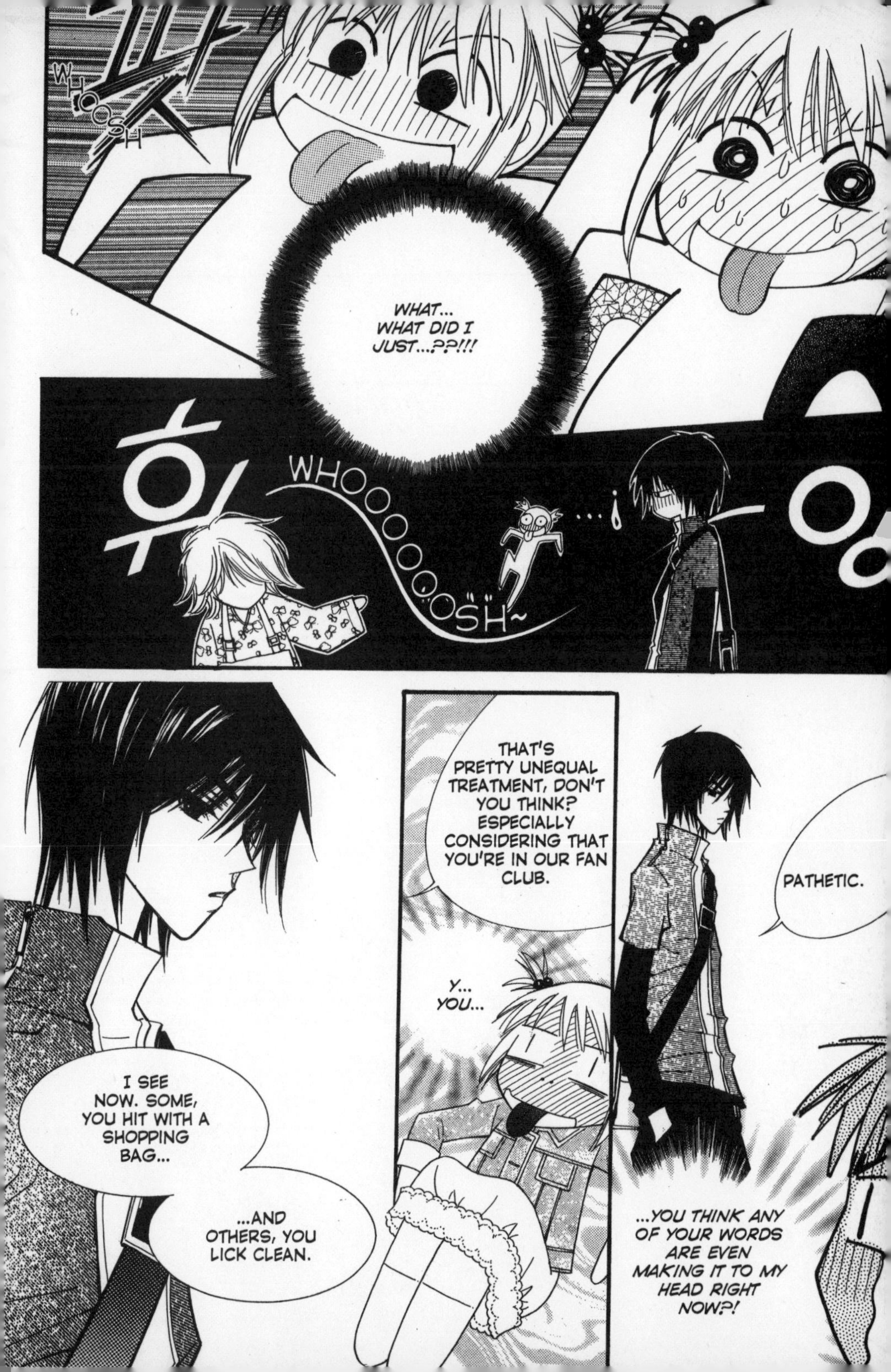
WHOOSH
WHAT... WHAT DID I JUST...??!!!
WHOOOOOOOOSH~
THAT'S PRETTY UNEQUAL TREATMENT, DON'T YOU THINK? ESPECIALLY CONSIDERING THAT YOU'RE IN OUR FAN CLUB.
PATHETIC.
Y... YOU...
I SEE NOW. SOME, YOU HIT WITH A SHOPPING BAG...
...AND OTHERS, YOU LICK CLEAN.
...YOU THINK ANY OF YOUR WORDS ARE EVEN MAKING IT TO MY HEAD RIGHT NOW?!

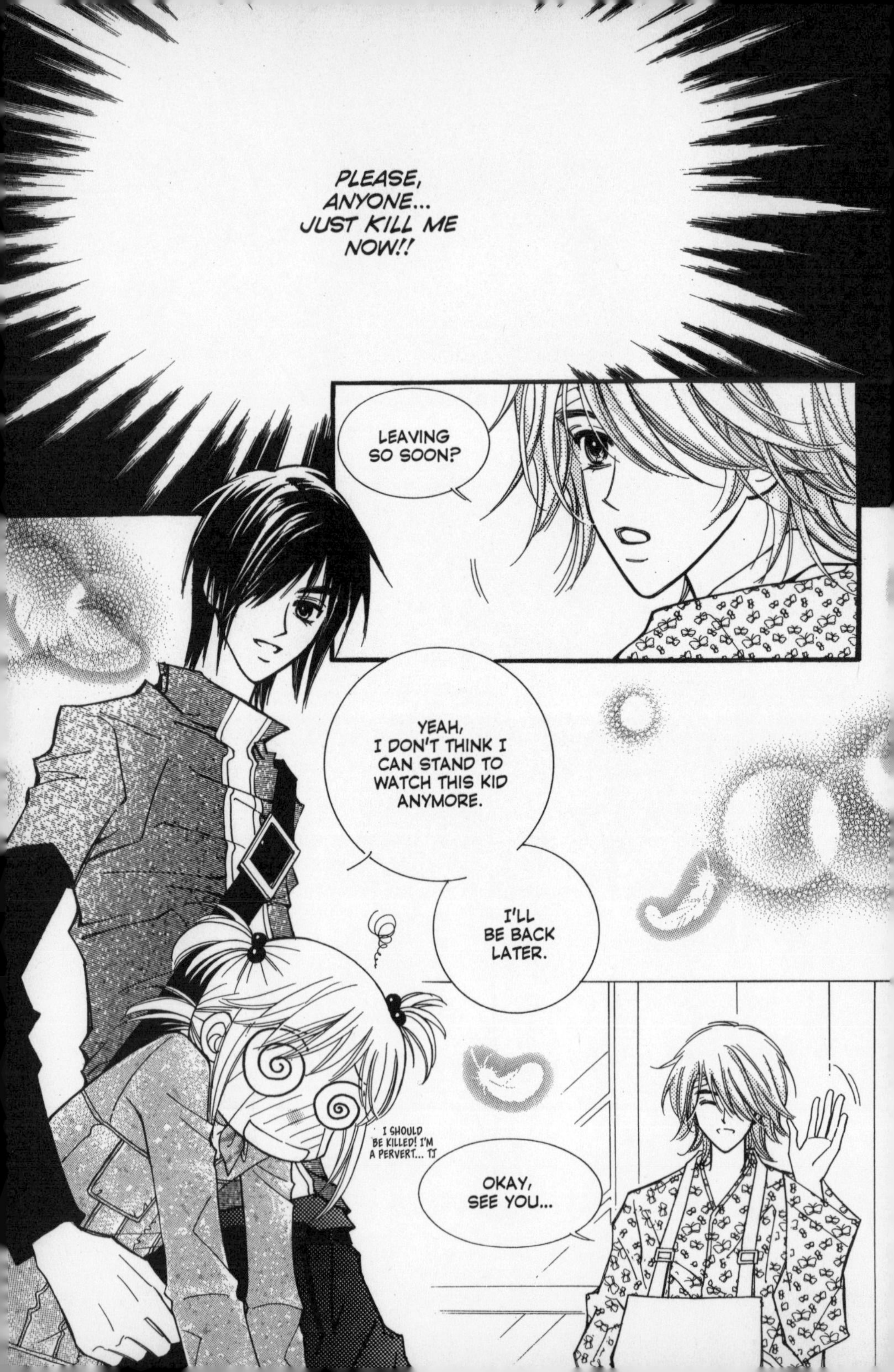
PLEASE, ANYONE... JUST KILL ME NOW!!
LEAVING SO SOON?
YEAH, I DON'T THINK I CAN STAND TO WATCH THIS KID ANYMORE.
I'LL BE BACK LATER.
I SHOULD BE KILLED! I'M A PERVERT... TT
OKAY, SEE YOU...

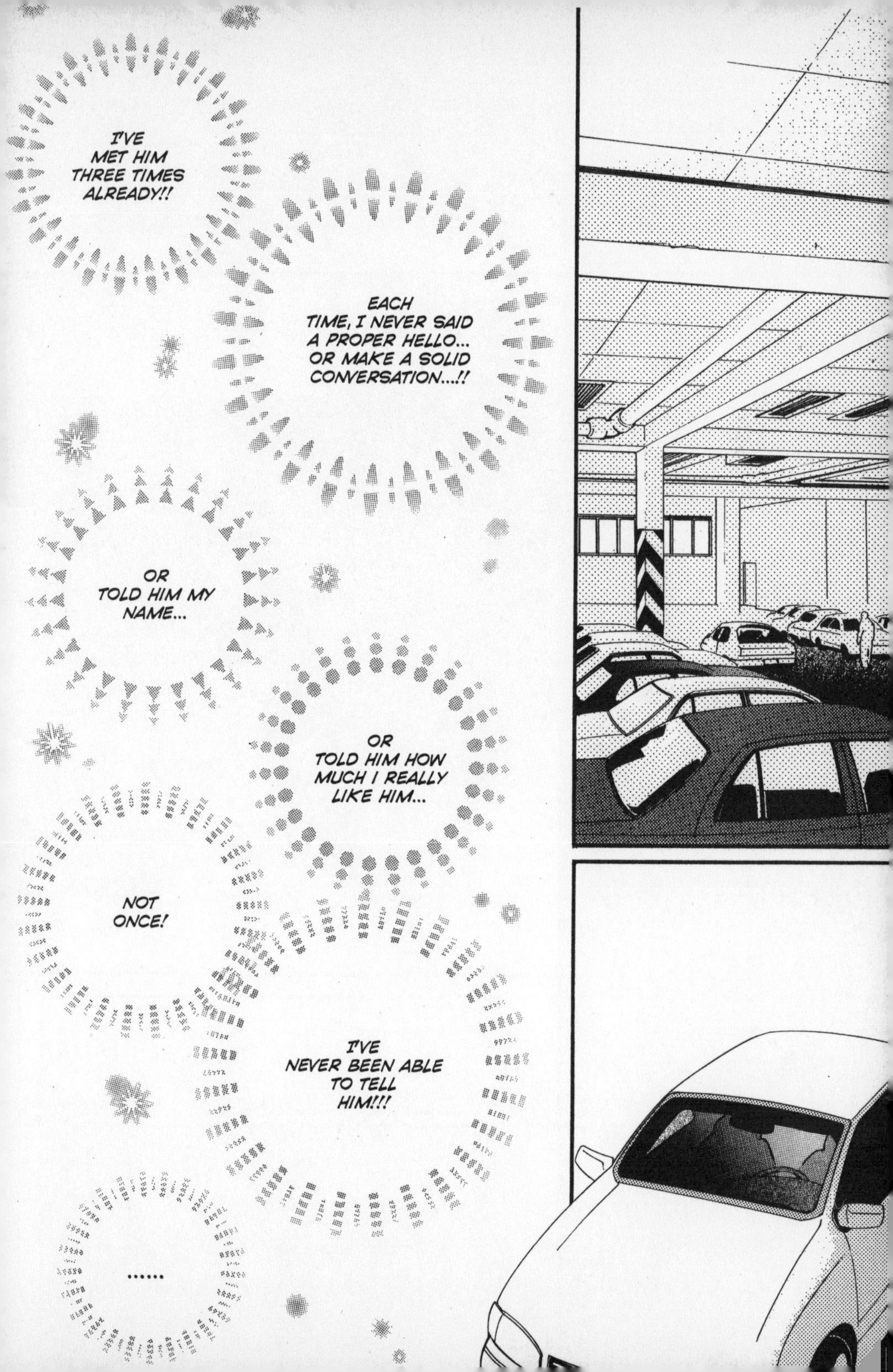
I'VE MET HIM THREE TIMES ALREADY!!
EACH TIME, I NEVER SAID A PROPER HELLO... OR MAKE A SOLID CONVERSATION...!!
OR TOLD HIM MY NAME...
OR TOLD HIM HOW MUCH I REALLY LIKE HIM...
NOT ONCE!
I'VE NEVER BEEN ABLE TO TELL HIM!!!
......

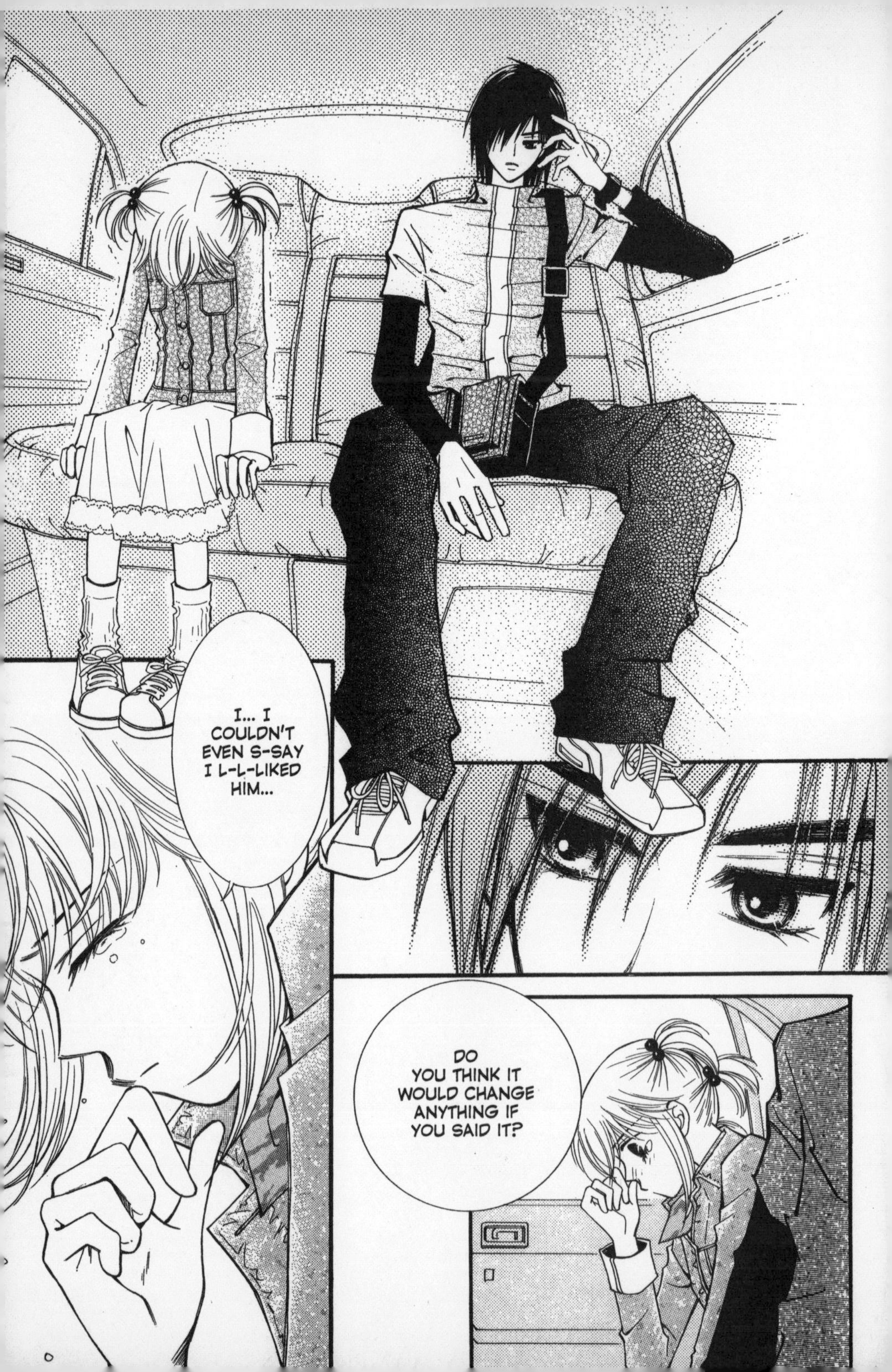
I... I COULDN'T EVEN S-SAY I L-L-LIKED HIM...
DO YOU THINK IT WOULD CHANGE ANYTHING IF YOU SAID IT?

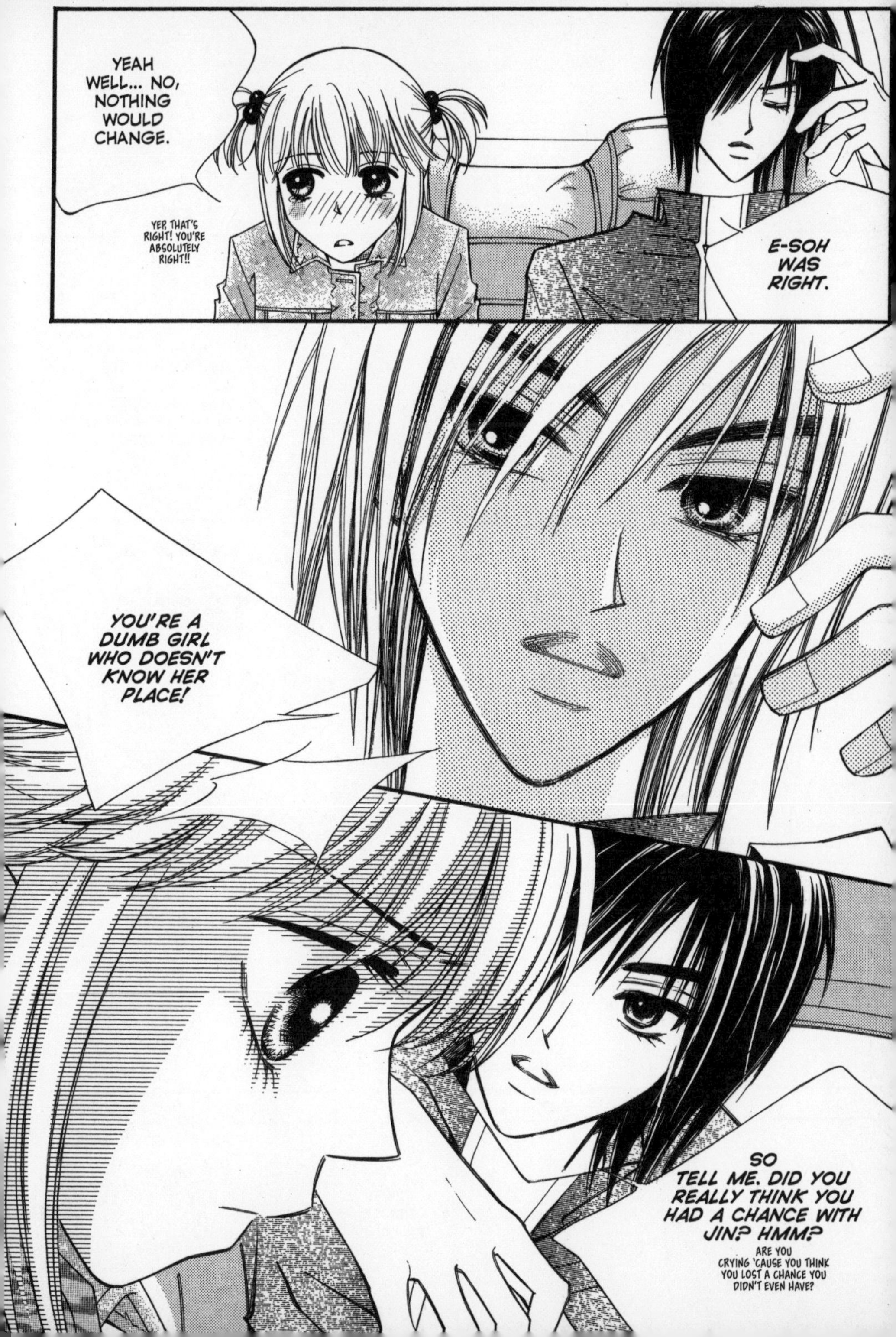
YEAH WELL... NO, NOTHING WOULD CHANGE.
YEP, THAT'S RIGHT! YOU'RE ABSOLUTELY RIGHT!!
E-SOH WAS RIGHT.
YOU'RE A DUMB GIRL WHO DOESN'T KNOW HER PLACE!
SO TELL ME. DID YOU REALLY THINK YOU HAD A CHANCE WITH JIN? HMM?
ARE YOU CRYING 'CAUSE YOU THINK YOU LOST A CHANCE YOU DIDN'T EVEN HAVE?

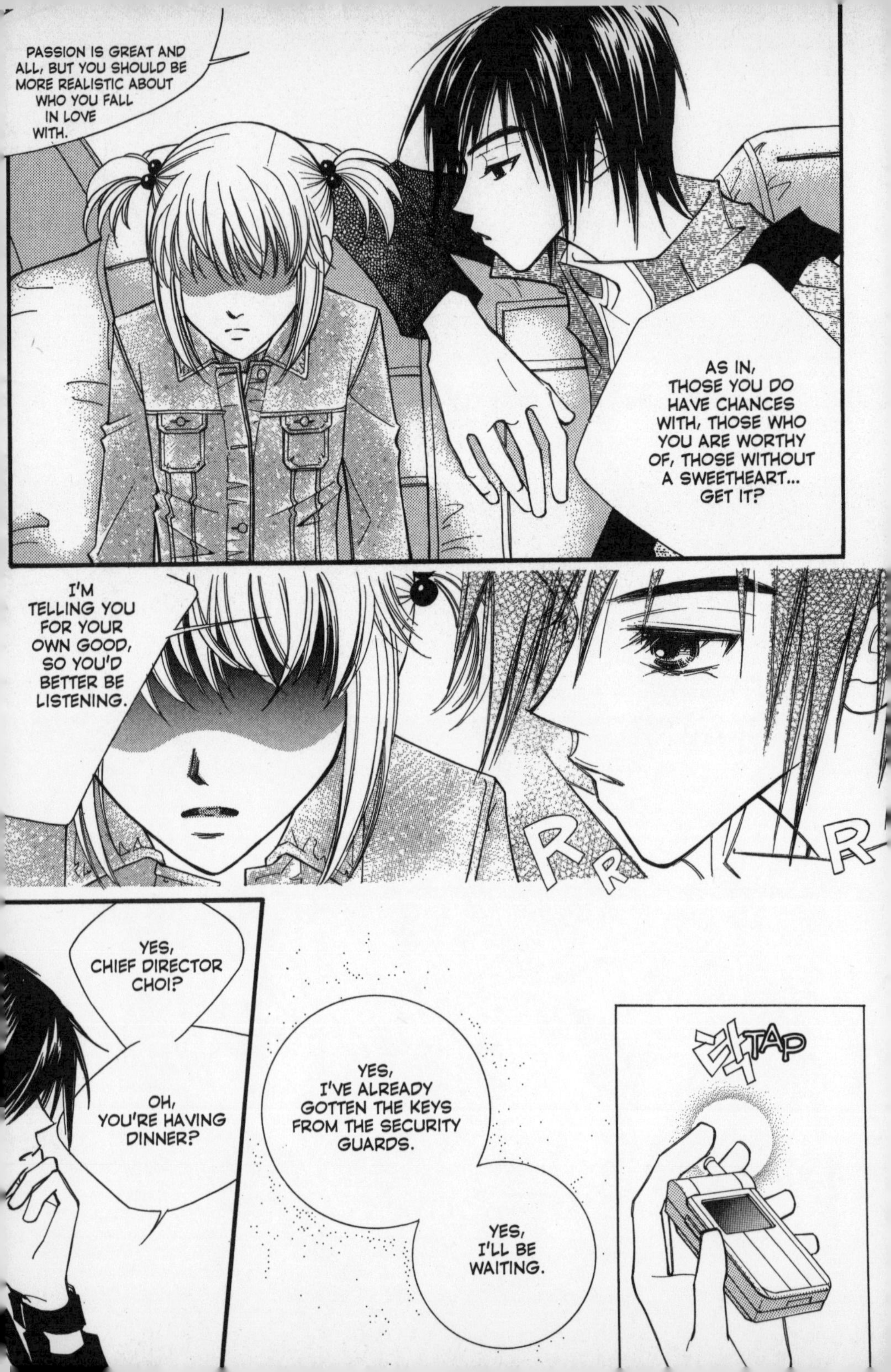
PASSION IS GREAT AND ALL, BUT YOU SHOULD BE MORE REALISTIC ABOUT WHO YOU FALL IN LOVE WITH.
AS IN, THOSE YOU DO HAVE CHANCES WITH, THOSE WHO YOU ARE WORTHY OF, THOSE WITHOUT A SWEETHEART... GET IT?
I'M TELLING YOU FOR YOUR OWN GOOD, SO YOU'D BETTER BE LISTENING.
RRRR
YES, CHIEF DIRECTOR CHOI?
OH, YOU'RE HAVING DINNER?
YES, I'VE ALREADY GOTTEN THE KEYS FROM THE SECURITY GUARDS.
YES, I'LL BE WAITING.
탁 TAP

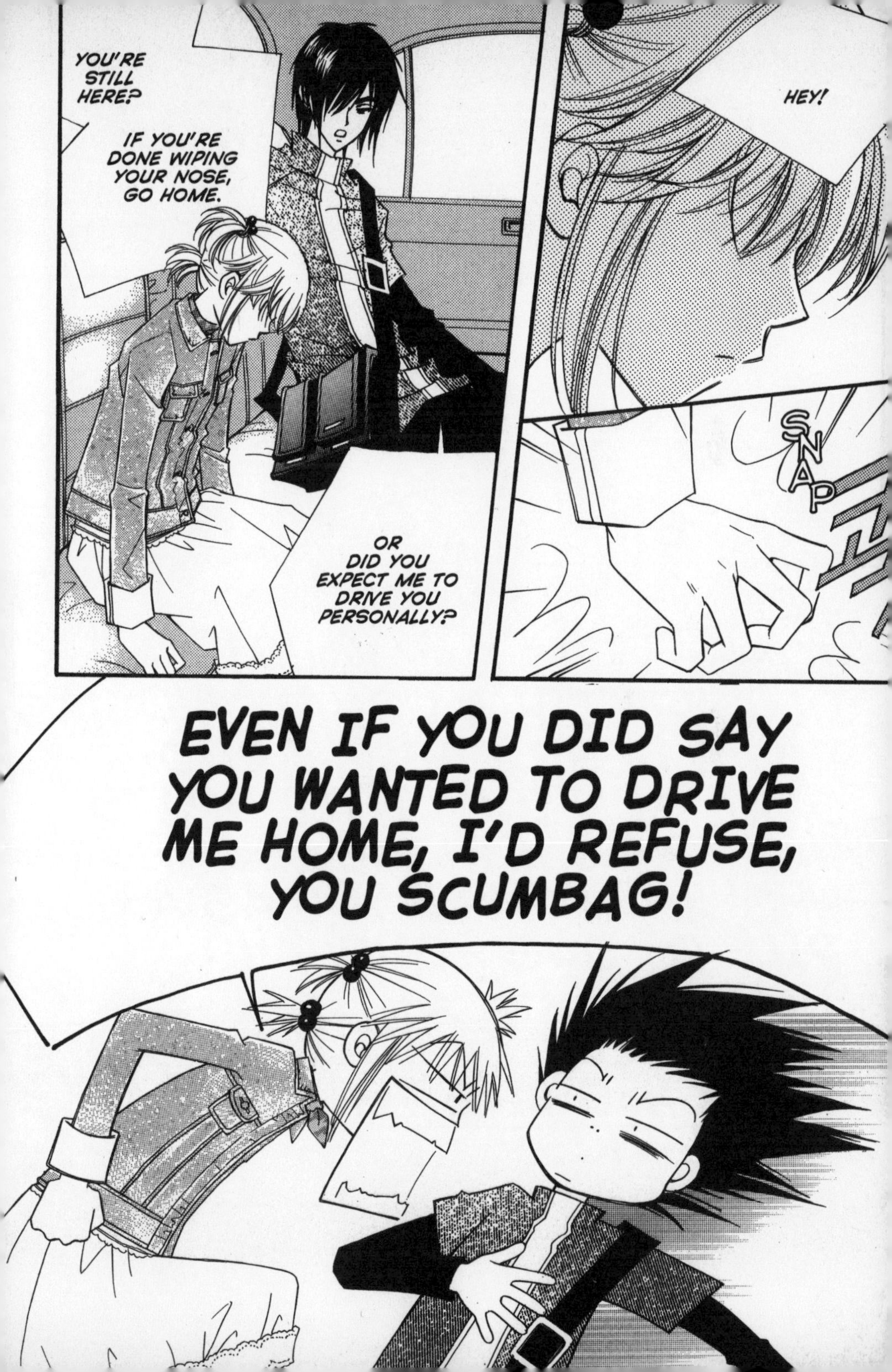
YOU'RE STILL HERE?
IF YOU'RE DONE WIPING YOUR NOSE, GO HOME.
OR DID YOU EXPECT ME TO DRIVE YOU PERSONALLY?
HEY!
SNAP
EVEN IF YOU DID SAY YOU WANTED TO DRIVE ME HOME, I'D REFUSE, YOU SCUMBAG!

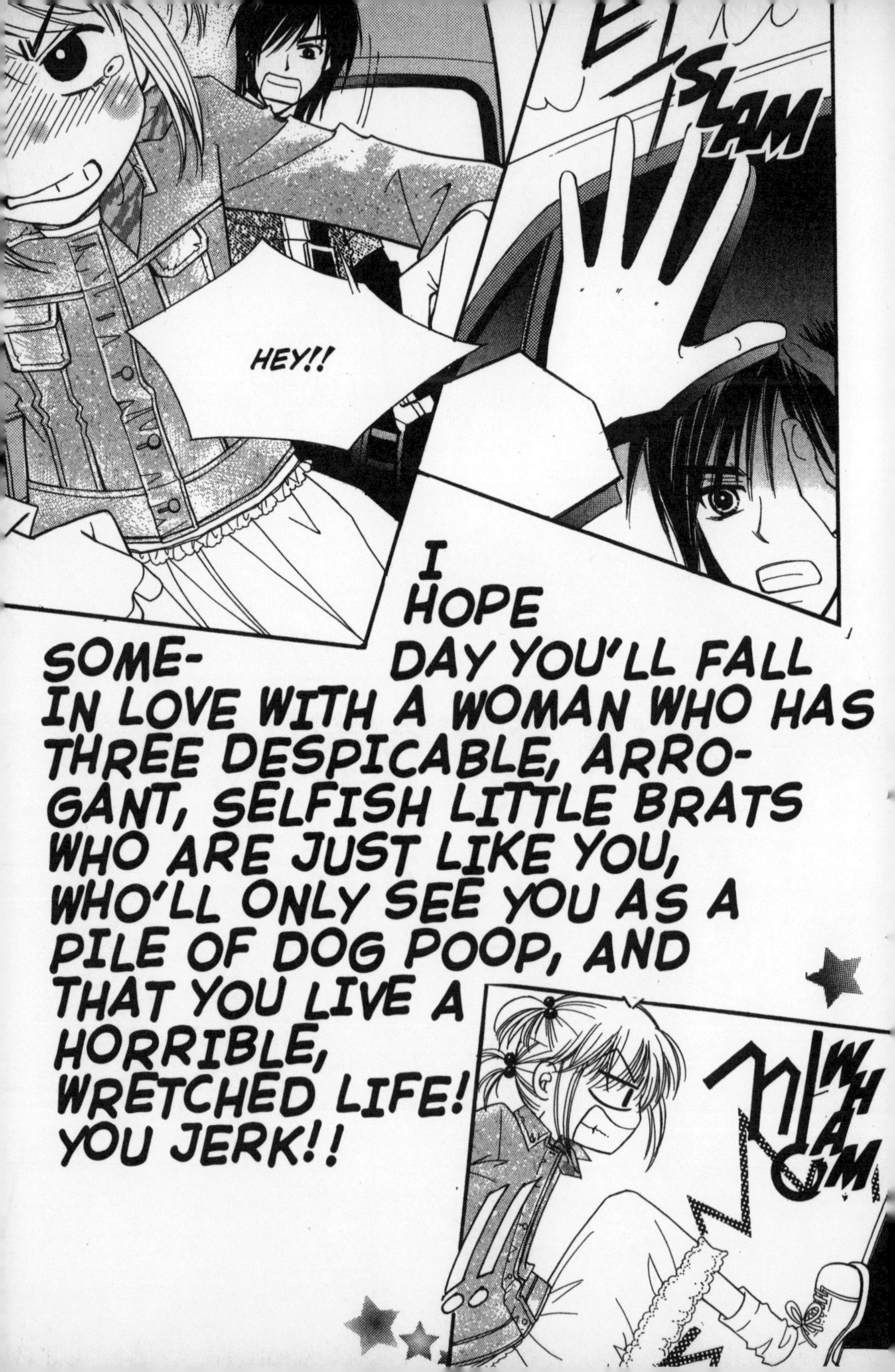
HEY!!
SLAM
I HOPE SOME-DAY YOU'LL FALL IN LOVE WITH A WOMAN WHO HAS THREE DESPICABLE, ARRO-GANT, SELFISH LITTLE BRATS WHO ARE JUST LIKE YOU, WHO'LL ONLY SEE YOU AS A PILE OF DOG POOP, AND THAT YOU LIVE A HORRIBLE, WRETCHED LIFE! YOU JERK!!
WHAM

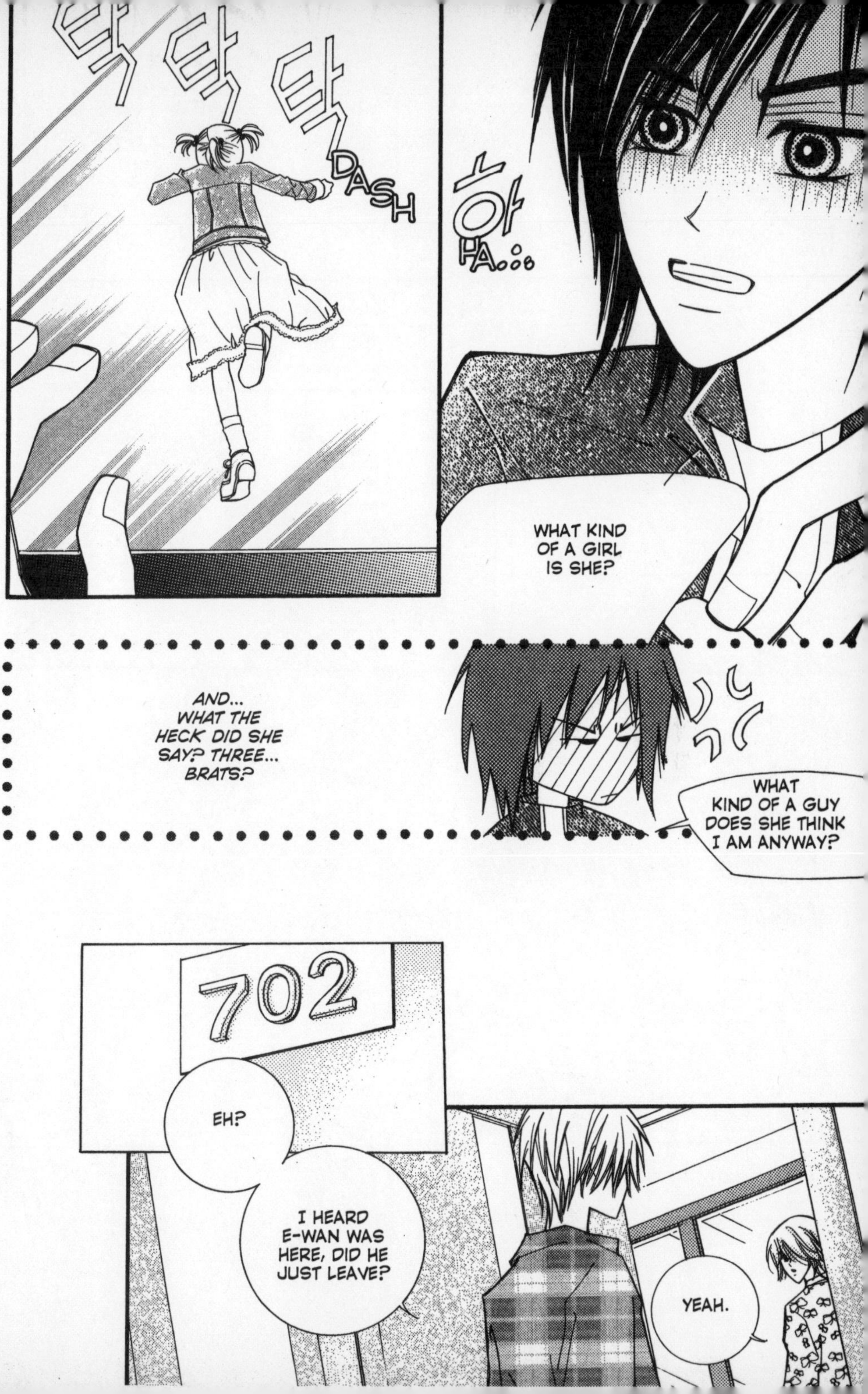
탁 탁 탁
DASH
하
HA...
WHAT KIND OF A GIRL IS SHE?
AND... WHAT THE HECK DID SHE SAY? THREE... BRATS?
WHAT KIND OF A GUY DOES SHE THINK I AM ANYWAY?
702
EH?
I HEARD E-WAN WAS HERE, DID HE JUST LEAVE?
YEAH.

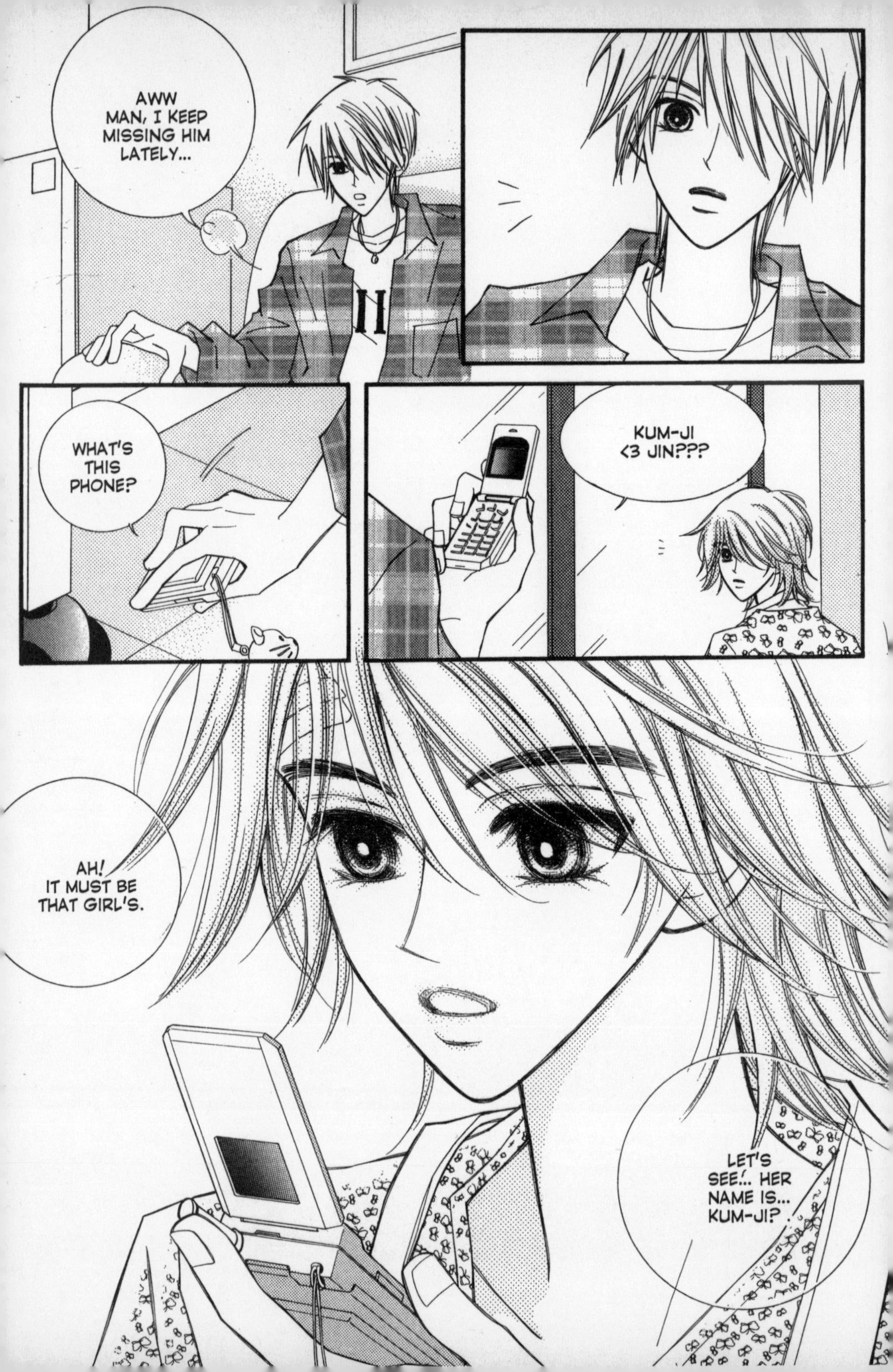
AWW MAN, I KEEP MISSING HIM LATELY...
WHAT'S THIS PHONE?
KUM-JI <3 JIN???
AH! IT MUST BE THAT GIRL'S.
LET'S SEE... HER NAME IS... KUM-JI?

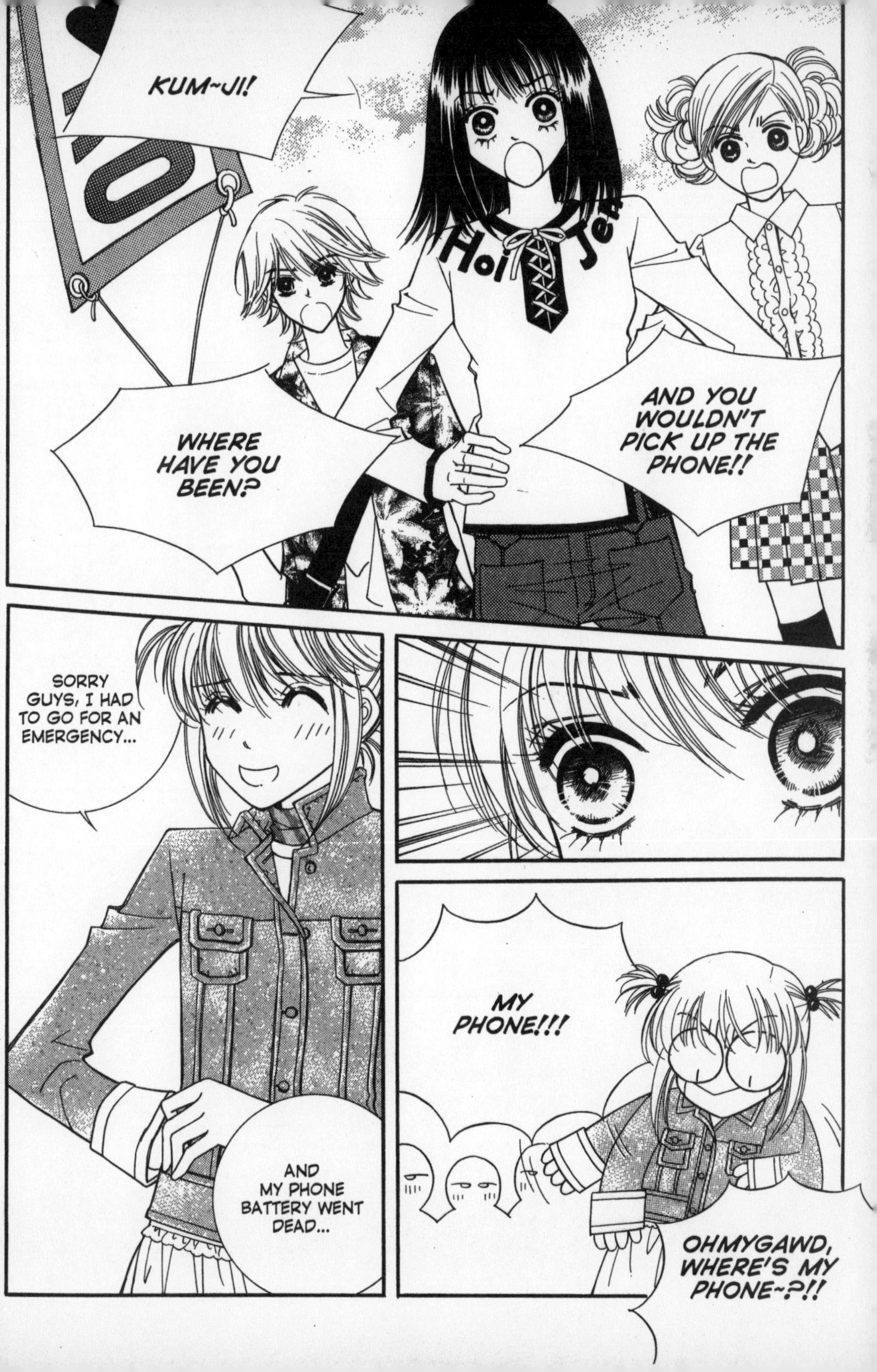
KUM~JI!
WHERE HAVE YOU BEEN?
AND YOU WOULDN'T PICK UP THE PHONE!!
SORRY GUYS, I HAD TO GO FOR AN EMERGENCY...
AND MY PHONE BATTERY WENT DEAD...
MY PHONE!!!
OHMYGAWD, WHERE'S MY PHONE~?!!

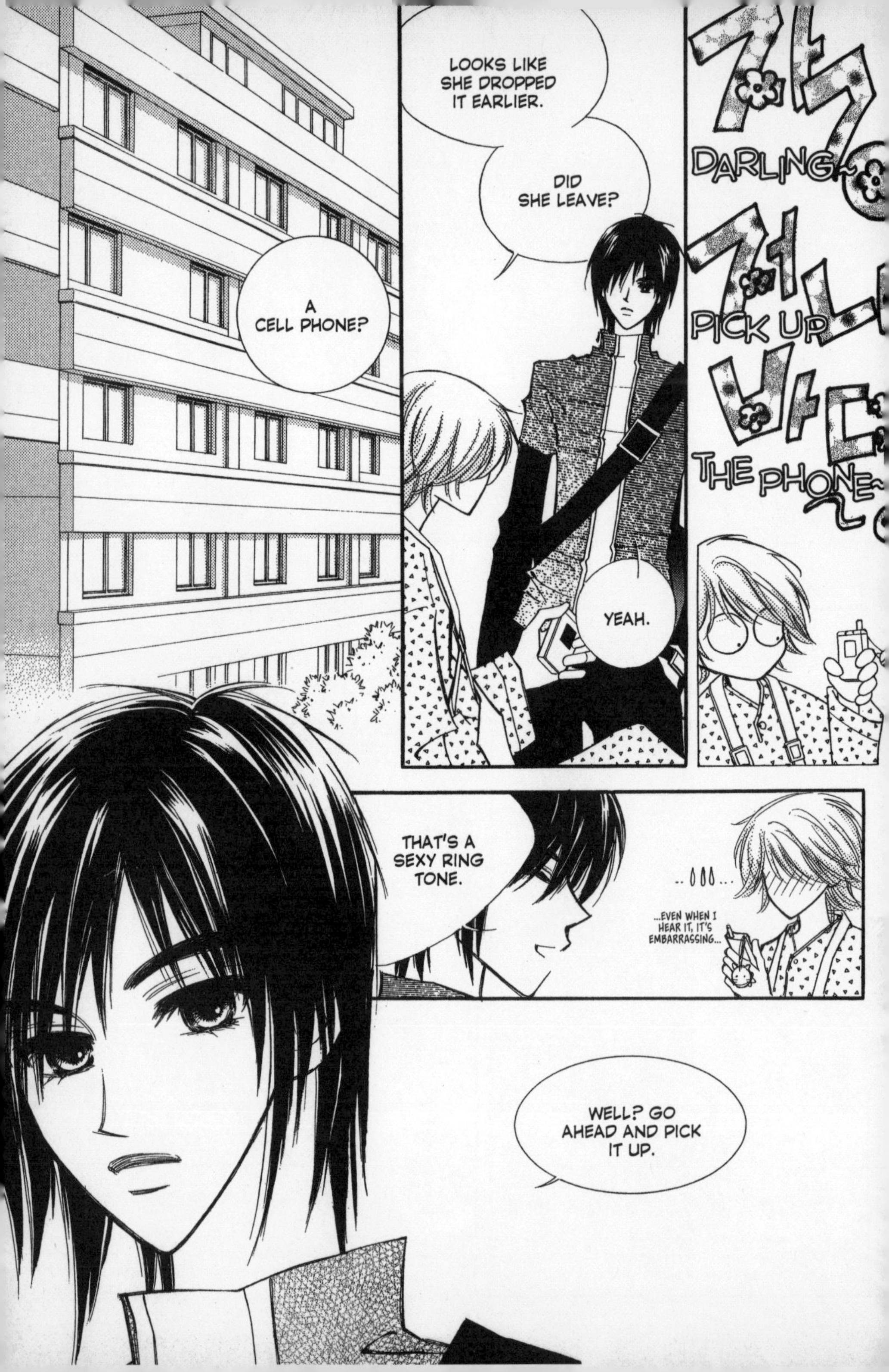
A CELL PHONE?
LOOKS LIKE SHE DROPPED IT EARLIER.
DID SHE LEAVE?
YEAH.
DARLING~ PICK UP THE PHONE~
THAT'S A SEXY RING TONE.
...EVEN WHEN I HEAR IT, IT'S EMBARRASSING...
WELL? GO AHEAD AND PICK IT UP.

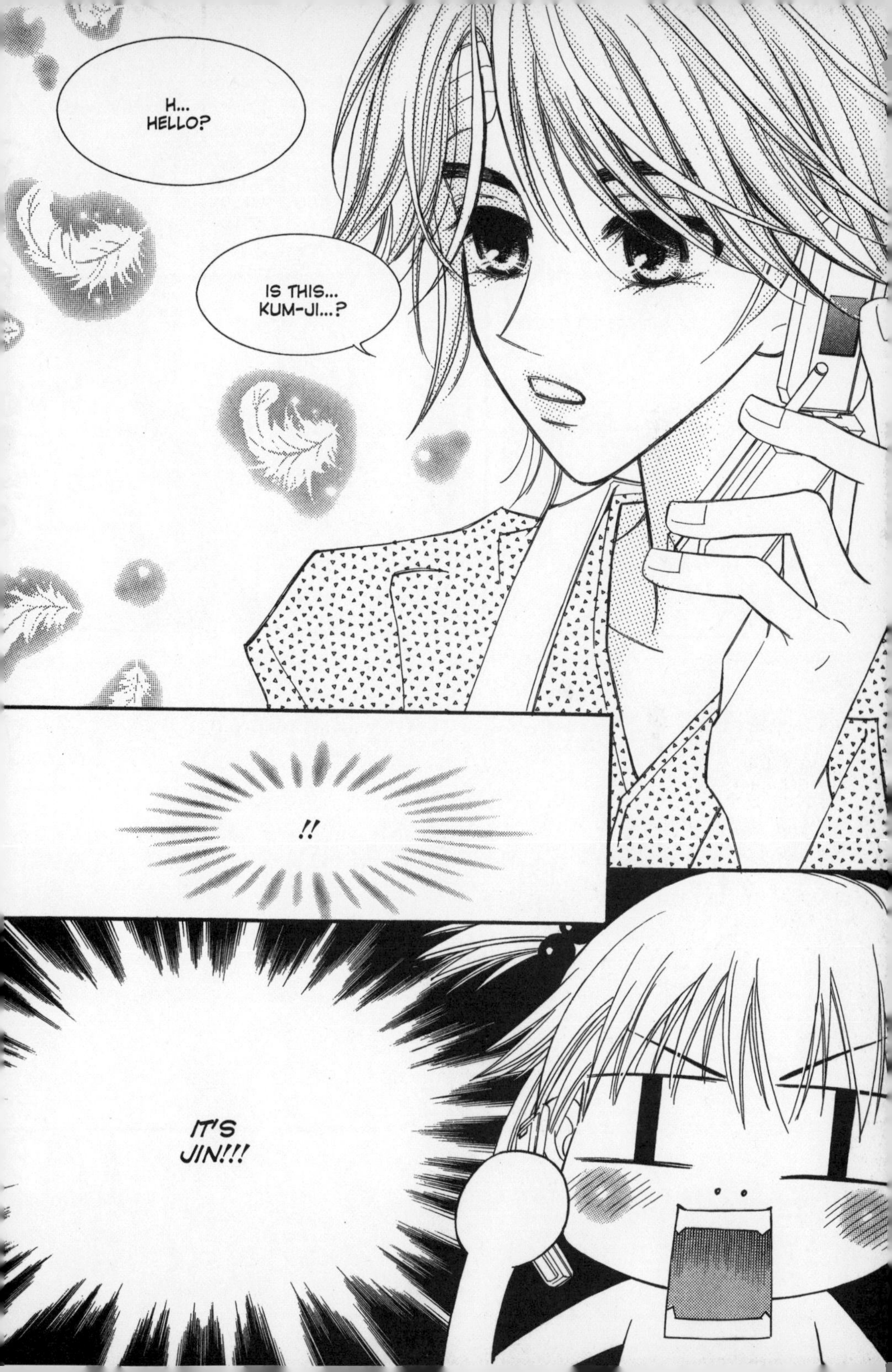
H... HELLO?
IS THIS... KUM-JI...?
!!
IT'S JIN!!!

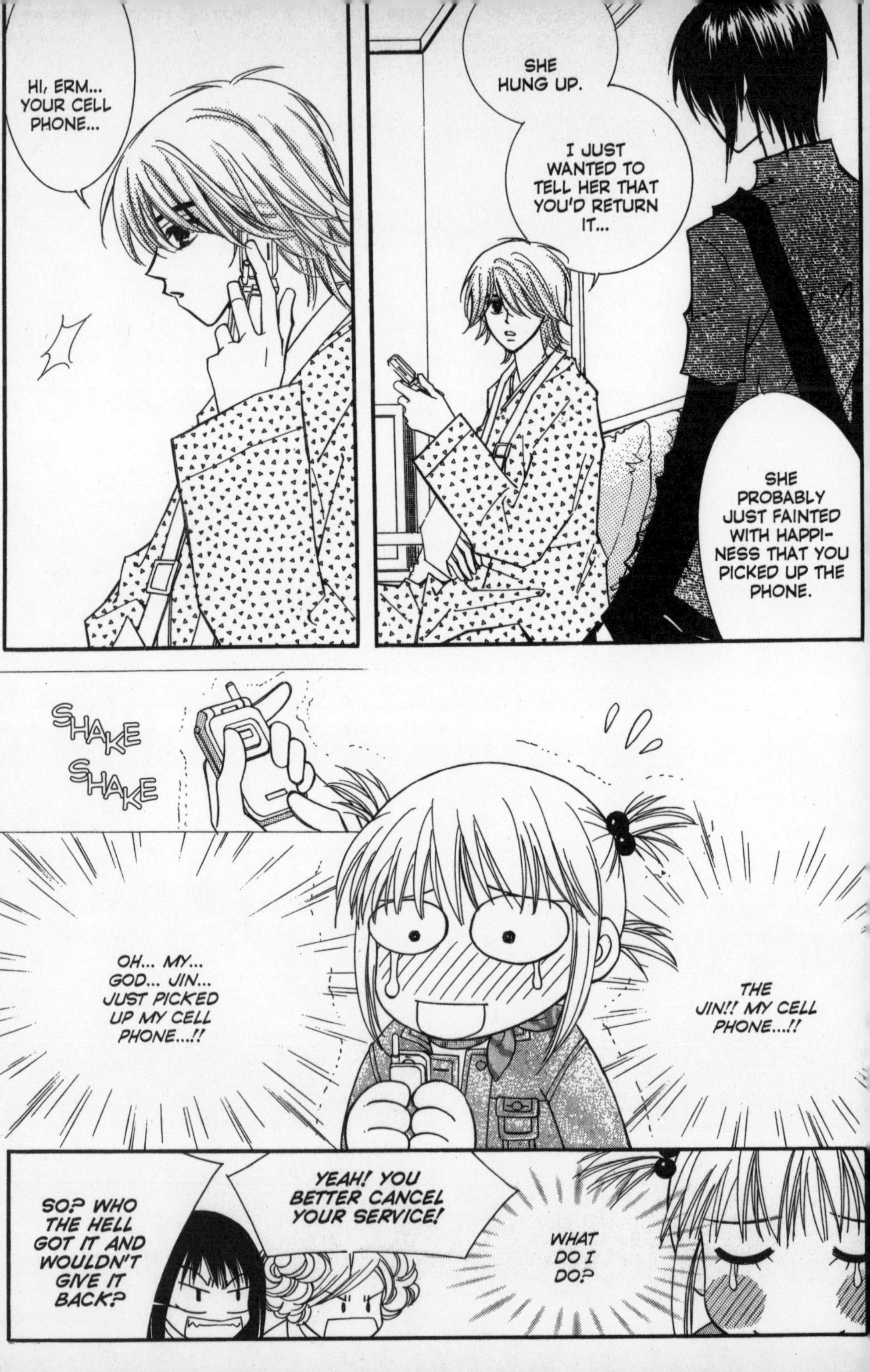
HI, ERM... YOUR CELL PHONE...
SHE HUNG UP.
I JUST WANTED TO TELL HER THAT YOU'D RETURN IT...
SHE PROBABLY JUST FAINTED WITH HAPPINESS THAT YOU PICKED UP THE PHONE.
SHAKE
SHAKE
OH... MY... GOD... JIN... JUST PICKED UP MY CELL PHONE...!!
THE JIN!! MY CELL PHONE...!!
SO? WHO THE HELL GOT IT AND WOULDN'T GIVE IT BACK?
YEAH! YOU BETTER CANCEL YOUR SERVICE!
WHAT DO I DO?

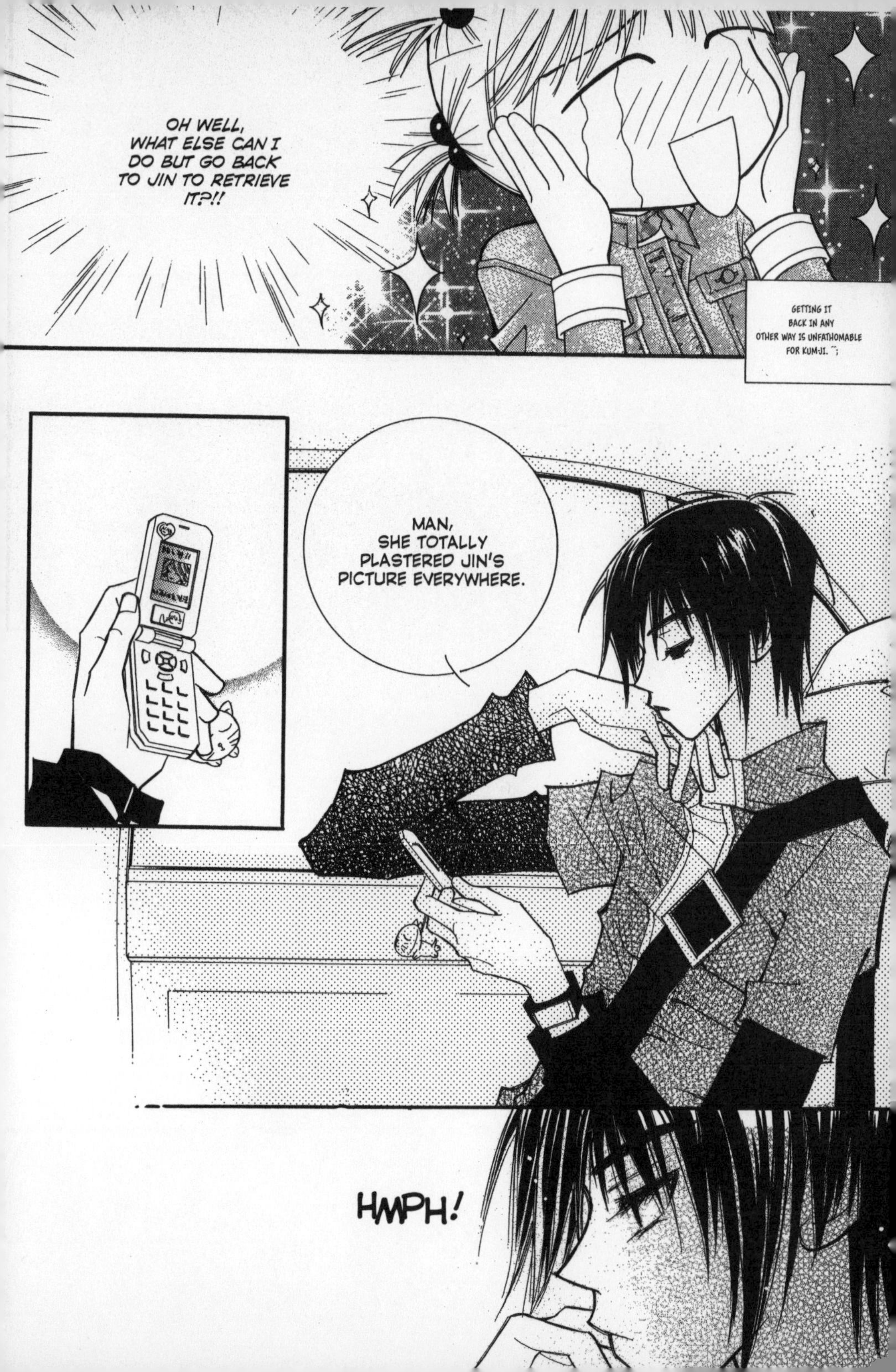
OH WELL, WHAT ELSE CAN I DO BUT GO BACK TO JIN TO RETRIEVE IT?!!
GETTING IT BACK IN ANY OTHER WAY IS UNFATHOMABLE FOR KUM-JI. ^^;
MAN, SHE TOTALLY PLASTERED JIN'S PICTURE EVERYWHERE.
HMPH!

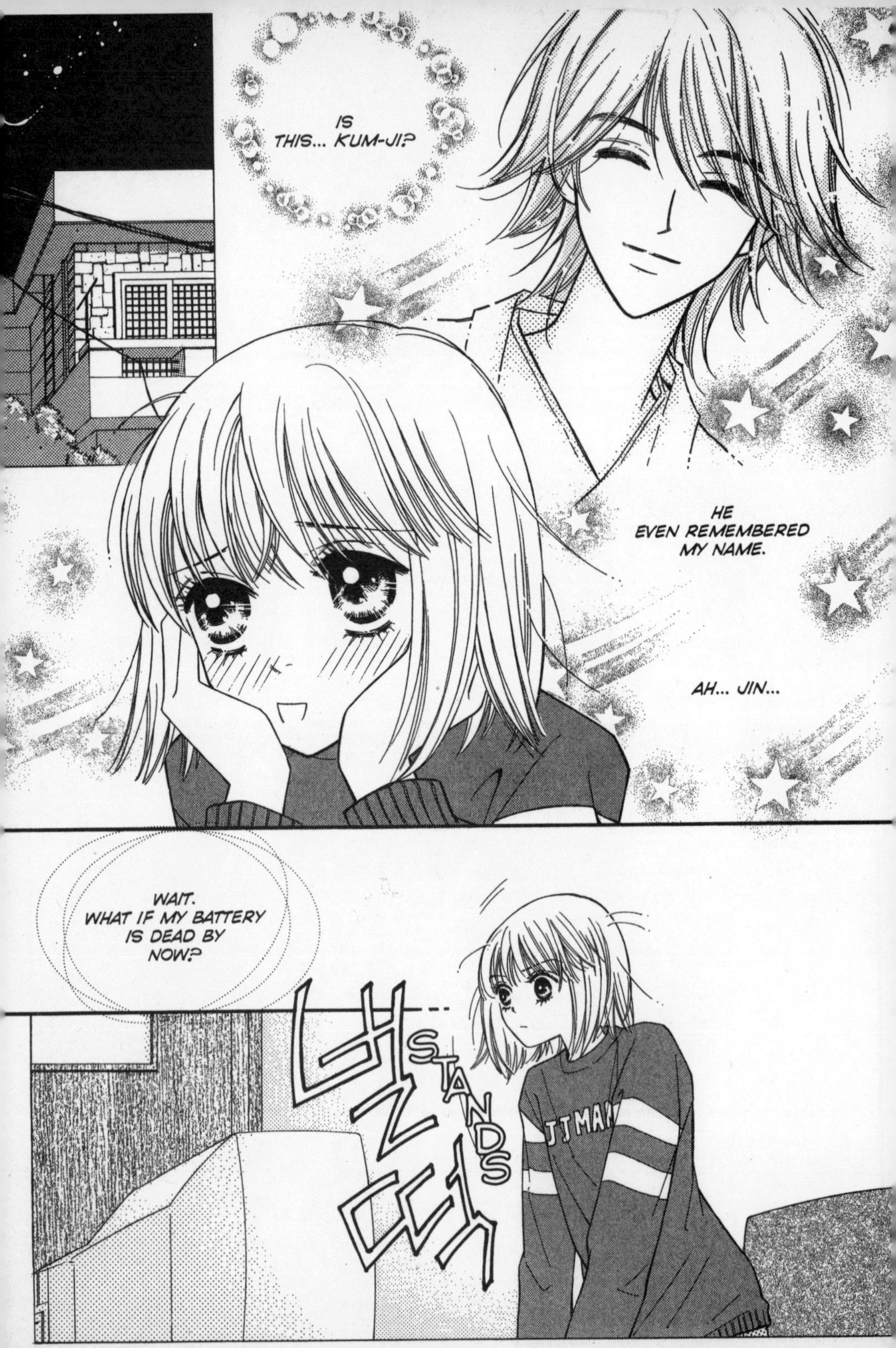
IS THIS... KUM-JI?
HE EVEN REMEMBERED MY NAME.
AH... JIN...
WAIT. WHAT IF MY BATTERY IS DEAD BY NOW?
STANDS

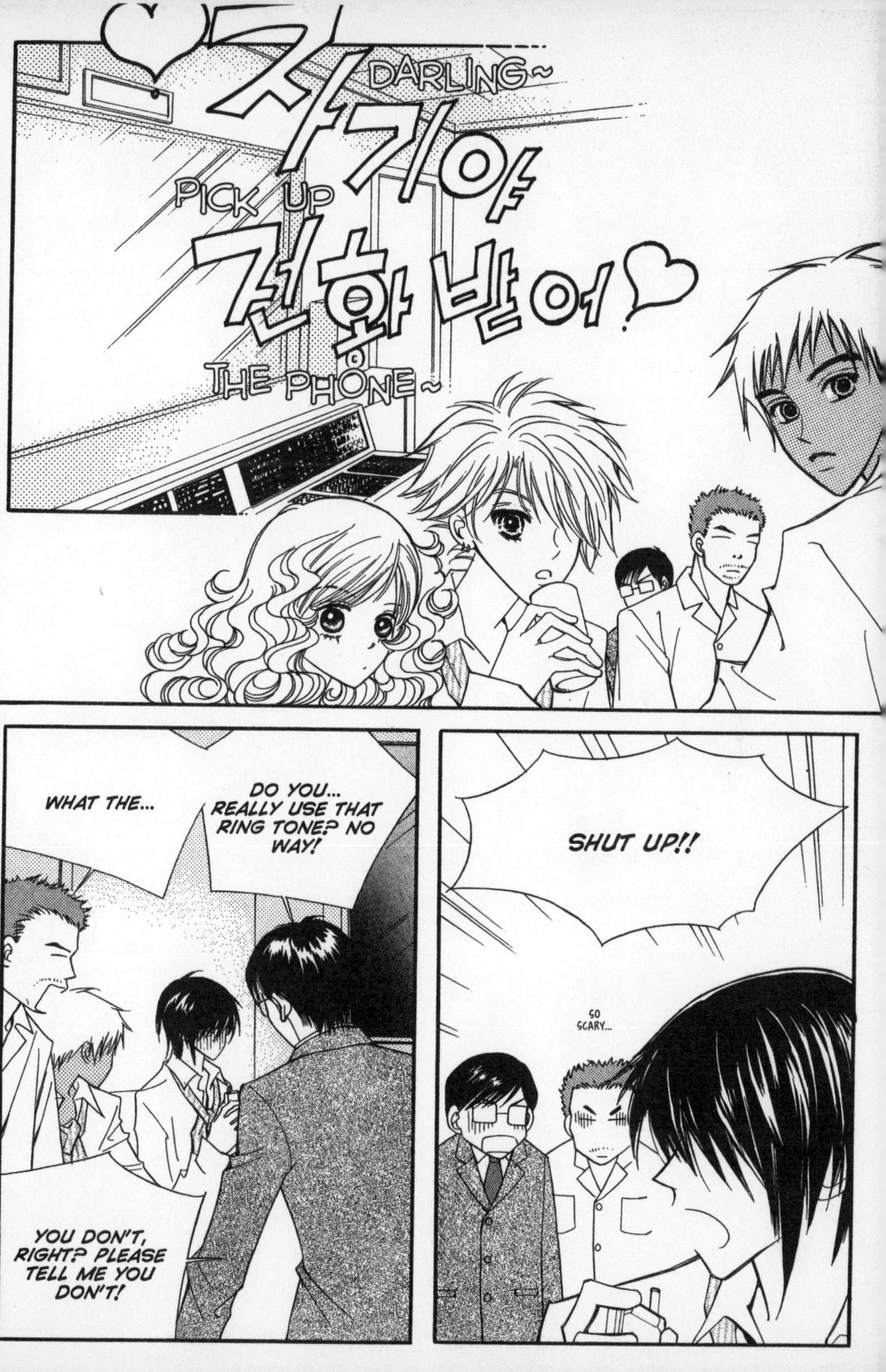
자기야
DARLING~
전화받아
PICK UP
THE PHONE~
WHAT THE...
DO YOU... REALLY USE THAT RING TONE? NO WAY!
YOU DON'T, RIGHT? PLEASE TELL ME YOU DON'T!
SHUT UP!!
SO SCARY...

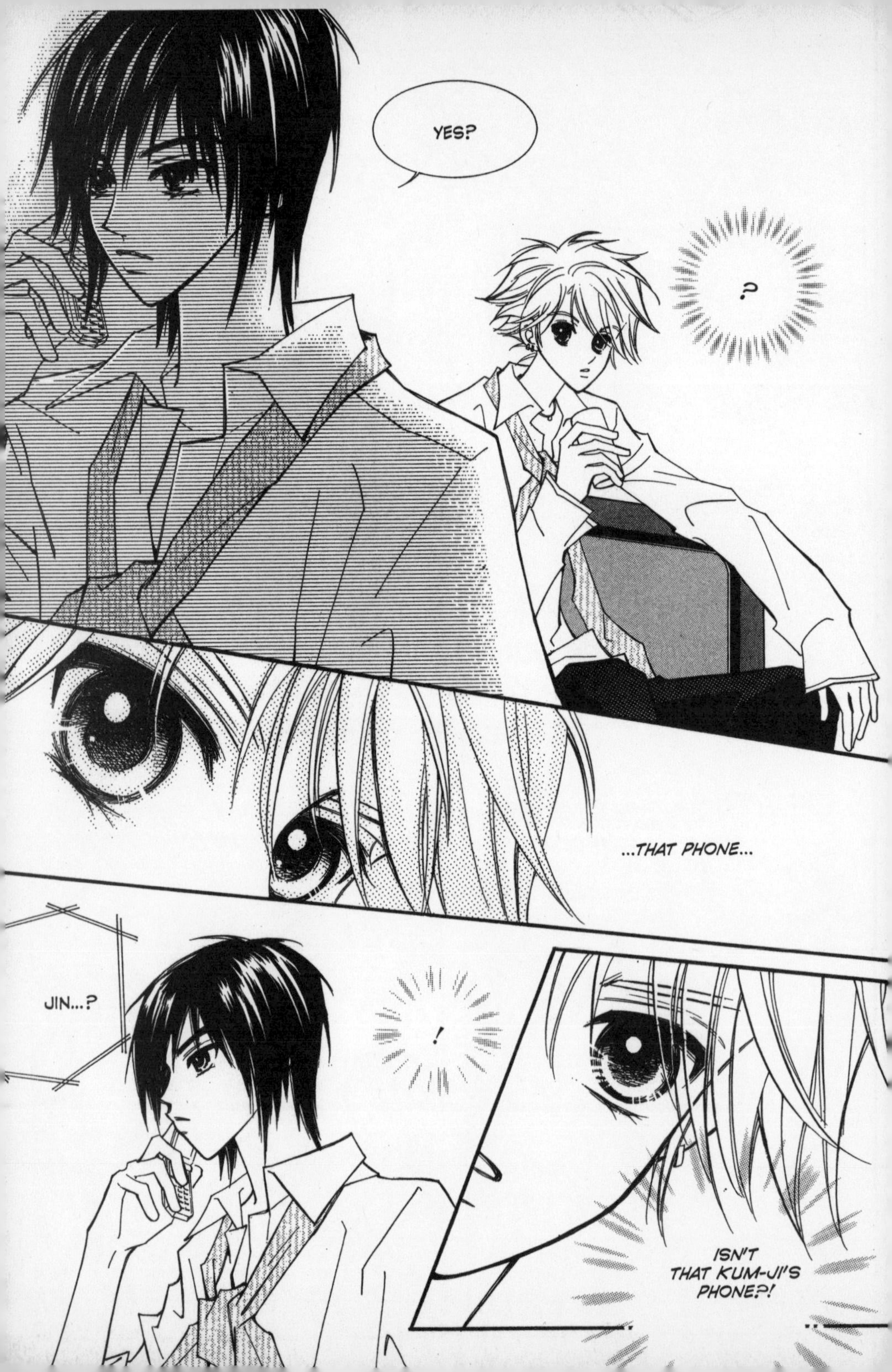
YES?
?
...THAT PHONE...
JIN...?
!
ISN'T THAT KUM-JI'S PHONE?!

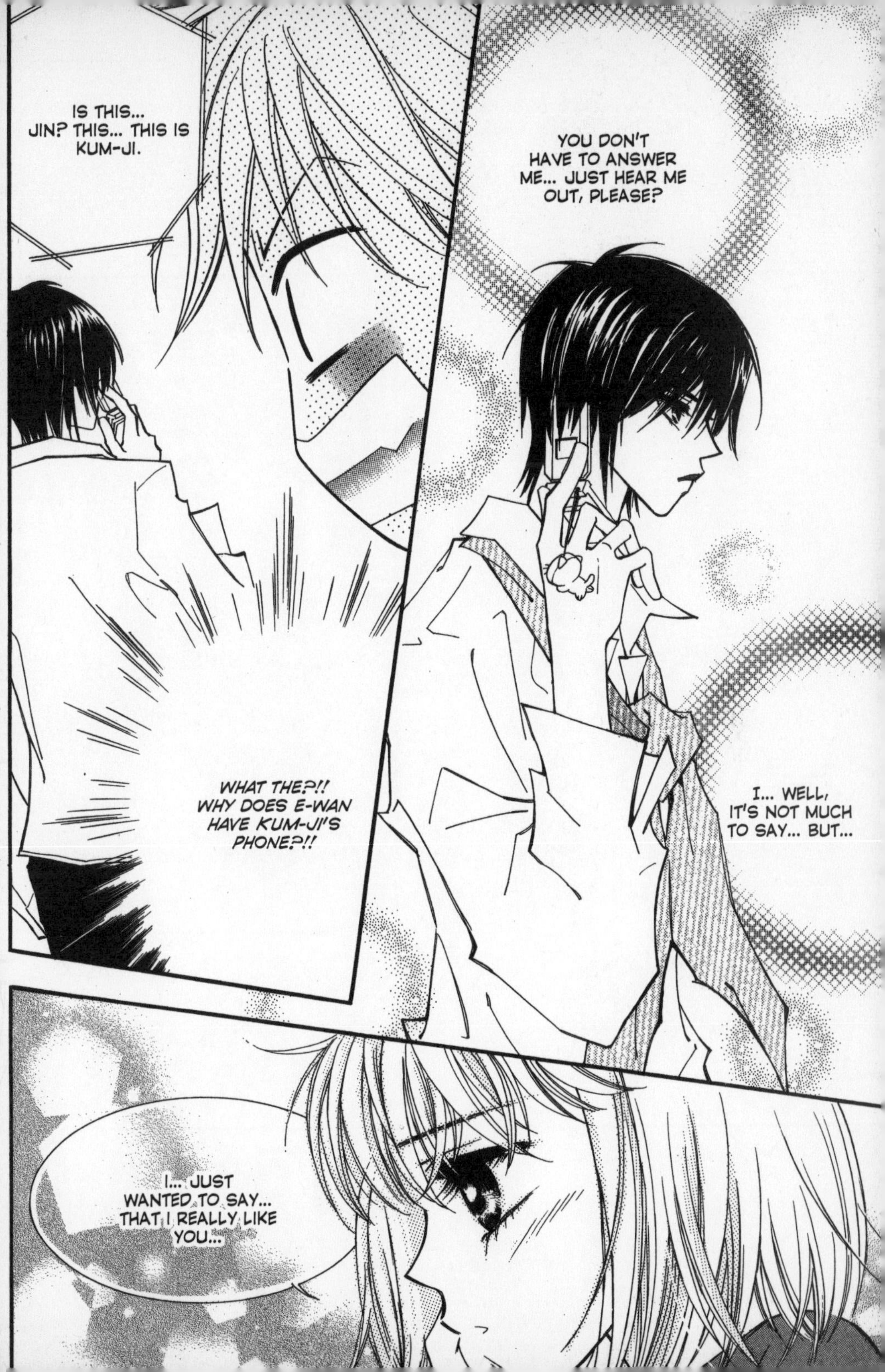
IS THIS... JIN? THIS... THIS IS KUM-JI.
WHAT THE?!! WHY DOES E-WAN HAVE KUM-JI'S PHONE?!!
YOU DON'T HAVE TO ANSWER ME... JUST HEAR ME OUT, PLEASE?
I... WELL, IT'S NOT MUCH TO SAY... BUT...
I... JUST WANTED TO SAY... THAT I REALLY LIKE YOU...

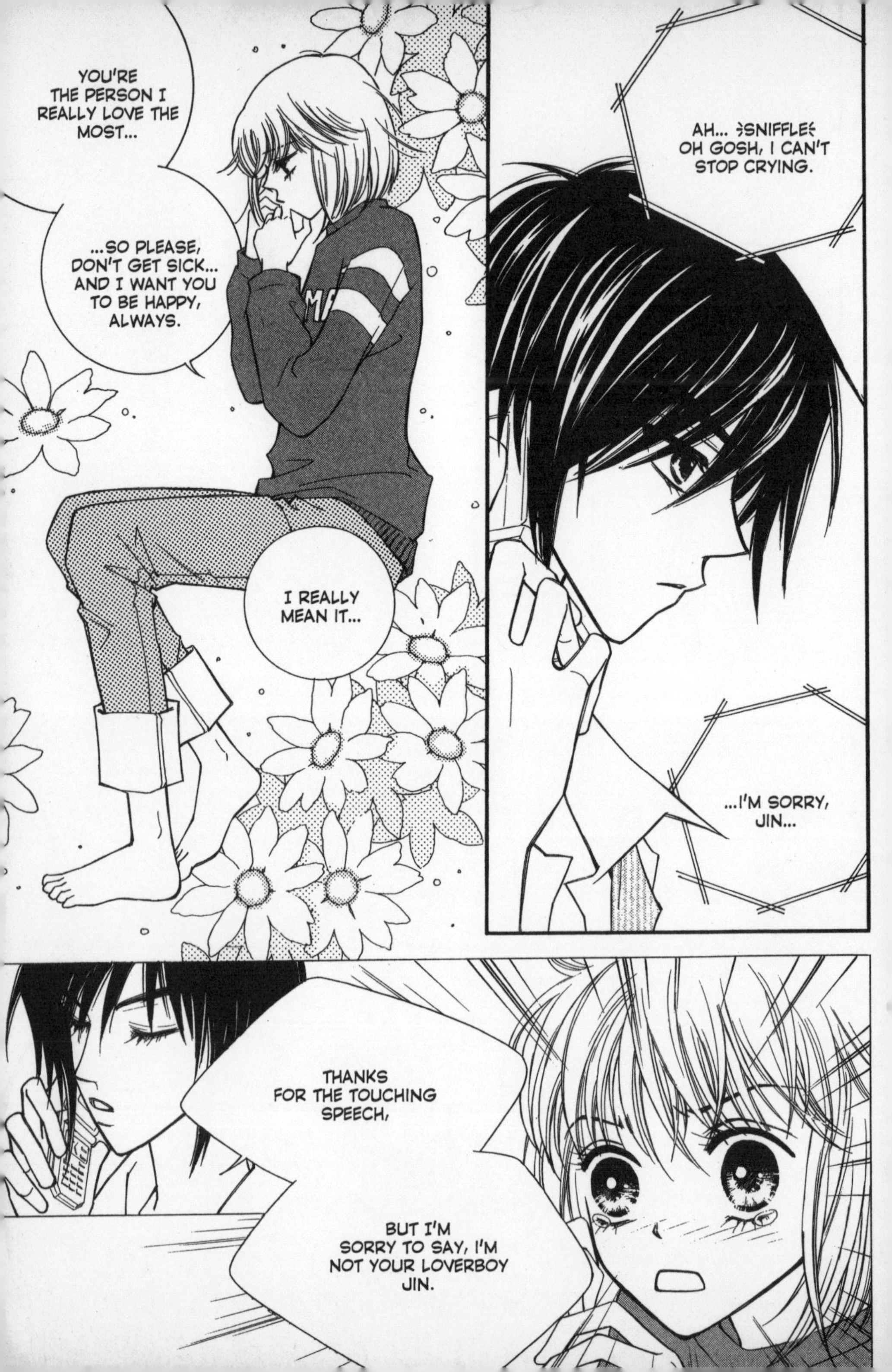
YOU'RE THE PERSON I REALLY LOVE THE MOST...
...SO PLEASE, DON'T GET SICK... AND I WANT YOU TO BE HAPPY, ALWAYS.
I REALLY MEAN IT...
AH... ⋟SNIFFLE⋞ OH GOSH, I CAN'T STOP CRYING.
...I'M SORRY, JIN...
THANKS FOR THE TOUCHING SPEECH,
BUT I'M SORRY TO SAY, I'M NOT YOUR LOVERBOY JIN.

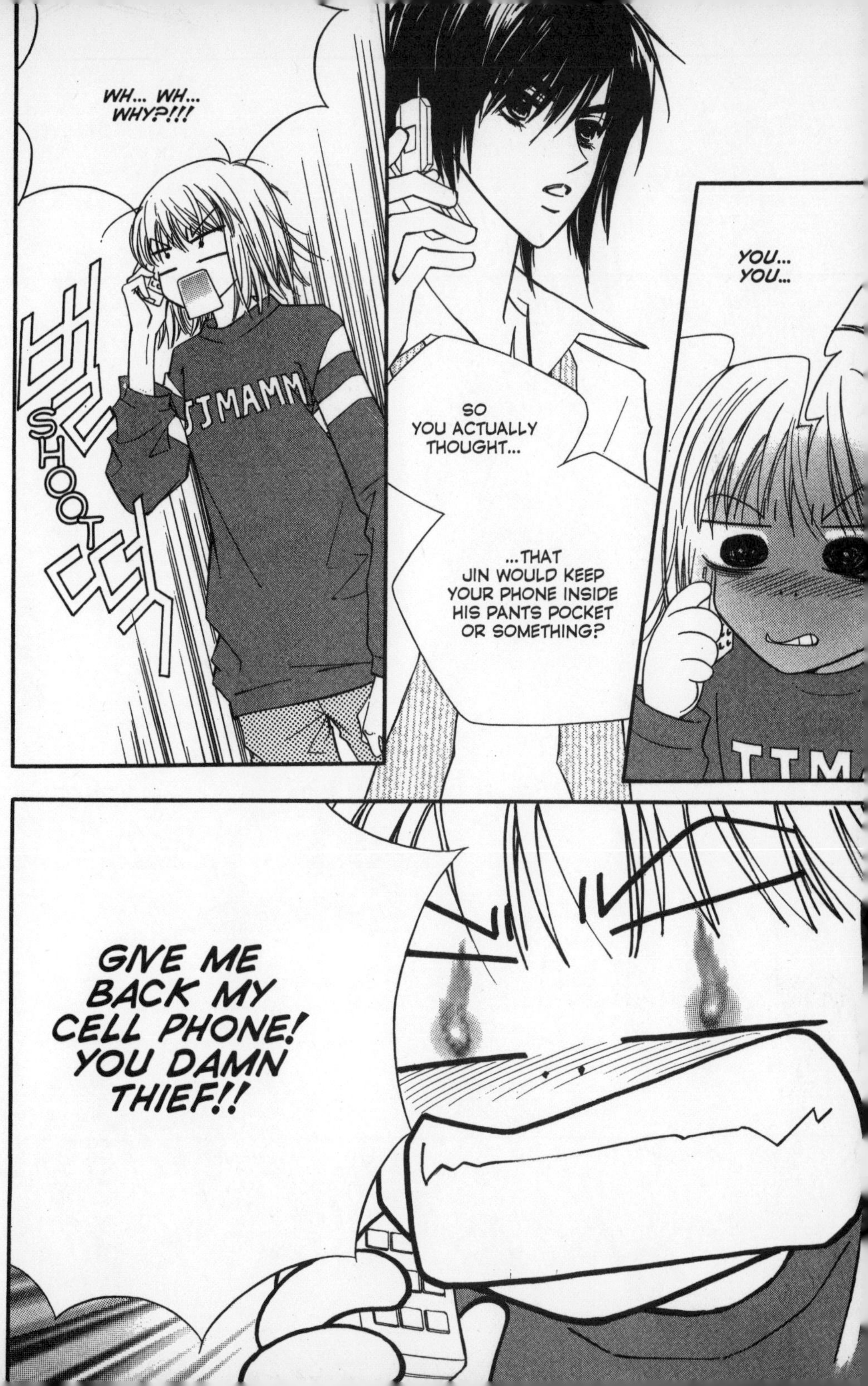
WH... WH... WHY?!!!
SHOOT
SO YOU ACTUALLY THOUGHT...
...THAT JIN WOULD KEEP YOUR PHONE INSIDE HIS PANTS POCKET OR SOMETHING?
YOU... YOU...
GIVE ME BACK MY CELL PHONE! YOU DAMN THIEF!!

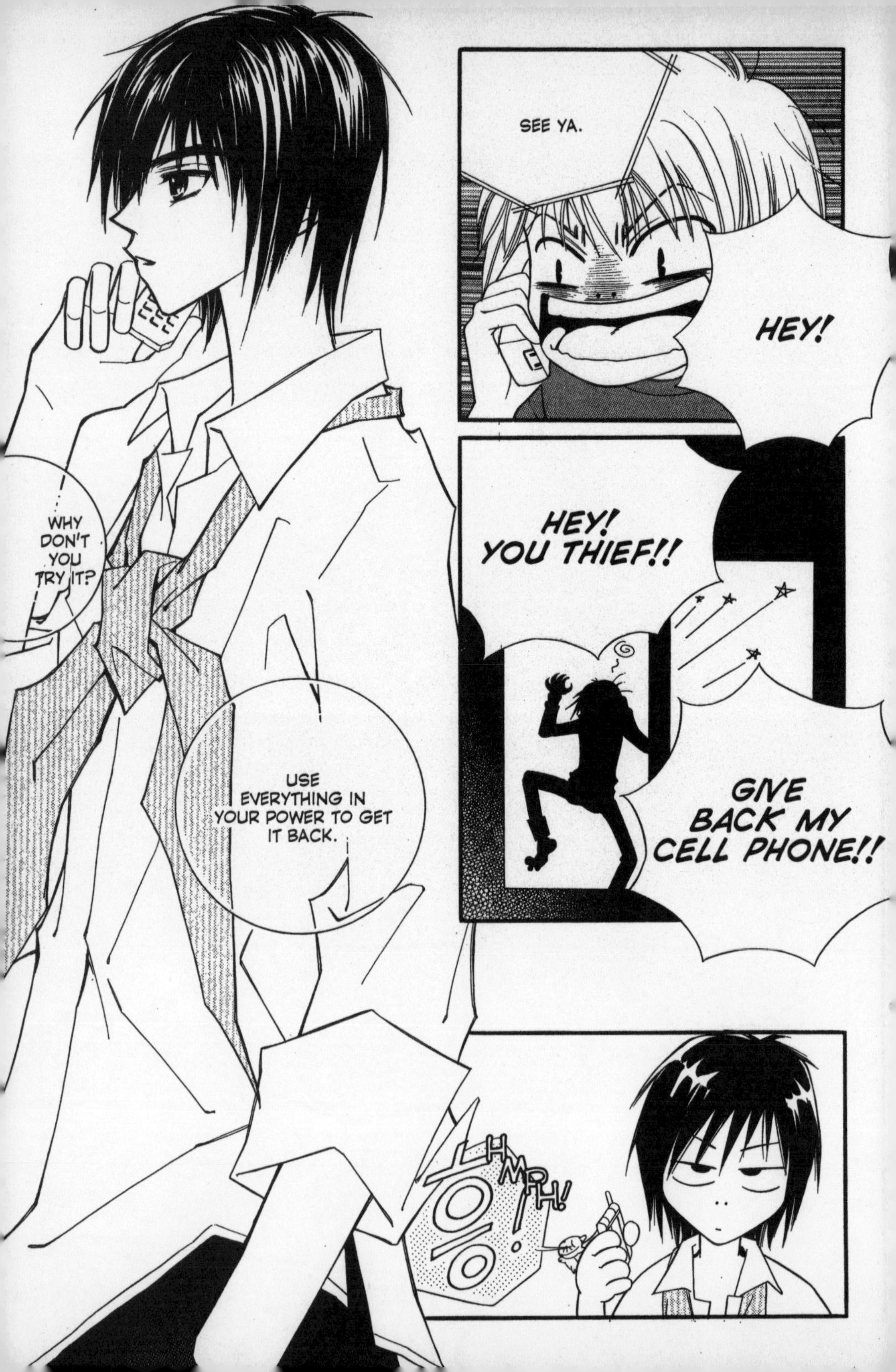
WHY DON'T YOU TRY IT?
USE EVERYTHING IN YOUR POWER TO GET IT BACK.
SEE YA.
HEY!
HEY! YOU THIEF!!
GIVE BACK MY CELL PHONE!!
HMPH!

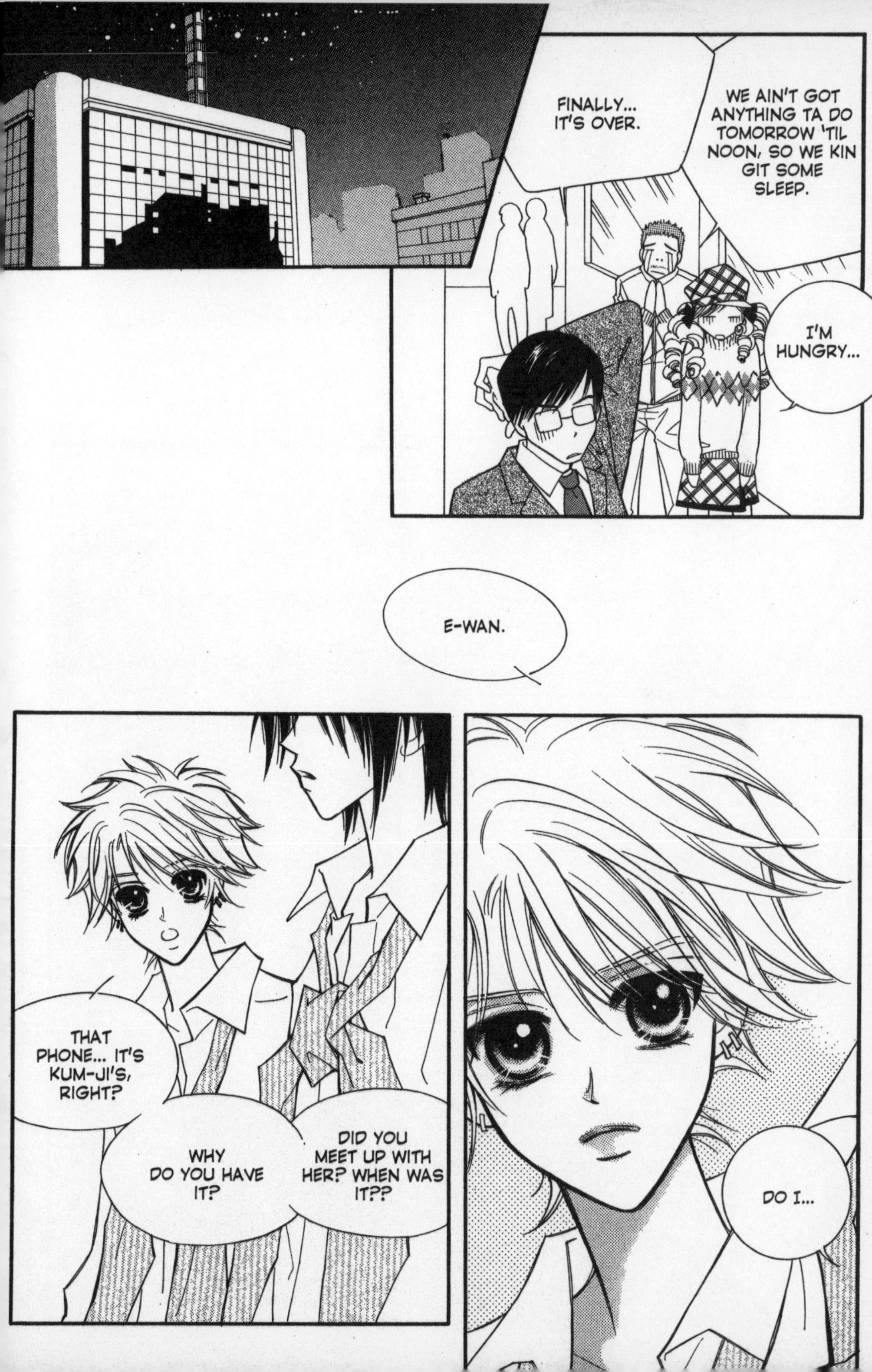
FINALLY... IT'S OVER.
WE AIN'T GOT ANYTHING TA DO TOMORROW 'TIL NOON, SO WE KIN GIT SOME SLEEP.
I'M HUNGRY...
E-WAN.
THAT PHONE... IT'S KUM-JI'S, RIGHT?
WHY DO YOU HAVE IT?
DID YOU MEET UP WITH HER? WHEN WAS IT??
DO I...

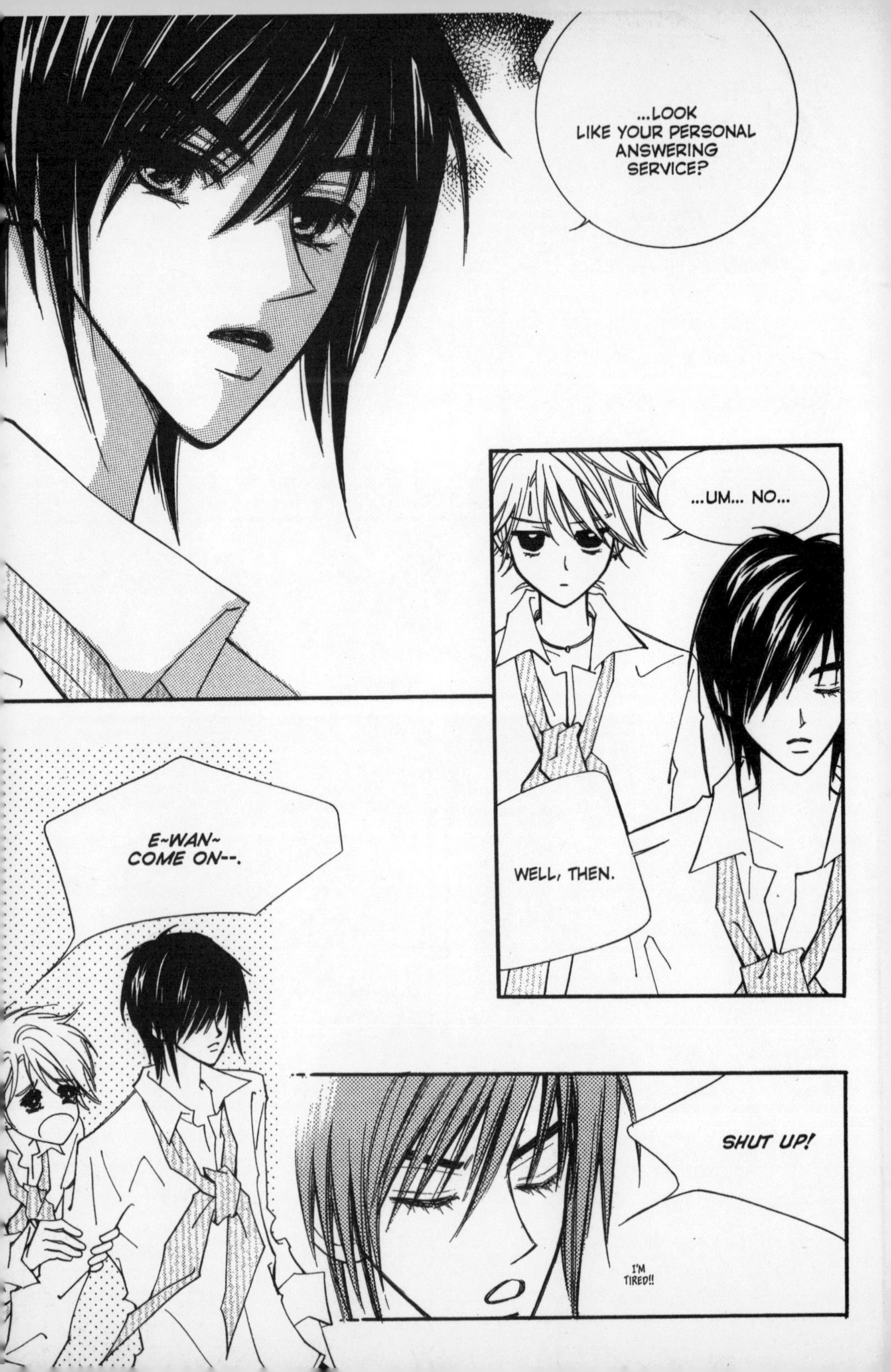
...LOOK LIKE YOUR PERSONAL ANSWERING SERVICE?
...UM... NO...
WELL, THEN.
E~WAN~ COME ON--.
SHUT UP!
I'M TIRED!!

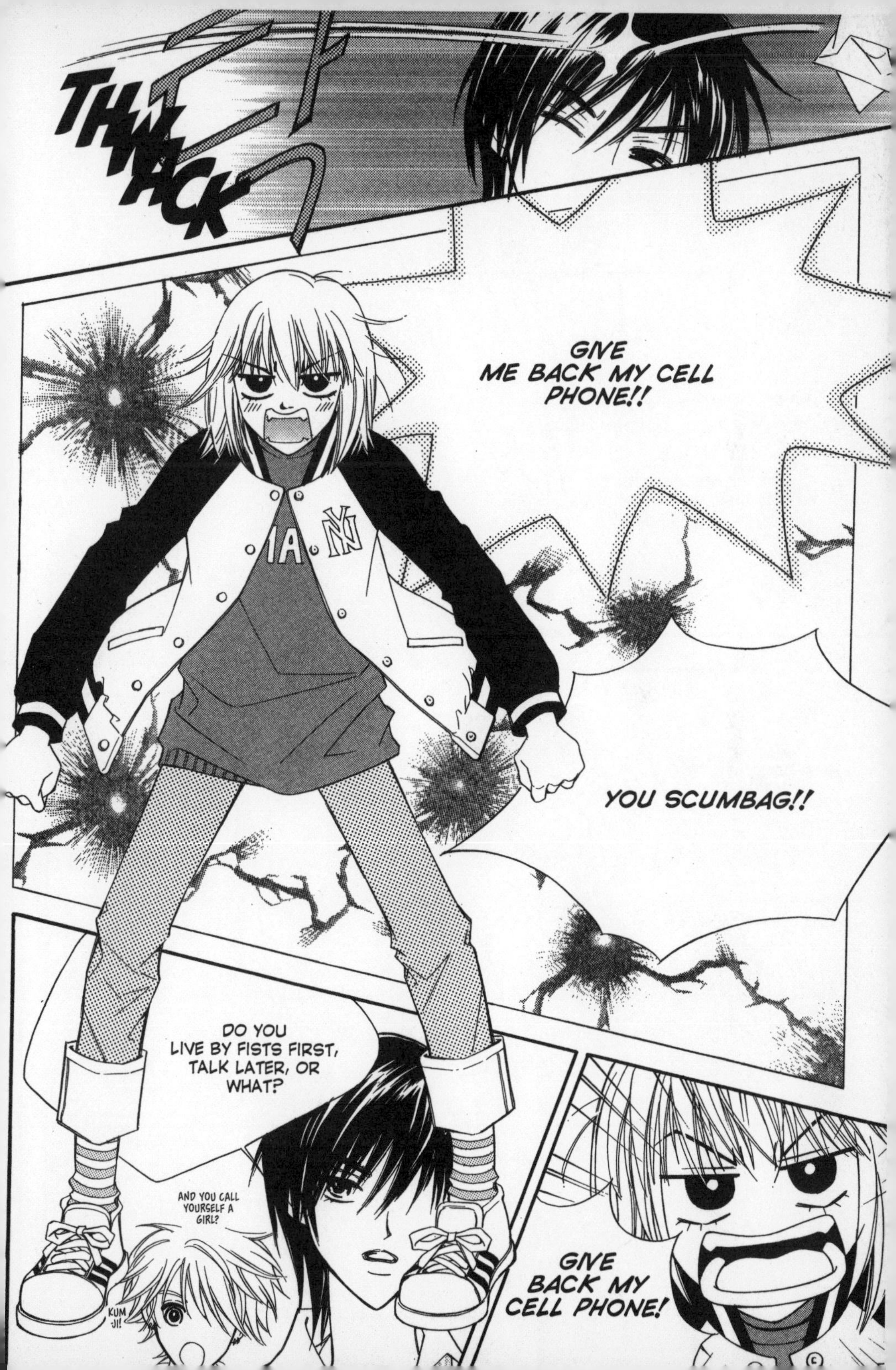
THWACK
GIVE ME BACK MY CELL PHONE!!
YOU SCUMBAG!!
DO YOU LIVE BY FISTS FIRST, TALK LATER, OR WHAT?
AND YOU CALL YOURSELF A GIRL?
KUM JI!
GIVE BACK MY CELL PHONE!

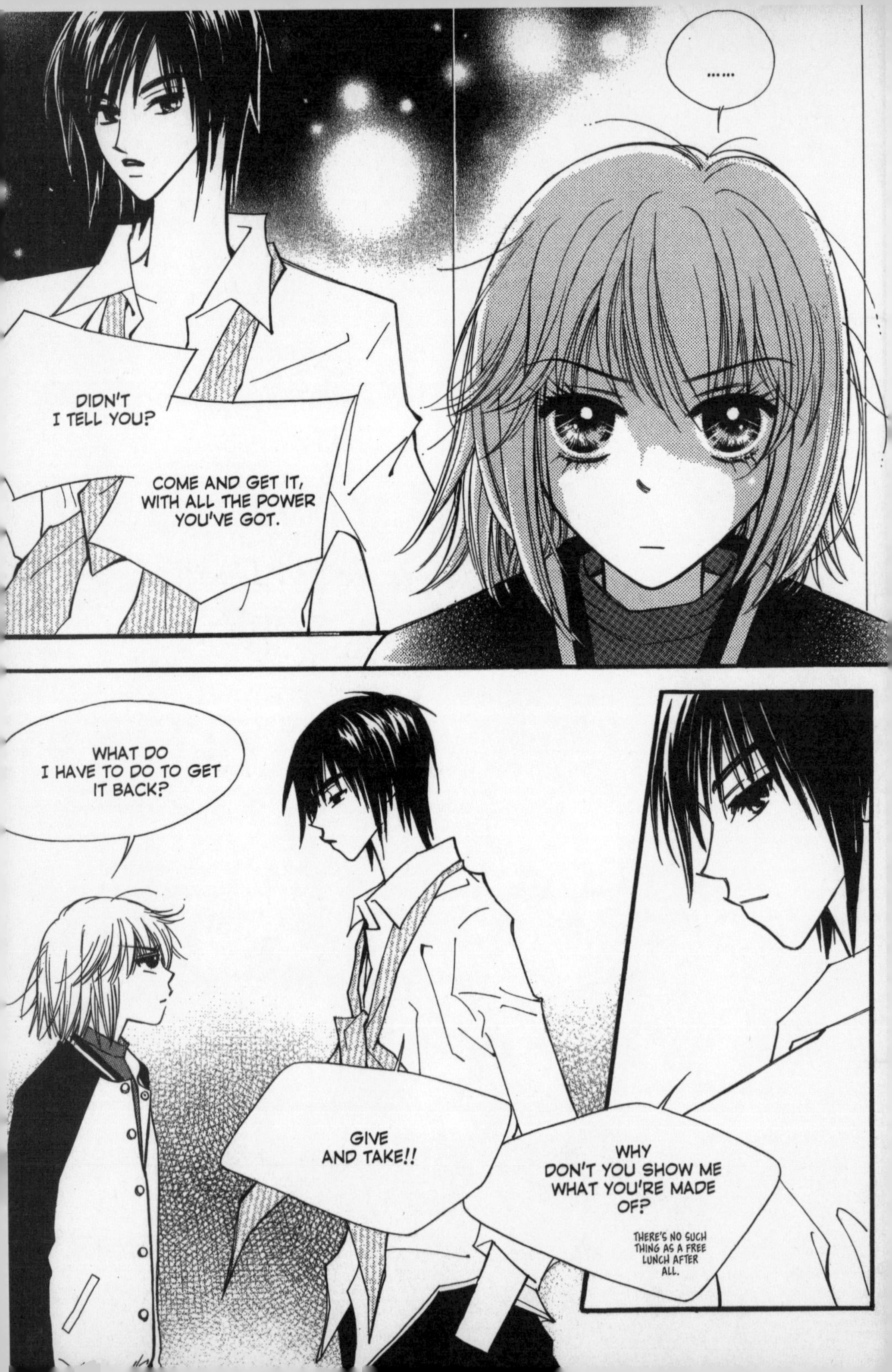
DIDN'T I TELL YOU?
COME AND GET IT, WITH ALL THE POWER YOU'VE GOT.
......
WHAT DO I HAVE TO DO TO GET IT BACK?
GIVE AND TAKE!!
WHY DON'T YOU SHOW ME WHAT YOU'RE MADE OF?
THERE'S NO SUCH THING AS A FREE LUNCH AFTER ALL.

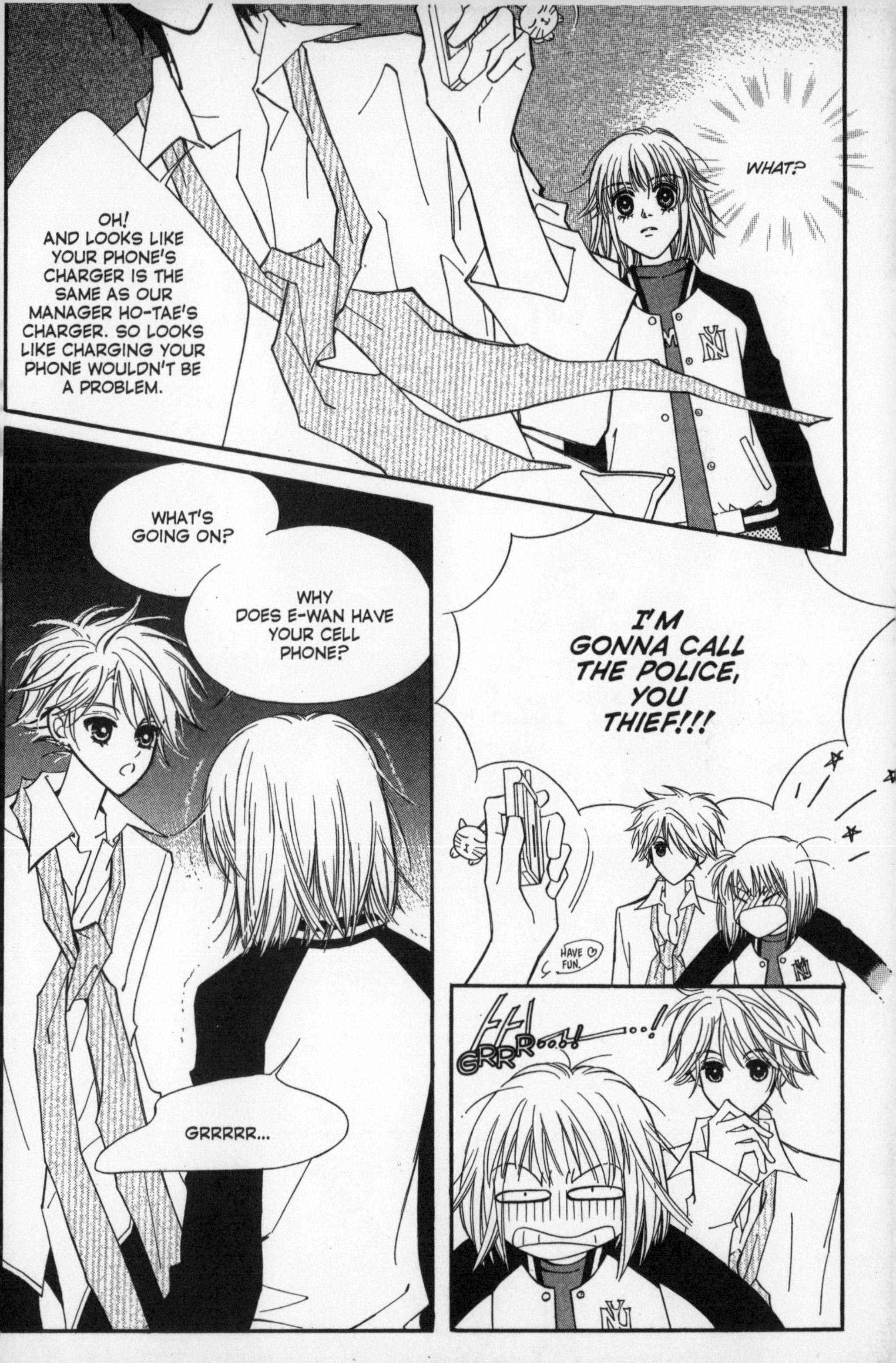
OH!
AND LOOKS LIKE YOUR PHONE'S CHARGER IS THE SAME AS OUR MANAGER HO-TAE'S CHARGER. SO LOOKS LIKE CHARGING YOUR PHONE WOULDN'T BE A PROBLEM.
WHAT?
WHAT'S GOING ON?
WHY DOES E-WAN HAVE YOUR CELL PHONE?
GRRRRR...
I'M GONNA CALL THE POLICE, YOU THIEF!!!
HAVE FUN.

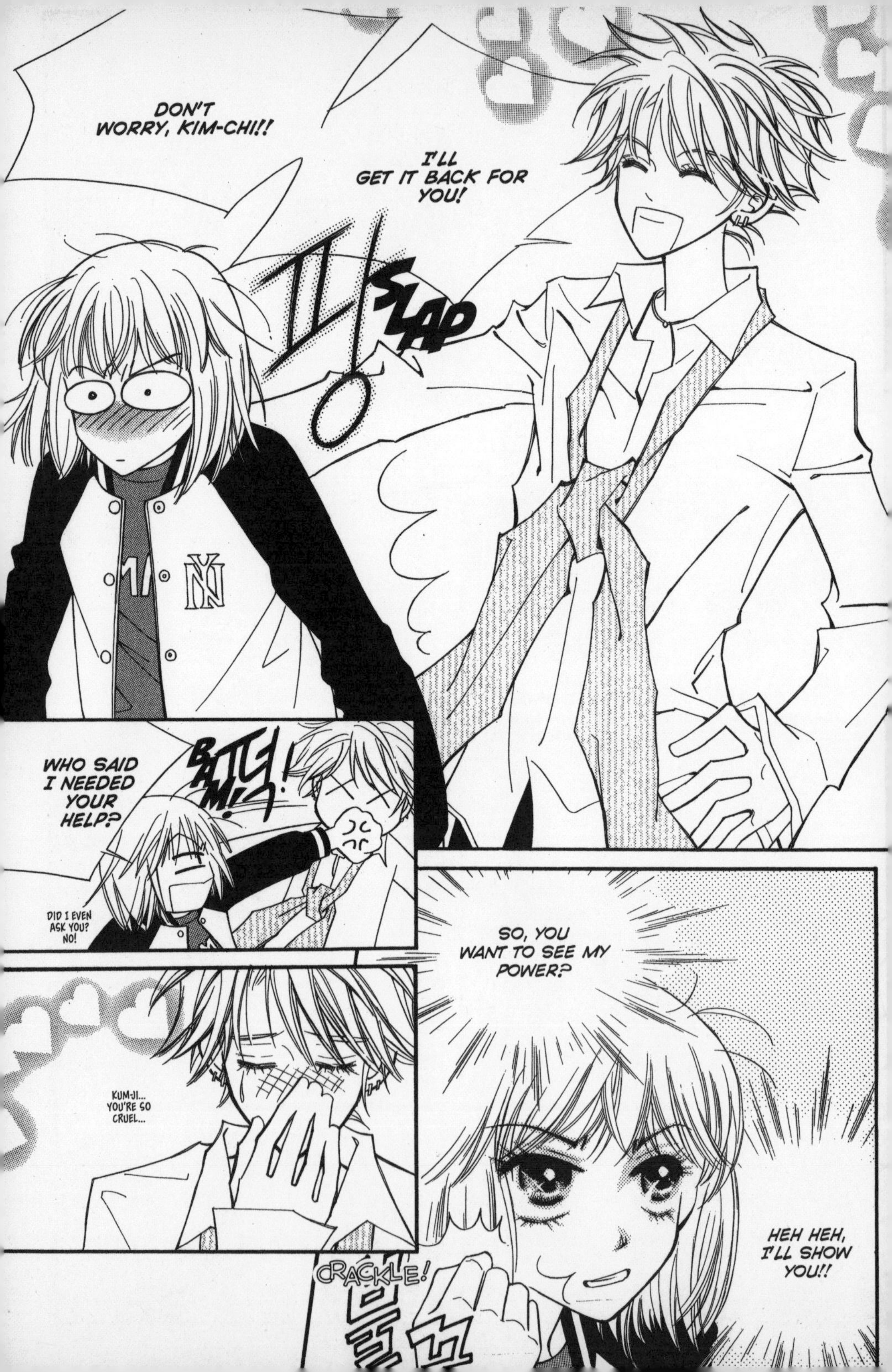
DON'T WORRY, KIM-CHI!!
I'LL GET IT BACK FOR YOU!
SLAP
WHO SAID I NEEDED YOUR HELP?
BAM!
DID I EVEN ASK YOU? NO!
KUM-JI... YOU'RE SO CRUEL...
SO, YOU WANT TO SEE MY POWER?
HEH HEH, I'LL SHOW YOU!!
CRACKLE!

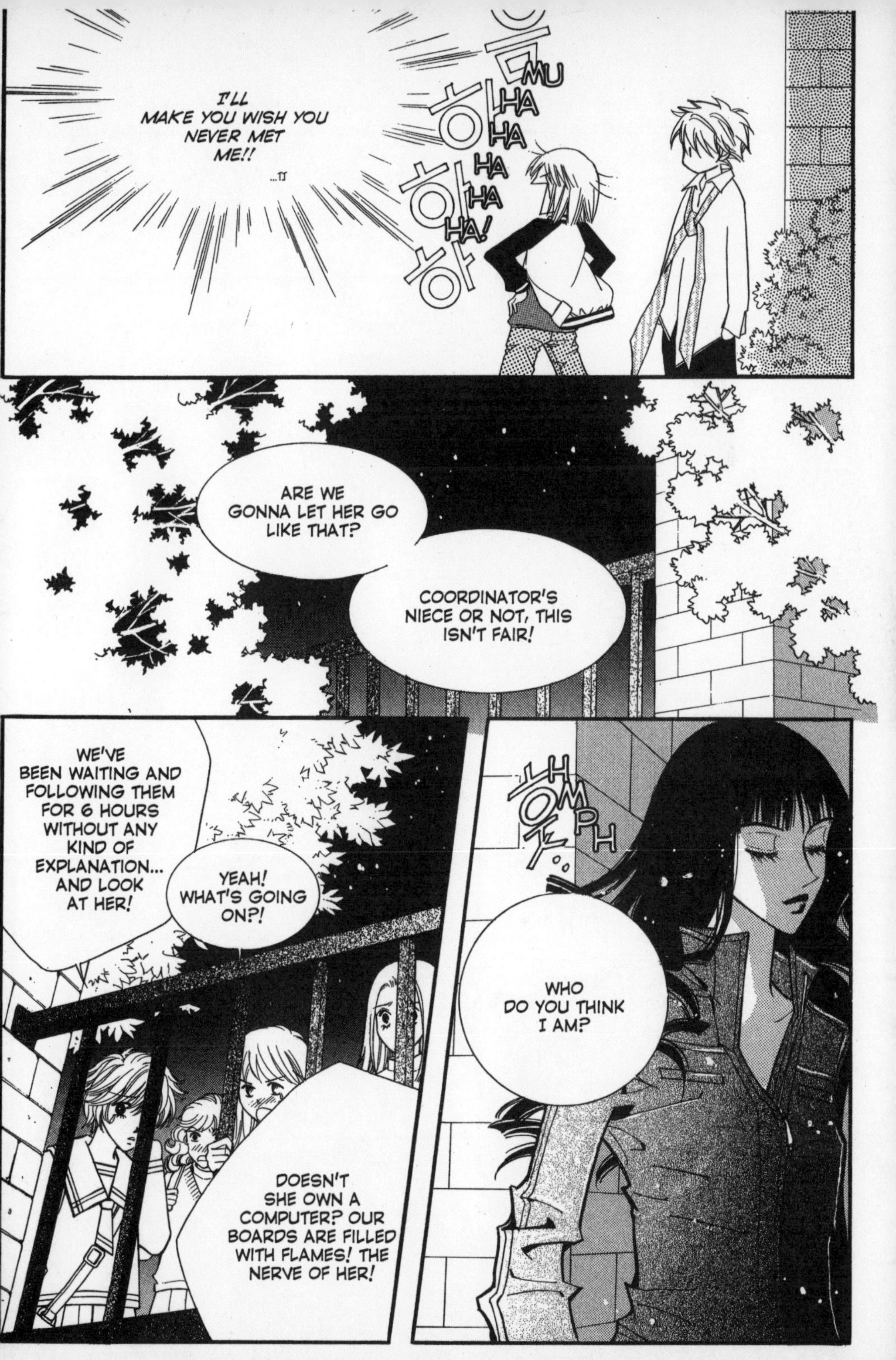

I'LL MAKE YOU WISH YOU NEVER MET ME!!
음하하하
MU HA HA HA HA HA!
ARE WE GONNA LET HER GO LIKE THAT?
COORDINATOR'S NIECE OR NOT, THIS ISN'T FAIR!
WE'VE BEEN WAITING AND FOLLOWING THEM FOR 6 HOURS WITHOUT ANY KIND OF EXPLANATION... AND LOOK AT HER!
YEAH! WHAT'S GOING ON?!
DOESN'T SHE OWN A COMPUTER? OUR BOARDS ARE FILLED WITH FLAMES! THE NERVE OF HER!
HMPH
WHO DO YOU THINK I AM?

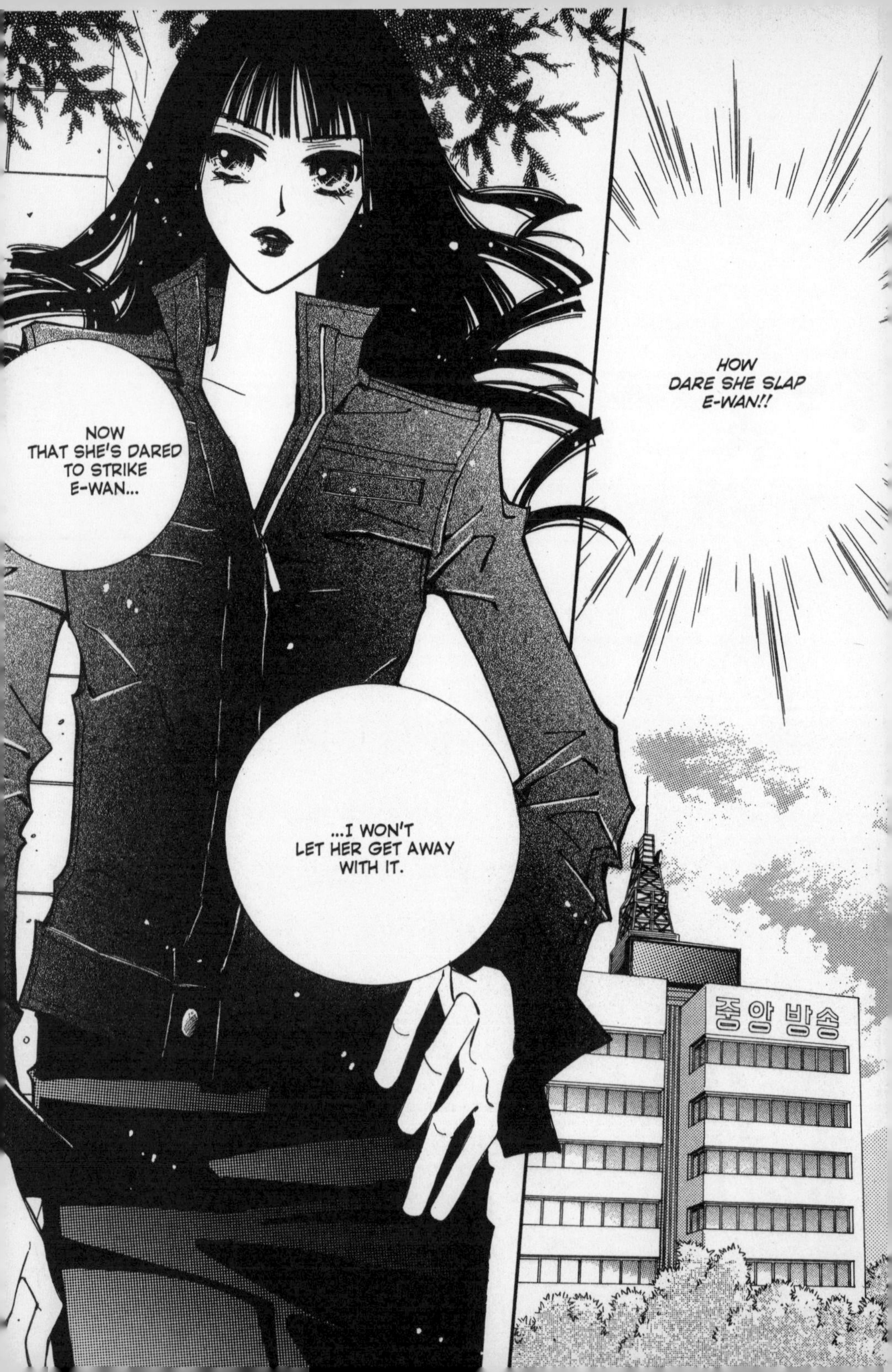
NOW THAT SHE'S DARED TO STRIKE E-WAN...
...I WON'T LET HER GET AWAY WITH IT.
HOW DARE SHE SLAP E-WAN!!
중앙 방송

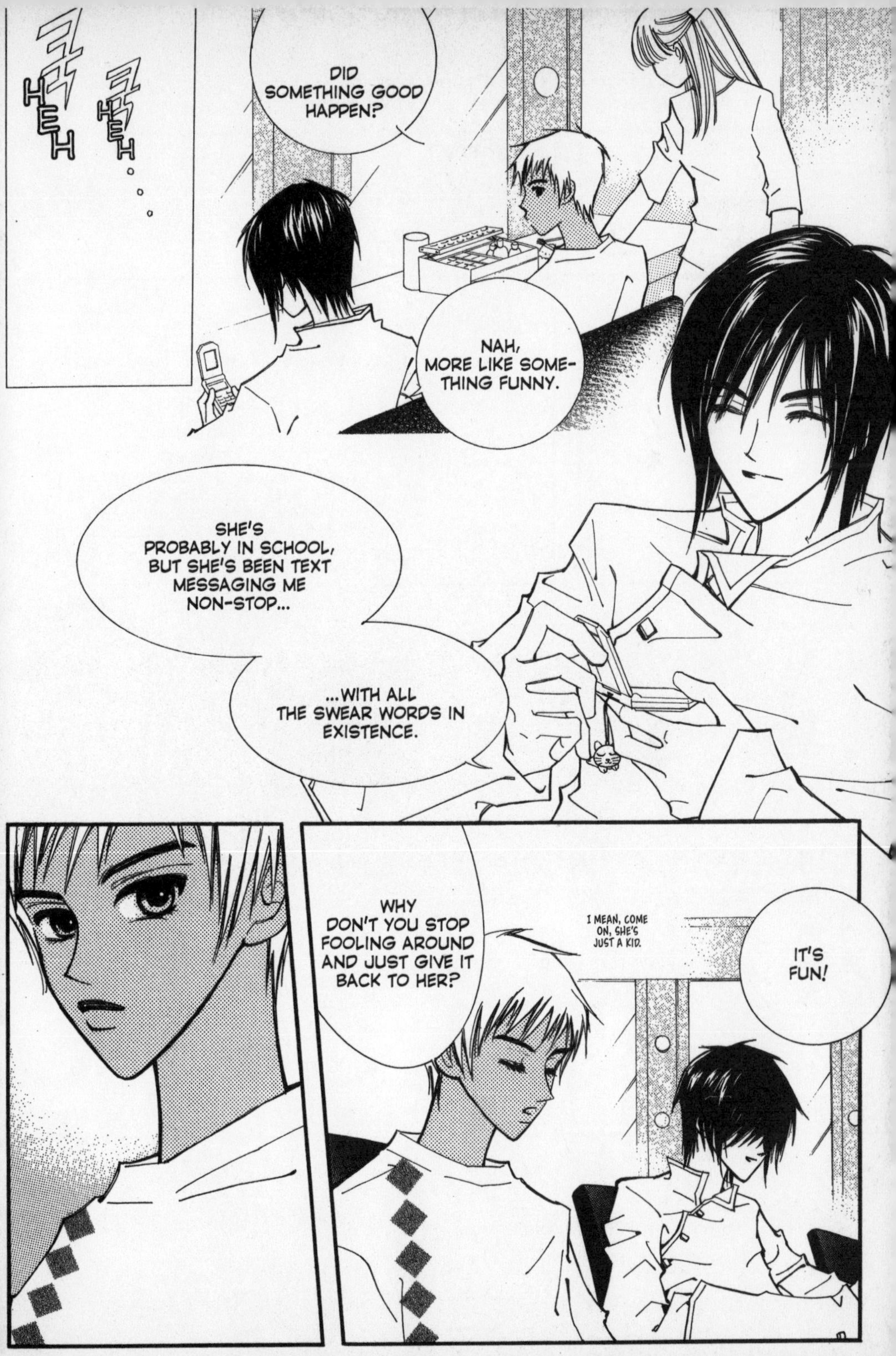
HEH HEH
HEH HEH
DID SOMETHING GOOD HAPPEN?
NAH, MORE LIKE SOME-THING FUNNY.
SHE'S PROBABLY IN SCHOOL, BUT SHE'S BEEN TEXT MESSAGING ME NON-STOP...
...WITH ALL THE SWEAR WORDS IN EXISTENCE.
WHY DON'T YOU STOP FOOLING AROUND AND JUST GIVE IT BACK TO HER?
I MEAN, COME ON, SHE'S JUST A KID.
IT'S FUN!

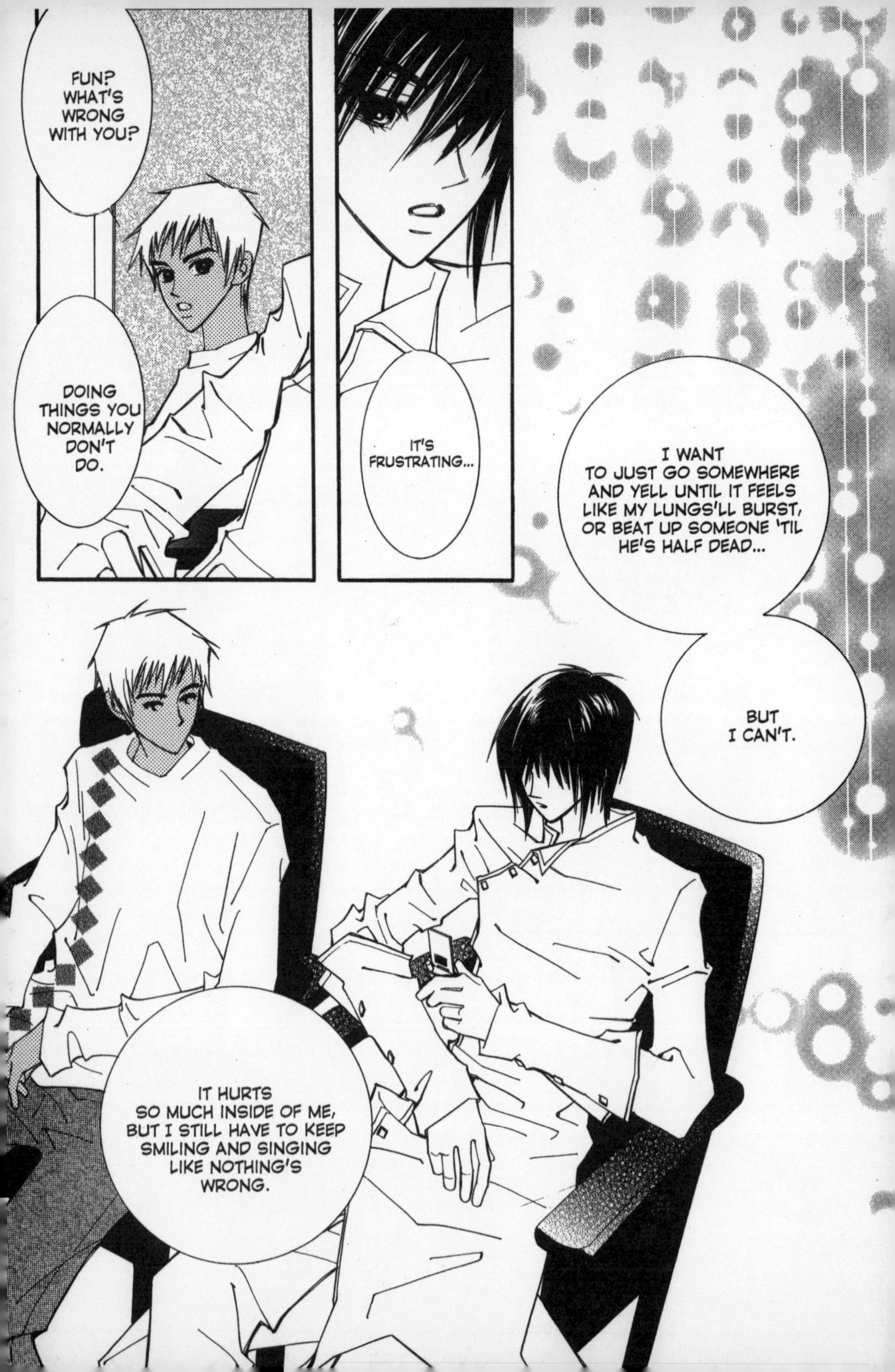
FUN? WHAT'S WRONG WITH YOU?
DOING THINGS YOU NORMALLY DON'T DO.
IT'S FRUSTRATING...
I WANT TO JUST GO SOMEWHERE AND YELL UNTIL IT FEELS LIKE MY LUNGS'LL BURST, OR BEAT UP SOMEONE 'TIL HE'S HALF DEAD...
BUT I CAN'T.
IT HURTS SO MUCH INSIDE OF ME, BUT I STILL HAVE TO KEEP SMILING AND SINGING LIKE NOTHING'S WRONG.

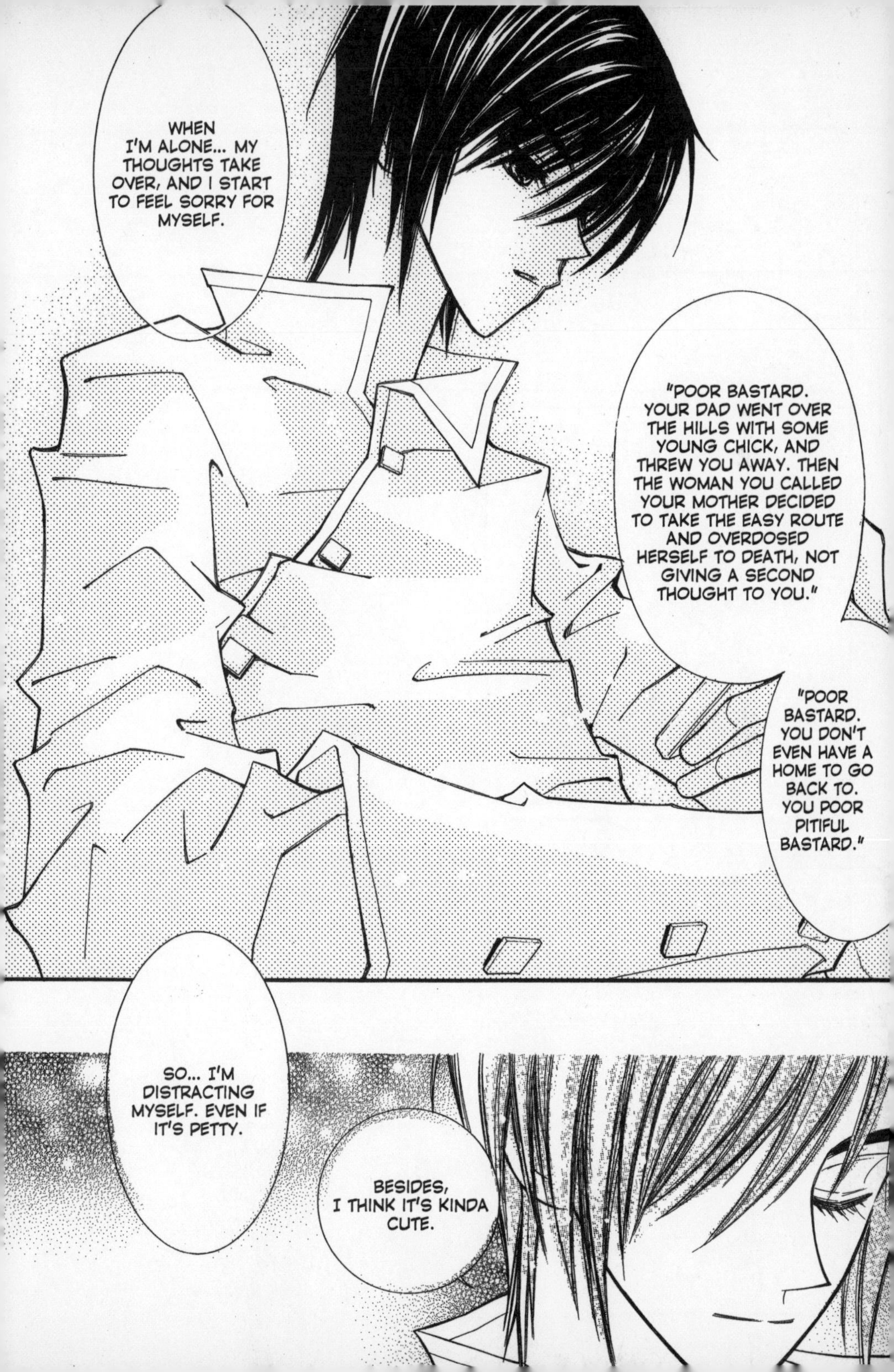
WHEN I'M ALONE... MY THOUGHTS TAKE OVER, AND I START TO FEEL SORRY FOR MYSELF.
"POOR BASTARD. YOUR DAD WENT OVER THE HILLS WITH SOME YOUNG CHICK, AND THREW YOU AWAY. THEN THE WOMAN YOU CALLED YOUR MOTHER DECIDED TO TAKE THE EASY ROUTE AND OVERDOSED HERSELF TO DEATH, NOT GIVING A SECOND THOUGHT TO YOU."
"POOR BASTARD. YOU DON'T EVEN HAVE A HOME TO GO BACK TO. YOU POOR PITIFUL BASTARD."
SO... I'M DISTRACTING MYSELF. EVEN IF IT'S PETTY.
BESIDES, I THINK IT'S KINDA CUTE.

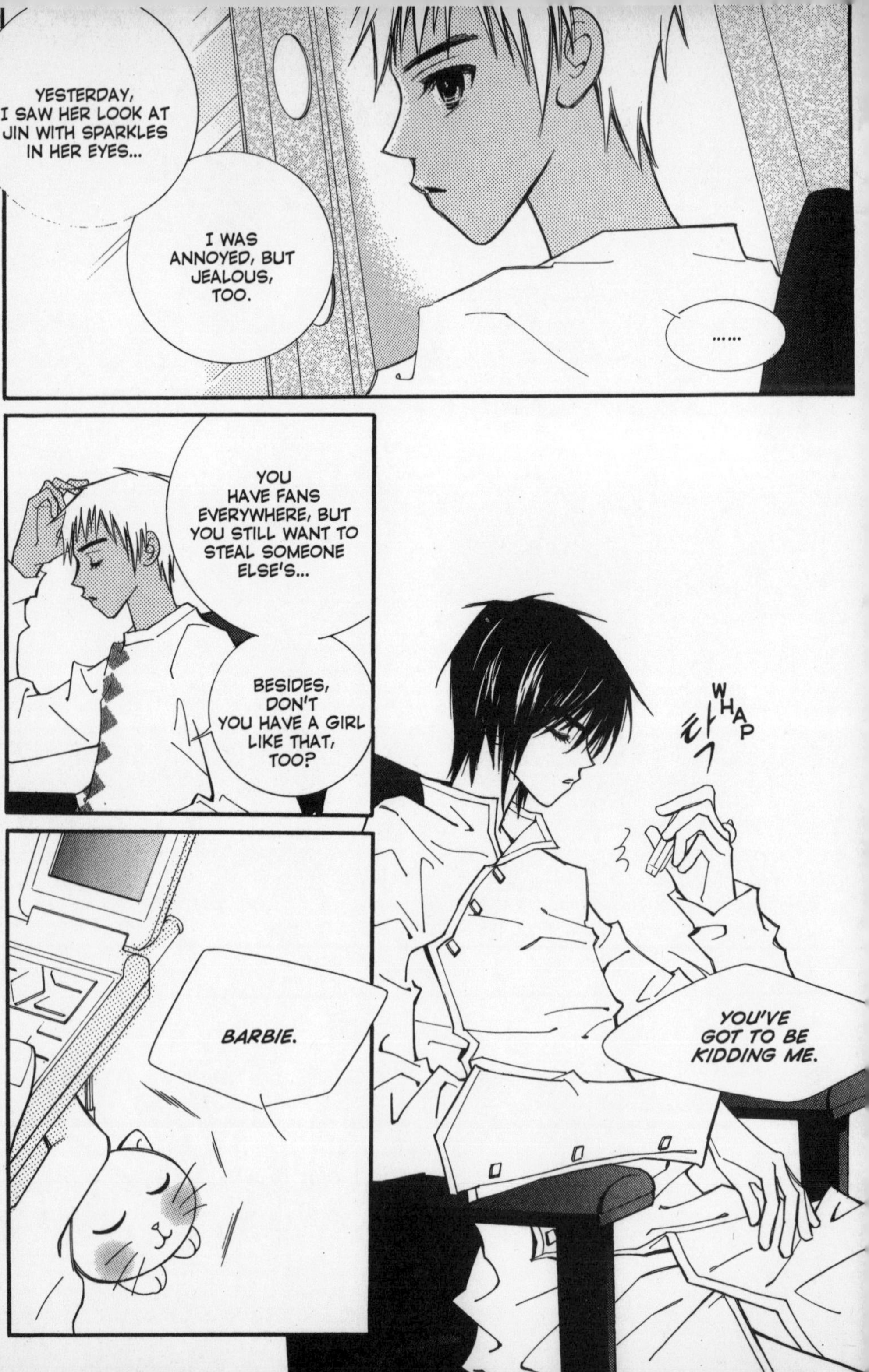
YESTERDAY, I SAW HER LOOK AT JIN WITH SPARKLES IN HER EYES...
I WAS ANNOYED, BUT JEALOUS, TOO.
......
YOU HAVE FANS EVERYWHERE, BUT YOU STILL WANT TO STEAL SOMEONE ELSE'S...
BESIDES, DON'T YOU HAVE A GIRL LIKE THAT, TOO?
WHAP
BARBIE.
YOU'VE GOT TO BE KIDDING ME.

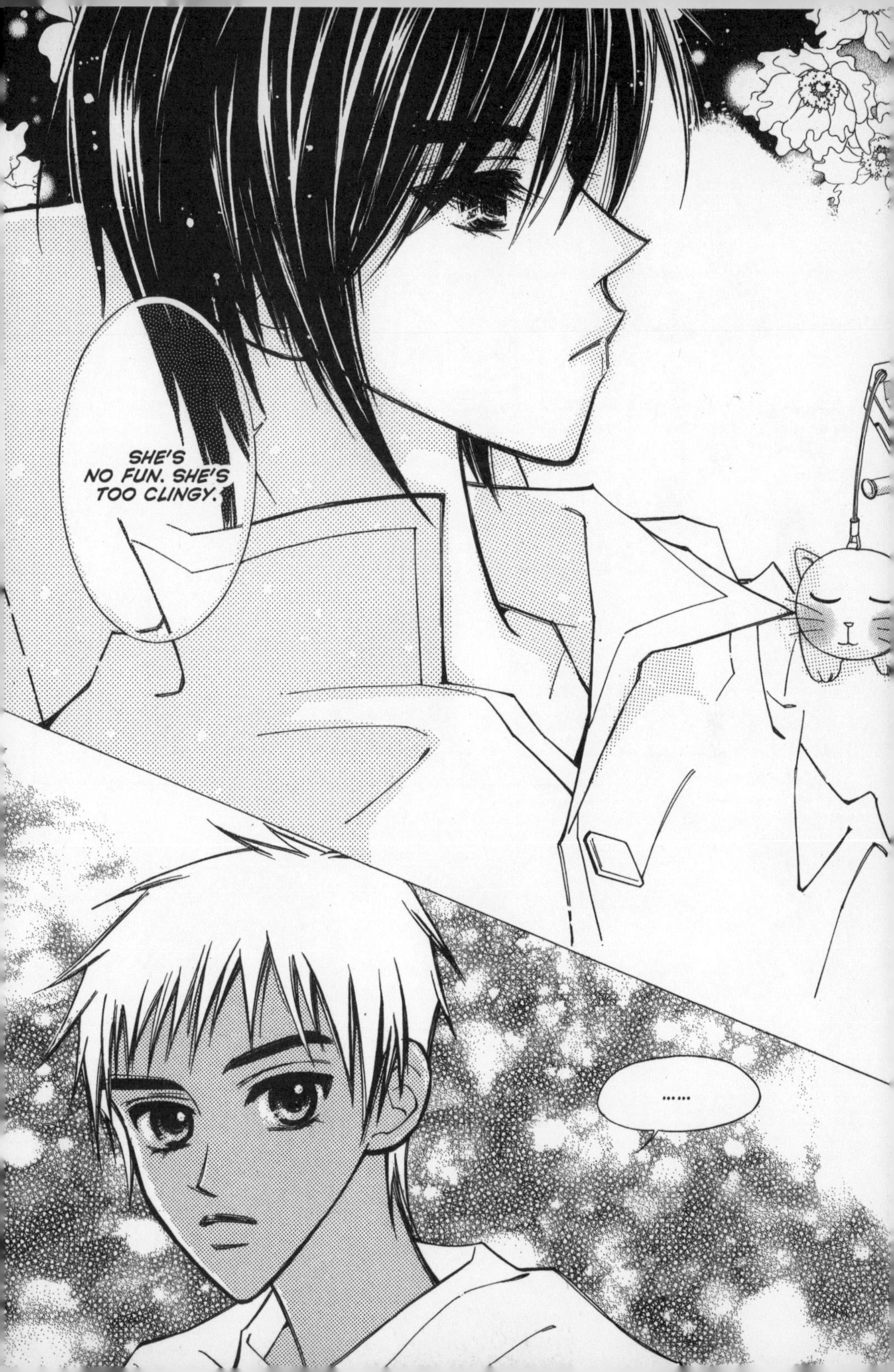
SHE'S NO FUN. SHE'S TOO CLINGY.
......

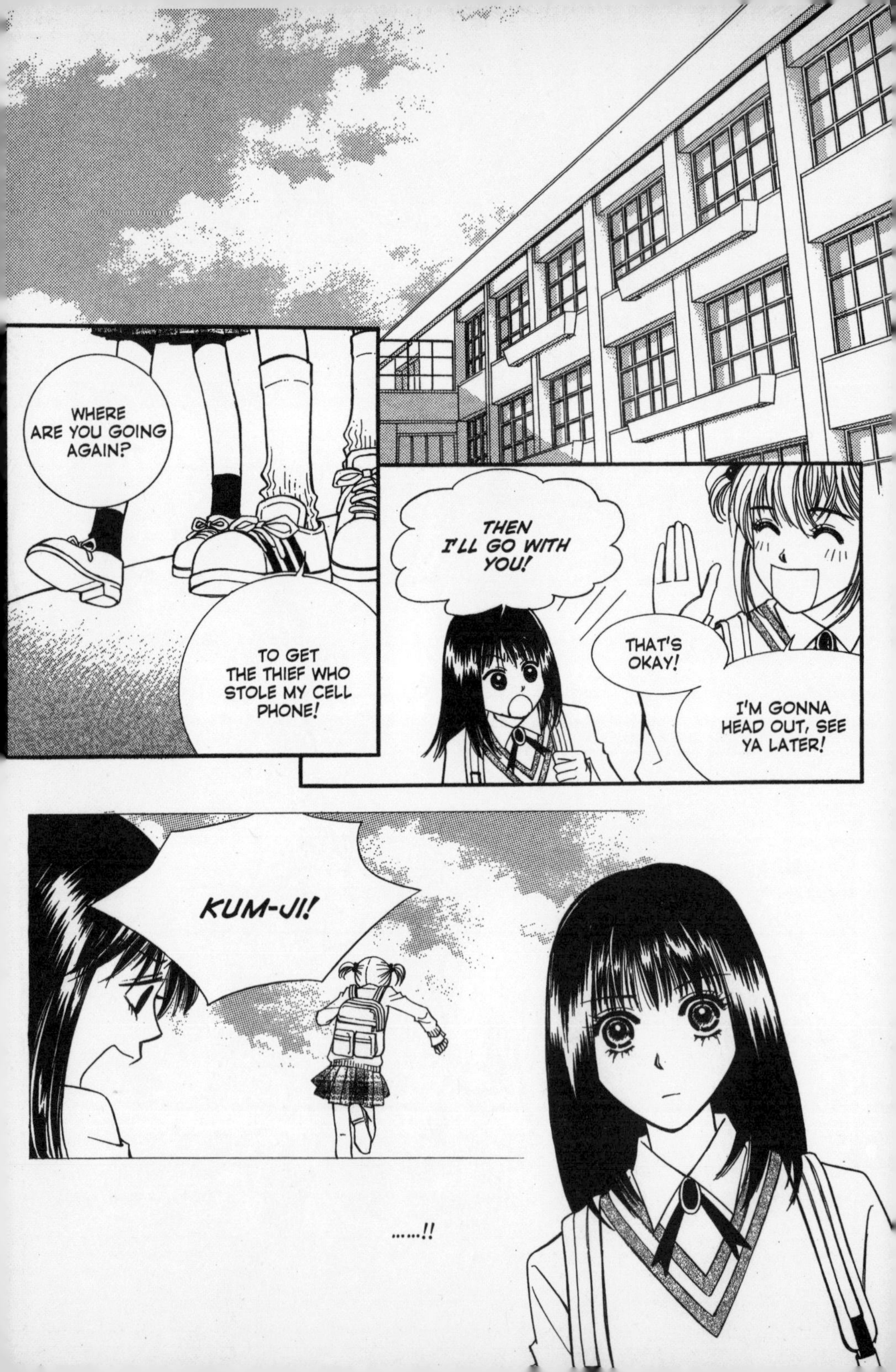
WHERE ARE YOU GOING AGAIN?
TO GET THE THIEF WHO STOLE MY CELL PHONE!
THEN I'LL GO WITH YOU!
THAT'S OKAY!
I'M GONNA HEAD OUT, SEE YA LATER!
KUM-JI!
......!!

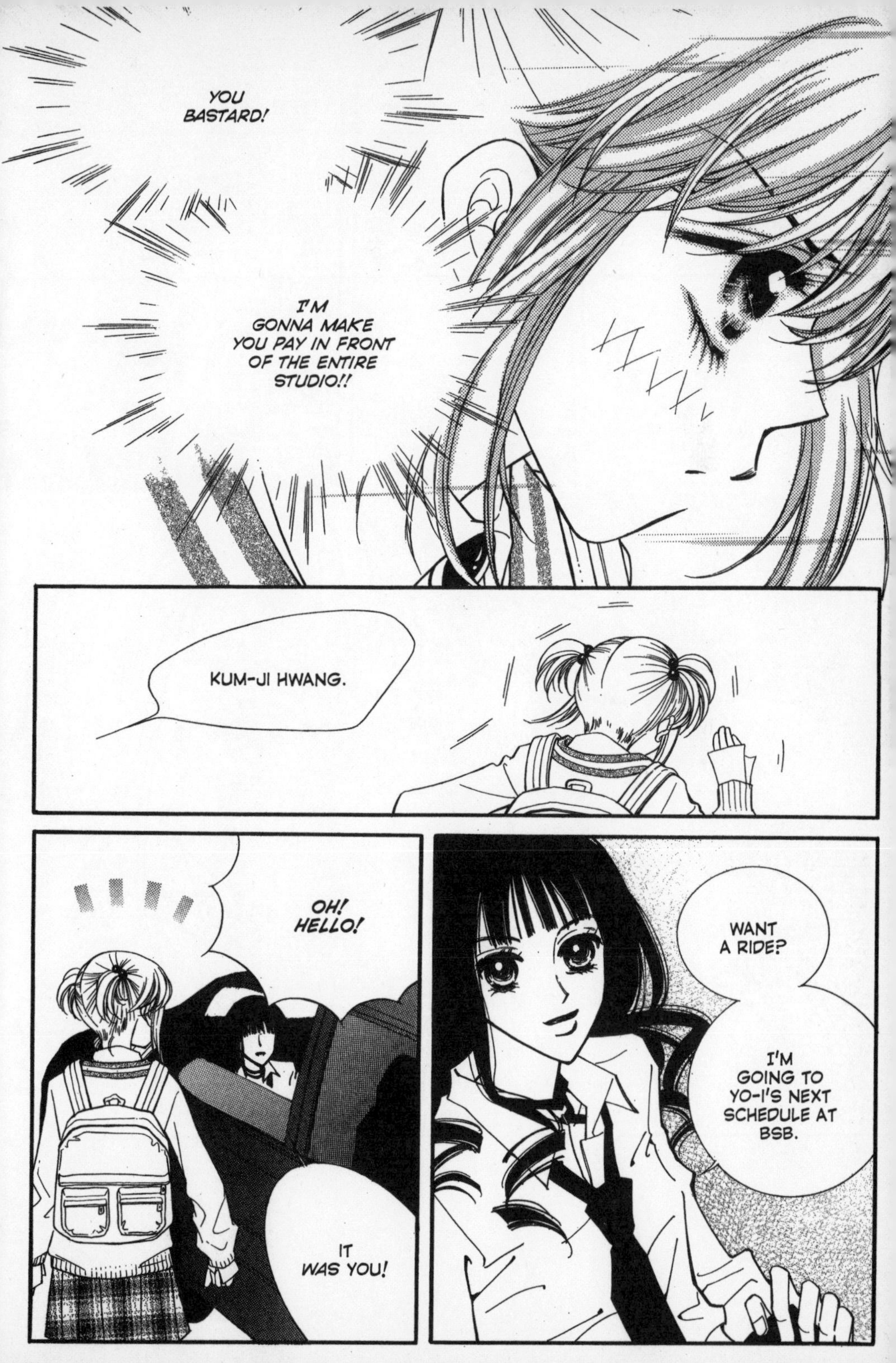
YOU BASTARD!
I'M GONNA MAKE YOU PAY IN FRONT OF THE ENTIRE STUDIO!!
KUM-JI HWANG.
OH! HELLO!
IT WAS YOU!
WANT A RIDE?
I'M GOING TO YO-I'S NEXT SCHEDULE AT BSB.

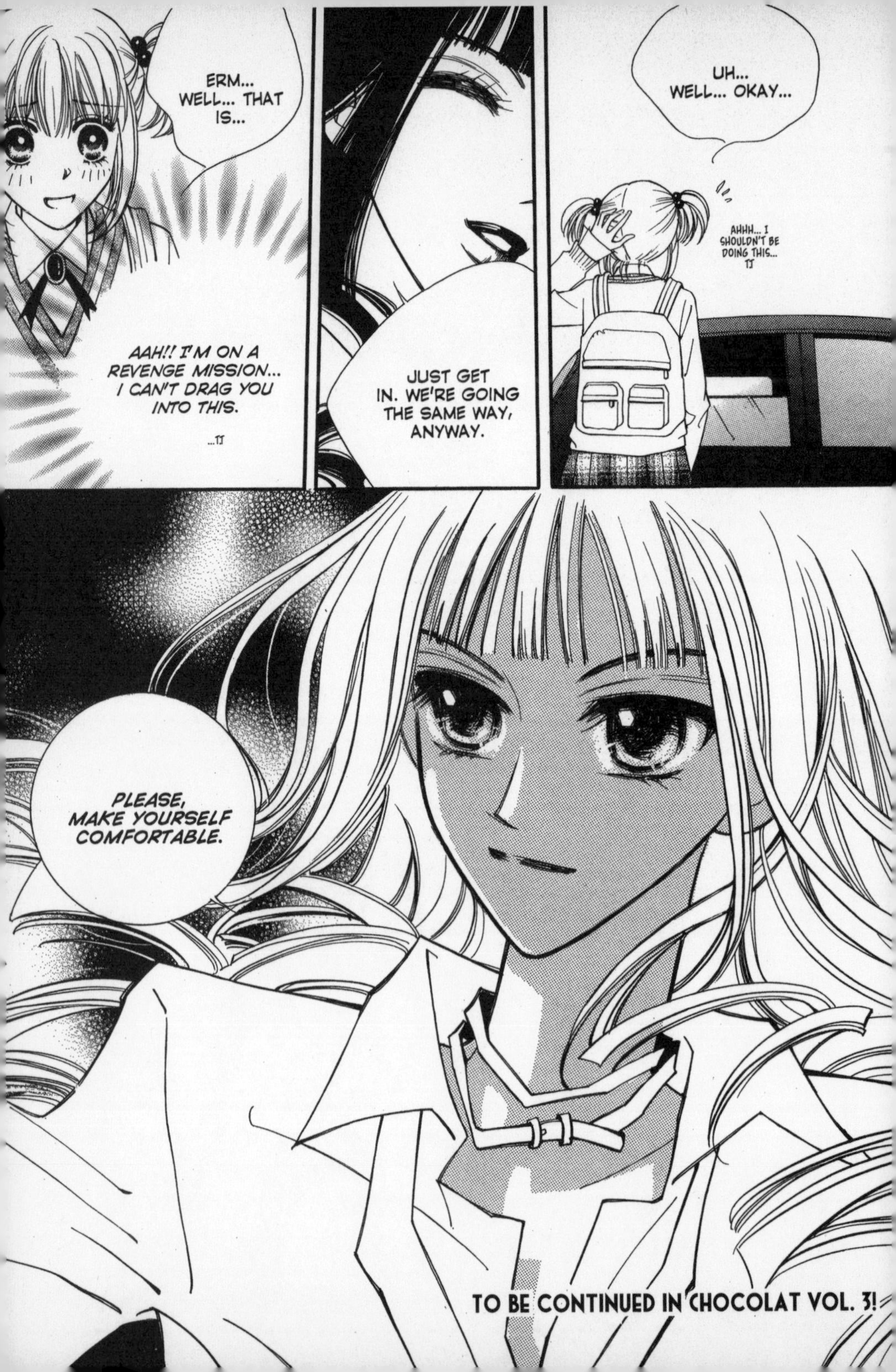
ERM... WELL... THAT IS...
AAH!! I'M ON A REVENGE MISSION... I CAN'T DRAG YOU INTO THIS.
...TJ
JUST GET IN. WE'RE GOING THE SAME WAY, ANYWAY.
UH... WELL... OKAY...
AHHH... I SHOULDN'T BE DOING THIS... TJ
PLEASE, MAKE YOURSELF COMFORTABLE.
TO BE CONTINUED IN CHOCOLAT VOL. 3!

Preview

Bring it on!

vol.2

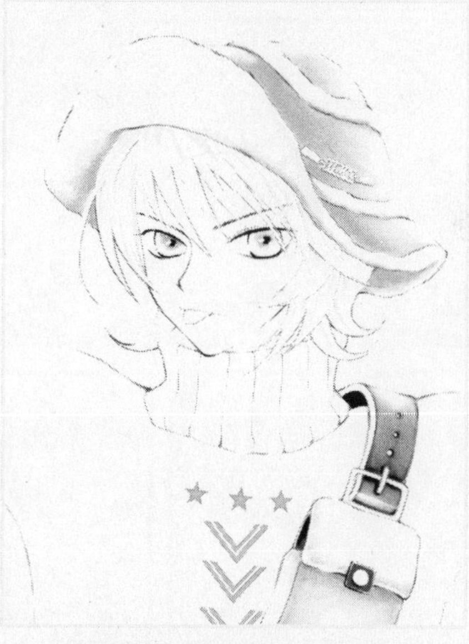

Baek HyeKyung

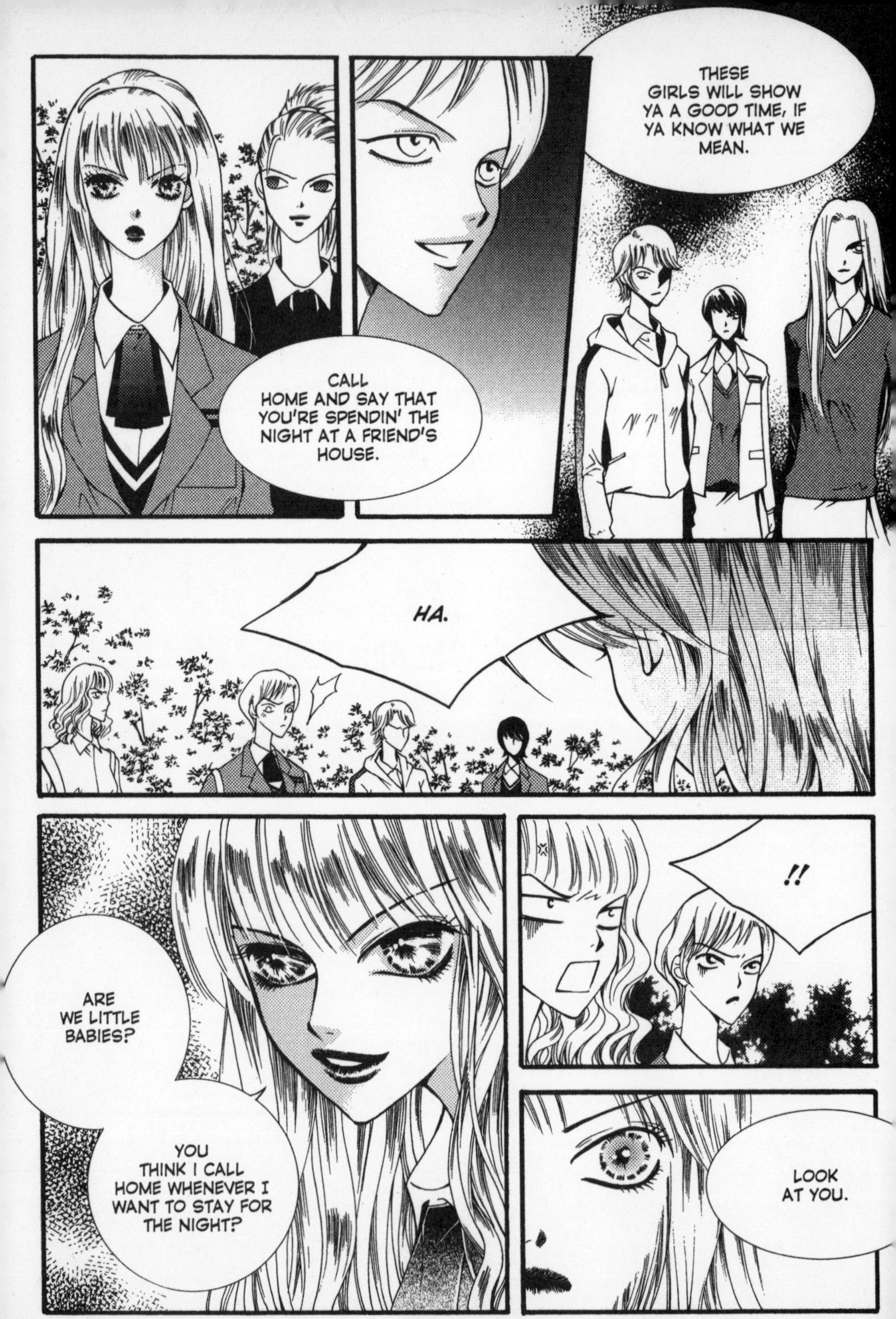
CALL HOME AND SAY THAT YOU'RE SPENDIN' THE NIGHT AT A FRIEND'S HOUSE.
THESE GIRLS WILL SHOW YA A GOOD TIME, IF YA KNOW WHAT WE MEAN.
HA.
ARE WE LITTLE BABIES?
YOU THINK I CALL HOME WHENEVER I WANT TO STAY FOR THE NIGHT?
!!
LOOK AT YOU.

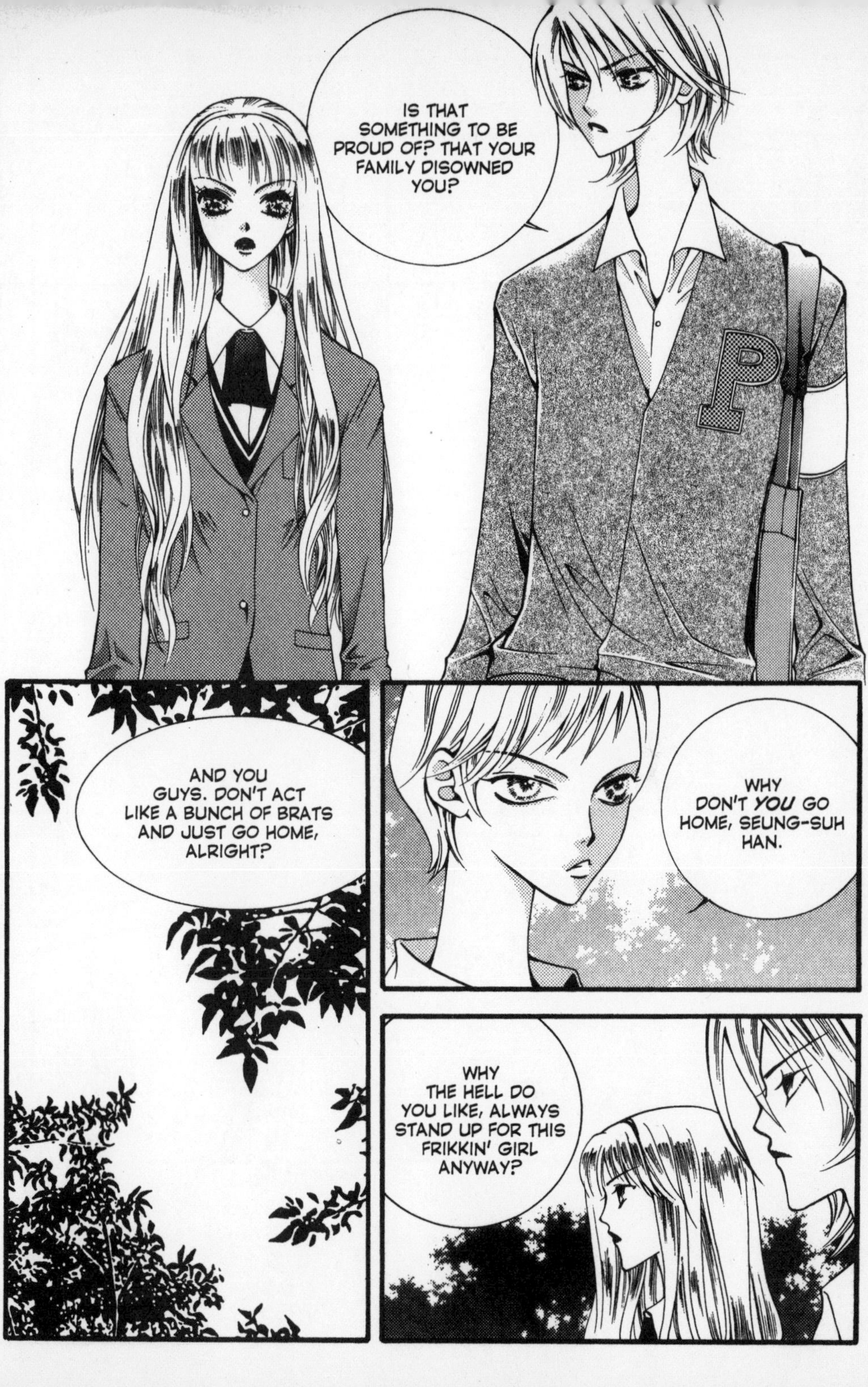
IS THAT SOMETHING TO BE PROUD OF? THAT YOUR FAMILY DISOWNED YOU?
AND YOU GUYS. DON'T ACT LIKE A BUNCH OF BRATS AND JUST GO HOME, ALRIGHT?
WHY DON'T *YOU* GO HOME, SEUNG-SUH HAN.
WHY THE HELL DO YOU LIKE, ALWAYS STAND UP FOR THIS FRIKKIN' GIRL ANYWAY?

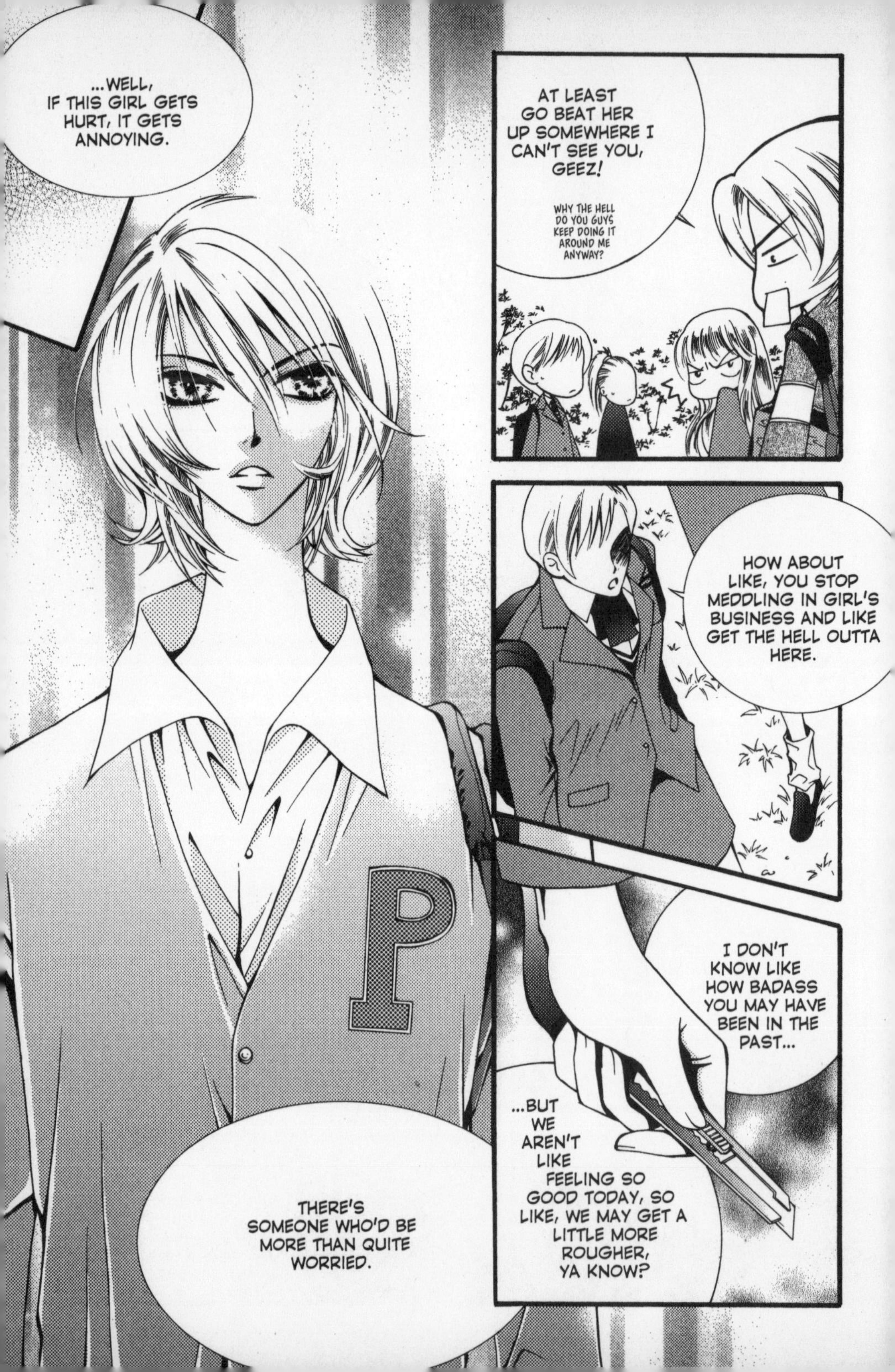
...WELL, IF THIS GIRL GETS HURT, IT GETS ANNOYING.
THERE'S SOMEONE WHO'D BE MORE THAN QUITE WORRIED.
AT LEAST GO BEAT HER UP SOMEWHERE I CAN'T SEE YOU, GEEZ!
WHY THE HELL DO YOU GUYS KEEP DOING IT AROUND ME ANYWAY?
HOW ABOUT LIKE, YOU STOP MEDDLING IN GIRL'S BUSINESS AND LIKE GET THE HELL OUTTA HERE.
I DON'T KNOW LIKE HOW BADASS YOU MAY HAVE BEEN IN THE PAST...
...BUT WE AREN'T LIKE FEELING SO GOOD TODAY, SO LIKE, WE MAY GET A LITTLE MORE ROUGHER, YA KNOW?

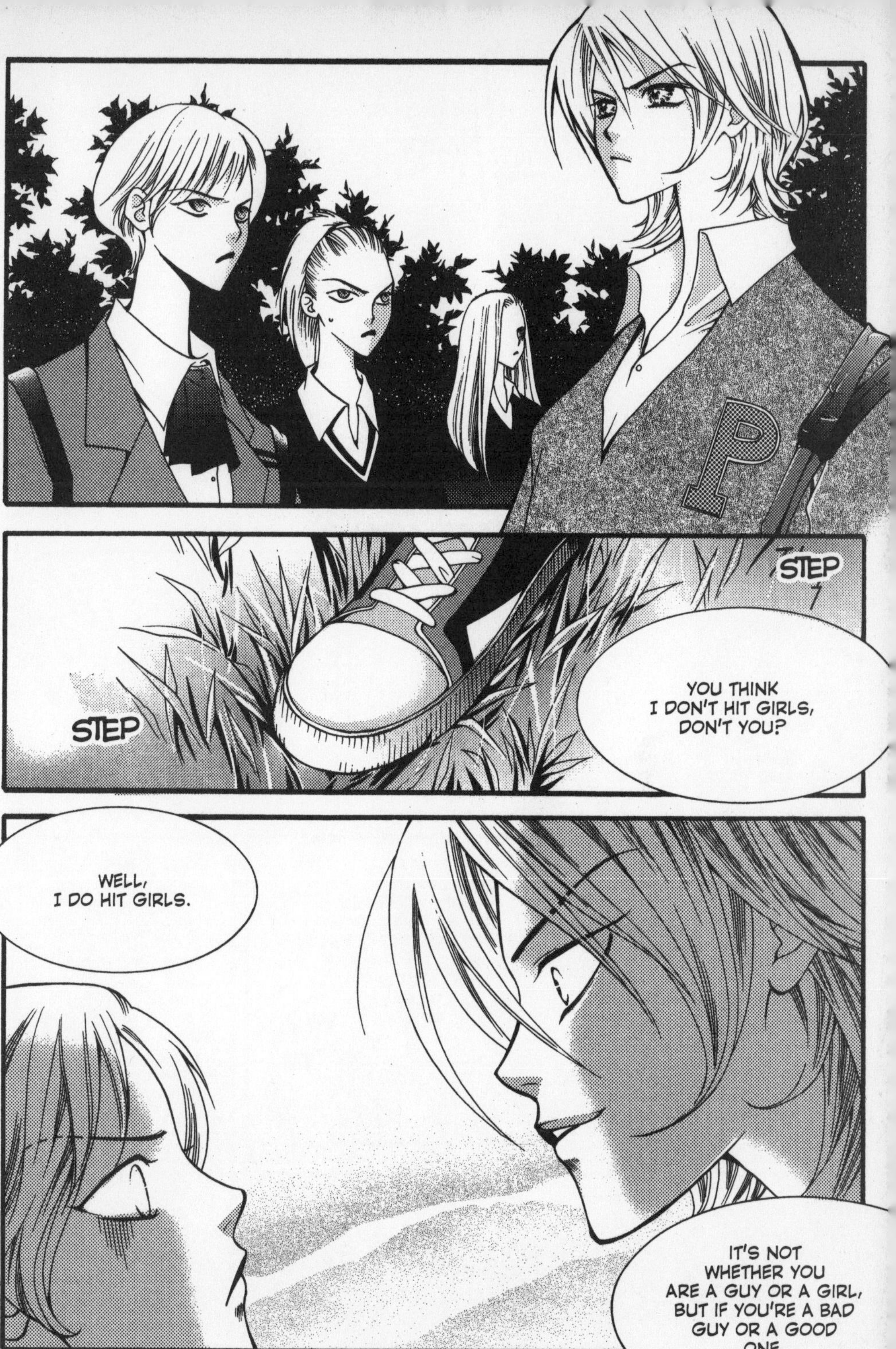
STEP
STEP
YOU THINK I DON'T HIT GIRLS, DON'T YOU?
WELL, I DO HIT GIRLS.
IT'S NOT WHETHER YOU ARE A GUY OR A GIRL, BUT IF YOU'RE A BAD GUY OR A GOOD ONE.

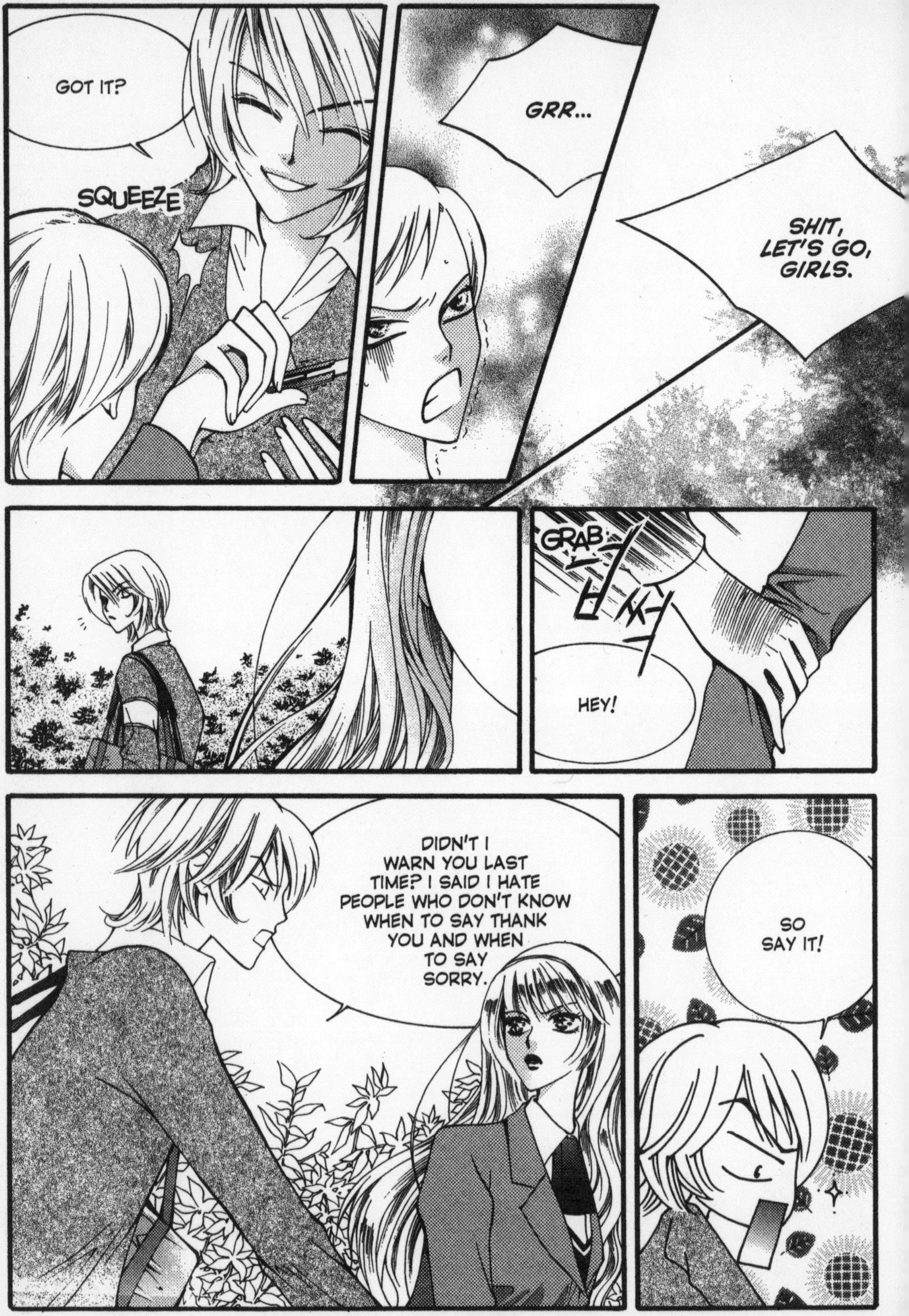
GOT IT?
SQUEEZE
GRR...
SHIT, LET'S GO, GIRLS.
GRAB
HEY!
DIDN'T I WARN YOU LAST TIME? I SAID I HATE PEOPLE WHO DON'T KNOW WHEN TO SAY THANK YOU AND WHEN TO SAY SORRY.
SO SAY IT!

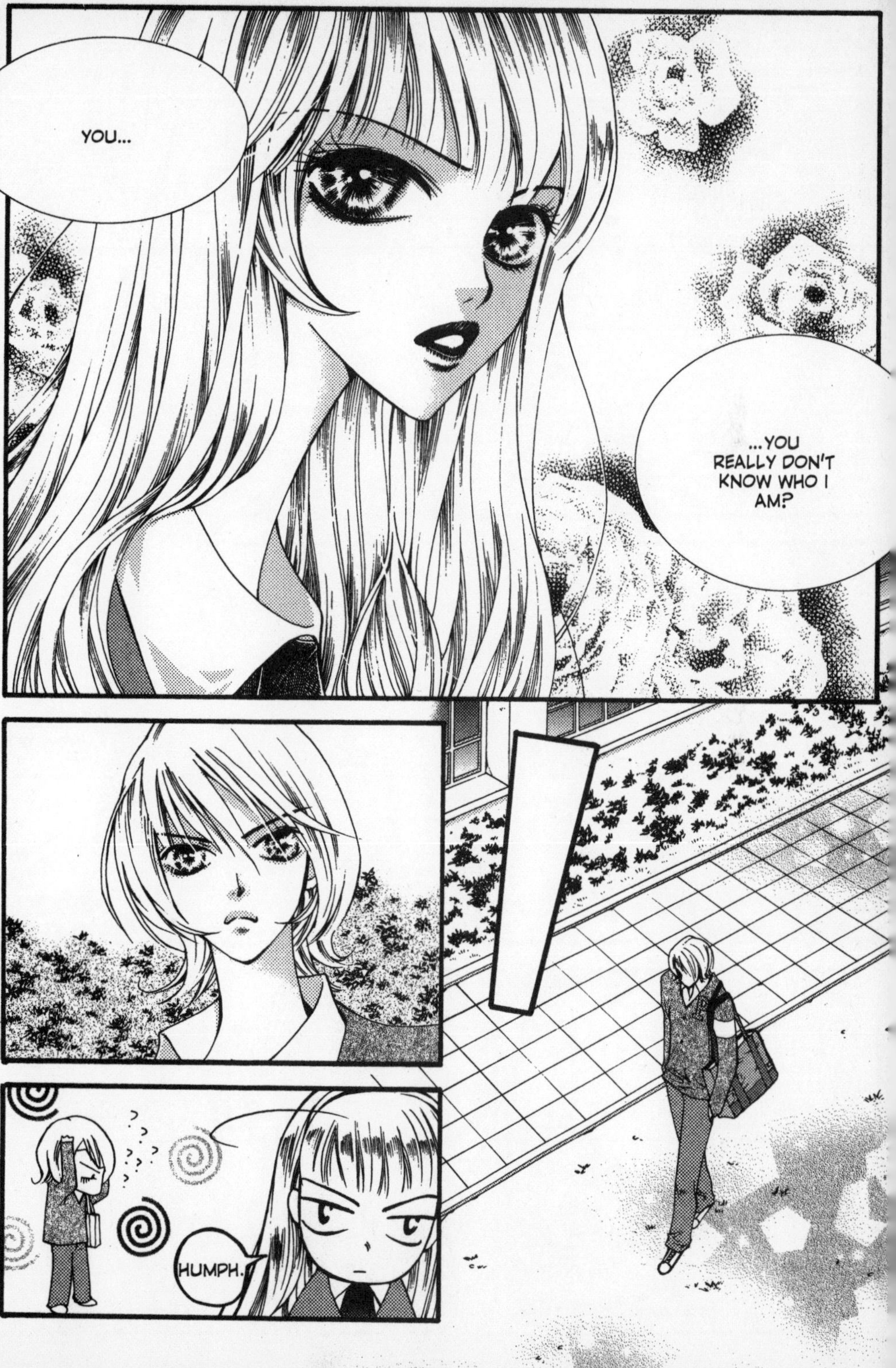
YOU...
...YOU REALLY DON'T KNOW WHO I AM?
!
HUMPH.

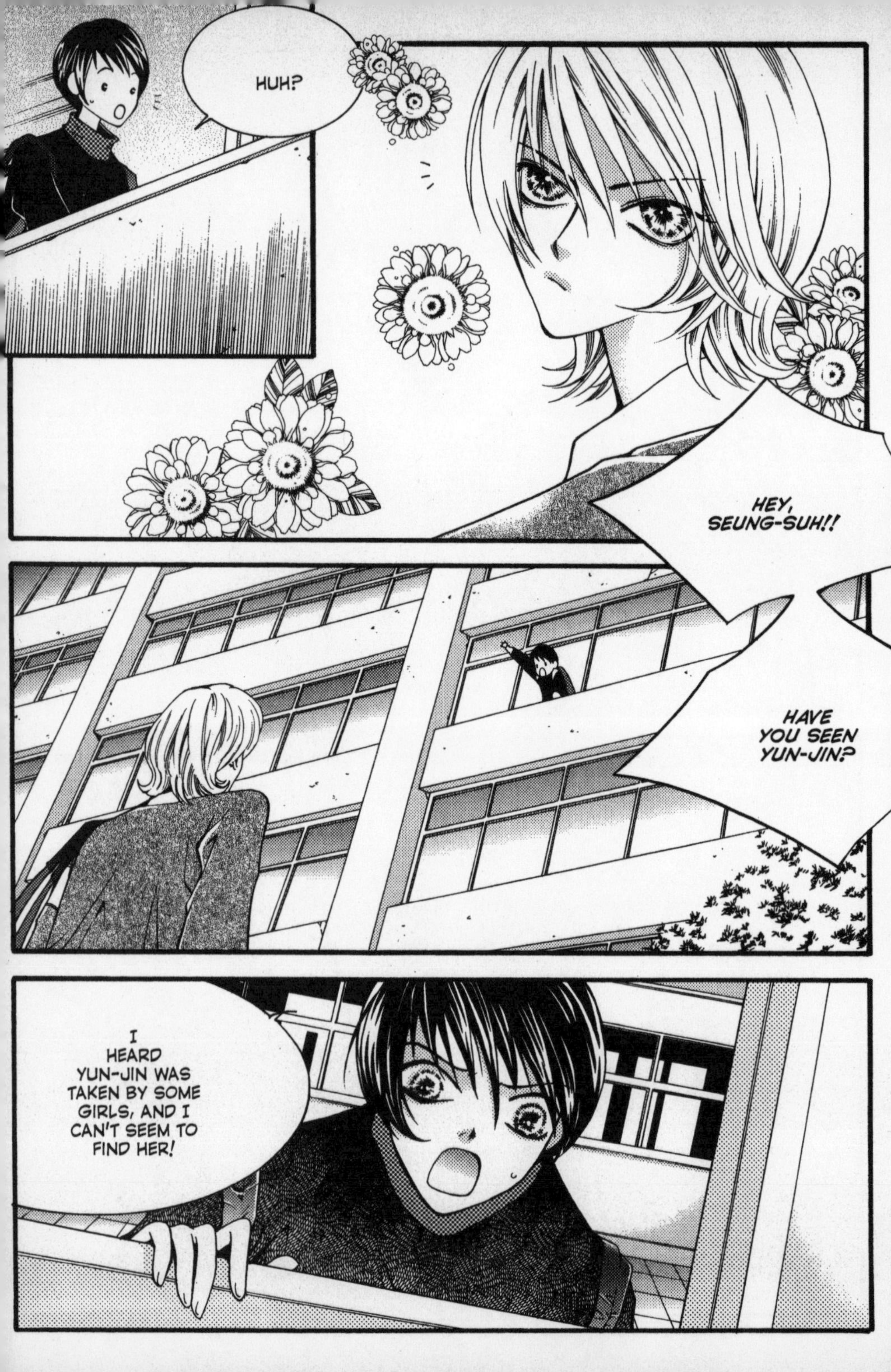
HUH?
HEY, SEUNG-SUH!!
HAVE YOU SEEN YUN-JIN?
I HEARD YUN-JIN WAS TAKEN BY SOME GIRLS, AND I CAN'T SEEM TO FIND HER!

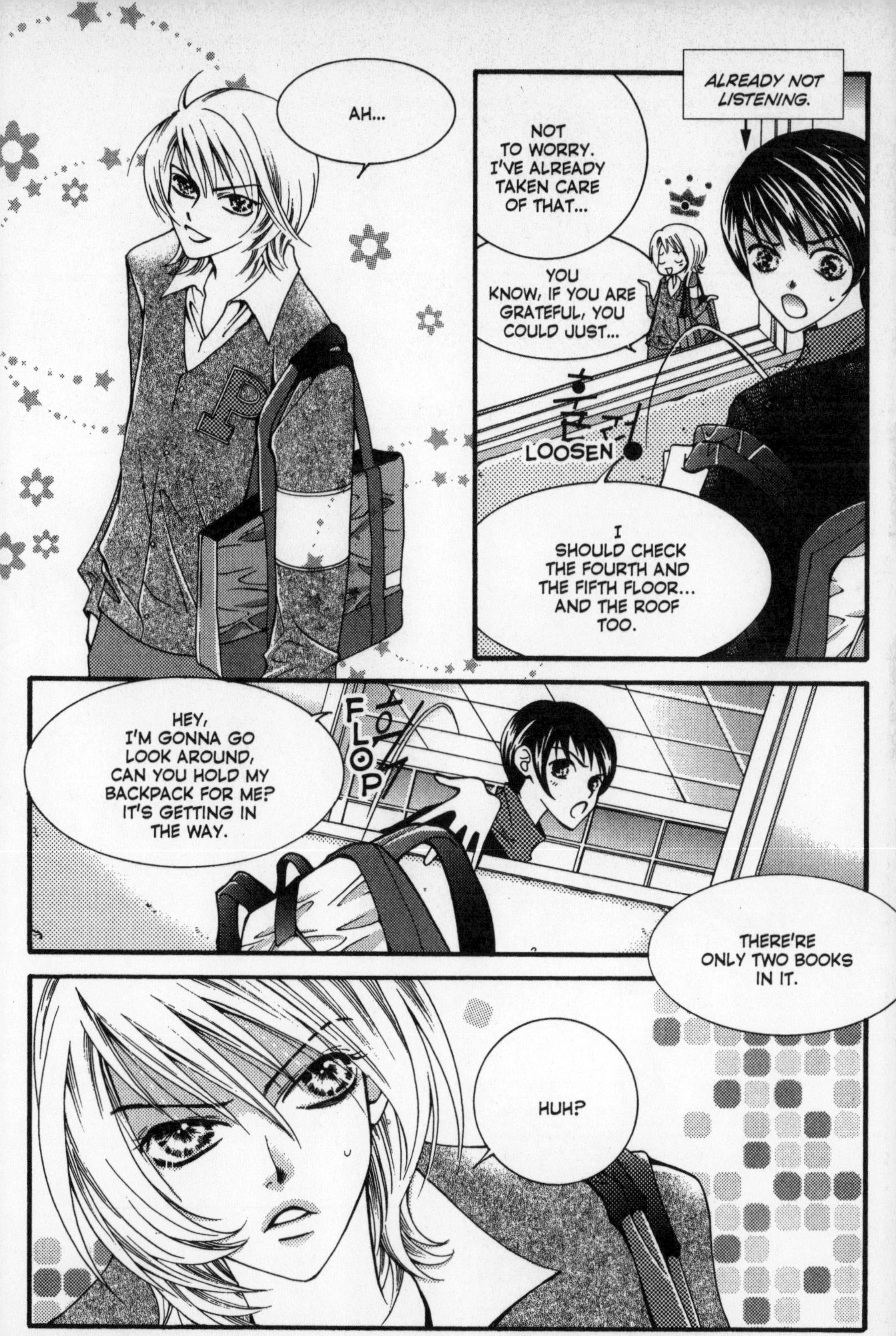
AH...
ALREADY NOT LISTENING.
NOT TO WORRY. I'VE ALREADY TAKEN CARE OF THAT...
YOU KNOW, IF YOU ARE GRATEFUL, YOU COULD JUST...
LOOSEN
I SHOULD CHECK THE FOURTH AND THE FIFTH FLOOR... AND THE ROOF TOO.
HEY, I'M GONNA GO LOOK AROUND, CAN YOU HOLD MY BACKPACK FOR ME? IT'S GETTING IN THE WAY.
FLOP
THERE'RE ONLY TWO BOOKS IN IT.
HUH?

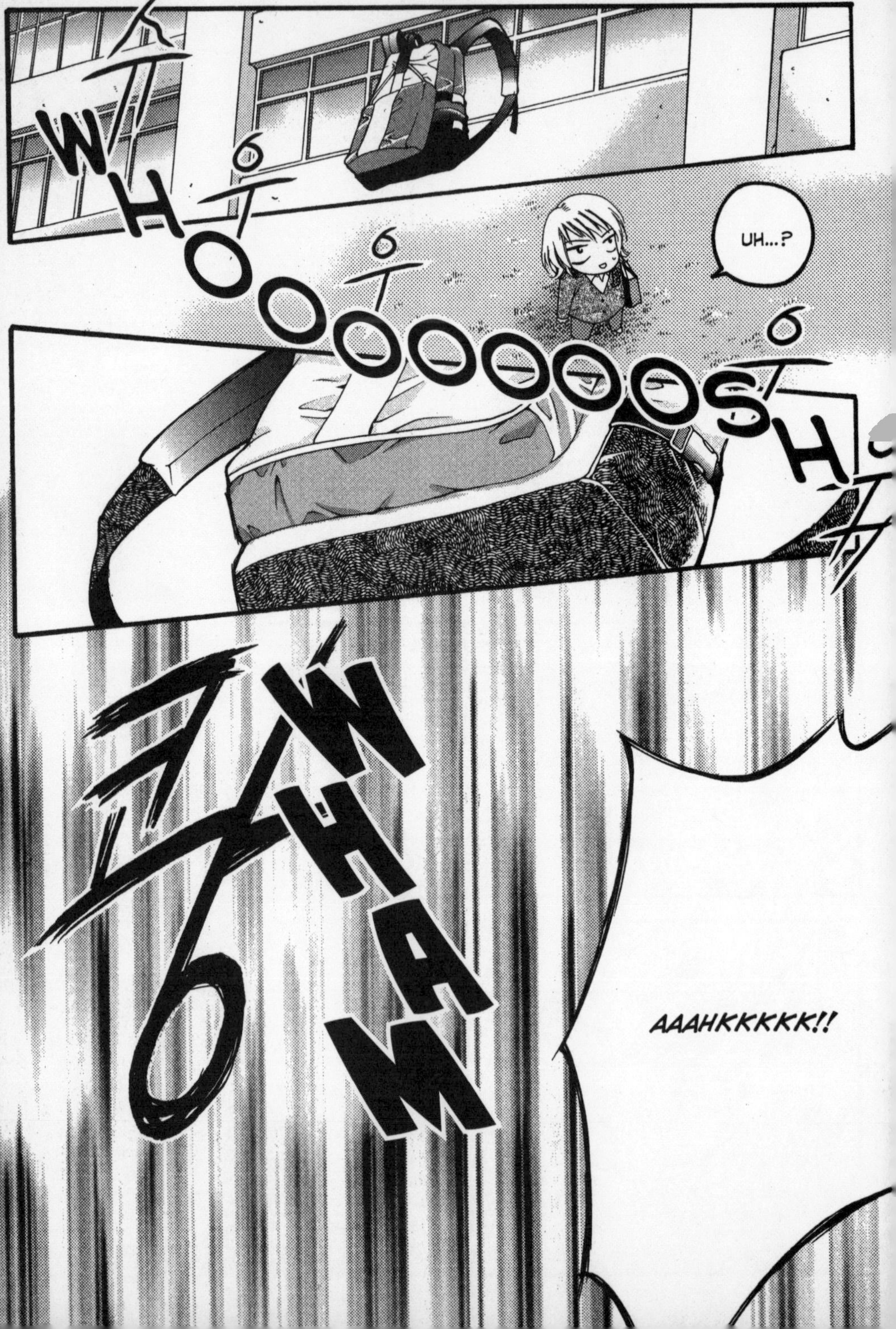
WHOOOOOOOSH
UH...?
WHAM
AAAHKKKKK!!

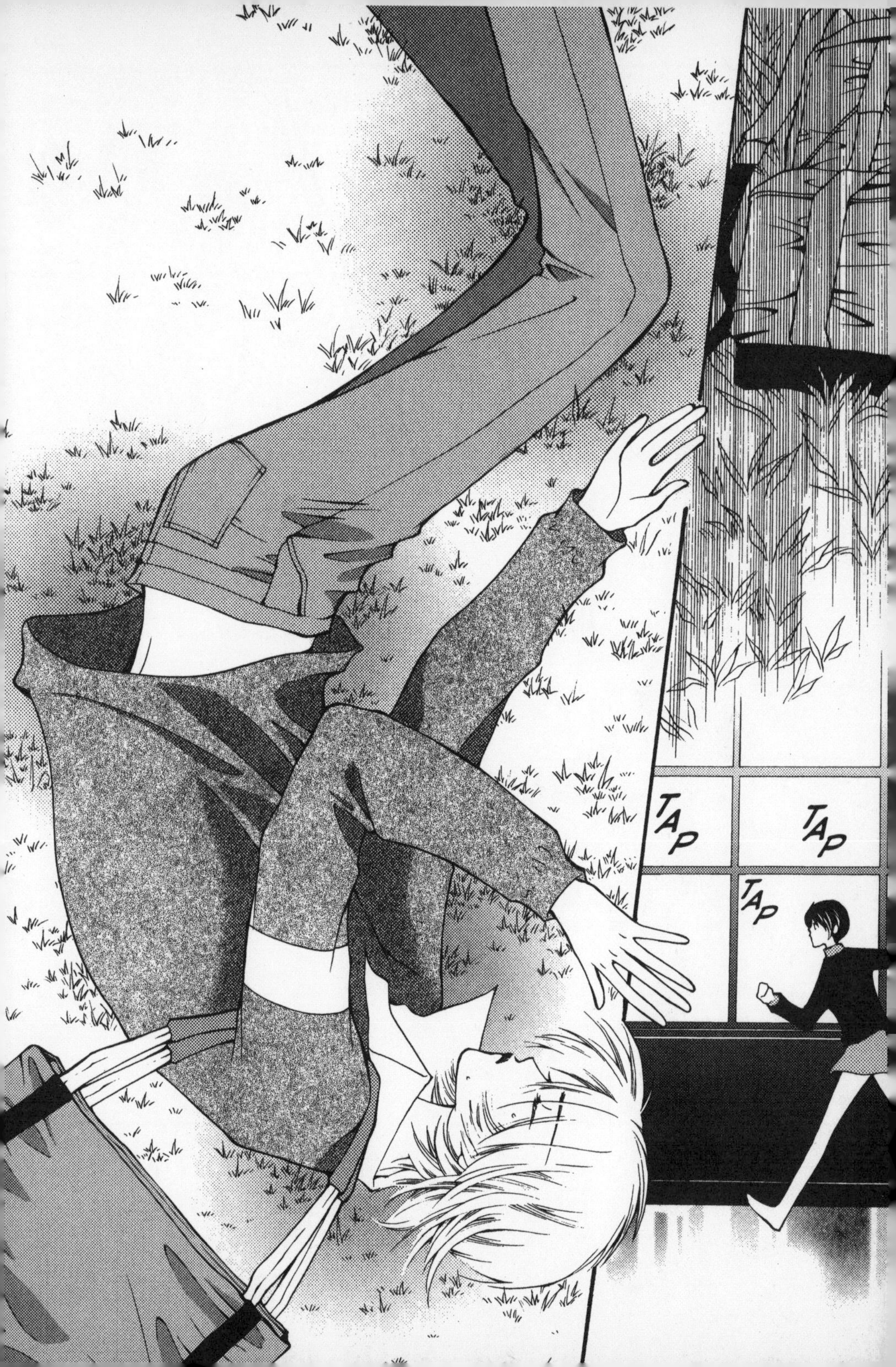
TAP
TAP
TAP

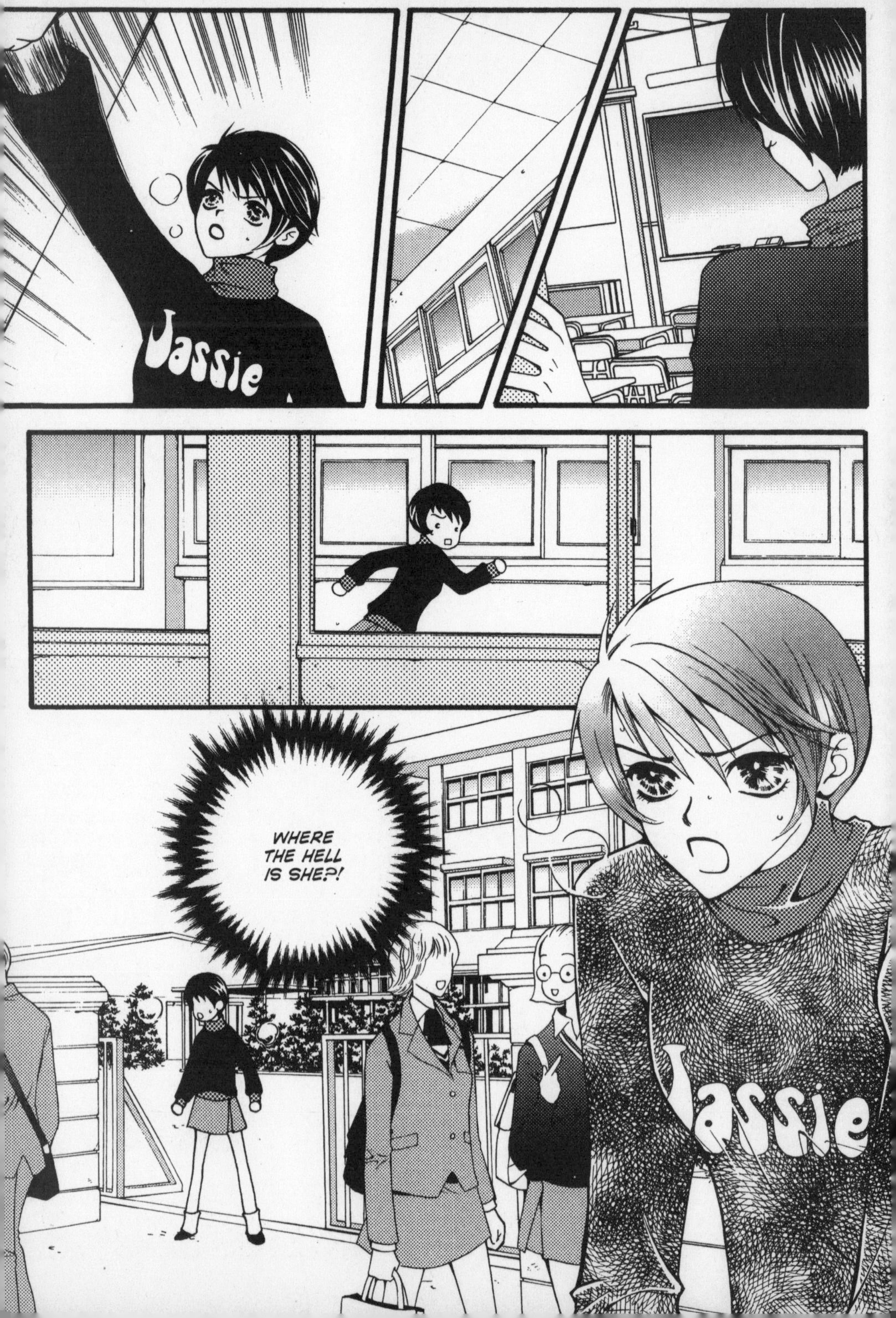
Jassie
WHERE THE HELL IS SHE?!
Jassie

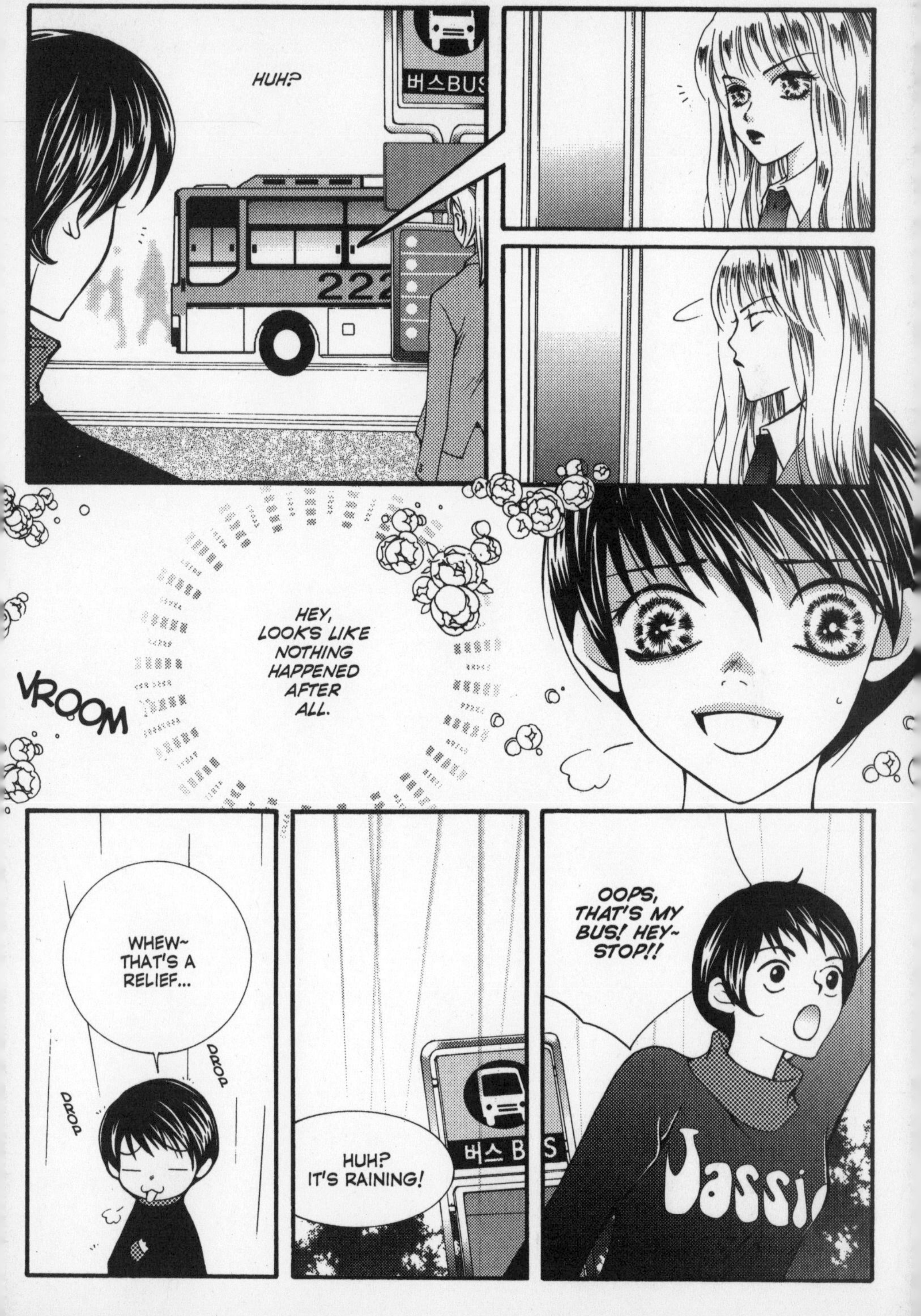
HUH?
버스BUS
222
VROOM
HEY, LOOKS LIKE NOTHING HAPPENED AFTER ALL.
WHEW~ THAT'S A RELIEF...
DROP
DROP
버스 BUS
HUH? IT'S RAINING!
OOPS, THAT'S MY BUS! HEY~ STOP!!

Danbi Original

Chocolat vol.2

Story and art by JiSang Shin · Geo

Translation Sunny Kim
English Adaptation Jackie Oh · Audra Furuichi
Touch-up and Lettering Terri Delgado · Marshall Dillon
Graphic Design EunKyung Kim
Editor JuYoun Lee

ICE Kunion

Project Manager Chan Park
Managing Editor Marshall Dillon
Marketing Manager Erik Ko
Editor in Chief Eddie Yu
Publishing Director JeongHyun Chin
Publisher and C.E.O. JaeKook Chun

Chocolat © 2005 JiSang Shin · Geo
First published in Korea in 2002 by SIGONGSA Co., Ltd.
English text translation rights arranged by SIGONGSA Co., Ltd.
English text © 2005 ICE KUNION

Published by ICE Kunion.
SIGONGSA 2F Yeil Bldg. 1619-4, Seocho-dong, Seocho-gu, Seoul, 137-878, Korea

ISBN : 89-527-4472-1

First printing, January 2006
10 9 8 7 6 5 4 3 2 1
Printed in Canada

www.ICEkunion.com/www.koreanmanhwa.com